Adele
PARKS

HUSBANDS

headline
review

First published in Great Britain in 2005
by PENGUIN BOOKS

This edition published in Great Britain in 2012
by HEADLINE REVIEW
An imprint of HEADLINE PUBLISHING GROUP

2

Cataloguing in Publication Data is available from the British Library

ISBN 978 0 7553 9425 8

Typeset in Garamond MT

Printed and bound in Great Britain by
Clays Ltd, St Ives plc

Headline's policy is to use papers that are natural, renewable and recyclable
products and made from wood grown in sustainable forests. The logging
and manufacturing processes are expected to conform to the environmental
regulations of the country of origin.

HEADLINE PUBLISHING GROUP
An Hachette UK Company
338 Euston Road
London NW1 3BH

www.headline.co.uk
www.hachette.co.uk

For my husband and my sister

Contents

1. Tomorrow is a Long Time

Sunday 9th May 2004

Bella

'OK? I'll call you tomorrow, Amelie. You're OK, aren't you?'

'Yes,' says Amelie with a sigh. Her tone isn't reassuring.

I press the red button on the handset and disconnect my lovely friend. I'm left with an overwhelming sense of inadequacy and grief. Grief is so lonely. It stains everything it touches and builds huge divisive walls. I should know, my mother died of cancer when I was nine. I will never stop feeling cheated. I'd wanted to say something meaningful, calming, consoling and true to Amelie but I couldn't. I've tried to find those words for nearly ten months now but they don't exist. Sighing with frustration I push my fists into the sockets of my eyes and rub hard. When Amelie called, I'd just finished my night-time round of pelvic-floor exercises and I'd gritted my teeth through eight reps of stomach crunches. I was mid my cleanse, tone and moisturize routine but now I can't find the emotional energy to continue. All that vanity stuff seems so pointless in the face of Amelie's pain.

Loving is such a risk.

I look at my husband, Philip, who has fallen asleep

while I was on the phone. He's clasping a copy of *The Economist*. I turn on the bedside lamp and turn off the bright overhead light, ease the magazine out of his hand and kiss his forehead. I always love him even more after talking to my widowed friend; grief makes us selfish. I wish that every time I spoke to Amelie I didn't think, 'There but for the grace of God,' but I do. Which probably means I'm not as nice a person as I'd like to be.

I nip around to my side of the bed, climb in next to Phil and hold tight to his strong, bulky body. My breathing slows down and I can't feel my heart thud quite as furiously inside my chest. During my conversation with Amelie it raced so violently that I was convinced it was attempting an escape bid.

I often think my heart would like to escape.

Philip makes me feel safe. He's nine years older than me, which is undoubtedly part of it. He is kind, respectful and thoughtful, even after sex. The men that I dated before Philip had not often been these things, even before sex. We met not quite two and a half years ago – I was working as a waitress in a cocktail bar, which makes me a tribute to a Human League song that I can barely remember but Philip enthuses about. An interesting dinner-party anecdote maybe, but working as a waitress in a cocktail bar is in fact a fairly grim existence. Philip is a highly successful City trader and while I'm not sure exactly what City traders do, I know that they get paid an awful lot of money to do it. So Philip charged into my life armed with the traditional gifts of dinners in fancy restaurants, flirty lingerie (wrapped in tissue paper and hidden in thick cardboard bags) and even the occasional meaningful CD and book. He also brought with him a new array of courtship tools. He was a grown-up. Philip talked about ISAs, pension plans and stocks and shares with the same passion as other men talk about football league tables, PlayStation and bottled beer. He remembered stuff I found difficult to retain, like when the hunk of junk I called a car needed to be squeezed through its MOT, or if my household insurance needed renewing, and his DIY knowledge actively turned me on.

When I met Philip I was, I suppose, a bit of a mess. The most substantial thing about me was my overdraft and my most meaningful relationship was with my bank manager. In fact, thinking about it, I hadn't actually met my bank manager, so my most meaningful relationship was with the girl at the call centre (probably in Delhi) who I rang regularly to explain my latest embarrassment.

It wasn't as though I squandered money on designer labels and expensive lotions and potions. I didn't own much; not a flash car or a property. Not even a shoe collection; hard to believe, when you consider that most women who have been brought up on a diet of *Sex and the City* and *Friends* think that a to-die-for shoe collection and wardrobe is, well . . . to die for.

It wasn't as though I'd been idle. I'd worked pretty much every day of my life since I graduated with my middle-of-the-road degree. The problem was I hadn't been consistent in my career progression. I had been on the bottom rung of several career ladders but had never clambered to the top of any of them. The thing is, I don't know what I want to do or be. I try to view it positively that, after several years, I can confirm that I don't want to be an accountant (too many exams), a banker (I don't like wearing suits), a calligrapher (anyway there isn't much calling), a dental hygienist (other people's mouths – yuk), something in PR or anything in the music industry. I still think being a chocolate buyer for Selfridges might be good but the opportunity has never arisen.

In fact fewer opportunities arise as the years pass. On leaving university starting and failing to complete one graduate trainee programme is acceptable but after several years of failing to finish any trainee programmes, potential employers became wary of what they (rightly) identify as my inability to commit.

I'd been seeing Phil for nineteen months when he popped the question. I like to round up and say two years; it sounds more . . . appropriate. Actually, he sort of blurted it rather than popped, in a very un-Philip moment. If I was a betting woman I'd have put money on Phil being the type of man to propose in a controlled environment, like a restaurant or in front of some significant building or beautiful sunset. I'd have guessed that he'd buy a ring in advance, go down on one knee and recite a rehearsed speech asking me to do him the honour etc etc. In fact he yelled over gushing water (he was wearing Marigold rubber gloves at the time). I think his exact words were, 'We'd better get married before you cause any more trouble.' How could a girl resist?

At the time I was flat-sitting for a flamboyant and wealthy fashion designer friend of Amelie's, while she flittered around the globe to be inspired by spices in Morocco and sunsets in Cape Town, or similar. She had exactly the sort of job I could see myself being good at, even though I wasn't sure what she did, it didn't even sound like work to me (undoubtedly part of the attraction). Real work, as far as I am concerned, is a series of dull temp jobs and late-night shifts serving cocktails to wanker bankers.

I found the fashion designer's Clerkenwell 'space' horribly intimidating. It was too trendy to be described as anything as mundane as a flat, which says it all. There were acres of glossy wooden floors and I thought the place would have benefited from a couple of cosy rugs. There were impressive skirting-board-to-ceiling windows which let in plenty of uplifting light but left me with as much privacy as a goldfish. And while stripping the palette to a single colour – white – apparently achieved 'monochrome drama on a grand scale', it was almost impossible to live with. Of course, I was grateful to be staying in such a stunning and stylized 'space' for a next-to-nothing rent but my gratitude was all about the rate not the stylized nature of the gaff. I'd never say so; it would be regarded as the epitome of crassness.

While my responsibilities were hardly tasking I did, disappointingly but somewhat predictably, manage to muck things up. I was charged with switching lights on and off, drawing blinds and setting alarms when I went out. I just had to live there, but all the same I found my position arduous. I was surrounded by white walls, white sheets, white settees, white crockery and white towels. All of them waiting for me to stain, spoil, scuff or spot. I lived in a state of perpetual nervousness for three months. Inevitably, the horror I imagined became a reality; I blocked the state-of-the-art waste disposal unit with the remnants of a very average Chinese takeaway and I left a tap running as I rushed out to work. I returned to find a blocked sink and a flooded kitchen.

Philip arrived thirty minutes after I called him. He unblocked the sink, mopped up the spill and assured me that he'd source, buy and refit the water-damaged kick boards and tiles. I agreed to marry him that instant.

Besides, while Philip was being photographed by speed cameras as he dashed to East London to help me, I took a call from Amelie, who with an eerie calmness – that I later identified as shock – told me that Ben, her partner for eleven years, had been knocked over by a bus.

What are the chances of that? You hear people say, 'Go on then, I'll have a second piece of cake. Sod the cholesterol, I might walk out of here and get knocked over by a bus.' But no one expects to, do they? No more than we expect to be abducted by aliens or win the lottery. But he was. Dear, dear Ben. Exuberant, amusing, vibrant Ben was buying a copy of *Esquire* and a packet of chewing gum one moment and the next, he was dead.

It was the bus, not the blocked U-bend, that most encouraged me to accept Philip's proposal but I never, ever acknowledge as much. Sadness and fear seem inappropriate reasons to accept a marriage proposal.

2. One Broken Heart for Sale

Laura

Although it is 10.45 p.m. I consider this a perfectly acceptable time to call my bezzie mate, Bella. She knows it takes me until about now to find space in my day to talk. It's not that my friends are a low priority; it's just that Eddie, my son, is four years old and while he appears more than moderately intelligent, he seems to have a deaf spot where certain phrases are concerned. 'Can't you amuse yourself for a moment? Mummy has to make a telephone call,' and, 'Time for bed,' being the ones that spring most readily to mind.

I have tried to hold conversations while he's still up and about, but my friends (particularly the child-free ones) find it infuriating that I never finish a sentence without having to break off to yell, 'Don't touch that!' Or, 'No, you can't have a lollipop, eat an apple,' which I say for the benefit of the person on the other end of the phone while I feed Eddie kilos of sweets in an effort to buy time for adult chatter. Even when Eddie does fall asleep the next couple of hours are lost in a blur of household duties.

Not that I am a domestic goddess. I wouldn't like to mislead and give the impression that I am the sort of woman who pre-packs her kid's lunch for kindie the night before it is actually needed. A lunch full of home-made goodies, organic whatsits and fruit and veggie thingies. I am (sadly) far more of a seat-of-my-pants type of girl. The chores that gobble up my time are scraping tomato sauce and leftover fish fingers from plastic plates into the bin, scraping yogurt from any and every surface that Eddie can reach in the flat, sticking a load of washing on, maybe doing a bit of ironing (if I can't smooth the crinkles out by hand) *and* drinking at least half a bottle of wine. By the time the washing is on the spin cycle the wine has usually taken effect and I feel sufficiently cleansed of the day's grime to call Bella.

We never run out of things to say. For quite some time we talked about my divorce and my bastard ex-husband, Oscar. Then we discussed Bella's wedding and now, as neither of us is facing any particular life-changing event, we talk about what colour I should paint my bathroom and what colour she should paint her toenails.

It really doesn't matter if I put a late call in, keep Bella up into the small hours of the morning, as she doesn't have to get up for work or a demanding child. I won't even try to pretend that I'm not jealous.

When I met Bella, over three years ago, things were very different. In those days she didn't visit beauticians, expensive hairdressers, food nutritionists or the gym to fill her day. Between approximately 8.30 a.m. and 7.45 p.m. she was a lackey in some PR company because she had a vague notion that she wanted to 'get into PR'. People kept telling her she'd be good at it. Not that she is a particularly good communicator but she is pretty and a disproportionate amount of pretty girls are advised that

PR is the career for them. As these girls often labour under the mistaken belief that a career in PR means attending lots of swanky parties, they try it out for a while, despite having little genuine interest in the industry. This is the category Bella fell into.

Some evenings she did a bit of waitressing in a seedy cocktail bar and other evenings she did an IT course because someone had told her she needed to improve her PC skills. Once she cleared up the misunderstanding that PC stood for 'personal computer' and not 'politically correct' she enrolled for evening classes. She used to joke that she might as well be an IT girl if not an 'it' girl. At weekends she worked as a waitress in a café, which is where I met her.

In those days she was overworked, underpaid and not glossy. Now, the opposite is true.

I was newly separated from my husband. Oscar left when Eddie was six months old. He said he needed to find himself, which is male-coward-speak for, 'I've met someone else.' This left me in what the British would call 'a tight spot' and we guys from down under would call 'up shit creek without a paddle'. My family were all thousands of miles and an expensive flight away. I'd packed in work just before Eddie was born, I didn't know anyone well enough to ask them to come over and dish out the Kleenex. Most of my other friends were halves of couples that had been *our* friends and while many tried to be helpful and sympathetic about Oscar's speedy exit, it was difficult. I felt I couldn't talk to them in case they repeated things to their husbands who might let stuff slip to Oscar. For 'talk' read monstrously slag off, bitterly condemn and continually revile – obviously. Eddie was able to consume my hours with demands for food, nappy changes, cuddles and baths but he didn't offer much in the way of feedback beyond 'google ga, ma, ma, ma, ma, ma, ga ga'.

I was lonely.

Bella and I met just two months after the, frankly, gob-smacking catastrophic event. At that time the greatest distance I'd managed to wander from home was to the local child-friendly café in the high street. Its appeal was that I didn't really have to make any effort at all there. All the customers had squealing babies or unruly toddlers. Looking rat-shit, rolls of post natal fat and gaunt, sleep-deprived faces were de rigueur. I was sure that I merged into the noisy fray and that's what I wanted. Ideally, I'd have liked to fade away altogether; it's a common state of mind when your marriage is done for. However, it appeared my trust in my camouflage (elasticized daks, grey face, and scungy hair) was misplaced. I still stood out. I discovered as much when one day a waitress (Bella) said to me, 'You really are quite fucking miserable, aren't you?'

I intended to ignore the comment and just move to another table. However, instinct and curiosity took over and I couldn't resist a peek at the perpetrator of such an 'out-there' un-English comment. I looked up and was greeted by the broadest smile and biggest brown eyes; both assets were shimmering at me. For the first time in a couple of months I saw kindness.

'Totally,' I confessed.

Bella put a plate on to the table. There sat two large sticky buns, covered in icing sugar and cinnamon; they glistened temptingly. I felt disproportionately grateful. I hadn't eaten much since Oscar had left. Or rather I'd eaten loads but nothing nice. I found going to the supermarket (chockers with happy housewives), an overwhelming task so I made do with whatever was in the house. At first I ate reasonably but as the freezer and cupboard resources depleted I found myself eating increasingly weird combinations, such as fillets of skinless, boneless fish (good) with cornflakes (slightly odd) or cold baked beans with spaghetti. That particular lunchtime I'd eaten a jar of anchovies and tinned rice pudding. My taste buds had been abused.

'These are my favourite. I thought you'd like them,' said the waitress, pointing to the buns.

'Thanks,' I muttered. Did I know this pretty woman with a dark, curly bob and a big grin? I didn't think so but she was behaving as though we were friends.

'Eat,' she demanded. Obediently I picked up a bun and bit into it. Tiny flakes of cinnamon and sugar stuck to my lips. Warm dough melted on my tongue and it felt like heaven.

'I'm Bella.'

I managed to mutter, 'Laura,' before I started to cry. Bella handed me a tissue. I think she'd used it but I didn't care.

That was how Bella became my bezzie mate.

Bella and I recognized in one another certain similarities. Not that she had been abandoned by her husband and left holding the baby, far from it. Bella had never been married and from what I could gather, back then, she wasn't capable of staying interested in a relationship with a guy much longer than the initial three-month oh-la-la stage. But we were both travellers, both searching for something.

I was born in Wollongong, Australia. It has everything a girl could ask for; a big port and a smelting and steel plant. Wollongong is the Oz aesthetic equivalent of Slough. Or so I'm told; I haven't been to Slough so I might be doing one or the other of the two places a disservice. I'm the youngest of four children. My older brothers and sister all grew up gracefully, sat and passed exams, went away to uni, moved back home, married the neighbours and settled down to live the same lives as my parents had lived.

For as long as I can remember I have wanted more. Not more money. When I was growing up we always had enough money but not too much, and as a consequence I've never given money much thought. I wanted more experiences. I wanted to see more, do more, feel, taste and touch more. I didn't go to uni: instead of getting a degree I got several part-time jobs and started to save up for a ticket that would take me around the world. I wanted to see the Taj Mahal, the Empire State Building, the Eiffel Tower and all those other monuments that end up inside plastic domes that scatter snow.

I wanted to meet different people from the ones in my neighbourhood; who were very lovely but scarily similar, in a Stepford wives sort of way. I left Oz in 1993, aged twenty-one, and set off on my big adventure. In truth, most twenty-one-year-olds embark on an adventure; it's called life. But my adventure seemed to be more significant, more vital because it was *mine*.

I worked my way across Europe. And it was every bit pure gold, just as I'd imagined, and sometimes it was as terrible as my poor mum feared. The highlights included working in a circus – not that I was doing anything exotic like a trapeze artist or a flame thrower – I sold tickets and mucked out elephants. Another highlight was meeting a French lesbian who became a great mate. Briefly I wondered if we should become lovers, just for the experience, but she introduced me to her brother who was just like her but with a dick so I had a thing with him instead. I saw the Eiffel Tower, the Vatican and the tulip fields in Holland. The low lights included being employed as a dunny cleaner in public loos in Spain and sleeping on a floor for three nights in Florence train station because I couldn't get a job and I'd run out of money. Best not dwell.

I met myriad people; some fascinating, some so dull they brought on rigor mortis, some astute – I'll always remember their soundbites of wisdom. Some were totally nong yet their nonsensical chatter pops into my head at inconvenient moments. In 1998, aged twenty-six, I met Oscar. I'd never believed I was looking for 'the one', that my search and wanderlust were born from something as prosaic as that. But when I met him I thought I heard the pieces of my life drop into place.

Oscar was twenty-eight, just two years older than me but he seemed the epitome of grown-up sophistication. He owned his own flat, a small one-bedroom thing, above a dry-cleaner's in Fulham. He had a car. He threw dinner parties. It was only a few short months before he suggested that it was time for me to hang up my travelling boots and hinted that maybe he could swing a job for me as a receptionist at the media buying company he worked for. I never saw the Empire State Building or the Taj Mahal.

Not that I had a problem with that at the time because I felt a seismic shift. Something like relief washed over me and I hastily agreed. I believed that meeting the love of my life had answered all my questions and needs. And he *had* to be the love of my life, didn't he? He was clever enough, good looking enough and even though he hadn't travelled (because you can't class two-week package holidays to Crete or Ibiza as travel) he seemed happy enough to listen to my boisterous recounting of adventures *and* I fancied him so much I practically fizzed when he walked into the room. It seemed like love to me.

Three years, a white wedding, a baby boy and a decree absolute later I realized I was still on life's journey. Far from Oscar answering all my questions, his existence just forced me to ask new, harder ones.

Bella hadn't actually worn out her passport and crossed continents like I had but she was always seeking out new experiences too; she was a stone that gathered no moss. Bella looked Latin although born in Scotland and had moved to London in her early twenties. I'm not sure how she passed her time before that, she doesn't yak about her family much. My guess is that she has a perfectly respectable middle-class background and a respectable 2:2 degree to boot. This hardly fits in with the bohemian lifestyle that she likes to pursue and portray so she is tight-lipped about her teen years.

We bonded because we were broke and knew well

the tedium of temping. We bonded because we soon discovered that we love a decent paperback, our Boots loyalty cards, window shopping and white wine. We bonded because we believe you have to laugh or else you'd cry and we believe that there's something in horoscopes. We bonded because Bella said nice things about my son (even while he was in his buggy and asleep she noticed his above-average intelligence and creative temperament). We bonded because, in short, she is kind.

Bella's line rings. She picks up the handset quickly. Philip is probably asleep and she won't want to wake him.

'Hiya.' I don't need to introduce myself.

3. I Need Somebody to Lean On

Monday 10th May 2004

Bella

Philip has already eaten half a grapefruit and two slices of wholemeal toast by the time I make it to the kitchen. He is standing at the sink rinsing his plates before he stacks them in the dishwasher. He does this because, he tells me, a build-up of crumbs, rice or even tomato sauce will eventually cause the dishwasher to break and, he points out, nobody likes putting their hand in the filter bit to scoop out soggy spaghetti or peas. He is undoubtedly right but still I am aware that I rarely rinse. He smiles and pats his hands on a tea towel before turning his attention to brewing me a cup of the strong, black, Colombian coffee that I need to kick-start my morning.

'You didn't need to get up,' he says. 'It's not yet seven.'

It's true that I don't need to get up, I'm officially resting, that much Philip and I agree on. What I am resting from and for is far more complex. I think I am resting from a lifetime of catapulting from unsuitable job to unsuitable job. I live in hope that a bit of 'me-time' will give me the necessary space to discover my vocation. Philip thinks I am resting to prepare my body for pregnancy. Look, he might be right. I might conclude the same after my 'me-time'. Or I might not. I have issues. It's complex.

I can see that some kids are nice kids. My friends' kids, for example. Amelie's eight-year-old, Freya, and six-year-old Davey, and Laura's Eddie, are 'nice kids'. If they weren't I probably wouldn't see their mums or at least not until the children were safely tucked up in bed. If, one day, I was ever to have kids I'd definitely want 'nice ones', like Freya, Davey and Eddie. But 'if' and 'one day' are the phrases I'm most likely to use when I talk about kids, whereas Philip has chosen names and picked out schools for an entire football team.

I keep telling him there's no rush, I'm just thirty. Phil and my friends view my considered approach out of character; I'm famed for making rash decisions (few of which, in retrospect, are ever too brilliant, which is my point). In the past I changed job and home with the same frequency as other people change their sheets. Historically, I haven't been too reliable with men either. So, I'm rather proud of my cautious and considered approach to motherhood. Philip doesn't see it that way; he thinks I'm being obstreperous. We've been married just shy of six months and in his ideal world I would now be five months up the duff. I'm just getting used to ordering for *two* when I ring the pizza delivery guy.

'I like getting up to see you off to work,' I smile and I plant a fat kiss on Phil's lips. He pats my bum and grins appreciatively. Secretly, he likes the fact that I always scramble out of bed to wave him off to work in the mornings; he values any effort I make. I yawn widely.

'Were you on the phone to Amelie until late last night?' he asks.

I nod. 'Amelie and then Laura.'

'How are they?'

'Amelie was a bit quiet. It was Ben's birthday yesterday. He would have been thirty-seven.'

'That poor woman. She's done so well.'

'I know. She's endured Christmas, the children's birthdays, her birthday. It's so sad, isn't it? Previously, these were such joyous occasions, now they are just horrible days she has to get through. It just keeps going on and on.'

I met Amelie Gordon six years ago when I got a job as a cleaner and general dogsbody at Richmond Rep Theatre. At that time I had a vague notion that I might like to 'get into theatre', perhaps be a make-up artist or a set designer. Ben was a playwright and, that season, Amelie was producing one of his plays. It soon became apparent to me that Amelie was a trooper. Not only had she just given birth to Davey but she managed everything from ticket sales to resolving artistic differences between the cast. She even rolled up her sleeves and painted scenery alongside me. Lots of Ben's success can be attributed to Amelie's talents and dedication.

Amelie is the sort who glares back at the bullying brutality and realities of life with courage and humour. I haven't got the same va-va-voom. I'm not a shrinking violet but then nor am I the sort of woman who faces problems full on. When inevitable difficulties or even inconveniences come my way, I try to ignore them. I can be very boy-like. I fill my life with inconsequential concerns; I dance, duck and dive past harsh realities. I used to hate it when it came to handing in my notice, however frequently I did it. Invariably I'd resort to sending an e-mail as I walked out of the office on Friday night. Neither I nor my staple gun was ever to be seen again. I was also a bit of a wuss when it came to giving guys the elbow. I'd ignore calls, break dates and let bunches of flowers wilt rather than say that I didn't fancy someone any longer.

If Amelie is an owl, then I'm an ostrich and my friend Laura is a swan. She'd tell you she is a duck because her self-esteem isn't what it should be. But she is a swan.

Even though Amelie is one of my best friends I was astounded when she came to my wedding only months after she lost Ben. Throughout the day, if I caught her eye, guilt slashed me to the bone. It seemed irresponsible to be pretty and happy in front of Amelie who, despite the disguise of a wide crimson hat, was clearly stricken. If I had been in her position I'd have sat at home with a big box of tissues and an even bigger box of tranquillizers. But Amelie came to the wedding and behaved with unimaginable dignity, bravery and poise. She embodies the twenty-first-century equivalent of the British war spirit. I live in awe of her.

'Things will get easier for her,' says Philip. He kisses the top of my head.

'And will Laura meet the man of her dreams and fall head over heels in love?'

'Definitely,' grins Phil.

I love his calm, confident responses. Whenever I talk to Amelie I cannot imagine her grief fading and it's hard to imagine the man who will make Laura happy; for one thing she never meets a soul. But when I talk to Philip I do believe their lives will be joyful again.

Phil and I are not alike yet we are well suited. His ambition complements my lack of it. His direction and drive have stopped me meandering aimlessly and I was in serious danger of doing that, ad infinitum. My gregarious nature compensates for his shyer moments. My dress sense has saved him from being labelled a young fogey. *And* he makes a perfect cup of coffee.

'What are your plans today?'

'I'm meeting Laura for a coffee. I'll probably go to the gym and I'm thinking of tidying out my winter wardrobe. Bagging stuff up for the charity shops, deciding what I'll need to buy for the summer.' I try to sound as industrious as possible despite my day being essentially one of mooching and lolling. Philip has the good grace not to notice my idleness, or at least, not to comment on it.

'Sounds fun. I'm going to shave.'

'Kiss me,' I demand.

'I'll scratch you,' he warns.

'I don't care.'

We kiss and I know I am the luckiest woman on the planet.

4. Money Honey

Laura

This morning, like most mornings, I got up approximately two hours before I woke up. Eddie's disregard for sleep is directly proportional to my dire need for it. I operate in a zombie-state. I can sing, recite rhymes, answer an unending string of 'why' questions and still not be fully conscious.

I try to keep Eddie in either my or his bedroom until at least 6 a.m. when kids' TV starts, then I let him charge, like a cork from a champagne bottle, into the sitting room. I leave him alone with the remote (mastered aged two) and I return to patchy sleep, often interrupted as I hear him switch from Noddy to Teenage Mutant Ninja Turtles. I can hear him stampede around the room insisting that some imaginary baddie *die*. I long for thicker walls. Not that thicker walls would mean my child would display fewer signs of delinquency, but at least I wouldn't be as aware of them.

At seven I drag myself into the shower and turn the water on full blast. It's freezing cold which makes me scream.

'Problem, Mummy?' asks Eddie with his trademark composure.

It strikes me that currently Eddie has no concept of

real problems. Happily, he still lives in the state of nirvana where I can solve any problem by proffering an ice cream or agreeing to take him to the park on his bike. I wonder how I'll cope with him enduring any difficulty as he grows up. My heart almost breaks when I think that some floozy, one day, might bin him because his car is not cool or because he can't dance. I already want to rip off the heads of little morons who don't play nicely with him in the playground.

'No problem, just cold,' I mutter, as I towel dry and plunge one foot into a trouser leg. 'No hot water, again,' I add. Eddie could not care less. I know I'll be lucky if I get to slosh a sponge around his face before he goes to kindie, he has a predisposition towards filth. 'The bloody builders must have altered the timer,' I mutter.

'Bloody builders,' he echoes, which makes me think I ought to look for someone else with whom I can discuss the trials and tribulations of having building work done.

The builders arrive just as I am dragging a comb through Eddie's hair and trying to close the deal on the contents of his lunch box. He wants to pack jam sandwiches, biscuits and a slice of chocolate fudge cake. I open my pitch with ham sandwiches, an apple and a yogurt. I already know that we'll settle on ham sandwiches, biscuits and the fudge cake. He's by far the better negotiator.

They arrive at exactly 8.30 every morning. This is half an hour later than we agreed the preceding evening. As soon as they arrive, Henryk the foreman reiterates his all-too-familiar lecture on the importance of punctuality. This immediately disarms me and I lose my ability to point out that he's late, which is of course his intention.

I shrug mentally, and reason that 8.30 a.m. is early for the appearance of a builder, no matter what time we agreed. Besides, they defy stereotype by being clean-ish, tidy-ish and very thorough. They do, however, revert to type in so much as they have now camped with me for a total of three months when initially I thought I'd be enjoying their company for four weeks, tops. Henryk likes to chat to me; he's Polish and enjoys practising his English and because I'm short on adult company I encouraged this for a while. But, it transpires, Henryk can chatter for an Olympic sport, which is one of the reasons that the job is taking longer than estimated.

The second reason is there are plenty of things to fix in my dilapidated two-bedroom flat, and Henryk and his team keep finding them. 'Builders' is a catch-all phrase; they are electricians/plumbers/decorators/general 'all-rounders'. When I mentioned as much to my father, on my bi-weekly telephone call to Wollongong, he said the phrase that came to mind was 'jack of all trades, master of none'. I didn't find this helpful. Then he asked if I was paying them by the hour, as if I were some sort of an idiot. Dad also questioned whether all the work was strictly necessary. Annoyingly, the answer is yes. Henryk is not a cowboy. The things that he points out as ugly, dysfunctional or impractical in my home are just that.

I think Dad was just a bit jealous because I described Henryk as the bane and saviour of my life. Clearly, a parental role. Dad pointed out that as a qualified plumber, he could do all the jobs for free. I reminded him that, while this was excellent in theory, we live on separate continents and the flight would cost more than Henryk's bill. Sadly, I doubt this to be the case and besides, both my father and I know that he doesn't want to fly to the UK, he and my mum want me to fly home. They've wanted this since they saw me disappear through passport control back in 1993. The ferocity of their desire increased when Eddie was born and again when Oscar split. As they are not especially demanding parents I feel all the more mean for denying them this one thing.

Henryk is in his early fifties. He has a moustache and a paunch. I mention this immediately not because I'm particularly shallow and judge people by the way they look but because *Bella* is and does. I was verbose in my praise of Henryk, so delighted was I to find someone who could and would stop my leaking shower and unblock my toilet, and Bella became convinced that I fancied him when I started to refer to him as 'Big H'. She said my giving him a nickname was proof positive that I fancied him. I found this very depressing. No disrespect, he's fair dinkum but I think of him as a father figure. Clearly, my best mate sees me as a sad divorcee who fancies her tradesmen. Bleak moment.

Henryk is clever. He has about a dozen degrees, as most Eastern Europeans seem to, and over the months of chatting I've learnt that he has an understanding of literature, art and history that would allow him to hold an intelligent debate with the guys at Sotheby's. He's cheerful and has a twinkle in his eye. OK, he might have been fun in another century, even attractive, but I don't, don't, *don't* fancy him.

Clear?

I make him and his team a cup of tea and give in to

the inevitability of being late dropping Eddie off at kindie. Henryk is complaining about the stupidity of some house-wife or other, who has three times changed her mind about the tiles she wants in her bathroom. I already resent the woman, assuming that she'll be choosing between phenomenally expensive textured slate, classy marble or criminally priced mosaic. I went for bog-standard white ceramic with a blue trim which looks quite pretty but I ached for mosaics like you see in the loo of really trendy pubs. Or at least, I think you do. It's been a while since I went to a really trendy pub. The loo might be decorated with oak panels again for all I know, mosaic might be passé.

Suddenly Big H changes tack, 'You're happy with that door?' We both stare at my front door, the one that opens out on to the corridor of my apartment block.

'Yes,' I mutter defensively, sure that admitting as much has exposed some appalling ignorance or at the very least a frightening lapse in taste.

Big H shakes his head and tuts. I look at the door again.

'Maybe it could do with a lick of paint,' I concede. Henryk is not comforted.

'You're happy with gap, causing draught? Heat escaping?' he asks with incredulity.

'The gap?' I ask.

'Gap under letter box and at the top of door. It's been hung incorrectly. Monkeys. Look at your floor.'

It's horribly scratched. I'd noticed it before but blithely accepted it just as I accept so many imperfections in the way I run my life. I don't floss on a daily basis. Neither Eddie nor I eat five portions of fruit and veg every day;

we average about four every other day. I'm only human.

I look at the letter box. The gap is growing in front of my very eyes. Suddenly, I am ambushed by a vision of my hard-earned cash flying out. Ten-, twenty-, fifty-pound notes fluttering away down the stairwell.

I sigh and ask him if he can fix it. He says he can and will. He has the sense not to scare me by telling me what it will cost. Nor have I any idea how much it cost me for him to fix the banging radiator or the flickering lights in Eddie's room. I wonder when he will present the bill and how much cash selling my body would raise (we have no family silver). I doubt it would cover it so I instantly decide against it. Besides, I'd rather do overtime than show anyone my naked body. It's a long time since it was exposed to anything more radical than the communal showers at the swimming pool.

I break free from Henryk and dash to drop Eddie off at kindie. He goes there Monday mornings and all day on Tuesday, Wednesday and Friday, so that I can work as a receptionist at the local doctor's surgery for three days a week and act like a normal, independent human being on one morning; Monday – when I meet Bella for coffee. It kicks off my week with a high point and gives her something to get out of bed for; without our date she'd probably be languishing there on a Friday.

Big H's chatter means that there is no chance of my running a comb through my hair or dabbing on some lipstick. It is probably a good thing that my only dates are with girlfriends to drink coffee. Messy hair and a harassed expression are hardly this season's 'must-haves'.

5. How's the World Treating You?

Bella

Laura is late but only forty-five minutes, which for her isn't too bad. What do I care? The treadmill at the gym won't get arsey if I don't turn up.

She bursts into Starbucks with more enthusiasm than the venue deserves. I know some nice Starbucks, which have managed to remain intimate despite the cookie-cut approach to decor; this isn't one of them. This building used to be a butcher's and I am sure I can still smell the blood. It isn't the right shape to accommodate a long bar and leave space for clusters of tables and chairs; necessary to facilitate gossip and giggles. The chairs fall into an awkward line and always need shuffling.

'Morning,' says Laura. She bends and kisses my cheek. One not two because we don't work in the media and neither of us is French.

'You look lovely,' I say.

'I look terrible,' she states with no self-pity.

Neither of us is accurate. She looks OK. She could look lovely. She could be a total babe but usually she looks like what she is, a fraught mum. Her babe status would be immediately more attainable if she stood up straight. She's tall, about five ten. I'm not quite five two. Clearly, God gave her the extra four inches that were supposed to come my way. A clerical error among the angels, no doubt. She doesn't know how wonderful it is to be tall. She doesn't understand the frustration of not being able to see your way to the bar in a busy club or having to lop a good four inches off every pair of trousers purchased.

I'd love it if she was able to somehow recapture the magnificence I have seen evidence of. Old photos of Laura in her early twenties show a curvy woman, with big breasts, strong shoulders and thighs. I think Laura started to shrink after Eddie was born. By the time he was two years old he weighed three stone and Laura had lost the same amount. Every spare scrap of fat and flesh seemed to fall and melt from her. When Oscar left she seemed to lose height too. She stoops so badly now that her shoulders almost meet in the middle of her chest.

Laura also has lovely hair; naturally blonde and curly. She generally scrapes it back into a functional, no-nonsense ponytail. On the rare occasion when she lets it escape it bounces energetically around her face, in a mass of intoxicating ringlets which bring her sprinkling of freckles to life. Her curls defy the truth of her life as they insist everything is fun and merriment, one long crazy giggle. I think this is why she keeps her hair tied up; she doesn't like to be sardonic. Today she is wearing a T-shirt I haven't seen before and I feel it's polite to acknowledge it. 'Nice top.'

Laura grins, 'It is, isn't it? I got it in Top Shop. You know how cool their stuff is.'

I do. We used to shop there together. Saturday mornings would be spent pawing over the messy rails of disposable fashion. We would arm-wrestle for the last pair of (deeply unsuitable) purple hot pants. We'd take turns at guarding Eddie's pushchair and trying on shimmery, flimsy tops and pretty embroidered skirts. It was a fun way to spend thirty quid.

We don't see as much of each other at weekends now. Laura and Eddie sometimes pop by on a Sunday morning but Saturdays are for me and Philip. I sometimes feel a bit guilty about this but Laura assures me there is nothing to feel bad about. She insists that I should spend time with my husband, that it is 'only right'. I love being with Phil so in that sense it is 'only right' but somehow, when Laura says as much, she manages to sound more traditional than Mary Whitehouse.

'Why do we meet here?' asks Laura. 'There are dozens of lovely little coffee shops in Wimbledon or Shepherd's Bush and Starbucks is so soulless.'

'Because it's central for us both and we've tried the wee independents and they sell tepid instant coffee,' I remind her.

'Oh yes, why aren't things like I imagine them to be?' She grins.

'Rough morning?' I ask sympathetically. Despite the new T-shirt and almost permanent smile both Laura and I know that her lot is not a carefree one. It would be patronizing if I totally bought into her cheery persona.

'Not especially. Except when I dropped Eddie off at kindie he clung to me and sobbed.'

'I thought he was settled.'

'He was. He is. He's probably just playing me.' Laura carries more Catholic guilt than the Pope and she's not even Catholic. 'When he sobs I forget that his kindie is a perfectly pleasant place and that the carers do actually care. I imagine it to be a fascist dictatorship, where tearing out fingernails is an acceptable response to a four-year-old refusing to eat his carrots.'

I pat her hand.

'He seemed so distraught this morning that I seriously considered making a run for it.'

'Did you?'

'No. Eddie's key care worker, Linda, scooped him into her large breasts.'

'Did he smile appreciatively?' I ask.

'No, he's about twelve years too young. He just looked at me with his sad, blue eyes. Linda firmly and fairly declared that it is "silly to be clingy".'

'Bit harsh, he's only a tot,' I comment sympathetically.

'She was talking to me,' explains Laura with a grin.

I go to the counter and buy two more coffees and a blueberry muffin each. We always wait until our second coffee before we eat cake. Our ritual puts me in mind of my mum, who would never let alcohol pass her lips until after 7 p.m. She insisted it was important to have 'standards'. Her approach was rare. Like me, she was born and bred in Kirkspey, a small village in a colourless, dreary corner of the north-east of Scotland: a community that historically had been dependent on the fishing industry. In Kirkspey whisky was known as 'the water of life' and was as appreciated as mother's milk. I guess it dulled the pain and terror of the ever-present threat of injury or death. Events that were dreaded but not unexpected in a fishing town. Now, the area is blighted by drug addiction, high unemployment and incurable economic decline. You can't spit without hitting a forsaken boatyard but the passion for 'the water of life' is unabated. If anything it's more ferocious. I mean, I enjoy a glass or two with friends (well, three or four sometimes) but in Kirkspey I'd be regarded as pretty much teetotal.

In Kirkspey, riotous mood swings, unjustified insult, physical and verbal invective against strangers, vomiting and urinating in the streets, self-harm, lewd exposure, memory blackout and insolvency are rife. All because too many people worship 'the water of life' and don't have my mum's 'standards'. Blueberry muffins, of course, are a lot less damaging.

'You know what you need?' I ask Laura, pushing all thoughts of Kirkspey from my head, not a difficult task as I'm practised at doing so.

'A six-foot-two, handsome millionaire, who dotes on my every word and wants to make an honest woman of me,' answers Laura succinctly.

'I wasn't going to say that.'

'Good thing – you got the last one of those. Lucky bint.'

'I was going to suggest a night out.'

'I can't afford it.'

I am used to Laura's stock answers: she has been reeling them out for all of the three years I have known her and has recited them with increased vigour since I married Philip. When we were both on the pull she was prepared to launch herself into bars, pubs and clubs every second Friday but she is much more reluctant now. Who can blame her? It's a disaster movie out there.

'We don't have to go anywhere expensive,' I counter.

'But even if the venue is cheapo I have to pay a babysitter, that's if I can find one who doesn't come with a million terms and conditions. The last babysitter specified which takeaway pizza supplier she wanted *and* she wouldn't let me record *Footballers' Wives* because she wanted to watch it and tape the other side!'

I've heard this before; it is shocking.

'You could come to my place, bring Eddie. We could open a couple of bottles of wine.'

'But the cost of a cab home.'

'Stay.'

'I'd be in the way. Philip works hard – he doesn't want to come home to a house full.'

'Philip is away most of this week and won't be back until very late Friday night. I could do with the company.' I can see that she is tempted. She's probably thinking how delightful it will be to live in a dust and power-tool-free environment for twenty-four hours. I seal the deal by adding, 'I think Amelie could do with a night out too.'

Laura looks at once thrilled and stricken but agrees immediately. She's thrilled at the idea of a girls' night in/out and stricken at the mention of Amelie's name. Amelie's loss has that effect on everyone. In our heads we both refer to her as 'poor Amelie' and occasionally we slip up and do so out loud, although Amelie would be outraged to know we feel like this.

We agree to meet on Friday and then I pull a copy of *Heat* from my bag. We dive into it, hungry for our gossip fix. I buy this mag religiously on the day of publication, and, in a unique act of friendship, I don't even peek inside it until I see Laura so that we can take a virgin look together. This isn't a completely unselfish act as she always comes up with the most amusing and scathing comments. The conversation turns to the rash of B-list celebrities exposing their pregnancy bumps.

'Hers is nice,' comments Laura.

'It turns my stomach. Not just because they'll use their fertility to secure a few column inches, but because they look so gross and don't seem to know it.'

'You'll feel differently when it's you,' grins Laura and then she does that thing that so many people have started to do since I married Philip. She gives me a knowing wink.

I bite into my muffin and concentrate on the sweetness because unaccountably I can suddenly taste fear.

6. Guitar Man

Laura

Bella and I leave Starbucks together and stop for a minute or two to look in the window of a shop that sells children's T-shirts with funny slogans such as 'Granny Target' and 'Been Inside for Nine Months'. I resist buying Eddie the one with 'Mummy's Little Man' emblazoned across the front. Mostly because it is true and therefore seriously unfunny.

Eddie is my utter love and the only reason I don't completely hate Oscar is that he had something to do with Eddie's existence, although I don't dwell on exactly what that involvement entailed. I sometimes worry that I love my child too much. It might have been better if Oscar had left me with two children (a girl, perhaps) so I could have spread my love a little more evenly and Eddie would not grow up thinking that the world revolves around him. But then, imagine the extra washing and the increased chances of standing on those tiny little bits of Lego in bare feet (there is no pain like it).

I leave Bella sauntering towards Soho where, no doubt, she'll spend a couple of hours gazing in shop windows at the retro film posters, cute stationery and large silver dildos. I tear off in the opposite direction and head for the tube. We were having such a great time being cruel

34

to celebrities that I'd completely lost track of time. I now have only thirty-five minutes before I'm supposed to collect Eddie. I hate being late for pick-up. Besides the haughty looks that rain down on me from the kindie staff and the enormous fine (they charge an extra £7.50 for each unscheduled hour, or part hour) the biggest punishment is catching sight of Eddie's face. There is a huge stigma attached to being the last child that is picked up. I know that the shame is only ever a delayed tube away.

I dash down the first escalator towards the depths of the Piccadilly line. Halfway down my sense of urgency is hijacked by Elvis. Not the real Elvis. I know he's dead. But someone singing as though he were Elvis. 'All Shook Up' bounces up the escalator and I find that I am playfully tapping my toes and gently patting my fingers against my hip. If I'd been in the privacy of my own sitting room I would undoubtedly have been clicking my fingers and shaking my hips with real enthusiasm. Remarkable, when you consider that the sentiment could not be further from my reality. I am not in love and I can't remember when last someone left me aquiver except with anger or disappointment. Yet, it's impossible not to smile and sing along. It doesn't surprise me that Elvis songs are still played at just about every wedding reception even thirty years after his death. Elvis was put on this earth to make it better for all of us. I'm not fanatical. I don't own a pair of sparkly gold sunglasses, just the CD, *Elvis' 30 #1 Hits*. Someone bought it for me for Christmas, a few years back, and I played it all Boxing Day, although I think that was the last time I played it.

The music stops abruptly. The busker is being moved

on. Some are supported by London Underground; certain areas of some platforms have been declared official busking sites. I imagine you have to apply to perform there; clearly the Elvis guy hasn't.

As I mount the second escalator I can see an official insisting that the busker pack up and move on. I notice that the guy has a guitar which surprises me. He really is good; I'd assumed he was singing along to a beatbox. It's a shame he's been made to move. He was only brightening commuters' day.

I flash a sympathetic half-grin/half-shrug at him as I pass and comment, 'Really cool, thanks,' and flick a pound coin into his open guitar case. The official stares at me and mutters that busking is illegal. I flash him a look that tells him I don't care.

The tube arrives within a remarkable three minutes and, more surprising still, there are empty seats. I fling myself into one and rummage in my bag for my novel. Someone sits next to me. This is not a good sign. Only nutters choose to huddle up when there's plenty of space. I steadfastly refuse to look up.

'Thanks for your support,' says the nutter.

I take a sneaky glance around the carriage to see if he might be talking to anyone else. This frail hope disappears when I see that there isn't anyone else at this end of the carriage. Bad news on two counts. First, the nutter must be addressing me and, second, there's no one to help me if the situation turns nasty. I'm not a pessimist but if a complete stranger talks to you on the tube the chances are the situation is going to turn nasty. I didn't always understand this urban law. When I arrived from Oz I would innocently insist on commenting 'g'day' to complete strangers. I noticed that they always changed seats or got off at the next stop. It didn't take me long to realize that speaking to strangers on tubes wasn't so much considered a break in etiquette, more like a certifiable act.

'I feel I owe you a quid, though. You didn't really get chance to listen. Hardly what you'd call value for money.'

I look up and recognize the guitar case before I recognize the busker, to whom I hadn't given much more than a cursory grin.

'That's OK,' I reply cautiously. I'm not prepared to be overly friendly. Just because he's a busker doesn't exempt him from being mad. In fact, I'd have thought that anyone who was trying to make a living off the charity and generosity of Londoners probably does have a screw loose.

The busker grins and holds out his hand, 'Stevie Jones, pleased to meet you.'

I decide it would be rude not to shake his hand at exactly the same time that I decide Stevie Jones has the most beautiful smile I have ever seen. His eyes aren't bad either. The smile breaks across his face creating a similar sensation to that of cracking an egg in a frying pan. I love that moment. The moment when the frail shell snaps under the pressure of my fingers and the egg metamorphoses into something that promises imminent yumminess. It's a moment of change, expectancy and release. Stevie Jones's smile is the same.

'Laura Ingalls,' I reply. Fireworks explode in my knickers. Wey-hey, sexual attraction. Undeniable. I am completely shocked by this. I am, after all, wearing prosaic grey/white cotton numbers that were not designed to entertain flutters of any description. More, I'd forgotten that my body was capable of entertaining flutters. I have come to think of it as a vessel for food and something for Eddie to cling to and climb on. How odd.

'Laura Ingalls? You're kidding,' he laughs.

'No, I'm not. My parents hadn't seen or heard of *Little House on the Prairie* when they named me. More's the pity,' I mumble.

Can people see sexual attraction? Does this man know I'm imagining him naked? I hope not.

'I bet you hated it when the programme was a hit,' says Stevie.

'I did,' I agree.

Most people assume that *Little House on the Prairie* must have been my favourite programme as I shared my name with the precocious tomboy who was the lead character. It takes unusual insight to guess that I wouldn't have appreciated sharing my name with a freckly, goofy kid who had a penchant for big bonnets and bloomers.

'Still, it could have been worse. You could have been called Mary.'

Stevie and I shudder as we consider the full horror. Mary was the prettier character in the show but she was mawkish and irritating too.

'Back then I hankered after a zappier name. Zara, Zandar or Zuleika were my favourites.'

'Did this discontent with your identity last long?'

Stevie is smiling his fried-egg smile and the fear that he is a fruitcake recedes at about the same rate as realization dawns that he's flirting with me.

'Throughout the seventies and a large proportion of the eighties until I started to accept that being called Zara, Zandar or Zuleika wouldn't guarantee that I was more popular or the captain of the netball team.'

He laughs. 'I think Laura is a really pretty name.'

All at once I *love* my name.

'*Top Cat* was my favourite cartoon as a kid.' The non-sequential comment makes perfect sense to me.

'I loved *Wacky Races*,' I enthuse.

And so we start to chatter about stuff, rather than things. And we just keep on chattering until the train flies through Barons Court. 'I get off at the next stop,' I tell him.

What am I saying? Kiss me: this is our brief encounter. Get a grip. His eyes are a bright, clean green that reminds me of jelly: sparkly and rich. I realize I'm describing him as though his face is a plate of food at teatime but it has been a while since I've looked at men with any real interest. By contrast, food is an enduring passion.

'Mine too,' says Stevie.

'I change on to the Hammersmith and City line. I live near Ladbroke Road,' I blather, giving away more than is wise or cool.

'I'm going to Richmond. I have a sort of job interview.'

'Really?'

'The possibility of a regular gig. That's what I do. I'm an Elvis impersonator, or at least it's my night job.'

'Really?' I smile hoping to show my approval and interest, although I seem incapable of articulating it.

All too soon the tube pulls up in Hammersmith. We both alight and for a moment we hesitate. Clearly, we both want to say something, *anything*, but nothing ground-breaking comes to mind.

'Well, good luck with the interview – er, the gig thing,' I say.

'Thanks, see you around,' offers Stevie.

We both know we won't see each other again. Not if he disappears into the throng getting the District line and I merge with the masses passing through the turnstiles for the Hammersmith and City line. I shouldn't care. But I do.

'Bye then,' I mumble.

Then he kisses me. Stevie Jones leans towards me and after an intimacy of approximately fifteen and a half minutes, he kisses me. Very gently on the cheek, a fraction away from my lips.

A number of possible responses spring to mind. I could slap his face – unlikely as I'm not a star in a black and white, pre-Second World War movie. I could grab his scruffy, scrummy body and pull it close to mine and snog his face off. Also unlikely. Although I have now had chance to notice that he *is* scruffy and scrummy (longish hair, over six foot, broad shoulders, lean – almost lanky – with neat bum). But it isn't a long enough acquaintance for me to be that forward.

The kiss had been soft and kind. Interested and promising. I am not used to being touched with such tenderness. It was a good kiss.

So good, in fact, that the only response that seems appropriate is for me to run. As fast as I can. Up the stairs and out of his life, not leaving behind so much as a glass slipper.

7. All Shook Up

Friday 14th May 2004

Bella

I have made a special effort for the house to look lovely. Since Philip is paying such an enormous mortgage the least I can do is fill it with friends and buy a few fresh cut flowers now and again.

When we got married I moved out of the trendy Clerkenwell space and Phil sold his flat in Putney. I would happily have moved in there with him but Philip wanted to start afresh. We bought a five-bedroom house in Wimbledon, Philip said it was the perfect home to fill with bonny lasses and strapping lads. Who am I to object? It's not as though I have to keep it tidy. Gana, our Thai housekeeper, does that.

Despite Philip's plans for us to build a home together, he decorated the place on his own. It wasn't supposed to be like that but whenever I brought something home he would shake his head and say that it was lovely but not right for a Victorian family home. I sometimes disagreed but not enough to make an issue of it – and he might have had a point when it came to the glitter ball and the jelly bean loo seat. We both got what we wanted; me, a ready-made, middle-class identity, him, the knowledge that he'd tried to do the right thing.

Philip surrounded us with antique bureaus, shelves, chests, chairs and tables that needed to be protected with mats or glass. It was the tiny things that told me that I'd grown up. We kept spare loo rolls in the bathroom cupboard and light bulbs in a box in the garage. I had Christmas decorations in the loft. We have a Poggenpohl kitchen that's packed with gadgets – only a few of which have been taken out of their boxes.

This spring, we made the most of any mild weather and in the evenings Philip and I often sat in the garden to enjoy a drink. We watched as the trees slowly came back to life and as the tiny buds opened out into fleshy leaves. I'm planning on spending most of my summer in the garden. It is so peaceful.

The five bedrooms are going to be put to use tonight. I have made sure that Laura and Amelie's rooms are aired. I've left *Vogue* and *Now* in Laura's room and *Tatler* and a holiday brochure in Amelie's. The boys will share a room tonight, which they'll enjoy, and Freya will get to sleep in a double bed on her own. Also a treat. Although I'm not in a hurry to be called mummy just yet, I adore being the fairy godmother. Whenever Freya, Davey or Eddie visit I make sure that I provide them with all the treats I can. I go to Blockbuster, hire a couple of kids' movies, buy massive bags of Butterkist and lots of chocolate. I buy comics, glitter glue, micro cars and Coke. Anyone who says money can't buy happiness is shopping in the wrong place.

Amelie arrives first. She brings with her an air of seriousness and purpose. She had this before Ben died but I notice it more now as it is no longer balanced with his irreverence and flippancy. Not that Amelie Gordon is dull. She is thoughtful and thought-provoking, she's simply less silly than any of my other friends. She reads the quality papers. She took a masters degree in religion and philosophy so she knows something about Scientology (beyond the fact that Tom Cruise practises it). Not only has she actually read the Bible but she can talk intelligently about Buddhism, Hinduism, Islam, Judaism, Shinto, Sikhism and Taoism. In short, she is the type of woman I'd like to be when I grow up; either like Amelie or a Charlie's Angel.

The children stumble into the house carrying large amounts of luggage. They always bring their own Disney sleeping bags, several spare sets of clothes and a mountain of toys. Amelie is also oblivious to the idea of packing light. She's arrived with the entire Estée Lauder skin care range, clean clothes for tomorrow (two outfits; one befitting a walk in the park, another an amble down King's Road), nightwear, flowers (for me), several huge bars of chocolate (for everyone), books, articles cut out from magazines that she thinks are interesting and hopes I might too (Amelie assumes other people find thorny issues appealing and she has a higher opinion of my intellect than anyone I've ever met), and a bottle of Chablis (already chilled).

'I'm thinking of buying some ceramic hair straighteners and thought you might have a set I could try,' says Amelie, in a timely reminder that she enjoys frivolity too. I confirm that I have the latest type and that they work miracles.

'Aunty Bella, will you pierce my ears?' asks Freya who

has watched *Grease* about fifty times and definitely sees herself as Olivia Newton-John.

'No,' her mother and I chorus.

The doorbell rings.

'The oven should be hot now, will you stick the pizzas in?' I ask Amelie. The kids are already searching through the DVDs and arguing over whether they should watch *Shrek* or *Honey*. Amelie wanders through to the kitchen and I answer the door to Laura and Eddie.

They arrive with similar noise and commotion. Eddie is just in time to cast a deciding vote in favour of *Shrek*. Freya looks crushed but is somewhat comforted when I say there is time for both films. Amelie and Laura stare at me as though I'm insane as they see the chances of getting their offspring in bed before 10 p.m. recede. I shrug off their concerns as I know after they've had a couple of glasses of wine, they'll be less tyrannical.

It's about fifteen minutes before the children are safely ensconced upstairs in front of the TV. The pizza is almost ready and the wine is already affecting our brain cells. We lounge around the kitchen, propping up the breakfast bar. Whenever I'm with Amelie my first instinct is to ask her how she is.

'How *are* things Amelie?' I cock my head to one side – I read in a magazine that this stance encourages confidences.

'Oh, you know,' Amelie holds up the box of chocolates I've bought – Swiss – they cost a packet but are worth it. 'Should we open these before the pizza? Can we risk it? Sweet before savoury?'

'My mum's not here,' laughs Laura, 'no one is going to tell us off.'

Amelie opens the chocolates and pops one in her mouth, I wait for her to answer my question. She doesn't. Instead she turns to Laura and says, 'You look lovely.'

I haven't had a chance to do more than glance at Laura, since she arrived – I've been focusing on the children and Amelie – but Amelie's right: Laura does look great. Really great, not just the-new-T-shirt-demands-attention great. She's smiley and relaxed. She's taken the time to wash and scrunch-dry her hair, allowing her curls to celebrate their bounce. She's wearing another new top, a pink, floral-print one, it's cool, not mumsy. And besides these outward changes, I can see that something has shifted on the inside too. She is gleaming.

'I've met someone.'

'You have?' Amelie and I sound delighted and incredulous at once.

'Where?' I ask. 'At nursery? Do I know him?'

Laura grins mischievously. She's enjoying the attention. 'I met him after I left you on Monday.'

'You met him on *Monday* and you've taken until now, *Friday*, to tell me about him?' I'm mildly offended. Considering Laura sometimes rings me to talk about a new brand of washing powder, I can't understand why she'd hold back something of this magnitude.

'I wanted to see your face and . . . well, nothing is concrete.'

'Tell us everything,' says Amelie, hopping on to a bar stool and patting the one beside her.

'Well, at first, and I can hardly believe this now, I didn't notice how cute he is. I just heard him busking—'

'He's a *busker*,' I say with indecorous astonishment.

'Yeah. So?' demands Laura tetchily, suggesting that she already knows what point I'm going to make. From the look on her face she is warning me not to pour cold water. 'He was being moved on by an underground official.'

'Not even an authorized busker?' Did I say that? I hadn't meant to.

'Actually, that's not his real job. He's an Elvis impersonator, a tribute act,' declares Laura – as though he is more important than the chancellor of the exchequer.

I feel sick. Is there anything worse? I want to tell her that tribute guys are never more than that. I object to the whole premise: if you have to be an entertainer, why be an imitator? Why not be yourself? I can see her now in the audience of working men's clubs, surrounded by wasters and alcoholics, sipping Blue Nun as her man squeezes himself into his sparkly suit – changing room nothing more than a curtain pulled around a makeshift stage. I contain my criticism as a discontented mumble.

'Well, that should impress the bank manager.' Laura glares at me. 'Sorry, no more interruptions. Go on.'

'And then I got on the train and the next thing I knew he was sat in my carriage and we got chatting. He's got the most beautiful smile.'

'What did you chat about?'

'*Little House on the Prairie.*'

'Oh.'

'And as I got off the tube he kissed me.'

'He kissed you?' Even Amelie is taken aback but she's

grinning as though this forward, stalking busker is a good thing!

'When are you going to see him next?' she asks.

'I don't know. That's the problem. I didn't take his number.'

'But you gave him yours,' said Amelie.

Laura shakes her head. She then retells the story of her brief encounter with gory detail. She goes on about 'connections' and feeling 'something in the air'. I tell her that's smog. She pretends not to hear me.

'You are insane,' I pronounce and then I panic. 'He could have been insane. Really, I mean.'

'I thought that at first but he was too cute,' smiles Laura.

'Insanity comes in all sorts of guises, even practised flirts,' I point out. I feel like her mother.

'I'm so glad I was wearing my new T-shirt,' she says dreamily.

Visions of the countless eligible guys that I've trailed past Laura for her inspection clamber into my head. None of them ever raised an iota of interest. None of them made her so much as twinkle, never mind glow as she is glowing now. She looks fantastic. This brief flirtation, not much more than a fleeting moment, that wouldn't even have registered on my sexual Richter scale, had clearly sent her into a spin.

'I wonder how you can track him down,' muses Amelie.

'Why would she want to do that?' I demand.

'Look at her. She's all shook up.'

Amelie and Laura collapse into giggles. I pour some more wine and search for something else to talk about.

47

It's not that I don't want Laura to be happy – I want her to be *very* happy – I want her to have everything I have but she is not going to find it by hooking up with an Elvis impersonator. There would be no happiness that way. No stability, no regular income. I didn't marry Philip for his money but I'm glad he has money. Laura needs someone who can help support Eddie. Or if not that, then at least she needs to avoid anyone who is a bigger financial drain and has a similar income capacity to Eddie's.

'I bet we could find out which pub he performs at in Richmond, assuming he got the job,' suggests Amelie.

'She can't just turn up like a groupie,' I argue.

'Why not?' asks Amelie. She smiles at Laura. Laura beams back hopefully.

I make lots of noise clattering plates as I serve up the pizza. I hope my protest is registered. My neck clicks with tension and my stomach seems to be performing a complex crunch that isn't taught in any gym but has a similar agonizing effect to hundreds of sit-ups. I imagine someone pulling out my guts, putting them in a boxing ring to do a few rounds with Tyson and then shoving them back down my throat. I've never liked Elvis.

I take pizza and napkins up to the kids although both the mums warn me that I'll be scraping tomato sauce off the wool carpet for years to come. I ignore them, partly to show how relaxed and easy-going a host I am, and partly because I don't care about the carpet.

When I come back downstairs my friends are talking about reruns of *Heartbeat* but Laura keeps drifting off into a daydream and the smile on her face makes it clear that she is thinking about her busker. I refuse to indulge her and so we stumble through conversations about Delia Smith recipes, TV adaptations of great novels and how Amelie should wear her hair (she's planning a revamp). At midnight, after we have drunk more than a bottle of wine each, I decide to hit the hay. Both Laura and Amelie insist that they want to stay up and watch some terrible eighties movie. As I close the sitting-room door behind me I hear Amelie ask, 'So, what was he singing?'

I feel strangely excluded and unreasonably narky, even though I know it is self-inflicted exile and the only person I'm annoyed with is me.

8. If I Can Dream

Tuesday 18th May 2004

Laura

Amelie isn't really my friend; she's Bella's, although I've met her on a number of occasions at 'Bella Parties' (and more recently 'Bella Events' as nowadays she is more likely to host something spectacular that outgrows the party category). Obviously, I know all about Amelie's tragic loss. I want, if at all possible, to make her life a little more bearable – ideally a little more pleasurable. It's as good a basis for a friendship as any, probably better than a shared postcode.

In my experience women are generally territorial when it comes to friendships. They don't like mixing. I think the issue is that loose lips sink ships and invariably Friend A has had a good old gossip with Friend B about Friend C's boring husband/imminent affair/terrible way with money, therefore can't possibly let Friend B meet Friend C in case a clanger is dropped. To Bella's credit, she is always trying to get her friends to mix. Take last Friday for example, it was so sweet of her to invite Amelie and me for supper. The kids all got along brilliantly, and that gave Amelie and me the opportunity to get past 'nice canapés' and 'yummy, champagne, how lovely' which is as deep as our conversations get at 'Bella Events'. That said, I'm not sure Bella will be overjoyed with the subject matter that Amelie calls me about today.

'I've found him.'

'How?'

'It wasn't so difficult. I went online and got a list of pubs in Richmond. I called them all and asked if they had an Elvis impersonator performing. I got lucky on the ninth pub. Apparently Stevie Jones has just been employed to be Elvis, on the third Friday of every month at The Bell and Long Wheat. Peculiar name, don't you think?'

I assume she is referring to the pub. 'Oh, Amelie, so many calls. What a purler!'

'Meaning, you're pleased?'

'How can I thank you?'

'I wanted to do it,' she says firmly.

I didn't press the point. I figure I must be a pretty desperate case if a friend of a friend thinks I need help with my love life.

'I could babysit for you, if you like,' offers Amelie.

'So you think I should go and see him?'

'Well, yes, obviously. The landlord of the pub said he's expecting your Stevie to pull a big crowd. Didn't you want to see him again?'

Yes. No. Maybe. Suddenly, I am terrified and delighted all at once. Stevie Jones has fallen into my lap.

'I couldn't go on my own.'

'Take Bella,' suggests Amelie. We both fall silent. 'No, maybe not.'

Bella has only mentioned Stevie twice since last Friday and both times as the 'loony, stalking busker'.

'OK, we'll get her to babysit and I'll come with you,' suggests Amelie. 'We don't even have to tell Bella where you're going if you think it will cause difficulties.'

'What if he doesn't remember me?'

'He'll remember you.'

'I've nothing to wear.' The age-old excuse.

'Nonsense,' says Amelie, in a tone that suggests she knows nonsense when she hears it and will not be accepting any.

I scramble around my brain for another excuse but the cupboard is bare.

It has been years since I fancied anyone. I hardly dare admit it to myself but the truth is I can't remember ever fancying anyone as much as I fancy Stevie. I'd been with Oscar forever and while I remember thinking he was a total stud when I first met him that oh-la-la feeling had faded after we'd been together a few years. It was stamped out altogether once I'd got to the stage of searching through his coat pockets for receipts and other incriminating evidence.

After we split I had a brief fling with my osteopath. We rooted energetically every Thursday night. We did not eat together, sleep together or even talk to one another much. I viewed him as a pleasant alternative to Prozac. The affair stopped as abruptly as it started when my backache receded and he got himself a proper girlfriend (someone without a child and a looming divorce case). I don't believe I ever missed him.

But I miss Stevie already. For days I've thought of nothing and no one else. I've found it easy to be pleasant to Big H and I am patience personified with Eddie.

Yesterday, I played Captain Hook and Peter Pan with him for over four consecutive hours. This involves me being endlessly tied up with a soft toy snake, rolling around on the floor until I escape, then being captured again so that I can walk the plank (a line of cushions on the floor). I did it and smiled, so lusted up am I.

I've endlessly replayed *The Conversation* and *The Kiss*. Stevie Jones thinks Laura Ingalls is a pretty name, which warms me like a cashmere-covered hot water bottle. I think about his smile, his fingers and the tiny hairs on his ear lobes. I am immortalizing him. Bugger. I've only just managed to control the situation by reminding myself that Stevie Jones is a fantasy figure: my feelings for him are not dissimilar to those I harbour for Robbie Williams and the chances of it developing into anything real are similar too. Amelie has taken away the safety barrier. She seems hell-bent on making Stevie more than a hazy mess of ill-defined desires and daydreams.

I wonder if I dare go to The Bell and Long Wheat. Amelie makes it sound so easy.

'Wear your pink floral T-shirt, your Wonderbra and your best smile,' she insists.

'What would we talk about?'

'You'll think of something,' she says confidently. 'Come over to my place at seven thirty. Bring Eddie. I'll sort out babysitting with Bella.'

9. I Really Don't Want to Know

Friday 21st May 2004

Bella

I protest at being dragged into this farce. Every sensible bone in my body is screaming objections but it would be infinitely more terrible to be left out.

Amelie rang and nonchalantly asked if I was doing anything this Friday. I said I wasn't and she asked if I would babysit for her. Delighted to, I said. Then she added that as she and Laura were having a night out could I babysit Eddie too. I was furious. Of course, I couldn't admit it.

'Oh, going anywhere nice?' I squeaked.

'A pub in Richmond. The Bell and Long Wheat.'

She didn't have to explain.

'The loony busker?' I demanded.

'The first guy Laura has shown any interest in for as long as I can remember,' replied Amelie, calmly; her criticism of my standpoint implicit but loud enough. 'She's really keen. A bit of fun would be good for her. Life's too short not to take all your chances.'

I thought the 'life's too short' line was a mean trick but an effective one. I agreed to babysit.

'You know what would make her most happy?' asked Amelie.

'No.'

'If you went with her, rather than me. It would mean so much to her if she thought you approved.'

'I don't.'

'You're her friend, I'm a stand-in.'

'Ohhh,' I moaned, flattered by Amelie's assessment of my importance, irritated that I was being manipulated.

At 7.52 p.m. exactly I find myself pushing open the door of The Bell and Long Wheat. I'm overwhelmed by the smell of cigarettes and alcohol and by the profligate confetti of leopard-print tops, huge hooped earrings and sequined Elvis Presley handbags. I didn't think people still dressed like that, not unless they were starring in sitcoms. The wine bars I frequent are inhabited by people wearing dark suits, smart shirts and discreet ties.

'Isn't it fantastic?' asks Laura.

'It's OK as pubs go,' I mutter ungraciously.

I object, so strongly, to the idea of my best friend falling for a loony busker that I feel miserable about everything associated with him and I'm not going to admit that the pub oozes charm. The windows are original stained glass; the tiny coloured diamonds throw interesting hues around the bar and dance merrily on the optics. There are baroque cherubs climbing the walls, leaving behind them trails of gilded laurels. The chairs are mismatched and worn; the wood has been polished by skittish bottoms and the velvet on the benches is shabby to threadbare. A number of huge ornate mirrors hang on the walls, aged to black in parts. Under any other circumstances this pub would have earned my praise, but

I grumble that it is very smoky and it will be difficult to get a seat.

'How do I look?' asks Laura. She's too excited even to be decently nervous.

Despite myself I grin. 'Amazing, he's a lucky man.'

We push our way to the bar and order a couple of Pernod and blacks (not our normal tipple but Laura wanted to blend in), then drive our way to the last couple of overlooked seats squashed into the corner of the room.

'I'm surprised by the crowd in here,' I comment.

'You mean the large number of ladies past a certain age?' asks Laura.

'No, I expected a fair showing of wrinklies. I'm surprised to see young guys and girls.'

'I guess they've come with their mums to keep them out of trouble,' giggles Laura.

You can almost taste the anticipation in the air. Some diehards, with their beaded Elvis T-shirts, sit in silence, grimly guarding their table.

Laura and I steal a glance at our watches. The loony busker is due to appear in fifteen minutes.

'Pop stars never start their gigs on time,' asserts Laura.

'He's hardly a pop star, is he?' She ignores me and insists on continuing to look expectant and radiant.

I glance around at the women wearing heavy eyeliner and too-red lipstick and I am back in a place I never wanted to revisit. 'Don't you think it's weird and morbid that these women spend their Friday nights idolizing a mimic of a corpse?' I ask.

'No. I think it's romantic that one man affected the lives of so many,' replies Laura.

'Jesus,' I mutter.

'No, Elvis.'

I am unsure as to whether she deliberately misunderstood my exasperation.

'Everybody has a face like a slapped arse.'

'They're just normal people, Bella. It's because you're used to mixing with the beautiful people.'

'I prefer the beautiful people, call me shallow.'

'Shallow.'

I glare at her, so she offers to get us both another drink. Laura fights her way to the bar and this time comes back with a couple of vodkas and orange. We drink them far too quickly. Laura is either nervous or excited and I've decided this whole evening will be less tedious if I'm drunk.

'Do you think we've got time to get another in?' I ask.

'Better had,' agrees Laura.

It's my turn to shove my way to the bar. At first I smile flirtatiously as people make way for me, but soon I'm forced to dig my bony elbows into people's backs. It's a dog-eat-dog world. Everyone wants to buy their drinks and get back to their seats or viewing point before the loony busker appears. I can smell other people's perfume and aftershave only just masking the more raw smell of sweat produced by their sense of urgency. My hair starts to curl in the heat, betraying my faux sophistication. The last time I wore my hair curly was on my wedding day when I noticed approx one hundred of my two hundred guests wore theirs straight – the guys were mostly bald.

Just as I pick up our double gins and tonic, the crowd lets out a cheer. I start to inch my way back through the throng. Elvis is in the building. Suddenly, the room is awash with the uptempo beat of 'Return to Sender'. A good opening number, I suppose, and I know the words – doesn't everybody? Certainly everybody in The Bell and Long Wheat seems to. The pub is a mass of swaying hips and wide grins, people are singing along, clicking their fingers, tapping their feet. The old grannies smile, showing their dentures, and the girls twirl, showing neat waists and high bums. It's depressingly familiar.

Slowly, I shuffle forwards. Laura is beaming inanely at the stage. She's swaying and nodding with more enthusiasm than I was expecting to see for the first track. On the rare occasion that we go to a club Laura forgets she's an up-for-it Aussie girl. She follows etiquette dictated by British shyness and shuffles on the spot for ten tracks before dancing. But tonight she has rediscovered her roots and is refusing to be intimidated. Amelie is right, the girl has got it bad. I turn towards the direction of her stare, to see for myself this object of her adoration. My world screeches to a dangerous halt and I'm viciously whiplashed by bad karma, spiteful fate or simply sod's rotten law.

Elvis is Stevie Jones.

10. His Latest Flame

Laura

Bella missed the first song as she was at the bar. Which is a total bummer. Stevie Jones is even better than I remembered him. Who would have thought it possible?

Although my fantasies over the last twelve days have been elaborate, I had not considered what he would be wearing at this gig (in most of my fantasies he is naked or on the way). My overwhelming image of him is as a slightly grubby figure, standing on Hammersmith platform. Tonight he is groomed to within an inch of his life and looks even sexier than I remembered. He is wearing high-waisted trousers and a ruffled dress shirt; the style Elvis favoured in his early years. His wide shoulders and trim bum are displayed for optimum impact. His shaggy surfer hair is greased into a quiff and somehow he looks cooler than anyone with a quiff deserves to look. I hadn't noticed his broad forearms before.

The room is buzzing and yet at the same time everyone is transfixed. All hearts and minds are paying homage to Stevie. He sang and danced his opening number, 'Return to Sender', with perfection. In witty, flawless imitation of Elvis, he faithfully mimicked the suggestive hand gestures, the boxer's shuffle, the self-deprecating shoulder shrugs.

I am in love. The lusty type of love, not the real type.

Besides, so is every other woman in the room and some of the boys too. Bella makes it back to the table. She looks anxious.

'Pisser about the crowds,' I comment sympathetically, 'but you can understand it, can't you? He's mesmerizing.'

'I can't stay here,' yells Bella.

'What?' I am not sure I've heard her properly. 'He's bloody good, isn't he?' It is a rhetorical question although it would give me untold satisfaction if Bella agreed. My man is sex on legs and talented. Women are clambering on to the stage to have their photos taken with him. When I say stage I mean the slightly raised area, about a metre and a half long by a metre wide and thirty centimetres off the ground. Still, some of the fans stumble, or at least pretend to, requiring Stevie to catch them. I glare my hostility.

'You've got to admit, he's not just a busker. Not when you see him like this. He's special,' I add.

Bella is always going on about making her mark, making a difference. It's one of the reasons she admired Ben so much. He left something behind him. His droll, poignant plays make people think.

Stevie is making a difference; he is making people happy. Even if he isn't performing to thousands at the Royal Albert Hall, even if it is only in a pub in Richmond. Bella can laugh but people are holding up their mobile phones and texting photos of him to their mates.

Stevie begins 'Jailhouse Rock'.

'It's crazy that we all know the words to these songs. We weren't even born when they were released. I never think of myself as an Elvis fan but it's all there.' I tap my skull and turn to Bella, hoping she'll enthuse. She doesn't. She looks as though she's going to puke or faint or spontaneously combust. 'Christ! Bella, are you ill?'

It's as though she hasn't heard me. I put my arm round her shoulders and shake her. She's not normally a big drinker and we've been mixing irresponsibly tonight. She doesn't seem aware of me. The only time I've seen her like this before was when we went to Brighton to see a hypnotic act. She was picked out of the audience and the guy convinced her she was an egg-laying chicken. I so wish I'd had a video camera with me that night. I click my fingers in front of Bella's eyes and shake her again. Slowly she returns to me. Her eyes darken and the pupils shrink.

'I'm going. You should come too,' she snaps.

'No, Bella, don't do this to me. I know you think I should meet a banker or even an estate agent but I like Stevie. Like *like*. I want to stay.'

'We don't belong here,' she says as though I've just asked her to join a mad religious cult, rather than stay and have a few jars and watch hunk of the month gyrate on a stage. What is her problem?

'These people are not like us. Not our sort.'

'What are you talking about?'

'The smoke's making my eyes sting and I think I might have an asthma attack.'

'You're not asthmatic,' I point out.

'I have to go. Please come.'

'No, Bella.'

I glance around the room to assess the people Bella has taken a disproportionate and inconvenient dislike to. The room is full of people who eat too much cholesterol, exercise too little, dream more than average. They seem very much my sort. I turn to say as much to Bella but she has gone.

Bugger, bugger, bugger her. I reach for my handbag. I'll have to go and find her, as much as I want to kick on and drool over Stevie Jones, Bella is my best friend – even if, right now, I could cheerfully throttle her. The moment I start to push through the crowd the music changes from 'Jailhouse Rock' to 'Stuck On You'.

Stevie's voice, deeper than I remembered – a touch more gravelly – breaks through the noise. 'Ladies and gentlemen, I dedicate this track to Laura Ingalls.'

The crowd throws out a mindless cheer. They have no idea who Laura Ingalls is, other than a freckly, goofy kid with a penchant for big bonnets and bloomers, but they cheer anyway, such is their intense, albeit transient, love for Stevie.

Stevie locks eyes with me and beams. It is the widest, happiest grin I have ever seen on an adult. I'm stunned. Even before Oscar stomped on my self-esteem, I knew my limits. Generally, men look at me and think 'best mate' rather than 'total goddess'. I'm the type of girl men fall in love with after they have got used to my weird sense of humour and my inability to put the cap back on the toothpaste. If I was ever foolish enough to ask a man why he loved me, he'd invariably reply that he appreciated my extensive film-trivia knowledge. I am not the sort of woman who stops traffic (unless I'm stood at a Zebra crossing), but right now, I know, *absolutely know*, that the way Stevie Jones is looking at me is important. It means he thinks that I'm important.

And so do many of the other people in the room. The men turn with interest, the women with ill-disguised envy, to see who Stevie Jones is singing to. Suddenly, I'm not so sure of the words to 'Stuck On You'. So I listen carefully. Initially, I try not to read too much into it. I tell myself that it's not as though he is saying that if *we* were together *we* couldn't be torn apart.

It's just a song.

It's not as though Stevie is planning on catching *me*. He doesn't even know me. No doubt he does this every night; he picks some woman from the crowd, sings something that seems poignant to her and throws out that smile of his. He makes her feel as though she is the only woman on the planet. I'm probably in the epicentre of a horribly shoddy, humdrum moment. I don't even have long black hair, like the lyrics specify. I remind myself that logically speaking I am not special. This is not a special moment.

Yet . . . while my brain is telling me that this is a tacky, predictable move, my heart is pounding with such ferocity that I think it is about to break out of my chest and jump up on to the stage to join Stevie and dance a jig. It *feels* extremely special. And, if I'm not completely deluded or plastered (both are possibilities but not probabilities) Stevie looks as though seeing me is the equivalent to all his Christmases and birthdays coming at once. I don't think that his reaction is entirely because he thinks I'll be an easy lay. I realize that by allowing an absolute stranger to kiss me after exchanging approximately one hundred and fifty words on a train then I have, perhaps, given off 'available' signals (if not 'slapper'). But even so, it is obvious that Stevie is not without options. If an easy lay is what he requires, just about every woman in the room will happily oblige.

I start to sway my hips. And my shoulders. For about six tracks I am the most beautiful and accomplished woman in the universe. I see myself as a sort of Kate Moss/Keira Knightley mix, with a bit of Liz Hurley mystery thrown in for good measure. Throughout '(Let Me Be Your) Teddy Bear' and 'A Big Hunk o' Love', I believe that I have a higher butt than Kylie's. As he sings 'Wooden Heart', I am sure that I can do mental arithmetic faster than Carol Vorderman and I am perhaps more green-fingered than Charlie Dimmock. I could scour an oven, clean behind the back of a settee and descale the taps in my bathroom faster than Kim and Aggie, those cleaning women with their own TV show. I am *invincible*. Although, the more I stare at sexy Stevie, the more convinced I am that these housewifery skills, which I have long admired, will not be required. I start to focus along the lines of imitating Lucy Liu's gymnastic ability instead.

I have the best night, ever. Stevie dedicates tracks to me, he blows kisses to me, he tells the audience that they ought to cheer the wonderfulness of me. And they do. Complete strangers buy me drinks. They clink glasses and yell congratulations although it is unclear what they imagine I have achieved. In the fans' eyes winning Stevie's attention deserves extensive praise and I'm inclined to agree with them.

I drink most of the drinks proffered, which certainly helps cement the illusion that I am the most beautiful woman in the universe and stops me considering that I am potentially making a complete arse of myself.

I ache for the gig to be over. While I'm enjoying watching Stevie perform, I don't want to have to share him. I hardly give a thought to Bella. And when I do, I reassure myself that she will have got a taxi and besides, she doesn't like people fussing when she is ill.

11. You Don't Know Me

Saturday 22nd May 2004

Bella

Amelie rings me at 8.30 a.m. I wonder what took her so long.

'You'd better have a good reason for running out on Laura,' she says.

'I have.'

'Well?'

I turn to look at Philip sleeping peacefully beside me. He looks almost babyish swaddled in thick white cotton sheets, cushioned by a large amount of pillows. He's exhausted. He spent yesterday in Switzerland, seeing a client. His plane was delayed and the cab from the airport got snarled up in traffic, we arrived home at approximately the same time. Like Amelie, Philip had been surprised that I had cut short my girls' night out and wanted to know why.

I told him that I'd felt overwhelmed by a need to be with him and, more than anything in this world, I wanted to be away from the pub, full of fat, blowzy women, cigarette smoke and the smell of booze. I wanted to be in our clean, stylishly decorated, south-west-facing home. I wanted to drape my arms round his neck and squash myself against his chest. Philip had been delighted with this response and we'd made urgent love on the stairs. For once, our needs overwhelmed our desire for comfort.

'I just wanted to be with Philip,' I tell Amelie truthfully.

There is a pause while she considers this. Unlike Philip, there is no probability that Amelie will be flattered into distraction.

'Why? What's going on?' she asks with more perception than I appreciate.

I shiver even though it's a bright spring day and sunshine is flooding through the bedroom window. I choose not to answer the question and ask, 'What time did Laura get home?' Suddenly I'm panicked. 'She did come home, didn't she?'

'Are you worried that she is lying prone in an alley somewhere?'

'No, I'm worried she slept with Stevie Jones,' I blurt, with more truth than I intended.

'What's going on, Bella? What on earth made you leave her like that?'

I hesitate again. Eleven years of rigorous training battles with fleeting instinct. Can I cast aside the stringent code I've put in place? Can I tell her the truth? I touch Philip's face gently. I trace his eyebrow and cheekbone. I have so much to lose. There's everything to lose.

Despite the needy and energetic sex last night I had not fallen into my usual deep, contented sleep, whereas Philip could barely drag himself off the landing and into bed before his eyes closed. I tried reading but the words jumped about, spitefully cheating me out of a distraction. I drank a glass of warm milk but it just left a funny cloying taste in my mouth so I lay awake all night, replaying the past, imagining the future. One was depressing, the other bleak. I last remember looking at the clock at 5.45 a.m. After that, I must have finally fallen asleep. Amelie's call woke me from a miserable dream where I was being chased by Big Ben and I kept standing in gigantic piles of dog faeces.

'Amelie, can I come over? I can't talk about this over the phone.'

'The coffee's on,' she replies, mirroring my ominous tone.

Amelie opens the door to me and is clearly torn between ticking me off and giving me a hug.

'I guess you're in some sort of tricky spot?' she asks.

'You could say that. I need a coffee.'

Amelie leads me into her kitchen where, as she promised and as is usually the case, a pot of coffee is brewing. She pours me a cup and tops up her own. I reach for the warm croissants without waiting to be offered.

I choose to say nothing because I don't know how to start. I stare out of the window and watch Freya and Davey who are playing in the garden. They are wearing their pyjamas, under their coats, accessorized with trainers. This sartorial chaos is nothing to do with the fact that Amelie is a grieving widow, although to the uninformed observer this may seem the case. Amelie, Ben and the kids often stayed in their nightwear throughout an entire weekend, unless they ventured out or invited company round. Ben always said that this was to symbolize a release from the tyranny of a working week. Although in reality, as he worked from home, his working week wasn't hampered by a dress code. Amelie has continued the bohemian tradition after his death. It strikes me that she has managed to hit the correct balance of changing some things and leaving others well alone.

'Amelie, what do you think of me?' I blurt.

Amelie stares at me, probably reflecting that the question is borderline barmy. 'Where's this leading?' she asks cautiously. Of course she's right not to jump with both feet into a character assassination or even a glowing reference.

'Well, you're perceptive. You've known me for six years. We've seen each other through the good, the bad and the frankly bloody awful times—' I squeeze her hand. She smiles briefly. Bravely. 'You probably think you have me pegged, don't you?'

'I don't presume,' she replies, tactfully. 'You aren't easy to peg, as you put it. You're quite an impulsive woman.'

'Do you think so? Most people would look at my life and think it a scary amalgamation of clichés.' Amelie looks puzzled. 'Well, I am a thoughtless drifter, who can't make a go of it in any of the numerous industries I've had a stab at. I was working as a waitress when I met my husband, a wealthy, older man. I know people think I married Philip to get myself out of a hole.' I stare at the trail of flakes of croissant that sit on my lap, on the breakfast counter and the floor. I feel truly sorry for myself. I wonder if it's too early in the day to cry.

'Which people? Nonsense,' asserts Amelie. 'It's clear that you love him and he loves you. Have you had a row?'

I squeeze her hand again, poor Amelie, I didn't want to alarm her. 'No, nothing like that. The people who work with Philip, the other waitresses in the cocktail bar, people like them think I'm a cliché.'

Amelie tuts and waves her hand dismissively, 'No, they don't.' Then she becomes more assertive on my behalf, 'And even if they do, who cares? They don't matter to you.'

'I do love Philip,' I insist. 'I didn't just marry him because I couldn't face my arse being squeezed by one more randy, drunken customer. But I can see why people are doubtful.'

'Do you have any doubts?' she asks.

I take a deep breath and try to be as honest and clear as possible. I know it's vital that I explain myself to Amelie if she is to help me.

'The thing is—'

'I'm starving.'

I turn to see who is the source of the interruption.

'Morning, Eddie. Gosh, you must have been playing with your Buzz Lightyear late last night.'

Eddie looks wary: he probably thought that using a torch under the covers had fooled Amelie. Amelie doesn't pursue the issue – she always says the trick to being a calm mum is choosing the battles that are worth fighting; a late night at the weekend clearly doesn't fall into that category. 'Freya and Davey were up ages ago,' she adds.

'Oh.' Eddie immediately loses interest in food and runs to the back door. 'Can I go play too?'

'Don't you want some breakfast?' offers Amelie, far

too much of a professional to insist that Eddie should. He takes the bait.

'Maybe, OK. Hi, Aunty Belly.' Eddie smiles at me. Normally, I am unable to resist his smile and the private nickname. Normally, I'd sweep him up in a huge cuddle and plant kisses all over his face. This morning I find it hard to mumble more than, 'Hi, Eddie.'

Eddie is still here. Eddie spent the night at Amelie's. That means . . . I try not to panic. Maybe Laura is here too. Maybe she rang Amelie last night and they agreed not to wake Eddie and so Laura stayed here or just went home alone. *Alone* is the important bit. As though Eddie can sense the question I need answering he asks, 'Where's my mum? When will she pick me up?'

Amelie is busy pouring Rice Krispies into a bowl. She falters for a nanosecond, Eddie doesn't notice but the almost imperceptible hesitation tells me all I need to know.

'Mummy will pick you up before lunchtime,' she says. Eddie nods and accepts his breakfast.

Amelie and I sit in silence as he slowly eats his way through the cereal. Finally, when he has finished it and three pieces of toast (has the kid got worms?), after he has located his coat and trainers and flung himself out of the back door to start his day's adventures I am alone with Amelie and able to ask, 'She slept with him?'

'Well, we can't know for sure but she called last night and said they were going on some place after the gig. She asked if I'd look after Eddie until morning.'

'She slept with him,' I repeat. Saying it for a second time doesn't make it any easier to believe or accept.

'She's over twenty-one,' says Amelie reasonably. 'What's the matter, Bella? This can't just be about the fact that you don't like Elvis impersonators.'

I don't want to lie to her but I certainly don't want to have to tell her the truth either.

'I love Philip. I really do. It's not about the large home, although I do like him having a respectable job, I'm not denying it. Before Philip I had nothing more than a Boots loyalty card so I can barely articulate my joy at having a Selfridges store card. But that's partly because I like the yellow carrier bags, not because shopping at Selfridges means I'm rich. Of course I love our holidays in exotic places but they're only fun because we go together and . . .' I falter. 'I love all the add-ons but mostly I love him.' As the expression 'the lady doth protest too much' comes to mind, I snap my mouth shut.

'What's the matter?' demands Amelie again.

'I have so much to lose.'

'What are you talking about?'

I can no longer hold back the information that I've guarded aggressively for years. I am so lucky that I met Philip. Yeah, he took me away from the grind of a dead-end job and is paying the bills while I make my mind up about what I should do next. He's doing this patiently and without complaint, even though we both know it could be a long wait; think the siege of Troy. But more than that, I'm lucky because he is charming, funny, interesting, kind. He's a great husband and I want – wanted – want to be a great wife but I can feel the fates shift. My luck is running out, soon my secret will be exposed. I'm horrified.

'The thing is. The surprising, non-cliché thing about me, is technically I'm a bigamist.'

The words are out. They sit between Amelie and me for a silent and endless fraction of time.

She doesn't move and then, slowly, she asks, 'You're kidding, right?'

Her tone is cautious as though she is addressing an adolescent with a fresh outbreak of acne who has said she'd rather kill herself than go to school. I'm insulted but simultaneously understanding of her reaction.

'I wish I was,' I mutter. 'I'm married to Stevie Jones.'

'Elvis?' Amelie asks, with tangible disbelief. I nod. 'Laura's Elvis?'

'Mine, actually.' And the worst bit is, I am indignant that she described Stevie like that.

12. I Got Lucky

Stevie

I wake up before eight even though it's a Saturday and even though Laura and I were gassing till the small hours. I usually sleep late after a gig, rarely bothering to rouse myself before the big match is on TV but today is different. I'm full of energy. I have that feeling you get when you're a kid and you wake up on Saturday, knowing it's pocket-money day and there's no school and the world promises to offer unlimited, untold delights. A few of which are even legal.

I wander through to the kitchen and put the kettle on. I open the fridge and discover what I expected: nothing much. There is about a quarter of an inch of milk still in the carton but a quick sniff confirms it's no use to anyone other than a biologist. I pull on jeans, T-shirt and socks – I never bother with boxers at the weekend – I force my feet into my trainers, I grab a set of keys and set off to the shops.

It's only when I'm halfway there that I realize I should have left a note for Laura. There's a reasonable chance that when she wakes up she'll have no idea where she is. She was hammered last night when we staggered back to my place. She told me repeatedly that she'd never been to Highgate before and I told her repeatedly that she still hadn't, as I live in West Hampstead. I feel crap about not leaving a note. There is nothing worse than uncertainty. Personal bugbear of mine. Ancient thing. I resolve to hurry back as soon as poss.

'Morning, mate.' I nod to Mr Patel.

He smiles and nods back. He recognizes me from the countless midnight dashes I've made to his shop for bread, milk, cheese, frozen chips etc. He's unilaterally friendly – amazing considering that every day he has to deal with hordes of shoplifting teenagers, stinky winos and tight-fisted bastards who complain about his mark-up.

His mark-up is a disgrace, but I stomach it without murmur for a number of reasons. First, I'm not certain what anything does/should cost. When I do venture into a supermarket I rarely check the price tags. It's not that I'm loaded, far from it, but I can't see the point in getting worked up that a bag of crisps used to cost twelve pence and now they cost forty-five. I mean, Brigitte Bardot used to be a fox and now she's, well, not. That's life. Second, you pay for convenience and I have never found Mr Patel's doors closed, not even on Christmas Day in 2002 when I felt a desperate need for brandy butter. Third, I don't want to be grouped with complaining bastards who harass Mr Patel and similar. Once you start behaving like this you're only a step away from going out with your mates and splitting the pizza restaurant bill according to who ate what rather than in equal shares. It's not nice.

I pick up a basket and throw in a carton of orange juice, a loaf of bread, two cartons of milk (one tasty, the other skimmed, cos women like that). I can't decide whether to buy croissants or bacon, eggs and sausage. I have a feeling that Laura is a cooked-breakfast girl but I'm not sure if she'll admit as much to me at this early stage. Women always try to pretend to men that they eat less than they do. Which is ridiculous: we don't give a toss what they eat.

I decide to buy the lot and throw in a tin of beans and some fresh-ish mushrooms, which will probably look OK once they are cooked. Mr Patel has clearly seen this type of basket on countless Saturday mornings: he points out the fresh orange juice in the fridge which is tastier than the stuff I've picked up. I swap the carton for the tiny bottle of freshly squeezed chilled juice. Hesitate again, then grab another couple. I'm expecting Laura to be in dire need of vitamin C.

It's a beautiful spring morning. The air is cold but the sky is a calm, bold blue. A pleasantly high proportion of the wide undulating streets of West Hampstead are framed with fat, established cherry blossom trees that have started to shed their petals. Cars parked overnight under them look like they're dressed for a Hindu wedding. I have an almost girlish delight in the pink carpet (which I am, naturally, embarrassed by). It's disconcerting that I only just resist picking up a handful of windfall petals and chucking them into the air, just for the pleasure of seeing them flutter to the ground again. I content myself with banging into trees and hoping to dislodge a few petals. I've got to keep this impulse under wraps when I go out with the lads for a bevvy tonight or else I'll be ostracized from the darts team.

Laura is lovely.

Laura who kisses buskers, or at least let me kiss her when I was busking, is lovely.

I'm not a busker. By day I'm a music teacher at a local state secondary school. I like my job but it's not always easy. I seldom come across talent and confidence. It's not generally a good idea to show that you are a talented child in the state school system and if you do shine, it's cooler on the football pitch or in the end-of-term drama production. Passing grade seven violin is considered sad. Largely, the kids I teach have opted to take music because it's seen as a skive; there's no hint of verbs to be conjugated or algebra to be calculated.

I used to do the Elvis tribute thing more or less full time. I thought I'd make a career of it; lots of people earn a decent living that way. But it wasn't to be. Now I am Elvis from time to time because I like to see people enjoying music and that's not a sight I'm treated to when I'm teaching year ten and upwards. I limit myself to a few weddings and birthday parties and now I have this monthly gig at The Bell and Long Wheat.

The happy consequence of my gigs is that the extra cash comes in useful and the kids at school have developed a grudging respect for me since I turned up as the entertainment at Mark Barker's aunt's wedding. Mark Barker is as hard as nails and somewhat less pleasant than a bleeding, pus-oozing acne pock. Yet, while hating ourselves for doing so, staff and pupils alike court his good opinion. I'm lucky because Mark has never entirely despised me, as he does many other teachers; I haven't committed the cardinal sin of being post thirty-five (Mark doesn't deign to talk to coffin dodgers). Nor do I wear socks and sandals whatever the season. I believe that secretly Mark has always thought I'm a bit cool but he's never been quite able to forgive me for being a teacher. If I worked in web design or even ad sales Mark would have admitted I'm all right. Turning up as Elvis at his aunt's wedding could have gone either way.

Clearly the kids felt compelled to rip the piss out of me when they first heard I had a night job but I teach music, for God's sake, I couldn't have gone down in their estimation. For some time, my eardrums were assaulted with countless tuneless renditions of 'Jailhouse Rock' as I walked through the grey corridors and I'd accepted that I'd hear bastardized versions of 'Return to Sender' until I received my golden wristwatch. Kids are very consistent but not that imaginative when it comes to taking the mick. Then Mark Barker suggested I bring my guitar into his GCSE class. I'd been resisting turning into Robin Williams in *Dead Poets Society* because it all ends in tears, doesn't it? But I did relish hosting an impromptu and low-key jamming session.

Word soon got round that I 'wasn't completely crap' and my lessons became notably more animated, meaningful and, frankly, better attended. It was a thrill when the class discussed music with an enthusiasm and vigour that had previously been notably absent.

The kids seemed to view Elvis as the missing link between Beethoven and the hip-hop stuff they listened to. The misconception that anything with blaspheming and cursing in the lyrics was hot, and anything else was not, slowly eroded. We talked about the importance of music, the possibility of making a living from music and the value modern society placed on music. One of these discussions led to the bet/social experiment/barefaced dare that I could make money from busking. Mark Barker made the challenge, I couldn't pass it up.

So that was why the day I met Laura I was pretending to be a busker. But I guess pretending to be a busker makes you a busker, even if it is only for a couple of free periods and a lunchtime break. The same as, say, if you were pretending to be a hairdresser and you actually cut someone's hair, then you would be a hairdresser for that moment in time. Which I think is a great thought, as it gives us freedom to be many things.

When I met Laura I thought, quirky, which I always find attractive despite my experiences repeatedly demonstrating that quirky women ought to be avoided (quirky is one small step away from barking). I thought, pretty and nice accent. I like Aussie girls: they can throw frisbees. And when she kissed me, or at least let me kiss her I was like, yeah, cool. But I didn't expect to see her again. Three million people travel on the tube every day, it wasn't even my usual line but as my old grandad used to say, 'Never underestimate the lengths a woman will go to, to get what she wants.' And Laura, it seemed, wanted me.

This thought inspires me to do a little jump and click my heels mid-air. I make a mental note to execute this manoeuvre in front of Laura, if the opportunity arises or can be orchestrated. Women love it when you play around like a kid. I wonder if today I'll get to show her that I can walk on my hands.

I know she said her mate had tracked me down and

she'd been bullied along to the gig but that was rubbish. Where was the said mate, if that was the case? She was on her own last night. Not that I'm complaining. I think she's all the more gutsy and rare because of her sleuth work.

I put the key in the lock of my block of flats and bound up the stairs. I push open the door of my apartment quietly – I don't want to wake Laura if she's still asleep, with her young lad it's unlikely she often gets the chance for a lie-in – but my caution is unnecessary. Instantly, I'm ambushed by signs of activity.

The shower is gushing and Laura has found the MTV channel; she has the volume up far too high for this time of the morning – the bloke in the flat below mine will no doubt knock on the ceiling with a broom soon, as he does when I play MTV. I smile to myself. Further proof that Laura is a top lass.

I start to cook breakfast. I warm the croissants in the oven and fling everything else into a pan with a glob of oil. I'm ridiculously nervous. I say 'ridiculously' because I'm reasonably used to entertaining ladies, and breakfast is the meal I most often prepare. I'm not being pathetically braggie when I say that, if I wanted to, I could bed a babe (or at least a non-moose) after every gig. The women in my audience rarely present much of a challenge. And if there is nothing that takes my fancy I have actual groupies as a back-up. Groupies are girls who sleep with me while pretending that they are sleeping with Elvis Presley. Obviously, a bit weird but some of them are very cute and humming a couple of lines of 'Love Me Tender' is a small price to pay in return for enthusiastic and no-strings-attached sex with a cutie. It's not that I'm a bastard. It's biology. Few men would find it in their hearts (or their trousers) to say no.

But Laura is different.

Laura is a woman, not a girl. She knows how to have a laugh and yet after talking to her it is clear that her life is extremely serious. She's like a mate but sexy too. A sexy mate. I'm already looking forward to introducing her to my mates because John will make her laugh (and last night I discovered just how cool it is when Laura laughs) and Dave will reflect well on me, he's into the environment and saving whales and stuff, girls are impressed by blokes like that (they don't go out with them, though). And the lads will be impressed with Laura. They'll think she is funny and bright and cute. They're bound to.

'Hi.' Laura interrupts my thoughts of her. I jump as though she'd caught me looking through some hard-core porn. The knock-on effect is that I almost drop the frying pan.

'Hi,' I manage, sounding a bit lame. I cough and wave a tea towel over the pan to give the vague impression that the fumes have affected my vocal chords. I try again and hope my voice doesn't sound like a boy who is enduring his scrotum dropping. 'Did you sleep well?' I ask.

Laura blushes. Honestly, she's gorgeous. She puts me in mind of all those olde-worlde poems I read when I was studying English literature highers. Poems about coy mistresses who permanently wore the blush of a rose on their cheek. I used to think it was sloppy bollocks but now I see the attraction of shyness mixed with an almost imperceptible hint of wantonness.

'Did we have sex?' asks Laura. Hearing her say 'sex' causes my penis to shudder a fraction. This feels nice but vaguely inappropriate.

'Regrettably no,' I admit honestly.

Laura looks relieved. 'That's good.' She catches sight of my disappointed face. I make a point of blatantly wearing my disappointment, as experience has shown that wanting a woman is the best way to get one. 'I mean, I'd like to have remembered it if we had,' she adds.

I grin. 'You would have, I promise.'

She blushes again and grabs at the neckline of her robe, which is actually my robe. It feels good to see her wrapped in my robe. She thinks about it for a moment and then puts her hands at her sides, trying not to let me see that she opened the neckline a fraction while doing so in order to flash some cleavage. I really want her.

'We talked,' I add.

'I remember that,' she grins. 'Most of it. Was I talking absolute bollocks?'

'No. You were fascinating,' I tell her and we both know this isn't a line.

'What's for breakfast?'

'Sausage, bacon, eggs, beans, the works; even some dodgy mushrooms.'

'Great.' Laura grins.

'Great,' I confirm.

13. Girl of Mine

Philip

I surface from a peculiar dream about being at a race track and betting on a dog, who – happily – won. But then I noticed that it had the body of a dachshund and *my* head, which was somewhat disconcerting, even for the most rational type of guy who doesn't pay any attention to dreams; no one likes to see themselves as a mutant. I stretch out my hand and feel for Bella. She likes to know my every thought, both conscious and unconscious, so she likes me to tell her my dreams. She thinks they're significant and applies poppycock amateur psychoanalysis to them. Total nonsense, of course, but if it makes her happy then who am I to object? Besides, she sees the ones about Naomi Watts as a direct challenge and more often than not insists that we reenact whatever I've dreamt. A man can't lose.

We had good sex last night. Unexpected. Charged. Youthful. I *love* my wife.

I slowly stretch, wondering how it can possibly be the case that I notice when I feel youthful; is it the exception rather than the rule? I *am* much nearer fifty than twenty-one; a sobering thought. Not one I share with Bella, despite her longing to always know what's on my mind.

Her side of the bed is cold, suggesting she was up and

about some time ago. I pull myself out of bed and wander downstairs, hoping she'll be in the kitchen or the conservatory. Both rooms are empty and a cursory search of the house tells me that she's gone out. I check the calendar, which hangs in the pantry, and I scan the breakfast bar for a note. I'm not too surprised that I don't find either source at all fruitful; Bella is not the sort of woman to leave reassuring or even informative notes detailing her whereabouts. Sometimes she seems perpetually stuck in her rebellious teenage years. It's one of the things I find attractive about her.

I brew some coffee and consider breakfast. Bella would prefer it if I ate half a grapefruit and some of the muesli she prepares each Monday, with precise quantities of oats, nuts, raisins and stuff, to last the week; she'll know if I skip it. She won't hear of shop-bought muesli – too much salt and sugar. She worries about cholesterol (mine) and body fat (mine and hers).

The concern is at first glance endearingly mature but on closer inspection could be seen as a succinct embodiment of her almost split personality. A concern about fat intake is clearly very responsible, the fact that it was precipitated by an article in a women's monthly magazine that said 70% of all married couples put on over half a stone in the first year of their married life, is less mature. I begged her not to believe the statistic. I made her laugh by telling her that 87% of statistics are made up on the spot. Still, we lived on salads for weeks.

It concerns me how seriously Bella takes advice from not particularly legitimate sources. She is unlikely ever to read a pamphlet from the doctor's surgery. On the other hand she avidly reads article after article in tabloid papers on the latest food combination diet, ways to decorate your home, ways to interpret dreams, ways to impress your boss (particularly irrelevant when you consider she rarely has one). She'll also take the word of the woman at the dry-cleaner's, her friend's brother-in-law's dad, or the pleasant man who read the gas meter, as gospel. Bella, it seems to me, is always looking for answers. Often to questions other people don't even bother to ask. I often wonder if she would have been different if she'd had a mother. I think Bella losing her mother when she was so young has left her permanently lonely and a little bit lost, although she'd never admit it.

I choose the grapefruit and muesli because thinking of Bella's dead mother saddens me and I want to do something nice for her. Not that Bella would thank me for my disquiet, which she'd see as pity. Bella is, in many ways, fiercely independent. When I met her I wondered if I'd ever be able to chisel through her steely self-reliance and convince her that it is possible to be autonomous within a relationship. Once I saw her, I knew I had to have her. Not just for sex but for keeps. It was one of those big romantic falling-in-love moments that I'd never considered, let alone expected. At first, I thought she didn't want me. Or anyone for that matter. The shop was closed. I became driven by the desire to make her understand how fantastic it is to want and need someone, to be wanted and needed in return. I think I've succeeded. It's so clear that Bella, like most of us, needs looking after. Not all the time, not always by the same person but she does need a bit of help from time to time.

After breakfast, I rinse my china, stack the dishwasher, shower, shave and read half of the rainforest that is disguised as my Saturday paper. Bella still hasn't returned home. I call her mobile. It rings in the kitchen. I call Laura; her phone is switched off. I try Amelie.

'Hello, Amelie.'

'Hello, Philip. How are you?'

'Fine, except I've lost my wife.'

Bugger. What a tactless thing to say to someone who really has lost their partner. Mentally I beat myself soundly, then make matters worse, 'I mean I've mislaid her, not lost her.' I give up. 'Is she with you, by any chance?'

'Erm, she is and she isn't.' Amelie hesitates, which surprises me. I wait for her to be more specific. She's the clear thinker in Bella's group of friends. She's practical, efficient and easy to deal with. Normally. I wonder if I really have offended her as I can't see how my question about whether Bella is with her or not can be open to misinterpretation.

'She was here, minutes ago, but she's gone out.'

'Where?'

'With the children. Yes. She's taken Freya and Davey to the park. She wanted to give me a break.'

'Which park?' I ask. 'I could catch them up. I'm kicking my heels.'

'Do you know, she didn't say.'

'Well, it will be your local park, won't it?'

'Probably, but she might have gone all the way over to Kensington Gardens. Davey likes the Peter Pan play park.'

'Did she say when she'd be back?'

'No.'

'Maybe I'll pop over to the local park anyway.'

'I wouldn't waste your time – you know what kids are like, they'll probably get bored and be back home before you get there. You'd be better off calling one of your friends and seeing if you can get in a round of golf.'

'Maybe. Thanks, Amelie. Get her to give me a call when she gets back, will you?'

'Will do. Goodbye, Philip.'

I click the red button. How strange. I'm not often accused of having an overactive imagination but I definitely have the feeling Amelie was lying to me. Very odd.

But, on the other hand, why would she lie to me? No reason on earth. It is a lovely day, shame to waste it. I pick up the phone again, press my brother's number and arrange a round of golf.

14. I Just Can't Help Believin'

Laura

'That was delicious.' I smile as I mop up the last smudge of fried egg with a slice of white toast. 'A cooked brekkie. You're trying to impress me.' I smile, hoping I'm coming across as cute and astute. 'I should have guessed we hadn't slept with each other, you're still making an effort,' I add. Oops. It was supposed to be a joke but I wonder if I sound world-weary? Everyone knows that many a true word is said in jest.

Stevie looks a bit put out but doesn't say anything. But then what can he say? If he told me that I can trust him, that he won't let me down, that all he wants to do is sing to me and make me laugh and that he'd still be interested in me even *after* we've had sex – even if I am a single mum and a divorcee to boot – then I'd think he was pretty weird.

Yet, this is exactly what I want to hear.

My innards feel as though they are dancing a jig whenever I look at him, so it's not unreasonable that I'd like him to tell me that I'm the most interesting woman he's ever had the pleasure to meet. Or at least, that I'm not actively boring. I'd settle for that. I shake my head, bemused by my own inconsistency and fallibility. No wonder men don't understand us, I barely understand myself sometimes.

It's probably my hangover kicking in that's stopping me from thinking clearly. I don't *think* he thinks I'm boring or bogan. I steal a glance at him from under my eyelashes. I hope I look seductive rather than creating the impression that I have a fly in my eye. Stevie meets my gaze and he's grinning now, but that could be genuine amusement at me, not with me. He doesn't look bored, in fact, he looks eager to please. But I've been out of this game for a long time; it's easy to misread situations. I wish I could be the woman I was before I met Oscar, before my confidence and spirit had been trampled underfoot. The old Laura would have been able to make an accurate reading of the situation in a matter of seconds. I turn away, embarrassed at the situation and at the woman I have become.

I think it would be more productive to concentrate on recalling the events of last night. Hard facts will help me decide whether Stevie went to the effort of making a cooked breakfast because he's still hoping for a quickie but would then be counting the minutes until I got my jacket, or whether he was doing a nice thing because . . . well, because . . . he likes me.

I sit very quietly for some minutes before I decide that I'm *almost* certain we had a sweet-as time. And I mean *we*, not just me. Slowly, specifics come back to me. It seems miraculous that while I had unduly high expectations, the reality defied probability by exceeding them.

I can't remember ever being as happy as I was in The Bell and Long Wheat last night. I can't remember feeling so charged, so alluring, so positively fascinating. Stevie sang to me. The sweet words brushed my consciousness,

89

nearly bringing me to orgasm just as effectively as if it had been his fingers that were caressing my secret bits. He called to me when I was leaving because he didn't want me to go, he smiled at me, made a fuss of me. Every woman there wanted to be me. It was exhilarating!

We left the bar just after eleven. I'd already drunk more than was sensible but I'm pleased to say on the list of my talents, 'cheerful drunk' is quite high up. Neither of us considered going home, and once we'd made the phone call to Amelie, checking that Eddie could stay the night with her, we were free to go on anywhere we wanted. Of course, I didn't tell Stevie that Amelie had agreed to look after Eddie *all night*, I didn't want him to think I was too available, but I did say that I wasn't under any time constraint. Available enough.

Stevie stored his guitar and sound equipment at the pub and got changed into a pair of jeans and a T-shirt that were considerably more of this millennium. We caught a cab into Fulham and chatted all the way. It turned out that he wasn't a busker, with a breakthrough gig, he's a teacher and the gigging is a sideline.

'Are you disappointed or pleased?' he asked.

'Don't mind either way,' I answered truthfully, although I know Bella will be pleased.

We called in for a bite to eat at Vingt Quatre on the Fulham Road. I'd never been there before but remember passing it once, late at night, and seeing a queue outside the door. I was trying to flag down a cab to take me home after a dash to Chelsea and Westminster A&E (small piece of Lego up Eddie's nose, another story). I'd wondered how the restaurant pulled such crowds, it didn't look that special. It turns out that it has a double whammy of attractive plus-points. First, as the name suggests, Vingt Quatre serves terrific food 24–7 and is therefore a haven for clubbers with the munchies and, the best bit, at the end of the meal they bring a small bowl of Smarties with the bill. Who could resist? Certainly not Stevie or me.

We were led through the small noisy restaurant to a table at the back. I took in the decor (ubertrendy in a retro, not trying too hard, sort of way) and the clientele (eclectic – anyone from Sloanes sporting pashminas to hardcore cool, Diesel-clad clubbers). What everyone had in common was a surprisingly buoyant mood. Stevie ordered burger and chips. I went for smoked salmon and scrambled eggs on toast, although I seriously doubted my ability to swallow in front of him. I was being entirely a teenager.

Once the deeply trendy but unexpectedly affable waitress had taken our order I commented, 'People are champion in here, aren't they?'

'What do you mean?'

'Well, you rarely see Sloaney types smile, do you? Although I don't know why not, from where I'm sitting being beautiful, rich and pampered would seem reason enough to smile. And these trendy clubbers are so relaxed, even before they've taken their I-love-the-world drugs.'

Stevie had been a gent and taken the seat facing me and the wall so I had the best view of the restaurant. He turned to have a squiz.

'Everyone does look happy,' he agreed.

'And tonight at your gig, it was as though people had

been on laughing gas.' I was swamped by an overwhelming sense of love. 'I've never seen so many smiley people in one room since I left Australia. It must be you.'

I'd added this thought before my brain had checked the sentence for coolness. Luckily, before I could drown in my cheesiness, the waitress returned to our table. She chatted about how chockers it was and asked if we were OK sitting so close to the kitchen. She'd brought tap water rather than expensive bottled stuff, which was thoughtful. I stole a glance at Stevie. Miraculously he wasn't grimacing at my obvious compliment; he was grinning.

'The waitress is gold too.' I couldn't hide my astonishment. Stevie shrugged, clearly he hadn't noticed one way or the other, he would probably only notice the waiting service if the waitress accidentally spilt soup over his head and only then if she failed to offer a cloth to mop it up. Stevie was so laid back he was horizontal. I liked it.

'Aren't all waiters and waitresses pretty much the same?'

'No. The service and charm are usually inversely proportional to the beauty-slash-handsomeness of the server. The stunning ones know they're going to get a tip however surly they are, so they're rarely anything other. Mid-range try quite hard.' I was talking as an insider, I'd done my fair share of table waiting. 'This equation, however, has a point of no return. The incredibly ugly ones know that they won't get a tip no matter how nice they are, so they usually opt to be as unhelpful as the beauties.'

'That's a very sad theory,' commented Stevie, but he was grinning again, as though everything I said pleased him.

'Sad but true,' I assured him grimly.

'Do you really think the world is that superficial?' he'd asked.

'Lots of it. You must be bloody lovely not to have noticed, especially as you work in a school.'

Stevie's eyes widened. 'Did you just pay me another compliment?' he asked.

'No, I insulted you. I said you lacked perception.' I smiled again so that Stevie wouldn't take offence. He didn't. He laughed out loud. It was a laugh that came from the belly and rang clearly through the restaurant and all of London town too, I expect.

We talked, gossiped, told stories, swapped views and barely paused for breath. I got the opportunity to air my theories on the enormous quantities of sugar that builders, ostensibly, have in their tea (they must use it to mix cement or something). I talked about Eddie, a whole heap, so much so that I had to keep asking, 'Am I boring you?' Stevie assured me that he wasn't bored.

He talked about his work, his mates and his mum's Sunday roast. I was about to run a mile, I can't stand men with oedipal complexes and I don't buy into the theory of watching how a man treats his mum as an indication of how considerate he'll be as a boyfriend. An exceptionally close mother–son relationship at Stevie's age could only indicate a lack of proficiency with the washing-machine dial. I was relieved when, instead of telling me how friggn' A his mother's roast is, he confessed that she can't cook and that her gravy is often served with the question, 'One lump or two?'

After leaving university Stevie had bummed around

Edinburgh for a while, then galvanized and spent three years travelling around the world. I adore meeting other explorers. We talked about all the places we'd visited, and the ones we still wanted to see. Only another traveller can summon the appropriate interest to enthuse about a sunset not personally witnessed. Stevie seemed bright, animated, wise and relaxed. Characteristics that, pre-Oscar, might have been attributable to me.

It was past four in the morning when we fell out on to the street. We were giggling so much that I was bent double, although I can't remember what he'd said that was so funny. I was having a fantastic time, and from what I could gather, he was too. It seemed natural when he put his arm round me, and I don't think it was just to stop me falling over my heels and landing arse-up in the gutter.

'What do you want to do now?' Stevie asked.

I glanced along the Fulham Road and saw a cab's light in the distance.

'Do you have a girlfriend?' I asked, because although we'd discussed pretty much every other area of our lives we had both avoided discussing our love lives. I had done this for two reasons. First, I'm not sure I have a love life to discuss; and second, if I have, then it's one that has left me not quite bitter and twisted but certainly scared and scarred. Not, I believe, attractive qualities in a date. If we were on a date, and I'm pretty sure we were. It felt date-like.

What was Stevie's excuse for his reticence?

'No, the situation is vacant,' he said, with a broad smile.

I wanted to ask him if he was waiting for me to apply

but, even fortified by a large amount of drink, I didn't dare be so forward. He doesn't wear a ring but I thought I ought to check. 'Are you married?'

Stevie glanced at his shoes. 'The thing is—'

'You're married to your work, right?' I asked, cutting him off because of course he isn't married. What a stupid question. It's insulting to his integrity; I was immediately ashamed.

'I wasn't going to say that.'

Suddenly a depressing thought overwhelmed me. 'Are you gay?' I asked.

'Not last time I checked. Why? Are you homophobic?' he asked, mock-serious.

'No, of course not. I just don't want you to be gay. Even if it means I could say, "Some of my best friends are gay."'

'Am I going to be one of your best friends?' asked Stevie.

Was he flirting? He was. 'I hope we're going to be friends,' I reassured him.

Friends and a whole lot more but I didn't add that because just then a cab slowed to a standstill next to the pavement where we were stood.

'Need a ride?' asked the driver.

'Yes,' Stevie and I said in unison.

On our arrival at Stevie's flat I discovered I was anxious beyond precedent. I continually mixed up West Hampstead and Highgate and barely managed to articulate that I took my coffee black, one sugar.

'I've kind of forgotten how to do this,' I confessed.

'Do what?' asked Stevie.

'Whatever we're about to do,' I mumbled, wanting to kick myself. Had I just asked him to sleep with me? I had, hadn't I? Or as good as.

Stevie smiled away my nervousness. 'Well, I'm about to show you my enormous photo collection of my travels in India, Thailand and Malaysia. All you have to do is pretend to be interested. It's easy,' he joked. 'But be warned, if you do a convincing job I'll make you sit through the really old ones of me in South America too,' he added, as he rummaged around for packets of photos in an untidy cupboard. So that's how we passed the time until the sun came up and our eyes were stinging with lack of sleep.

I remember now that I fell asleep on the floor of his sitting room while he was trying to unearth some chocolate he was sure he had somewhere – maybe in the fridge, maybe in a cupboard, maybe in his sock drawer . . .

This morning is peculiar. This morning it is our easy intimacy that unsettles me. I'm almost sure we should be awkward with one another. Are we this comfortable because he doesn't feel the electricity that I feel, can almost touch and taste? Doesn't he fancy me? Are we just good friends? That damning, hopeless epitaph. And there is something else bothering me, something related. Have we kissed? Because if we have and he's this calm, I'm a lousy kisser. But, on the other hand, if we haven't, why not?

Maybe I'm out of my depth. Stevie is gorgeous – really, really special – therefore I'm not sure I want to stick around long enough to hear him say he doesn't think of me in the same way. It would be soul-destroying to discover that I'm a nice girl but not his type. It would be better to leave now with the beautiful memories of my sparkling night intact. I'm just about to say that I have to get dressed and leave because I have an oh-so-busy schedule when Stevie asks, 'Have you any plans for the rest of the day?'

'None. Well, I have to pick Eddie up but no, after that, we are totally free,' I blurt, which I realize doesn't help to create the impression that I am in demand, a girl with a crazily busy and very glamorous schedule.

'Me neither,' says Stevie. 'Do you think Eddie would like to go to the Science Museum? I loved that sort of stuff when I was a kid.'

'I think he'd like that very much,' I assure, nodding and smiling. Relief floods me. Truth is, Eddie would like that nearly as much as his mum would.

15. Baby, Let's Play House

Bella

'Don't ever, ever make me lie for you again,' Amelie hisses.

'I didn't ask you to lie,' I point out.

I hate it when my friends go all sanctimonious on me. Hey, like haven't I told the odd lie for Amelie in the past? I think about this for a moment and realize that, no, I have not. But I *would* lie if I ever had to, that's what friends are for. Blow it. This is why I've never told anyone my secret.

'You put me in an impossible position. I like Philip.'

'I love him.'

'Of course you do. That's why you married him while you were secretly married to someone else,' she snaps.

'But—'

Amelie holds up her hand to cut me off. She rummages in the drinks cupboard, pulls out a bottle of whisky and pours a generous measure into both our coffee cups, although it's only just past breakfast time. This gesture saddens me as it's exactly what I did for her on the countless occasions that we sat and talked about Ben, after his death, back when numbing the pain and shock was the only viable option.

'Well . . .' Amelie stutters to a stop before she starts, clearly she's unsure what to say.

I take a deep breath and tell my story. 'Stevie was my first love. He moved into our village when I was sixteen. He was like a glistening light in my humdrum existence. Unlike most of the other girls I'd never fancied the local boys I went to school with. Our village was so small that everyone knew each other since the day we were born so they had the familiarity of brothers. On the day I went into fifth form my only thought was which subjects I should take.'

Amelie, who is terrifically academic, is shocked into interrupting me. 'You hadn't chosen your subjects even though it was the beginning of term?'

'No. Amelie, I'm not like you or Ben. I don't have a particular talent or vocation. I never did. I was waiting to see which teacher was assigned to each subject then I'd choose according to who was the easiest about wearing make-up and who would set the least homework. But then Stevie Jones arrived at the school gate and all I could think of was how to get near him. I found out he was planning on taking literature, politics, music and history so I followed suit.'

'The work of the feminist movement has been so worthwhile,' murmurs Amelie.

'I didn't think it mattered, although, all these years later I can't help but think that I'd have done better if I'd picked geography and sociology instead of politics and music,' I admit. 'Anyway, aren't we getting off the point here?' Amelie nods tightly. 'Stevie was the talk of the school. He was a year older than everyone else because he'd had a year out, travelling around South America. Age sixteen. Can you imagine the cred that gave him? He'd travelled with relatives – cousins – and he seemed so sophisticated compared to the other boys. So knowledgeable. He was dark and moody and brooding. All the girls fancied him and all the boys wanted to be him. Three girls asked him out on the first day of term.'

'Not backward in coming forward at your school,' observes Amelie.

'We lived in a small town, you had to make your own entertainment,' I say. 'Luckily, he lived very near me and at the end of the day we found ourselves walking home together. It was a lovely early-September afternoon. Bright skies, leaves just turning to gold, there was a low sun glowing and throwing long shadows. We ambled along and I can still smell the sweet, wild grass and the hedgerow.'

It's a unique meteorological memory because, more often than not, the walk home from school was bleak and gloomy at best, or demanded an athletic feat of running while being stung mercilessly by lacerating rains.

'You know something, Amelie? Since Stevie I've had countless romantic evenings with a varied cross section of the male population. I've been courted, flattered, pursued, call it what you will, in the finest restaurants, on boats, beaches and even in front of two of the seven wonders of the modern world.'

'Really, which ones?' Amelie can't help her inquisitive mind.

'The Golden Gate Bridge in San Francisco and the Eurotunnel.'

'Is the Eurotunnel *really* classed as one of the seven wonders of the modern world? How marvellous.'

I stare at her and hope she can sense my exasperation. Our conversations habitually ebb and flow. Often, on leaving Amelie's house I think, 'Oh, I never told her . . .' or, 'I never finished the story about . . .' Today, I'm not in the mood for chit chat.

'Yes, I read about it on a website. Do you want the full account of those intrigues?' I snap, barely disguising my impatience.

Amelie considers for a moment. 'No, stick to your story. Keep the bridge and tunnel stories for another time.'

'I was just saying, nothing has ever been as romantic as that walk home with Stevie.'

'Nothing?'

'Nothing.'

'Except for Philip's proposal,' prompts Amelie.

'Not really,' I admit, refusing to comfort her with a lie. 'It turned out that Stevie wasn't dark, moody and brooding, just boyishly shy, but so clever and funny when you got chatting to him. He walked right past his house to mine, because he didn't want to leave me, and then I walked him back to his, and then—'

'He walked you back to yours.'

'Yes.' I grin, despite the seriousness of my situation. It's a wonderful, innocent memory. 'We did this from four o'clock until seven, when my dad got home and told me to stop messing around and come inside for tea. And then, in front of my dad and everything, Stevie kissed my cheek.'

'That seems to be his signature move,' observes Amelie.

I glare at her. 'So that was it. We were an item. He came in, had some tea with my dad and brothers and then we played Connect 4. I thrashed him,' I add proudly.

Until that night our house had existed in a bleak silence, punctuated by clocks ticking, coals sizzling and settling on the living-room fire and the occasional angry or drunken outburst. I think back to the cold, grey landscapes and seascapes of my childhood and fail to see their famed beauty but think of them as eerie and depressing. Stevie warmed the room with his irreverent chatter, even my father liked him and answered his questions about fishing with more patience than I'd ever enjoyed. Stevie was a sunrise on the horizon after a long, dark night. I thought he was the answer. To every question.

'We were inseparable all of fifth and sixth form. We were so in love, the way only teenagers can be. We studied together, read poetry, he sang and played his guitar. It seemed obvious that we would go to university together. I'd always thought Stevie would take me away from it all. His otherness was the main reason I was attracted to him. I waited until Stevie had made his choices, then I applied for the same unis. We ended up at Aberdeen, a great university, but even then I was a little disappointed that we weren't going somewhere further afield.'

'Where did he originate from, this knight in shining armour?'

'Blackpool.'

'Blackpool?' asks Amelie with understandable incredulity.

'I had only left Scotland twice in my life, both times

on school trips, one to the Lake District, the other to Whitby. Blackpool seemed exotic.' I blush at my naivety. Was there ever such an innocent?

'Didn't your father object to you going away together? Most parents encourage their children to try pastures new.'

'He never got involved in my private life.' Or any other part of it. 'I think he was just pleased that I was going away to study, not staying to kick my heels in the village.'

I'm glossing. I don't think Amelie would understand if I told her my father was glad to see the back of me and couldn't have cared less what I did with myself, as long as I didn't hang around him, being unlucky. He once muttered that a university education would do me no good, 'Being a lassie an' all, nae point.' And he told Stevie that he'd be better off getting a trade, 'Stick in at the skill, laddie, else ye'll end up wi' the rest of them, measuring the length of yer spit on the street corner.' I wonder what he'd say if he knew Stevie had stuck to his skill and was now a fully bona fide Elvis impersonator. I think my father was recommending a life as a fisherman or a roof tiler.

'Maybe it would have been different if Mum had still been with us.' I battle to keep the self-pity out of my voice.

Where do I start in explaining to Amelie? I bet if she was playing word association the word 'childhood' would provoke carefree responses such as 'summertime', 'TV' or 'pick 'n' mix sweets'. I'd say 'misery', 'fear', 'guilt'. My father thought confectionery, central heating and even smiling were indulgences we could do without. He believed that a north-eastern Scottish life was one in which hardship was inescapable, almost preferred. He liked firm chairs, cold winds and winter, but his biggest peculiarity was his distrust of me.

My father was a commercial fisherman. They're a superstitious lot. It goes back for centuries, and maybe it is understandable given that, before the advent of sophisticated navigational and fish-finding electronics, catching fish was in part good luck. It never hurts to hedge your bets.

The superstitions my father believed in and abided by were unending. Superstitions dictated what we wore, ate and said. It was considered bad luck to end a boat's name with a vowel, to paint a boat blue, to leave port on a Friday, to have a minister on your boat, to whistle on your boat. Rabbits were considered unlucky, as were pigs, salmon and women – especially women. I imagine this deep-seated distrust of women could be traced back to the myth of sirens luring boats to their doom or maybe it was just vicious misogyny. We weren't allowed near the boats and there were rules about how and when a woman should wash, do her household chores, bake and even brush her hair.

Having sired four sons my father considered himself especially fortuitous, but the day I was born he lost a man overboard. He blamed me. He didn't think of blaming the lousy weather and the high seas.

Victorian, isn't it? Laughable, really.

As a small child I was desperate to fish with my father and my brothers. Their lives seemed exciting and vigorous. Besides, nothing at all happened in Kirkspey except fishing and I didn't want to be left out. One day, I clambered aboard and tried to hide. I thought I'd stow away until we were at sea, then I'd reveal myself and join the boys with their on-board chores. A completely childish fantasy, of course, which was brought to an abrupt halt when I was discovered even before they set sail. Unfortunately that day my father slipped and broke his leg. Again I was blamed.

Proof positive that I was the devil in a skirt came when he caught me combing my hair when my brothers were at sea. He yelled at me, saying I was a curse, did I want to see them all ruined? My mum died that night; for a time he even had me believing in my ability to cause disaster. 'Nae whip cuts sae deep as the lash of guilt.' This superstitious claptrap seems total nonsense to me now as I'm sat in Amelie's clean, warm kitchen. I can't possibly explain it to her.

I'm not required to, because Amelie asks, 'What did Stevie's parents think?'

'They were divorced. He hadn't seen his dad for years. He lived with his mum, who liked me. She was pleased we were going away together. She had this old-fashioned and inaccurate idea that I would keep him out of trouble.'

'When did you marry?'

'I was nineteen.'

'*So* young.'

'I loved that. I loved the idea that we had so much time stretched out in front of us. I was sure we'd last forever.' I pause and think about a time when I believed in forever. It almost hurts. 'We were so in love, it seemed like the obvious thing to do, which seems madness now. Funny how hindsight can completely alter perspective.

The decision to marry was spur of the moment. We went to a registry office, still hungover from a wild party the night before. We pulled witnesses off the street. And while Scotland isn't the State of Nevada, we were both over eighteen so it wasn't at all tricky to get married. It seemed romantic. A big adventure.'

'What went wrong?'

'The obvious. We *were* too young. We were almost instantly ashamed and afraid and we didn't dare tell our parents or anyone what we'd done.'

'You thought they'd be angry?'

I didn't think it was anybody else's business. 'Sort of. We'd cheated Stevie's mum out of the chance to wear a hat. My dad would have been mildly disgruntled at missing out on a valid reason to have a drink although he'd have been relieved not to have had to pay for a bash.' I shrug apologetically, I'm apologizing for my youthful mistake. 'I thought marrying would make me feel independent but it didn't. I just felt daft. We knew everyone would dismiss our hasty ceremony as a silly, irresponsible joke because . . . well, it was, wasn't it? We kept silent because we didn't want to be told what we already knew.'

Amelie dashes to a cupboard, locates the biscuit barrel and then sits down again. She offers me a chocolate digestive; normally I'm partial but I shake my head. Amelie eats the biscuit in just two bites and then starts on another.

'Things were fine while we were at university. In a way we relished our wee secret. In halls of residence, we had no real responsibilities. We were two big kids playing house, playing grown-ups. The reality didn't hit until we graduated. We moved to Edinburgh and found it expensive. We had no money and no jobs and when we finally got jobs, crap ones, still had no money because we were paying rent.'

As I tell the story of this time in my life, the warmth drains out of my fingers and toes. I was always cold in our draughty flat. Cold and anxious. It wasn't different enough from Kirkspey.

'Stevie kept saying he wanted to be a musician but there weren't many opportunities in Edinburgh. Everyone said we needed to move south or even abroad. But Stevie didn't want to. He thought his talent would be revealed while he hummed and served chips in McDonald's. I started to hate him for that. It seemed so infantile, believing that one day someone would shout, "Hey, you with the salt shaker! I've been waiting to discover you." But things turned from dreadful to dire when he gave up on his dreams of entertaining with his own songs and style and fell into the Elvis tribute thing.'

'Fell into?'

'He'd done the Elvis gigs since he was a kid. His mother used to trail him round working men's clubs. I've seen the photos; you wouldn't believe it, Amelie. What sort of mother dresses her ten-year-old up in blue flares and gets him to perform to a room full of boozy strangers?'

'Did he hate it?' she asks with concern.

'No, he loved it.'

'Well, if he loved it his mother wasn't being cruel, was she?' I find Amelie's reasonableness infuriating.

'But what a seed of a dream to sow. A useless, tatty

dream. Couldn't she have encouraged his talent in another direction?'

'She was probably doing her best.'

'Yes,' I nod but I'm distraught at the memory. I never understood. 'When money got tight in Edinburgh, he got this crazy idea that he could start doing the circuit again. He was actually very good, more's the pity. We spent night after night in squalid dives; Stevie in fancy dress, belting out someone else's tunes. I couldn't see myself spending the rest of my life trailing around filthy pubs.' I sigh.

'Your loathing of Elvis impersonators makes more sense now,' says Amelie.

'But, then, my career prospects weren't much better. I had no idea what I wanted to do with myself and so I sat in our dingy flat, getting depressed. I wanted to move away but felt trapped by the marriage. Then some people started to ask if we were going to get married; we couldn't find a way to tell them that we already *were*. Other people, more perceptive people, started to ask why we were still together, when we clearly had different agendas now. It was impossible to explain ourselves to anyone. Our juicy secret became a sword hanging over us.'

I wish I smoked. This would be a good point to light a cigarette. Except that I hate the habit in others and have never dreamt of it for myself. Instead I take a swig of the whisky-coffee.

'It wasn't long before the bickering set in. Then we progressed to full-scale rows. We nosedived from love's young dream to a ghoulish nightmare with indecent haste. So I left.'

'Just like that?'

'Just like that.'

'Why didn't you get divorced?'

'We never got round to it.'

'You never—' Amelie is too incredulous to complete the sentence. 'How could you be so nonchalant? So irresponsible? People marry young, mistakes are made. Choosing who you want to spend the rest of your life with is a tricky one, lots of people get it wrong first time. But you should have got divorced.'

I nod. I've always known what I should have done, but doing the right thing is often hard. I'd wanted to pretend the whole thing had never happened.

'What the hell made you accept Philip's proposal? Why didn't you say something then?' she demands.

This is possibly the hardest question she could have asked. I gather my courage. 'He asked me minutes after I'd heard that Ben was dead. Before I'd even had time to tell him Ben was dead. I was scared. You must—'

I daren't finish my sentence. She must understand that. She must realize that I wanted to cling to life and that nothing seemed especially real or clear-cut, except that I loved Philip and he'd asked me to marry him. I wanted to feel safe and so I said yes.

It wasn't just the ISAs and the DIY that made me feel safe. It was something else. It was something I find difficult to put into words. Maybe something to do with his flat. Specifically, the thick creamy carpets, which were deeper and more luxurious than anything I'd ever come across. Or the large number of photographs in silver frames that showed Philip knew countless beautiful people who seemed devoted to having a great life. At least, that's what the numerous photos of friends and family said to me. Even the oldies in his pictures looked impossibly glamorous. Grandmas with silver bobs, black trouser suits and chic diamonds. Not a curler or saggy stocking in sight.

I was reassured by the enormous vases of fat, creamy lilies sitting on tables in the dining room and hall and on the shelf in the bathroom. I've always adored fat, creamy lilies, which seem to me the epitome of comfortable living. Somehow, waxy lilies embody summer, they smell sexy and expensive. We had dozens of lilies at our wedding even though everyone complained about the danger of the orange pollen staining their clothes. I ignored them. I wanted my wedding to smell of summer and wealth and sex. And security.

I hardly dare to look at Amelie. I wonder if she is going to be hurt or understanding.

'Are you blaming this on Ben?'

'No, no, Amelie you mustn't think that,' I say. I force myself to meet her eye so she can see I'm genuine. 'I loved Ben. I'd never try to use your tragedy as an excuse for my mess. It is *because* I loved Ben that I wasn't thinking clearly.'

Amelie seems to accept this. She breathes in deeply and then lets the air tumble out of her nose. 'Wasn't there an opportunity before the wedding to tell him that you were already married?'

'I tried. But you know when you get introduced to someone and you instantly forget their name? But you keep meeting them, and each time you mumble something barely audible, rather than admit that you have forgotten their name. It goes past the point when you can ask.'

'Yes.'

'Well, my situation was like that, only about a million times more difficult and more horrendous. When could I say, "By the way, Philip, did I not mention that I'm already married?" I wanted to say something, I really did. But, once the plans started to take shape, I got carried away—' I clamp my mouth shut. There is no explanation other than that I am a coward. A hopeful coward who thought I might get away with it.

Philip and I married in a hurry but in style. We had a great big do with over two hundred guests. I wanted to make a splash. Ben dying had left me feeling terrified and vulnerable. It wasn't just that I was scared that if I didn't grab at life and hold it really tightly, then the bus might get me next time – although that was certainly part of it. But the bigger thing was that I was also sick with the sense that if I died tomorrow I would die without making my mark.

Ben was a reasonably successful playwright. His works had been regularly performed on the local rep circuit for years, the critics had greeted his plays with considerable respect and there were always discussions about one of them making it to the West End. Ben had died – there was no doubt about it – on the cusp of huge financial and critical success. But he had always lived – there was no doubt about it – in the midst of huge emotional success. He was loved by Amelie, with an unequivocal and relentless love that I'd always found encouraging. He was an involved and inspiring father and an adored and respected partner. This made his death shattering but his life worthwhile.

That's what I wanted. A worthwhile life.

I couldn't write plays so I did the next best thing; I bought a wedding dress from Vera Wang and had a reception at a smart London hotel. Don't laugh. I felt it was a start. Like I said, grief doesn't make sense.

It's not true that a big wedding takes several years to plan and prepare for. In my experience it took exactly four months, one week, two days. Of course, I was in a fortunate position that my newly acquired status as Philip's fiancée meant that I was able to throw money at any potential hiccups. The harpist, the caterers and the vicar all insisted that they could not take any bookings at such short notice, until I offered to pay above the going rate and to make a sizeable donation to the church roof fund, at which point miracles occurred. My dress was stunningly simple and simply stunning. I had it all: Jimmy Choo shoes and Agent Provocateur underwear. My hair was teased into fat luxurious curls by one of London's top stylists. It was a very different affair to my hasty dash into the registry office with Stevie.

'The last I'd heard of Stevie was that he was back in Aberdeen. Bloody hell, I never expected him to turn up on my doorstep. Worse still, on my friend's doorstep. What am I going to do?'

'I wonder what Stevie's line is on all of this?' muses Amelie.

'Oh *my God.*'

The full awfulness of my situation hits me and I think I might throw up. Laura, one of my best friends, is possibly sleeping with my husband. One of my husbands, that is.

'We have to expect her to mention you to him,' points out Amelie. 'I wonder if he'll say, "Small world. The funny thing about your friend is that she's my wife."'

My mind is whirling so quickly that I almost miss Amelie's sarcastic tone, *almost*. I try to stay focused. 'No, we'll be fine. She'll call me Bella.'

'Yes, she will,' says Amelie carefully. 'That is, after all, your name.'

'Not then. Back then I was Belinda. That might buy me some time.'

'You changed your name?'

'I never liked Belinda, it's so—' I don't bother to finish.

'So Bella is a nickname?'

'No, I did it by deed poll. Bella *is* my name.'

'My God, you are a dark horse. I always thought you were one of those people who struggled to keep secrets about contents of Christmas stockings and all along you are an expert at being mendacious. I wish Ben was alive, he'd love this.'

I, on the other hand, am not loving this. I think I'm going to cry.

16. Is It So Strange?

Tuesday 25th May 2004

Laura

Since the breakdown of my marriage it is not uncommon for me to wake up and wonder why anybody chooses to live in London. I have no choice in the matter. I live in London because Eddie needs to see his father regularly and I doubt that would happen if I moved further afield. If I try, it is easy to spread and blur my loathing of Oscar so that I can find a way to blame pretty much everything that is uncomfortable in my life on him. My lack of money, decent career and self-respect are just the obvious ones. I can spend hours connecting Oscar's inadequacies with those of London's underground, London's lack of private gardens (or even parks that are dog-poop free), the cost of childcare, parking, council tax and housing.

Sometimes, I am clearsighted enough to see that there are many things that I adore about London and to remember that I spent half of my childhood dreaming of living here. I never link Oscar with these aspects of city life.

I love the fact that it is always possible to buy a loaf of bread, even at midnight, and the choice stretches between panini, bruschetta, cinnamon, cracked wheat, German pumpernickel and rye. I love that Eddie is surrounded by cultural diversity and won't grow up thinking *anyone* is different or odd. It's great that there is always something to do or somewhere to go and that most of the museums are free.

Invariably, I have a flare-up of resentment at living in London as I stand on a platform waiting for an over-priced, overpacked and already very late train to take me to work in Shepherd's Bush. Not today. This Tuesday morning as I head off to work at the surgery I'm amazed to discover that I don't find the crowded tubes particularly galling. Instead, I step back and let everyone off the tube before I rush forwards to try to secure, if not a seat, at least some floor space. I smile at . . . well, everyone. I don't even care that they don't smile back.

I arrive at the surgery before 9 a.m. and I am not churlish when I see that Sally, the colleague with whom I job-share, has once again left all the filing for me to do *and* I stay calm even though she has double-booked the first hour of appointments and the patients are all glaring at *me*. I work with unprecedented efficiency and pleasant-ness until lunchtime when I choose not to skulk around the pharmacy cupboard, eating my home-packed ham sandwich as usual, but I decide to get a breath of fresh air and wander along the high street. I might even treat myself to a sandwich from the little Italian café on the corner, Café Bianchi. It is a fabulously grubby, authentic Italian café run by an old couple and their innumerable, hot sons. They used to sell only cappuccino and espresso but a few months ago they branched out and started to serve panini. I could have a mozzarella and basil panini; the thought is exotic.

Shepherd's Bush is buzzing. I spot a nun, builders, grandparents, new mothers, posers and a gaggle of smokers. I'm stunned by the size of the world. It's so obvious, but it's as though I'm just noticing, that people all around me are living lives. They are doing ordinary things, drinking coffee, chatting, buying stamps and rocking prams, feeling losses, concern, outrage, kindness, love, friendship, exhaustion and exhilaration and none of them are connected to Oscar or my heartache. The realization hits me like a brick but feels like a release. It excites me. Oscar and my heartache are not perennial.

When I was a teenager and just discovering my love of a good novel I used to visit bookshops and stare for hours at the rows and rows of books on the shelves. I'd feel an excitement that threatened to overwhelm me, but never quite did. I always left the bookstore with another 'life' tucked under my arm, something else to grapple with, to empathize or repudiate. Books nurtured my longing to travel as they showed me that there was so much living being done. People were living spectacular, enchanting and amusing lives. And when I left to travel the world I did exactly that for quite some time; I lived a full and curious life.

I hadn't realized that heartbreak had scared me off and I'd started to live my life in tickover. Until now, *now* I feel that I might just be on the cusp of edging back up to full throttle. I feel as I did when I left Australia; excited, stretched and challenged. Shepherd's Bush is not the most salubrious part of town but it's interesting. There are shops, bars, cafés, hotels, even a trendy spa, a theatre, a gig venue. There is a green, a station, roadworks, skiving kids, overly industrious traffic wardens and police horses. Is there always so much going on? Have I been asleep? I look at all the people hurrying about their day and I don't feel passed by, superfluous or insignificant. The opposite. Because I am going about my day too. I am buying exotic sandwiches.

And sending flirty texts to Stevie.

Stevie is fun and reminds me that I am too. His witty, dry comments litter our conversations, as does his humming and singing. He listens. He seems to think everything I say is important or funny. Stevie, Eddie and I have enjoyed three glorious days together. I had no idea that the Science Museum was so fascinating. Obviously, there's a lot to learn about Newton's law, space travel, ecology etc. Fascinating, clearly. But I didn't realize the Science Museum had so much to teach me about the 'phwoar' factor.

For example, the tiny hairs on Stevie's forearms – under the blue light of one of the more spectacular foyers in the museum – look irresistible. It took every ounce of self-restraint not to reach out and stroke those hairs. The Science Museum taught me a lot about bone structure too, because while Stevie and Eddie spent an age looking at model rockets I gazed at Stevie's jawline and cheekbones. Without the costume he doesn't look much like Elvis. He wears his hair scruffy and longish, more like Noel Gallagher, and his jaw is much leaner than the King's. When he's Elvis he's enigmatic. Stevie is more straightforward. As Elvis he is a performer. Stevie is one hundred per cent 'what you see is what you get', a square-shooter. And I like that.

On Sunday we drifted around the lock and market stalls at Camden. The arty-crafty objects – mostly useless, and often verging on tatty – took on a charming quality. Vases, pictures, furniture and jewellery gleamed in the sunshine and with Stevie holding my hand I was tempted into several impulse purchases that I couldn't afford. I'm still trying to find a place in my kitchen for a large lavender-coloured wine rack. The candle (a sculptured couple pre-copulation) looks OK in the bathroom window. The thing is, being with Stevie makes me feel like I'm gleaming in sunshine too. A couple of celebratory impulse purchases doesn't seem too wild, under the circumstances.

The only fly in the ointment is Bella. She is sulking with me for not following her last Friday. That, or she's at death's door. I'm not sure which I'd prefer. I certainly don't like to be on the receiving end of Bella's strops. One of my biggest pleasures in life is calling her for a daily chat. Now, when I'm bursting at the seams with news, she's not returning my calls. She cancelled our Monday coffee date. The silent treatment is like water torture. A week ago I'd have sat this out until she called me: I hadn't the required confidence for confrontation. Now I decide to take action, even if it is only in the form of calling Amelie to see if she can throw any light on the situation. I reach for my mobile.

'G'day, Amelie, it's Laura.'

'Hello, Laura,' says Amelie, as ever her voice oozes warmth. 'How are you?'

'Sweet as. Things are as good as gold,' I giggle.

'Still getting on with Stevie, I take it?'

'Too right.' I force myself not to gush. 'Have you heard from Bella, recently?' I ask, hoping to sound nonchalant.

'I haven't seen her since Saturday.'

Bella had breakfasted with Amelie on Saturday morning but Stevie and I missed her when we collected Eddie. We must have missed her by a matter of moments because Eddie seemed to think she was still there. Ridiculous, of course, because there was no sign of her. She'd have had to be hiding in the shed.

'She blew me out yesterday, with no explanation. She hasn't returned my calls. Do you think she's ill?' I ask.

'Possibly very sick,' says Amelie but she doesn't sound unduly concerned.

'I wanted to tell her that Stevie isn't a busker, he's a teacher. She was so worried I was mixing with someone inappropriate. I just wanted to put her mind at rest.'

'Leave it with me. You get back to work. I'll call her and see if everything's OK,' says Amelie.

I thank Amelie and hang up. I'm happy to leave the situation with her. Without either of us having to say anything outright I sensed Amelie understood my belief that Bella has gone to ground because she's never liked Elvis impersonators. And she seems to have an almost pathological dislike of Stevie Jones.

17. It's Now Or Never

Thursday 27th May 2004

Bella

It was Amelie's idea that we should all meet for lunch. I'm torn. It's impossible to imagine ignoring Laura for the rest of my days, not least because she's rung me about ten times since Friday night. Initially, I let the answering machine pick up. The messages were as I expected: garbled apologies because she didn't follow me out of the pub and lots of giggling as she begged me to call her as she had 'so much news'. I do feel a bit guilty that she's sorry about Friday night, when it was me who did the runner, yet I could cheerfully wring her neck when I hear her schoolgirlish giggle. Doesn't she understand that Stevie was put on this earth to make me feel schoolgirlish, not her, not anyone else? Oh God, I'm married to one man and jealous about another. Another who I'm married to. How can I pick up the phone?

Laura must have called Amelie because Amelie rang me to say it wasn't fair to ignore Laura any longer, as she was beginning to imagine that I was ill.

'Laura has done nothing wrong,' said Amelie. She didn't need to complete the sentence, pointing out who has done something wrong. 'You have to face this Bella; it's not going to go away.'

But I want it to go away. Nothing material has changed. I am in exactly the same position I was in last week. Last week I was married to two men but I never gave it a thought. For years I have worked, with a steely determination, at ignoring this pertinent fact. It hasn't been easy and it has required sacrifices but I've managed it this far.

I told Amelie that one day I'd got up and left Stevie, which is true. 'One day' was a very particular day: the day of the final of the Greatest European Tribute Artist Convention and Competition – allegedly. A competition that was held in Blackpool, which in my book cast doubts on the claims 'greatest' and 'European'. As Stevie was born and bred there he was delighted with the idea of romping home to win the title of Greatest European Tribute Artist, King of Kings 1996.

In the months running up to that dreadful January evening Stevie had attended three qualifying heats in Britain. Attending the competitions had become a bone of contention between us. He qualified for the final with ease, and at the first event, so I didn't understand why he insisted on attending the other heats. He said that it was to get the measure of the competition; I moaned that he needed to get a measure of our overdraft. I refused to attend any of the heats with him. I'd started my illustrious waitressing career in a dodgy bar in Leith by then; I couldn't get Saturday nights off. Plus, we could barely afford coach fares for one, to Portsmouth, Saltburn and Newquay, let alone two.

Besides, the whole idea bored me.

Stevie, by contrast, was fired up with an enthusiasm I hadn't seen since the days he recited poetry to me in my childhood bedroom. He came home from each heat bursting with excitement as he assured me that Larry King had a good voice but terrible costume, Mike King wore a fantastic garb but was weak when singing the ballads, Kevin King was too short, Gary King too nervous. In brief, Stevie felt sure that he was in with a serious chance. He could be Europe's Number One. He could walk the golden mile in Elvis's blue suede shoes. Well, not Elvis's actual shoes, obviously, because they are sat in some museum in Vegas, but in a replica pair.

I used to stare at him amazed, and not in a positive sense. I'd make snide comments that it was a real coincidence that all the guys in the tribute acts shared a surname. Patiently, Stevie would explain to me that these weren't their real names, they were stage names, because he didn't credit me with anything as low as sarcasm.

The prize was a thousand pounds. No small sum, especially then. But I was sure we'd already spent hundreds on hotels, costumes and travel. When I pointed out as much to Stevie he would assure me that if, no when, he won the competition he could make a serious living on the bookings that he was bound to attract. Perhaps as much as thirty thousand a year.

'You also win a thirteen-hundred-dollar gift certificate for a red pinwheel suit and gold belt to be shipped in from the States,' he told me with a grin. I was nonplussed. 'Other colours are available,' he assured me. 'Elvis had the suit in three colours, you know.'

Fascinating.

Yet, Stevie is nothing if not persuasive. After months of listening to him rehearse in the bathroom and chat excitedly about the cool vibe at the competitions, I was curious enough to agree to attend the final. We'd been arguing bitterly and I saw the competition as a way of stemming the tide of fury that was washing between us. I told myself that it was important to *show* support, if not willing, and at least appear to be encouraging my husband in his chosen career – however ludicrous I thought the career was. I told myself that Blackpool would be a mini-break, a bit of fun. I imagined us holding hands while strolling up and down the prom, romping barefoot on the beach. We'd see the famous illuminations and laugh at people wearing kiss-me-quick hats. Stevie and I had been married for three years and we hadn't had a holiday in that time. Perhaps, this was what we needed. Perhaps, Stevie was right, his career as an Elvis tribute act might lead to great and glamorous things. *And* I'd get to see Stevie's hometown, few girls can resist a peek at their man's past. In the run-up to the competition, I told myself – over and over – that the weekend might be the best of my life.

The weekend was the worst of my life.

Part of Stevie's attraction was that he was from somewhere other than my hometown. I knew nothing about Blackpool, but had imagined it as far more elegant, sophisticated and promising than Kirkspey. My home, where I'd never felt at home. When we got off the coach at Blackpool and walked along the seafront in search of our B&B, I began to understand why Stevie fitted into Kirkspey so well: Blackpool was just the same.

Kirkspey was cold, dark, cruel and credulous, full of men who were too keen to hit the bottle and then each other just to ease the boredom. Headbutting was a finessed sport and hangovers were competitive. Slurred threats, irrational recriminations and unseemly brawls were celebrated. It was a poor and destructive place. Blackpool seemed the same but with more flashing lights and topless entertainers. I saw countless groups of men with bad teeth – all gold caps and spaces – modern-day pirates, they hung out on street corners and stared warily at one another, exuding loss and despair.

The B&B was miles out of town, no doubt that was why it was within our budget, so we caught a tram. It was bitterly cold outside, so the tram was crammed full. I hadn't considered the season in my fantasy version of our mini-break. Although it was only the afternoon many of the passengers were drunk. In Kirkspey most people were drunk most of the time too, that and/or pregnant, what else was there to do? Beer fumes and condensation blurred my vision. I've always hated condensation. To me, it signifies despair – used breath, used life. By the time we arrived at the B&B I knew that my fantasies of a happy mini-break were way off mark. I looked out of the bedroom window towards the cold and bleak coastline, another cold and bleak coastline, different but the same.

'Are the windows frosted?' asked Stevie.

'No, just filthy,' I sighed in reply, before curling up on the skinny, hard bed. The pillow smelt of someone else's hair grease. What attracted Stevie to this life? It was not glam, it was not even clean.

'Want to go for a walk?'

'No, too windy.' I knew from experience that the wind took the sand everywhere, in your knickers, in your bloodstream, ingrained in lines and wrinkles on your face. Stevie went for a walk on the prom on his own.

The contest was more horrible than even I'd imagined. It was held in a hotel that, about a million years ago, might have been considered posh. The chandeliers and cornicing were a testament to more elegant days; the modern-day clientele were rougher than high seas.

The audience was predominantly women – wives, girl-friends and mothers – either blatantly proud or pseudo-coy. They lived a life that I knew well enough not to want. I couldn't do it. I'd display my despair. I didn't want to be an Elvis wife. I didn't want to be an eternal onlooker.

In Blackpool, plunging necklines were obviously still considered de rigueur even after the menopause. Some of the women sported tattoos, on their breasts, which declared that they were once desirable and fancied, at least by themselves, but their skin now sagged under a forty-a-day habit and an excess of sweet white wine spritzers. The younger women were all yellow-blonde with black roots and perms were very popular. The older women had 'set' their hair that day; one was still in curlers and another wore gold sandals over her socks.

The walls of the room were lined with babies in push-chairs; no one considered the inappropriateness of bring-ing a bairn to a boozy, smoky bar. Older kids of seven, eight and nine years old ran around cussing and sipping from unguarded pint glasses. There were only a few blokes in the audience, occasional old rockers, fathers of contestants, I supposed. One grandad had a mullet that grew all the way down his back.

The compère introduced the judges. He was particularly proud and puffed up, as one of the judges was an in-law of a cousin to Elvis Presley. Another was a hairdresser of someone who once played with Elvis. I don't know who was more depressed, me or the guys who made their careers by being vaguely related to Elvis and were now judging two-bit competitions.

Stevie changed into his Elvis suit (the makeshift dressing room was an area curtained off, just to the left of the stage) and then he came to sit with me while we watched the other performances. Some contestants were nervous, others cocky, Stevie was quietly confident. I didn't care. There were nine Elvises waiting in the audience, which created a surreal effect. Everyone was vaguely familiar because they looked not quite like someone they were not, someone none of us had even met.

It soon became clear that the industry displayed too much charity. Everybody attending the event loved Elvis so much, that they were prepared to be polite and encouraging even towards the really talentless and ugly blokes. These guys inexpertly flung themselves around the stage, often mumbling corny lines and the audience clapped, with what looked like genuine appreciation. In no other industry would such averageness be tolerated, let alone encouraged.

'Superb, brilliant, where do you get the energy from?' asked Neil Curran, the compère, as he slapped another sticky Elvis on the back, following a piss-poor performance.

'Nice costume.' He grinned at another. 'You look bloody brilliant. Tell me, lad, why did you choose that particular track?'

The Elvis went on to explain it was his dear old, dead, granny's favourite. The audience gave up a big 'aahh' and threw out another round of applause.

'That's so stupid,' I muttered to Stevie. 'Every decision is made on some emotional impulse.'

'It's an emotional game. Elvis was an emotional man,' said Stevie. I noticed he'd clapped and whistled and cheered with verve throughout the evening.

'That guy picked his competition track because some old biddy said it was her favourite. Why not pick an entry because it's the one you sing best?' I asked. 'There is no killer instinct.'

'These guys are entertainers, not members of an elite government squad, protecting the crown,' argued Stevie.

'Well, I'm not entertained. I'm bored,' I replied. Bored by Stevie. The thought flicked across my mind. I tried to swipe it away but it stubbornly hung around. 'I think it's arrogant. No one looks and acts and sings like him, anyway. He was gorgeous.'

Stevie grinned broadly, 'I think that's the first nice thing I've ever heard you say about Elvis.'

And the last.

I didn't stay to see Stevie perform. I told him I was going to the Ladies and I never went back to finish my glass of warm Blue Nun.

Outside the hotel the air was fresh, even though it was drizzling. For once I appreciated a cold coastal breeze although smoke still lingered on my jacket and in my hair. I started to walk back to the B&B. I passed a building boasting a sign that read: 'Sinless go-go girls, entrance at rear'. Very funny, not. I walked past the hideous amusement arcades and countless stalls selling greasy, almost luminous food. At the guest house I packed the few things I'd brought with me and went to the coach station. I did not leave a note. I did not look back.

When I left Stevie and jumped on a National Express coach to London I'd expected him to follow me. I half believed he'd track me down and we'd start again. I reasoned that in London Stevie had a chance of becoming a musician, a real musician, not a mimic. And I could be ... well, I don't know, something glamorous too, no doubt. Wasn't everything in London glamorous? But Stevie didn't follow me. Not that I gave him any help or opportunity. I didn't leave forwarding addresses and when I sent him a postcard to say I was all right, I didn't commit beyond saying I was 'down south'. I wanted him to discover his own leads, make his own chances. I wanted him to prove to me that he wasn't the no-hope, no-ambition, no-get-up-and-go kind of bloke that I had come to think of him as. He did nothing to remove my prejudice. He did nothing at all.

So I started to rebuild my life. I put away the disappointment and heartache of our split and got a job. I can't remember which one. Maybe as a trainee recruitment consultant, or did I start in telesales and then try the recruitment thing? I honestly can't remember, neither job was particularly thrilling, rather disproving my theory that London was wall-to-wall stunning opportunities; but at the time I was dazzled with hope. At least I was bringing in some reasonable money.

I made new friends, moved into a cramped, untidy flat which was even more expensive than the one in Edinburgh but I preferred it. I loved everything about London. The things that most newcomers hate or find overwhelming, thrilled and excited me. I liked the size, the noise, the ridiculously complex tube map. I liked the fact that the corner shop never closed, I enjoyed the boisterous melody that makes up the capital's population. I had patience and goodwill for all; dawdling tourists, the busy, aggressive commuters, the aimless, desperately trendy students, the gangs of schoolboys, the gaggles of schoolgirls. I was fascinated.

I didn't tell my new friends that I was married. It was easier not to. I wanted to fit in and confessing to being a twenty-two-year-old runaway bride wasn't going to do that. My secret was always in the back of my mind but I never allowed it to spill into my consciousness, conscience or – worse still – spill out of my mouth. London was full of things that distracted me. I rushed around taking photos of Trafalgar Square, St Paul's Cathedral and the Tower of London. I lingered in bars and cafés. I ambled around shops and even spent some time in offices. Months turned into years, and one day I woke up and I realized that I hadn't thought of Stevie for weeks. *Weeks*. He was no longer part of my life, despite what a silly piece of paper lodged at a registry office in Aberdeen said to the contrary.

To keep my secret I had to give up things that other

people take for granted. True intimacy was impossible. I held boyfriends at arm's length; the girls I worked or shared a flat with thought of me as the ultimate commitment-phobe. Until Philip came along.

Bugger.

I am not a deliberately cruel person. I didn't set out to hurt anyone. Falling in love was exactly the complication I had tried to avoid. Even in my worst nightmares, I couldn't have imagined Stevie reappearing in my life because he'd become involved with one of my best friends. What a nasty twist of fate that is. I can't begin to imagine the nuclear fallout if Philip ever finds out what I've done.

Amelie isn't being much help. Her ludicrous suggestion was that I should come clean. Ha, as if! How does that work then? *Philip, darling, you know that forty-grand wedding we had six months ago? Well, sweetheart, it doesn't mean a jot because I'm married to someone else.* I don't think so. Luckily, Philip has had to go away on business this week so he's not around to witness my nervous catapulting from fear to fury.

I have a plan of my own.

Providing Laura isn't in too deep with Stevie (and she can't possibly be after just a few days), then I'll persuade her to ditch him asap. Once he's out of our lives we can all go on as before. I told Amelie my plan, but she said I'm deluded and arranged for Laura and me to meet for lunch anyway.

Amelie has booked Palais du Jardin in Covent Garden. Normally it's one of my favourite places but I'm finding it hard to concentrate on the utterly stylish decor or the tantalizing menu.

'A window seat! Perfect,' giggles Laura. She probably hasn't been here before and is feasting her eyes on the luxurious wood and leather, the subtle blends of taupe and browns that abound. She's paid for Eddie to stay at nursery today and worked an extra shift at the surgery to compensate. Her determination to behave like a normal person rather than a wrung-out dish rag is disconcerting. Delightful. Disastrous.

'Have you slept with him?' I demand. The question comes out louder than I expected and half of the other diners turn to stare at us.

'I can't believe you are asking me that before we've even looked at the menu,' she mutters.

I try to work out if she is being huffy, cagey or indignant and whether this is because she has or has not slept with my husband. One of them.

I look at Amelie for a steer. She glares at me and then picks up the menu. 'I think we ought to order champagne,' she suggests.

'Oh, fantastic,' agrees Laura, without pausing to worry about the cost as she usually does. Clearly, she's too happy for that.

Amelie secures the waiter's attention and orders champagne and a bottle of spring water. As soon as she has done so I ask again, 'Well, have you slept with him?'

'Stevie Jones seduced me with words,' said Laura grandly. I know she's been practising that opener, which I find a bit annoying. 'Not just the deep, melodious, soulful words of some of Elvis's songs and certainly not the silly, predictable, cheesy words of some of Elvis's other songs. Like that "Surrender" one. I mean – hearts on fire, going on about strange desires – I ask you?'

At this point Laura rolls her eyes to suggest that such clichéd words are ridiculous and beneath her. But the effect is ruined because if I had to describe Laura right now I'd say she looks just like someone whose heart is on fire, she looks exactly like someone in the grip of a strange desire. In the face of such evidence it's hard to laugh at the lyrics. I look to Amelie, she looks stunned too, I know she's seen it – Laura has grown again. She is straighter, stronger and more magnificent than we have ever seen her.

'He seduced me with my *own* words,' Laura declares, grinning broadly.

'What do you mean?' asks Amelie.

'Stevie Jones asks me questions, listens to the answers and asks more questions. I have never felt so interesting in my life,' Laura explains. 'I know I should be sorry that I stayed in the pub after you split, Bella. Am I off the hook?' I nod and hope that Amelie notices I have the decency to blush. 'It was crap of me. I know a good friend should have picked up her handbag and ignored the fact that he was singing to me.'

'He was?' I mumble.

'Yes,' Laura beams. 'I should have run straight out of the bar and chased you down the high street and found out why you'd suddenly turned all zombie on me, but I just couldn't. Sorry. How are you feeling now, by the way?'

'Still a bit nauseous,' I mutter, truthfully.

'I thought it must have been something you'd eaten or that we were mixing our drinks. Still, you should probably go to the doc and have it checked out. It's been hanging around for a while now, hasn't it?'

'I've felt sick for about six days.'

The waiter places a bottle of water on the table and brings the champagne to us in an ice bucket. No sooner has he poured than I've tipped mine down my throat. I pour myself a second.

'Cheers,' says Laura with a grin. 'You've some thirst on you, girl.'

I am only seconds away from yelling, 'Have you slept with him?' when Laura says, 'I can't believe I feel this happy when I still haven't slept with him.'

Hallelujah. I nearly punch the air, but such a gesture would certainly draw Laura and Amelie's attention.

'We've seen each other every day for six days and, let me tell you, I've been tempted. He's totally "ooh-ah".' Laura makes Meg Ryan-like fake orgasm sounds; under different circumstances I'd be amused. 'But I'm taking things slowly,' she declares, with a smile.

'Never a bad approach,' says Amelie, looking at me meaningfully.

Phew. Deep breath. At least she's not in this too deep. Now I know they haven't done the deed I can relax enough to order sea bass with fries. Amelie orders the same. Laura goes for a prawn salad even though she is rake thin and could do with putting on a pound or two. I doubt she wants to tuck heartily into a plate of carbs, I don't expect she's felt much like eating since the fateful busking incident.

'So what *have* you been doing, if not shagging?' asks Amelie. A question I find at once astute and helpful, yet a sad testament to the courtship rituals of the twenty-first century.

'On Saturday we took Eddie to the Science Museum.'

'Isn't it a wee bit early to introduce them?' I ask. 'It'll confuse Eddie if Stevie is a fixture one moment and gone the next.' Which is my intention.

'We went to investigate gravity and locomotion, we did not swing from the chandeliers,' laughs Laura. What is it with all this laughing and giggling? 'In fact Stevie was really considerate around Eddie. He didn't even hold my hand. He just acted like we were mates. He spent most of his time playing with Eddie, not me.'

'Maybe he doesn't like holding hands in public,' I offer. 'Some men don't. Usually the shifty ones.'

'Well, when Eddie was at his dad's on Sunday we went to Camden Market and had lunch in Islington. He held my hand all the time.'

'Is he the right type of guy for you, though?' I ask. 'A busker? It's hardly a settled career.'

'He's not a busker, he's a teacher. The busking thing was a bet,' says Laura with a dismissive wave of her hand.

I'm relieved. As silly as it sounds, a tiny bit of me was uncomfortable with the fact that one of my husbands was a busker, although obviously, him having a proper job doesn't help me with my case to Laura.

'He's so much fun. He has real spirit. You know what I mean?'

I know what she means.

'He makes me feel like I'm sixteen.'

I know what she means.

'On Monday he came round after work and we didn't do much. He helped me bath Eddie. We read him a story together and then tucked him in. After that we just, you know . . .' Laura blushes.

I'm unsure what can be making her blush if they haven't shagged.

'We just talked. Swapped viewpoints, put the world to rights. On Tuesday evening, after school, we went to a skateboarding exhibition over at Ally Pally.'

'You don't like skateboarding. That's not your cup of tea. Are you just doing these things to keep him happy? Have you considered you might not have that much in common?' I interject.

'Eddie loved it.'

'Well, that's probably because he stayed up late. Should he be staying up late on a school night? Is any of the compromise coming from Stevie or is it just your lifestyle that's being disrupted?' I sound like her mother and father rolled into one.

'On Wednesday he came with me to a kids' party that Eddie had been invited to. He spent two and a half hours giving piggybacks to kids with sticky hands and runny noses and tonight we've arranged a babysitter because we're going to see *Chicago*, the musical,' finishes Laura, triumphantly. We both know she's won her case. That's the problem with Stevie. He's, well, nice I suppose.

I stare at my sea bass, I've lost my appetite.

Throughout lunch I point out the possible pitfalls of a new relationship. It's not an easy argument to construct as it is generally accepted wisdom that falling in love is a good thing.

'You don't want to allow this flirtation to distract you from your studies.' Laura is studying on a part-time basis to become a reflexologist.

'I can practise my massage on him.' She grins.

'You're always saying that you have no time left after caring for Eddie, working and studying. Something will slip.'

'What? Like my career as the glorified gofer at the local surgery? I'm gutted,' she says sarcastically. 'Look, I don't know how to explain it but somehow Stevie has slipped into my life very easily. He isn't pulling me in another direction. He's pulling *with* me. I can't tell you how bewdy it was to have someone help with putting Eddie to bed.'

I want to point out Stevie's shortcomings: he lacked ambition, he wanted to live miles away from where I wanted to live and his obsession with Elvis was impossible. I'm not sure Laura cares about any of this. Besides, Stevie's a teacher now. He has a career while I'm still pottering – not a great thought. Even I can see that the long holidays would come in handy for childcare if Laura hooked up with him on a permanent basis. Not that I'm suggesting for a moment she should. It's just, if we weren't talking about Stevie and we were talking about some other guy who gave piggybacks and went to musicals, then we'd be projecting as far as the second baby by now. I remember Stevie's fab body; from my glimpse on Friday, it doesn't appear that he's let that go to seed. I remember he was kind, witty, deep and fun. I can't imagine these things will help me ruin Stevie for Laura.

'You don't know anything about him,' I point out. I realize I'm on dangerous territory. It's galling that the one piece of information that would put Laura off Stevie, the fact that he is a married man, wouldn't show me in a great light either. 'He might be . . .' I search around '. . . on the rebound or gay or a drug-user.' Laura looks at me pityingly.

'Will you excuse me? I need to visit the bathroom,' she says, with excessive formality.

Amelie waits until she's out of earshot and demands, 'What the hell are you playing at?'

'I'm trying to put her off him before she gets in too deep,' I reply. Amelie stares at me as though I've lost my mind. 'Well, they haven't had sex so it's not serious.'

'You are kidding, right?' asks Amelie. 'They might not have had sex but it is obvious that it is serious. She *calmly* referred to Oscar as Eddie's dad. That's more serious than sex. She's besotted with Stevie to the extent that she's already feeling less bitter about Oscar.'

'So you think Stevie is a rebound thing? A way to get over Oscar?' I ask hopefully.

'No. The osteopath was the rebound thing and he didn't help her get over Oscar anyway. I'm saying that Stevie must be the real thing.'

'No,' I yell, frustrated and angry with Amelie, Stevie, Laura and myself. Mostly myself.

'This is such good news,' says Amelie with a beam.

I can't share her enthusiasm. 'I'll have to move quickly to split them up.'

'I can't believe you're even thinking it. You of all

people. How could you be contemplating something so crass and selfish?'

'Survival,' I mutter.

'Laura was a messy heap when you met her. She embodied meltdown. She'd still be shuffling about in her cardy and maternity slacks if you hadn't befriended her. You gave her back her confidence and hope. You did such a good thing, Bella. How could you be thinking of doing such a terrible one now?' I hate it that Amelie thinks she's a good enough friend to give it to me straight. 'Sorry to sound harsh but what are friends for if not to keep you grounded?'

I want to say friends are there to discuss the idiosyncrasies of fashions with. Friends are there so you never have to drink copious amounts of vino alone, but I can't be flip.

'I've never seen Laura so cheerful and confident. She's glowing and – I hope I don't sound too tactless – he seems pretty keen on her too.'

I stare at Amelie, horrified. 'Do you think so?'

'Yes. He is taking her to see *Chicago*, for goodness' sake. You have to recognize that as an act of devotion.'

'He'll tell her,' I mutter ominously.

'You have to tell her first. And you have to talk to Philip.'

'No,' I shout. Again, dozens of necks snap in our direction. We are definitely the floor show at the Palais, this lunchtime. 'There has to be another way.' I ponder for a moment. 'Maybe I should talk to Stevie.'

'It's a start,' concedes Amelie.

'I could get a divorce, a quickie. They only take about

two minutes nowadays, don't they? After all, we've been separated for an age – there must be grounds. Then I can tell Philip that he and I are not quite legally married.'

Amelie scowls. 'I can't see the ambivalence of the situation. You are either married or you're not.'

'Well OK, we're not,' I admit reluctantly. It breaks my heart. I want to be married to Philip. I *feel* married to Philip. 'But it will be better than telling him now because I won't have to say I'm married to someone else. I could just tell him there was a legal technicality: that the paperwork for our wedding was filled out incorrectly. It's not even a lie.' I allow hope to glimmer for the first time in six days.

'It's hardly the truth, the whole truth, and nothing but the truth. He'll expect you to be specific. He's not the sort to be fobbed off with vagaries. It would be better to come clean,' argues Amelie.

'I'll fudge, I'll get round it.' I've been burying my head in sand for years; I have no intention of emerging now. 'And then Philip and I can get remarried, quietly. No one need ever know. And Laura and Stevie can do, well, whatever they want to do.'

I see this as the ultimate in self-sacrifice and magnanimity. I may not want Stevie now but gift-wrapping him for someone else is still hard. Deep down, somewhere untouchable, I had furtively believed that he was mine. He always has been, in a forever – since the start of time – sort of way. I may not have seen him for eight years, I may not even have thought about him for months on end but somewhere in my subconscious Stevie registered as mine. Amelie clearly doesn't see my sacrifice, because she pulls the face she normally reserves for Freya and Davey when they are squabbling.

Laura returns to the table. Her newly acquired glow has dimmed. I wonder if she was expecting a call and he hasn't rung or maybe he's just sent her a blowout text. Goodo. If he ditches her I won't have to meet him.

'Anything wrong?' I ask.

'Odd that you should ask me that, I was just going to ask you the same thing,' says Laura. 'Are you OK? You've been acting very strangely today.' I look at her blankly, not daring to allow any expression to flicker across my face. 'Look, I want you to be honest with me. What is your problem with Stevie?'

'I haven't got one,' I mutter.

'Good, because if you have, you should tell me. I know you objected to him being a busker but he isn't a busker.'

'Yes, you said, a teacher. That's great.'

'If you know of any *real* reason I shouldn't be going out with Stevie, then as a mate you should tell me now.'

This is my moment. I could confide in her as I have done with so many other, admittedly smaller, issues in the past. When I took slimming tablets Laura was the only person I told, and of course she convinced me that they were non-sense and sent me to the gym. When I missed my period just before Philip and I got married it was Laura who sat outside the bathroom door and waited for the results of my peeing on to a stick. It was a false alarm, stress had sent my body into disarray. Laura knew about the men I'd stood up, men I'd waited by the phone for. She knew when I highlighted my hair and that I always wore a Wonderbra on a first date. She knows everything about me – well, practically – she's been firmly ensconced on my side for three years now, I want to keep her there.

Fleetingly, I consider whether if I come clean Laura will conspire to keep my secret from Philip. Maybe I could persuade her to. But what if I can't? What if she is angry and confused at the situation, not an unreasonable response, and what if she insists on exposing me to Philip? I feel Amelie holding her breath, willing me to fess up, do the right thing. But I can't, daren't, do it.

My own plan has to work.

I shake my head, sick with shame. 'I'm just worried about you,' I mumble, which is true. The more shaming bit is I'm more worried about myself. 'I don't want to see you hurt,' I add. And I *don't* want to see Laura hurt. She has been through one massive break-up, which nearly killed her, and Amelie is right, she's fallen for Stevie. If I could put the bigamist thing to one side and think about Stevie and Laura as a couple I'd have to admit that they suit one another. I want my new plan to work, for everyone's sake.

'I'd like to meet him properly,' I say.

'You would?' Laura's former radiance reappears.

I smile despite myself. 'Yes. This whole thing has got off on the wrong foot.' That much is true. 'Why don't you and Stevie come to supper this Saturday?'

'That would be great. Oh, he has a gig then, a wedding. Can we make it the week after?'

I wonder how much damage can be done in a week. But, as I have no choice, I agree.

'He'll be so pleased,' enthuses Laura. 'He's dying to meet you. I've talked about you a lot.'

I take this comment and Stevie's keenness to meet Laura's friends at innocent face value because considering the alternative – that he might have an inkling that I am Belinda McDonnel from Kirkspey and not Bella Edwards of Wimbledon, would turn me to stone.

'And you'll come too, won't you, Amelie?' I offer.

'Wouldn't miss it for the world,' says Amelie.

Whereas I, on the other hand, would give the world not to have to throw this particular supper party.

18. Tonight is So Right for Love

Friday 4th June 2004

Laura

'Is he asleep?' I ask, as Stevie enters the kitchen.

'Almost. I read *The Man on the Moon*, *Fox in Socks* and *Peter the Pirate's Parrot*.'

'Ha, sucker.' I grin. They're all fairly long books. 'I always spell out the terms before I start the bedtime story. Two short ones or a long one. Never two long books. Three long ones is unprecedented. He'd have you in there all night, given the chance.'

'I don't mind. I quite enjoy it,' says Stevie. I steal a glance and can see the faintest trace of a blush on his cheekbones; clearly he wasn't one hundred per cent comfortable with the confession. But I am delighted.

'You're lucky you didn't meet us last year. Then he just wanted the same book over and over again. His favourite was this really annoying one about sounds in a builder's yard. I ask you! It's hardly got what I require from a novel. No tension, no big romance, no—'

'Resolution?' interrupted Stevie.

'Exactly.' Now I feel a little shy; it's time to change the subject. 'I think we're about done here. Why don't you grab a bottle of wine from the cooler and we can go and put our feet up while the steak marinates and the veggies are roasting?'

I've prepared dinner while Stevie supervised Eddie's bedtime. Eddie insisted that Stevie bath him, clean his teeth and read the story. Normally I relish that time of the evening – and not just because it signals that it's nearly time for sleep. I love the intimacy of curling up with Eddie and reading to him as we wind down from our frenetic day. I like to watch as his eyelids become heavier and heavier until the day's fun finally overwhelms him and his eyes close. I could look at his lengthy lashes resting on his rosy cheeks forever. I snuggle tightly, breathing in his essence and savouring his childhood. I thought I'd be put out when my services became surplus to requirements and I certainly hadn't expected it to occur quite so quickly, but when Eddie demanded that Stevie run his bath and read his story I felt totally comfortable.

I heard lots of laughing and splashing from the bathroom and when I went in to retrieve grubby clothes, the floors and walls were drenched; clearly bathtime is a much more boisterous occasion with Stevie than it is with me, no wonder Eddie was giggling so hard. I listened as Stevie read familiar stories in an unfamiliar way. He used different voices for characters and he insisted on acting out the swashbuckling scenes. I thought that Eddie would never settle, far too excited and enjoying the unfamiliar surge of testosterone in our home, then I heard Stevie sing a lullaby in a quiet, melodious tone. I had to swallow hard so as not to do anything really stupid like cry into the vegetables. It's not as though I was chopping onions, nor is it a particular time of the month.

I've promised Stevie a very special meal in tonight. We've had a night out this week and I wasn't happy about getting another babysitter. Stevie offered to pay, he said it was only fair as it was half the cost of the date. I explained it wasn't about the money, I just didn't feel right leaving Eddie again. It has been an exceptionally busy fortnight for us all and we need some chill time. I promised Stevie a home-cooked meal and I explained that while I didn't want to blow my own trumpet, I am pretty confident that my steak with rosemary will be the best he's ever tasted.

Besides the babysitting I have another important motive for staying in, lurking around my murky mind – I still believe that good cooking is the way to a man's heart. Put plainly, I hope that my steak and veg will be a way to Stevie's meat and veg.

It's the strangest thing. I am pretty sure that Stevie likes me – really likes me. After all, we've spent almost every evening together since we met. So, it's a little embarrassing to report that tonight, a whole fortnight after The Bell and Long Wheat gig, Stevie and I still have no carnal knowledge of one another. Absolutely none. We haven't even indulged in tonsil tennis. I'm at a loss.

I'm aware that my boobs have competitively challenged one another to a race to reach my waistline and I have crow's feet around my eyes (and God knows they can't be laugh lines because even Coco the Clown hasn't laughed enough to have that many lines). That said, I've caught Stevie looking at me with what I believe to be good old-fashioned craving. He couldn't take his eyes off my legs when I wore a micro-skirt to visit London Zoo last

Saturday – he missed seeing most of the animals. I'm pretty sure I don't repel him physically, and as he's spending all his free time with me he can't hate my company, which makes the whole abstinence-non-sexual-dating thing even more unfathomable. He's not shy. He's not inexperienced. To my knowledge, he doesn't have any awful diseases. So I'm at a loss.

I've considered calling Bella. She's normally so good at reading men. She doesn't see them as the alien species that I know they are. Besides, I always turn to her if I have a problem. Anything from not being able to get my meringue peaks to stand up high enough (her helpful advice was buy them at M&S), to how to handle my ex-in-laws, my 'out-laws', as she calls them. Yet I haven't rung her. The problem is, while we're all getting together tomorrow evening, and she says she wants us all to be friends, I don't believe her. I wish I did.

In the last two weeks I have seen Bella once and we have spoken on the phone twice. Both calls smacked of the perfunctory as we made arrangements for her supper. There's something wrong between us. I don't know what I've done to upset her. I get the distinct impression that she doesn't like Stevie, but that's impossible because she hasn't even met him.

Anyway, as I can't discuss Stevie with her, I'll have to rely on my own instincts. The conclusion I might have drawn in the past is that he has fallen for me, but not Eddie. As a single mum I make it clear that Eddie and I come as a job lot. I'm not looking for a father for Eddie – he has one of those – but, whoever I date has to be aware of my responsibilities and that the little man in my life comes first. It takes a special kind of guy to be so unselfish. But Stevie *has* fallen for Eddie. After lengthy internal debate and a brief bout of self-doubt, followed by several firm talking-tos, the only conclusion I can draw is that Stevie has not had the opportunity to get rude and cheeky with me. I'm not absolutely convinced by this but, for lack of any other reasonable explanation, I'm going with it.

I've decided to create an opportunity for him to make his move. I've pulled out all the stops. Besides the fine cooking, I've dimmed the lights, put on some soft music (a Costes CD bought especially for the occasion, even I could see Barry White was overdoing it) and lit dozens of candles. I have no shame. Blow it, I'm not trying to be subtle. I considered lying down naked in the pitch-black on the off-chance that he'd accidentally stumble across me. My patience is running short.

I've dressed to impress or, more accurately, I've dressed to be undressed. On Thursday after lunch with the girls, I nipped to La Senza, the normal girl's Agent Provocateur. I settled on a lacy underwired bra and matching hot-pant knickers. In red. I had a moment of panic when I wondered if the effect was a bit tarty. Eventually, I decided that wasn't a bad thing. As I said, I'm not going for subtle.

I follow Stevie through to the sitting room and stare at my feet, not quite brave enough to meet his eye as he confronts the music and more candles than Westminster Abbey burns at Christmas. Still, there's no place for last-minute nerves now. I collapse on to the settee, pat the cushion next to me and I wave the empty wine glasses I'm carrying. 'Come over here with that wine, I'm parched.'

147

Stevie obliges, sits next to me and pours the wine.

'What shall we toast?' I ask.

If that's not an all-time great opener I'm going to retire from this game, because while I haven't been dating for, well . . . too long, I remember endless occasions when I'd ask some guy that question, and he'd say, 'Us.' That's the script. It never failed. And, after the clink, he would lean in to kiss me. 'Us.' Clink. Kiss. Every time.

I carefully glance at my watch. The steak needs to marinate for another forty-five minutes. It is possible that we'll have got down and dirty before we even eat, which is favourite because my stomach will be flatter.

'Elvis,' says Stevie.

'What?' I gasp my disbelief. I start up from my slouched recline. That's it, I'm out of here. I *am* going to retire from the game. I am wearing red lacy underwear and shiny red lipgloss. I'm fluttering my eyelashes enough to cause a serious draught and I'm flashing a healthy dose of cleavage and he wants to toast *Elvis*.

'Let's toast Elvis.' Stevie has a huge grin on his face and if I wasn't choking on disappointment I might concede that he has never looked cuter. 'I've been dying to tell you. There's this annual competition. An Elvis Tribute Convention and Competition to find the King of Kings in Europe. I've already got through the UK heats. Babe, you might not have known it but I am the UK King.' His words are tumbling out in an excited cascade. I grin manically, trying to take it all in. 'But I never expected this. I'm in the final! And it's taking place in Las Vegas.' I smile and nod but can't get a word in edgeways. 'Vegas – can you believe it? Normally the convention is held somewhere like Blackpool or Newquay. But as it's the anniversary of what would have been Elvis's sixty-ninth birthday, there's been all this special sponsorship money thrown at it.'

'Why not wait until the seventieth anniversary, more of a round number?' I ask.

'To avoid confusion, because next year there will be a global event and the European one would be swallowed.'

'I didn't realize it was such a serious business.'

'But the very best bit is I get to take three other people with me. All expenses paid for a long weekend. Can you believe it? Dave and John are well up for it. What do you say?'

'That's fantastic.' It would be impossible not to be pleased for him. 'Is your mum chuffed?' I ask.

'My mum?' Stevie pulls away from me. In all the excitement I hadn't realized just how close his face was to mine. Just millimetres away. 'I haven't called her. Yeah, she'll be chuffed.' He sounds a bit confused.

'Has she travelled much?' I doubted it. Stevie comes from a background where there isn't much money spare for things like foreign holidays.

'God, I feel like an absolute shit,' says Stevie; his excited face folds like a pack of cards.

'Why?' I ask.

'I hadn't thought of taking my mum. Isn't that terrible of me? I was hoping you'd come.'

'Me?' I grin, astonished.

'But if you think I should take my mum . . .'

'Oh, no. Well, yes. Obviously, if you want to.' I try to swallow back my disappointment. Why couldn't I have kept my big mouth shut? I steal a glance at Stevie, he's grinning.

'Actually, she isn't too keen on long-haul travel. She thinks a train trip to the nearest market town is a major expedition and needs several weeks to prepare. Nor does she like the sun. Whereas I imagine you'd feel great stretching out by the pool, soaking up some rays.'

'Oh, I would, I would.' I laugh. 'But what about Eddie?'

'Couldn't his dad look after him? They'd have a bit of boy-to-boy bonding time. Or one of your mates – Amelie? Bella? They'd help out. You deserve a holiday.'

I *do* deserve a holiday. Or at least I want one so very much that I'm prepared to justify it on just about any grounds. I'm sure Oscar would have Eddie for a few days, Amelie would certainly pitch in. Bella too, of course. Probably. Besides, this isn't any old holiday. This is a once-in-a-lifetime opportunity. It's free and it's with Stevie. He's inviting me on holiday. He wants me there to support him in this competition.

'I'd love to go.' I grin, 'If you are sure.'

'I'm positive. Is that a deal then?'

'It's a deal. Shake on it.' I hold out my hand for Stevie to shake.

He takes hold but doesn't shake. He turns it over, then carefully traces one of the lines on my palm that curves around the fleshy bit underneath the thumb and then slowly up my forearm.

'The thing is, Laura, I was hoping we could seal the deal with something a little more intimate than a handshake.'

Yesssssss.

19. Baby, I Don't Care

Saturday 5th June 2004

Bella

'Amelie, do you think this is a stupid thing to do?' I hiss-whisper the question. We are in my kitchen and Philip is in the cellar choosing wine for tonight's supper party, but you can never be too careful. I am of course referring to inviting my ex-husband, or more pertinently my non-ex-husband, around for dinner.

'You've done the stupid thing already, marrying two blokes,' Amelie whispers back, with her signature brutal honesty.

I am disheartened. Doesn't she know that a girlfriend's role in life is to make the other girlfriend feel better, no matter what? Didn't she ever watch *Sex and the City*? She must have noticed that I'm less than happy with the situation because she adds, more sympathetically, 'Oh, Bella, what a mess. Still, at least you're trying to fix things now, aren't you?'

We stare at one another, trying to hide our fear and desperation. Amelie is a big one for fixing things. She's often sending flowers or chocs to cheer people up or to say sorry. Not that she ever has to apologize for anything worse than forgetting someone's birthday. But even

Amelie must see that Interflora isn't going to help here.

'Are you sure you don't just want to tell Philip?' she asks.

'Certain,' I reply forcefully. The idea of having a *tête-à-tête* with Stevie is horrible – my stomach has been churning all week – but it is nothing in comparison with having to come clean to Philip. He'd never forgive me. He wouldn't, couldn't understand. I don't really understand it myself.

'The man doesn't even cheat in Monopoly. He never returns to the same parking meter within the specified time, he sends his self-assessment tax return in *early*. He breaks out in a rash if he doesn't get his DVD back to Blockbuster on time. He is not a man who breaks laws,' I point out. 'He wouldn't take this well. Who would?'

Amelie nods patiently. 'I know but—'

'There are no buts. I got myself into this mess and I'll get myself out of it. I can do it. I have to.'

I realize that I have gone for the high-risk option. When I open the door to Stevie this evening he'll get a hell of a bolt. I'm hoping he'll be too shocked to say anything that will give me away until I've had chance to beg him not to. I turn back to the preparation of supper and put my energy into chopping the peppers as finely as possible. I try to blank out everything else – after all, I'm practised at that.

I wonder if Stevie will like fresh linguini with Roquefort sauce. When we met, his diet consisted entirely of Findus crispy pancakes, the chicken variety, with baked beans and brown sauce. His tastes weren't much more sophisticated by the time I left him. I wonder if he'll be impressed that I can cook now and that I have a six-ring Aga. Or will he think I'm a snob? The worst condemnation we lobbed at anyone way back when.

I shake my head and try to banish this thought.

Of course I'm not. I'm sure he'll be pleased I've done so well for myself, or at least I'm sure he would have been, if we'd met under different circumstances.

'What can I do to help?' asks Philip, as he emerges from the cellar, carrying several bottles of wine. He puts the two white ones in the fridge, then uncorks a red to allow it to breathe.

'You could pour some drinks,' I reply.

He pours me a gin and tonic and Amelie a vodka and cranberry: our preferred tipples.

'So what's this chap of Laura's like?' he asks.

'No idea. I haven't met him,' I say hastily.

'Well, he must be pretty special if we're going to all this effort for him. Oysters, fresh linguini, chocolate and orange soufflé,' observes Philip. 'And you, my darling, look fantastic. Is that dress new?'

I blush. 'I bought it ages ago,' I lie, wishing for the first time that Philip paid me less attention. Right now, I could do with one of those guys who think their wives are invisible.

The truth is, I have made an enormous effort with my appearance. Normally if friends are coming to supper, I change my top or I might pop on a pair of slightly smarter jeans. Tonight I am wearing a black Dolce & Gabbana knee-length dress. It has a tight bodice, no sleeves and very thin straps. It's laced at the back, which gives it low-key dominatrix-meets-shepherdess overtones.

I know I look hot. I want to look hot. I don't want to consider my motives here.

'He seems nice. He's making Laura very happy,' says Amelie.

'Have you met him?' asks Philip.

'Only briefly. I'd been looking after Eddie and they came together to collect him,' says Amelie, nonchalantly.

'You have?' I can't hide my surprise. 'You never said.'

I glare at Amelie but she refuses to look sheepish. Instead she says, 'Didn't I? Must have slipped my mind.'

It's not material but I feel betrayed. I can't help but think Amelie is trying to teach me a lesson. I want to yell at her that I bloody well know I've made a mistake, I don't need her priggish lessons. But the doorbell rings, saving us both.

'Damn! They're early.' I throw down the knife I've been using to chop spring onions and whisk off my apron. I check my reflection in the aluminium fridge door.

'No need to panic, sweetheart. I'll let them in,' says Philip.

'No, I will,' I say and push him aside. I charge towards the door, or at least I charge as much as is possible in three-inch-high shoes. It's important that I greet Stevie and Laura. I don't want Philip to have made Stevie feel relaxed by getting him a drink and chatting. I need to catch Stevie unawares, when he is most vulnerable and pliable. I just need him to keep silent this evening, and for a very short time afterwards, then everything will be OK. After that I can fix this whole sorry mess and we can carry on as normal.

'Laura,' I shout as I open the door. I fling my arms

round her and pull her to me. I look over her shoulder at Stevie. My husband. I can't deny I'm more than a wee bit curious. He is turned away, checking out Philip's Jag, which hasn't been put in the garage yet. Slowly he turns to greet me.

Poor Stevie. What was he expecting? The mate of his new girlfriend. A smart hostess? A former waitress turned housewife? How much had they talked about me? Had he already formed an opinion of Bella Edwards? Did he suspect that she might be a little spoilt, living in her huge home in Wimbledon? Or had Laura loyally retold our friendship? Did he know that I'd paid my dues, that I'm a good mate; that I've worked hard and played hard too? Does he know that I married Philip for love and life, not a lifestyle? I don't know, but whatever he was expecting it was not Belinda McDonnel.

Stevie turns to me and our eyes lock. He falters for a second, recognizing me but not trusting his vision, wanting, no doubt, to be mistaken. I was depending on this moment of shock.

'And you must be Stevie, I've heard so much about you.'

I lean in and hug him with just as much warmth as I hugged Laura. Normally this would be over the top but I'm hoping Laura will think I'm being super-friendly. As my body touches his it softens to merge into his harder, toned physique. He smells the same. He smells of my youth. Not Impulse and cheap hairspray, but that boy smell that he brought to my youth. I'd always assumed it was the scent of boy sweat turning to man sweat, combined with Clearasil and Imperial Leather, but I suspect he has left those brands behind. So, the smell that comforted me throughout my late teens and early twenties, must have been the smell of his skin. Simply Stevie. And smelling 'Simply Stevie' again now, makes me think I've missed it for nearly a decade.

I lean a fraction closer, hoping my move is indiscernible, and inhale gently. I'm trembling. And he is too. Damn.

'Don't say a word,' I whisper into his ear and then slowly – oh God help me – reluctantly, I pull away.

Stevie straightens and stares into my eyes. His gaze gallops past my pupils and explodes into my mind and soul. He looks confused, hurt and cross. Then he looks delighted: the most confusing response. I know how he feels. I've lived with this guilty mix of emotions for two weeks now. Something tiny and buried has been unearthed and Stevie is clearly pleased to see me.

'Come in, come in. Don't keep them on the doorstep,' says Philip, behind me.

There is the usual ten minutes of activity as introductions are made, drinks are requested and fetched. Laura hands me an enormous bunch of flowers. She doesn't normally bring flowers when she comes to us for supper, I suspect they are an acknowledgement that our easy intimacy has slipped. I thank her but don't really want to go to the kitchen to put them in water. I can't risk leaving Stevie alone with the others. I ask Amelie to see to them. She obliges without any enthusiasm, clearly she'd prefer to stay in the epicentre of the action. Stevie hands Philip a bottle of wine. He looks bashful. No doubt Philip will attribute this to the fact that he's a wee bit awkward about meeting Laura's friends – men rarely enjoy these social situations – but I know that under normal circumstances, Stevie would be delighted to meet his girlfriend's pals. He outgrew his teenage shyness and became gregarious and charming a long time ago.

I look at the two men standing side by side and I am struck by their similarities and their differences. They're approximately the same height, over six foot. Perhaps Stevie is an inch shorter than Philip. They both have dark hair and green eyes. Philip's hair is sprinkled with grey, which is to be expected – he has eight years on Stevie. Stevie's eyes flicker with mischief, excitement and anticipation as they always did. Philip's are calm, they tell the world that he's capable. Philip is bulkier. They both have big feet. The biggest difference is in the clothes they wear. Stevie is dressed in an up-to-the-minute Diesel T-shirt and low-slung jeans. I can see his underwear.

Which makes my throat dry. I take a large gulp of my drink.

Philip is wearing beige cords and a Gap T-shirt. Until today I've always thought that Philip looked smart but modern in that outfit. Now I'm wondering if he could carry off something a bit more cutting-edge. I blush at my shallow thought.

It's Philip I love.

Stevie is history.

My body is operating in slow motion yet at the same time my heart is racing. I wonder if these two diverging physical responses will tear me in two. Maybe splitting in two would be the perfect answer. I lift my glass to my lips and spill liquid down my dress.

'Are you OK, gorgeous?' asks Philip.

'Fine,' I mutter, blushing as I rub away the spillage.

'You don't want to go spilling things on your new dress.'

'It's not new.'

'Of course it is. I don't mind. Why don't you admit it? You look stunning.'

Philip is always OTT with his praise and thinks I'm far lovelier than I am. Normally it's a misconception I encourage but tonight I just want him to shut up. 'Doesn't she look gorgeous, Stevie?'

'Very nice,' mutters Stevie. Can everyone else see his embarrassment?

'Stop it, Philip,' I warn.

'You've made such a huge effort, why shouldn't you bask in compliments? And why can't I ask another chap's opinion? Laura doesn't mind.'

Laura grins good-naturedly. She's never looked better and therefore clearly doesn't mind her man being asked to compliment another woman. She's obviously secure. I can guess what's given her that dewy glow. Philip notices it too. 'You look stunning tonight, Laura. And you too, of course, Amelie.'

Amelie smiles, not offended that Philip's compliment to her was clearly an afterthought.

'Stevie and I are very lucky men to be surrounded by such a bevy of beauties.'

I know Phil is trying to be inclusive and fair but I wish he'd shut up. His excessive compliments sound pompous and insincere.

'Shall we eat?' I mutter as I stride towards the dining room.

20. You've Lost That Loving Feeling

Stevie

Holy fuck. Holy fuckity fuck. Belinda McDonnel. Belinda bloody McDonnel. My wife, ex-wife, I presume, is serving me . . . What the fuck is she serving me? I'm jolted out of my immediate shock by a plateful of slimy seashells. It looks a bit like the outflow of a seriously bad cold served up with doll's forks. Oysters? Belinda McDonnel is serving *oysters* to her mates for supper on a Saturday evening? It's too much to take in.

At first I thought I was mistaken. This Bella woman didn't seem to know me from Adam. So I doubted myself. This couldn't be my long-lost wife. There was a resemblance but then, as I've discovered, lots of women resemble Belinda. Over the years I have spotted women with the same gait, height or hair. I've heard similar laughs. I've chased women down streets and tapped them on the shoulder but when they've turned round, the illusion has always been blown apart.

I've imagined meeting my wife on countless occasions. I'd always thought we'd bump into each other at a gig or in a public library. Or maybe abroad somewhere, the Parthenon – yeah, that would have been good. Or in a rainstorm, because thunder and lightning are not without dramatic connotations. Despite having approximately a thousand scenarios filed away, I have never imagined meeting Belinda on the steps of a huge house in Wimbledon, as she welcomed me as a guest to her dinner party. For a start, Belinda McDonnel couldn't cook.

For a split second I wondered if this elegant lady might be a cousin of my long-lost wife. Because this Bella woman is married to this Philip, a good-looking older bloke, and as far as I know Belinda is still married to me. Oh, my God. Could we be divorced and I've never known? I move around a lot, post doesn't always find me. So, despite imagining this moment for eight years, on a more or less daily basis, when I was actually confronted with my ex-wife, I wasn't quite sure. For a split second the thing I had been longing for, was the thing I least wanted to believe. But then she hugged me.

She felt exactly the same. Any lingering doubt vanished in that instant. Belinda's body folded into mine and it fitted. She's only slight and she slipped under my arm, as though the space had been waiting for her to return, to fill it. I hadn't realized I was carrying around a gap. Or maybe I had.

She's changed quite a bit. Her hair used to be a mass of pre-Raphaelite curls but now she wears it straight like a newly polished sheet of glass. It's darker too – it hasn't seen a bottle of Sun-In for a while, that's for sure. Her face is thinner; she's lost her puppy fat. My Belinda McDonnel was pretty. This Bella, what's-her-name, is stunning. One of the most beautiful women I've seen for a long time.

As I hugged her, I breathed her in, and tried to fill my lungs with the essence of her. She wears a different perfume – something spicy and sophisticated. It suits her. And as she pulled away from me (why was that such a wrench?) I noticed her clothes. She was not wearing the Doc Martens, the thick woollen tights, baggy jumper, short cord skirt or large hoop earrings she wore in all my imagined reconciliation scenarios. Maybe it was a bit much to expect, it wouldn't be hygienic, let alone fashionable. She suits the sexy black number, no doubt about it. It's a posh dress, obviously. The type you buy in the shops I wouldn't dream of going in. Manned, or rather womanned, by intimidating ladies that look at me as though I'm too rough to even be their bit of rough. I wonder how much it cost as a percentage of my annual salary.

I hadn't expected her to have moved on quite so much. Moved quite so far away. Away from me. Which is perhaps a bit bloody naive of me, under the circumstances. There are those who would argue that she'd made it extremely clear that moving away from me was exactly what she wanted.

I watch Belinda closely as she fusses and serves up the food.

Belinda used to have a heavy North-East Scotland accent, now she sounds a bit like the queen. 'Do you think the rolls are the correct temperature to complement the oysters?' she asks the smiley Amelie lady, who shrugs indifferently – which suggests she's an OK type of woman. In my book the type of woman who cares if the bread rolls are the correct temperature to complement the oysters is not OK. Belinda can't be serious, can she? *I'm* sat opposite her. Me, her husband from Christmases past, here in her house bought with husband of Christmas present and she's worrying over the temperature of bread rolls!

The more I watch her, the more I think she has changed beyond recognition. It isn't just her expensive designer dress and haircut that sets her apart from everyone else I know. It isn't just that she's curbed her accent, changed her name and the colour of her hair. She is changed in a more fundamental sense. She is as hard as her beautifully manicured nails. I shiver.

The evening is a blur. Someone hands me a drink. Someone else hands me another. At the table I'm placed next to Laura and opposite Belinda. Someone pours me yet another drink. Who the hell is drinking them? This is too much. I've found her and lost her all in one night. She's married to Philip. She's wearing his diamond-encrusted, platinum wedding band. The simple gold one I gave her is nowhere to be seen. Not that it was constantly in evidence even when we were together. She was forever leaving it in her sock drawer in case we met anyone we knew and betrayed our marital status. When was I divorced?

I realize that I'm not being the entertaining and amusing boyfriend Laura would like me to be, when she digs me in the ribs for the third time. 'Did you catch that? Philip just asked how you got into doing Elvis gigs.'

Somehow, I mumble a response on automatic pilot. I'm sure lovely Laura will believe I'm nervous around her friends because I don't know them. Let's face it, she's not going to imagine how well I know her best friend, is she?

Lovely Laura. Oh, what a bastard I am. Lovely Laura. I call her that because, really, she is lovely. I adore the word 'lovely'. It's such a simple word but it conveys so much. Attractive, delightful, charming, kind. Full of love. Laura is all of those things and I have a history with her best mate and she clearly doesn't know a thing about it. Laura is sassy and fun and I know she wants me to believe that's all she is, but I know she's vulnerable and scared too. I don't want to hurt her. Should I say something? Should I pick up my fork and tap the glass – bloody crystal by the look of it. Who'd have thought of Belinda McDonnel owning anything more sparkly than a hair clip? Should I say, 'Sorry to interrupt such a genial evening but, Philip, mate, the thing is I was married to your wife. Just thought you ought to know. That is the case, isn't it, Belinda? Sorry, Laura. Sorry, everyone. Sorry.'

I reach for my fork.

'Aren't you keen on oysters?'

These are the first words that Belinda has spoken directly to me since she told me to keep my mouth shut. Her question coming at that precise moment makes me think she can read my mind. Something we both once believed. The memory of our past closeness sends a jolt through my body and stirs up some buried loyalty. I've thought of her over the years, of course I have. For years she was all I thought about, but nowadays I don't often look back. It's too confusing, too bloody . . . sad. Sometimes I've wondered what sort of life she was leading but I don't think about our history, our love. No way. I haven't allowed myself that—

Pleasure.

Because, oh God, she'd been a pleasure. I can almost smell the sunshine when I cast my mind back, so startling are the memories. So joyful, so real.

I can't make an announcement when she's asked me to keep quiet. I have to give her a chance to explain.

'Er, no. Don't like the texture,' I say.

'It's an acquired taste. You have to work at it.'

'But why would I want to?' I ask.

Laura nudges my knee. Obviously I sound rude. But fuck it, joyful, real, sunshine memories aside, Belinda is being so patronizing. I remember her using Typex to paint her stiletto heels, who is she to tell me which tastes I ought to acquire? I must stop drinking. I have to get a grip.

Belinda stretches across the table and takes my plate away. 'Maybe we can find you something you'd prefer. Eggs? A salad?'

'No, thanks.' I meet her eye. 'I haven't got an appetite.'

'It's probably the heat,' says Laura. She picks up a place mat and starts to half-heartedly fan herself. 'Not that I'm complaining. We don't get enough decent weather, this is really pleasant for early June.'

Laura is a little pink. It might be the alcohol, the heat, or it might be that she's been reduced to making small talk about the weather with her best friends. Poor Laura, clearly she's tense because she wants us all to get on. On our way over here she hinted that Bella (as she knows Belinda) had been a bit tetchy about our new relationship and Laura was at a loss to understand why. Well, there's a mystery solved.

'Would you mind giving me a hand in the kitchen, Stevie?' asks Belinda.

'Don't ask a guest, darling. I'll give you a hand,' says Philip. He's a nice enough bloke but clearly under the thumb.

'No, you sit still,' says Belinda placing a firm hand on his shoulder. I want to laugh that my mental image is not just symbolic but literal. I wonder if Belinda would think my joke was funny. I used to be able to make her laugh all the time.

I get to my feet and follow her. I hear Amelie say to Laura, 'Relax. She's going to grill the Roquefort, not Stevie. He's lovely.' Under normal circumstances I'd be chuffed but my head is too scrambled to care.

Last night I made love to Laura. And I mean made love. We didn't just shag or screw or even fuck or – what is that Aussie word she uses? Root. We didn't do any of those things. We really went for it. It was clear that we were both very much into each other. I'd been cautious about starting anything full-on with Laura. She's still reeling from the hurt of her divorce and she's too nice to mess around. Not that I'm keen on messing anyone around; I just mean that some ladies are more emotionally robust than others. Unless you think you might fall in love with a woman like Laura, it's kindest to leave her alone.

Last night I would have sworn I was in love with her.

I nearly did in fact. As we were lying exhausted and satiated in one another's sweat and stickiness I found myself a hair's breadth from muttering those three little words. It wasn't just that she gave the best head that

I have ever had the pleasure to receive. It wasn't just because we'd flipped and quipped our way through a fair amount of the *Kama Sutra* with a confidence and comfortableness normally reserved for established couples. I've spent two weeks with this woman and her son. She's fun and firm, loving and light-hearted. She seems the perfect mum to me and Eddie obviously thinks so too. I've seen her manner with her builders, her neighbours, shop assistants and mums at the school gate, and she's perfect. She has a laugh but doesn't allow anyone to take the piss. I know that sometimes, when she's feeling down, she's prone to seeing herself as a victim but her attitude is entirely victor. It's the mix of inward self-doubt and outward big clout that I admire so much. She even talked a traffic warden out of giving me a ticket. I've never seen that happen before.

Last night I was going to tell her I loved her. Or at least, I might have boy-fudged it and said, if not exactly that, then something like, 'I can see myself falling in love with you.' But one thing stopped me. Not the risk of making a total arse of myself and her laughing in my face. And not even the fact that we've only known each other two weeks and I might scare her off. The thing that stopped me was Belinda McDonnel.

How do you tell your girlfriend that you're not exactly sure of your marital status? I dunno. I really don't. And I've thought about this conundrum on and off for several years. My uncertainty about it has meant that it's easier to keep things casual with the ladies and until now, that hasn't been much of a problem. But all last night, today, and even right now, I've been thinking that I might be falling in love with Laura, that she's the ideal girl for me.

So why is it that as I follow Belinda into the kitchen I wonder if, once we are alone, we'll fall into each other's arms?

It's not an absolutely bizarre thought, well, not in the context of the evening. I don't actively *want* this to happen but as I watch her neat arse sway in front of me and recognize the mole on her shoulder, which I have kissed countless times, I feel a shudder in my trousers. I'm ashamed. And angry. Angry that she can still affect me this way. So instead of falling into one another's arms, the moment we're alone, I ensure that we fall into another old habit instead.

'Do you want to tell me what's going on, Belinda?' I snap.

'I can't explain here,' she hisses, casting a furtive glance at the kitchen door.

'You're going to bloody have to.'

'Look, I'm sorry.'

'Sorry? Sorry for what exactly? Marrying me? Divorcing me without telling me? When did we get divorced, by the way? Shouldn't I have received a solicitor's letter or something?'

The colour drains from Belinda's face. Her blusher stands out on her ashen cheeks like bruises. Her lips are a slash of bright red lipstick. For a moment her face loses its beauty and she looks like a clown.

'We're not divorced,' she mutters.

'We're – we're not?' I blindly feel around me, find a stool and plonk myself on it. Why the fuck am I pleased? She was mine and then I lost her. This evening I found her, but only briefly because I assumed, as she was married to Philip, that she was no longer married to me. For a fraction of a second I had felt intense grief as I flushed down the pan any latent fantasies I'd had about our reconciliation. Not that I truly want her, I don't. I've just found Laura. Meeting Belinda today must be viewed as a terrible, horrible inconvenience. So why the fuck am I feeling pleased?

'But you're married to—'

'Philip, yes.'

'You're a—'

'A bigamist, yes,' whispers Belinda. She sits on the stool next to mine and takes my hand. 'Look at me, Stevie. Please. This is important. We haven't got much time.'

I look at her. The sophisticated woman, who I have just watched calmly swallow oysters, has vanished. For some moments back there in the dining room I had almost hated Bella Edwards; she seemed smug and coldly unconcerned about my turmoil. The turmoil she'd caused. But Bella's grace and self-confidence have dissolved. I'm left with Belinda. I recognize the haunted, unsure look she's wearing now. Something inside me takes the blow and not just inside my trousers. I feel tender towards her, protective. Get me off this God-awful rollercoaster: I'm not enjoying the ride.

'I'm begging you, don't say anything. Please, give me some time. We'll meet. I'll explain everything. We're in such a mess here.'

'*We* are not in a mess. *You* are in a mess,' I point out.

'What about Laura? Don't you care for her?' Once

again she is Bella. She is cold and grasping to regain control. She snuffs out my feelings of warmth. She doesn't want me on her side, she wants a defeated opponent. She knows that because I've stayed silent and complicit for this much of the evening I am already in a weak position. It was probably part of her plan. There was always a ruthless side to Belinda.

'I do care for Laura. Maybe I'll just walk out there and tell everyone what you've just told me.'

'You can't do that.'

'Why not?'

'Because Laura would be devastated. Anything you are starting would be shot to pieces.' She could be right about that. Laura is fragile. I don't want to hurt or lose Laura. 'And —'

'Yes?'

'I'm asking you not to.' I stare at her impassively. 'I'm begging you not to. For old times' sake, give me this one chance to explain,' she adds.

'I don't know what to do,' I say, pulling my hand through my hair.

'Then just write down the address of your school and I'll be at the gate on Monday afternoon at four fifteen.' She points to a pen and pad. There's a long shopping list with groceries whose names I don't even recognize. What the hell do you do with calabrese and chayote squash? Bella picks up a large tureen and makes for the kitchen door. She stops and says, 'Look, Stevie. I really am sorry.'

I don't know what to believe.

21. Trying to Get to You

Philip

'Did you have a nice evening?' I ask as Bella finally comes to bed. She cleared away the entire dinner party, insisting that she couldn't bear to come down to the smell of stale plates in the morning. She ushered me up to bed, saying that I need to sleep at the weekends because on weekdays I have to get up early, which is true, but I wasn't convinced by her noble protest that she wanted to do the washing-up to give me a break; I had the feeling that she didn't want me around. When she came to bed and saw that I was still awake, reading *Newsweek*, her face showed a flicker of disappointment, which she immediately snuffed out with a broad smile.

'Did you have a nice evening?' I ask again.

She doesn't answer the question, just says, 'I have to do my exercises. Should I do them in another room? I don't want to keep you up.'

'Get into bed, Bella. You can't do sit-ups on a full stomach.' I pull back the duvet. Bella sighs and gets into bed. 'Why are you wearing pants?' I ask.

Normally, we sleep naked. I love the intimacy this suggests. It shows we're open to one another and open to sex, of course. Sometimes Bella comes to bed wearing frilly, sexy numbers; panties which clearly tell me she's feeling cheeky. At the moment she's wearing her period pants although I know she is not on her period. I wonder what she's saying.

'Full stomach, as you said. I feel fat,' she explains.

'That's ridiculous. You're beautiful.'

'I'm not,' snaps Bella, turning her back to me. I sigh, put down my book, turn out the light and snuggle up to her. I'm relieved when she pushes her bum into my crotch. This means that although Bella is feeling huffy, I'm not to blame. Next I have to establish who or what is.

'So, did you have a nice evening?' I ask for the third time.

'Yes, it was fine.'

'Just fine?'

'Fine.'

I'm stumped. Normally after our dinner parties she takes ages to wind down. She wants to chatter about who said what, who was wearing what, did they like our food? What did I think of pudding? Haven't we got great friends? Aren't we lucky? Tonight I was expecting a full grilling on my impressions of Stevie and a blow-by-blow analysis on what Bella thought of him and how much chance Laura's relationship has. I'd even practised a response because I often get ticked off for not taking enough interest. I'm a bit peeved not to get the opportunity to showcase my chatter.

'Delicious dinner, my love,' I say to kick-start the conversation.

'Thank you.'

'Shame Stevie wasn't keen on oysters.'

'Yes. What a waste.'

'Nice enough guy, though, wouldn't you say?' Silence. 'A bit shy perhaps, or do you think he was just nervous?'

'Why would he be nervous?' snaps Bella.

'Well, it's never easy meeting your partner's old friends and we're all protective of Laura. It must be the equivalent of meeting the parents.'

'Oh.'

'Did you like him?' I pursue.

'Didn't really get a chance to talk to him.'

'He mentioned that he went to university in Scotland. Do you—'

'There are lots of universities in Scotland. What makes you think he went to mine?'

'Darling, I know Scotland's a big place, not a village. I was just going to ask whether you'd discovered which one.'

Bella can be very tetchy about English ignorance of all things Scottish, and the general assumption that everyone in Scotland must know everyone else as it's such a parochial place. I change the subject. 'Good-looking chap.'

'Is he?'

'Come on, you must have noticed.' I squeeze her bum playfully. I have no problem with her noticing good-looking men, any more than she has with me noticing cute ladies. We're married, which means we're bound but not blind. 'Laura certainly thinks so. She's ga-ga about him.'

'Well, that's what counts.'

Bella still has her back to me and it seems that, despite my best efforts, she is not going to enter into a conversation. I could ask her outright what is bothering her but I know that the one thing guaranteed to make Bella close down is confrontation. Instead, I pursue a more convoluted route. 'I wonder if he plays golf.'

'No, he doesn't.'

'How do you know?'

'I . . . don't. I'm guessing. He doesn't look the golfing type.'

'He lived in Scotland for a while, there's a better than average chance that he plays. I'll ask him if he wants a round at my club.'

'Why?'

'To be friendly. You and Laura could go shopping one Saturday afternoon, like you used to, and Stevie and I could play golf.'

'I don't think that's a good idea.'

'Why not?'

'They may not last.'

'Well, if they don't I won't be heartbroken if I lose a new golf pal, and if they do last it would be nice to know him better.'

'Just leave it, Philip,' snips Bella, and she turns to me. 'Just leave it.' Her face, normally so composed, is sizzling with irritation.

'Why don't you like him?' I ask.

'I don't dislike him.' Bella stretches across me and turns off the bedside light. 'I have a headache. Can we just go to sleep now?'

I lie in the darkness counting on my fingers how far away from Bella's period we are. Never before have I encountered such a ferocious bout of PMT.

22. Love Me Tender

Laura

Stevie and I put Amelie into the first cab that comes along, then flag down a second one, only minutes later. We sit in the darkness and silence and, while I can't quite put my finger on why, I know that the dinner party was not a success. Bella had made a huge effort, there's no denying that. The menu was exquisite, as were the floral arrangements and her new dress. Perhaps that was what had caused the tension. Stevie must think my friends are completely ra-ra. I wish she'd opted for fish and chips or an Indian takeaway. I don't want to be ungrateful but her full-on 'hostess with the mostest' act rarely makes for a convivial evening.

Amelie wasn't herself either. She's been a real doll to me lately but there's friction between her and Bella. Twice tonight I saw Bella flash daggers at her and Amelie was really niggly and nit-picking with Bella. They are usually bosom buddies. Only Philip was his usual warm and relaxed self.

I steal a glance at Stevie and sigh inwardly. That was the worst of it. Stevie clearly didn't enjoy himself much. He drank too much and was monosyllabic most of the evening. I'm partly disappointed for him, that he didn't click with my mates, and partly irritated with him, for not understanding that Bella was trying her hardest. Couldn't he be a bit more perceptive? Couldn't he have told some of his funny tales or blue jokes and broken the ice?

He's leaning his head against the cab window, he appears mesmerized by the lights of London whizzing by. Is he bored, exhausted or just pissed? I wish I didn't care as much as I do. I should hold back and be all calm, cool and collected, sophisticated to the point of quasi-indifference. But then, it's a bit late for all that. I've slept with him. Last night I screamed and moaned enough to wake the dead and I didn't even have to fake it. It's unlikely that I can conjure up indifference now.

I'd waited so long for that first lip-kiss. I'd waited since he kissed me on the cheek on Hammersmith platform and I'd waited for thirty years before that. A kiss can mean so much or nothing at all. It amazes me that they are so varied and important. A kiss can be a way to say hello or goodbye. It can be an act of devotion or deceit. It can calm, comfort or arouse. The gentle kiss delivered on Hammersmith platform, a phut sound of his plump lips touching my cheek, was alarmingly ambiguous. Was the kiss one that meant the world to me but little to him? Or was it an opener? The phut sound had stayed with me and buoyed me up for three barren weeks, when sometimes I was afraid that our relationship would never be anything more than that damning epitaph of 'just good friends'. On Friday night, when he finally kissed me on the lips, the gentle phut sound was blasted away by the non-ambiguous force of a long, passionate, involved kiss.

His kisses were soft and careful. I responded eagerly; gently but decisively taking the kiss up a gear, I chewed and nibbled his lips and probed with my tongue. He softly kissed my jaw, my neck and my ears, which made me feel like a teenager, never a bad thing. It's surprising how, generally, men neglect kissing and yet it can be the most charged and erotic preamble. Stevie intuitively knew this; his kisses were diverse in intensity, he moved through the spectrum of polite to powerful, teasing to tenacious. I pushed my body close in to his. With my boobs squashed against his chest, I wondered if he could feel my hard nipples through my bra and clothes. I wondered if I dared lunge for his dick. Surprisingly, I did not feel nervous, anxious or inadequate – a state in which I'd existed more-or-less permanently since I split from Oscar – I felt charged, excited and curious.

He stroked my hair, he ran his fingers down my outer thighs and up my inner, pausing, hovering above my rudest bits. Drawing out the pleasure. He trailed his fingers down my shoulders and the length of my arms. He ran his touch over my ribs, my arse, my hip bone. His touch invited my confidence, stoked my desire and left me dizzy and energized with lust. His touch mended, calmed and reassured me. Then suddenly, he changed pace. He darted for my shirt and swiftly popped the buttons; one, two, three, four. I remember thinking it was a practised thumb and forefinger that managed such a swift disrobing but the thought didn't alarm me, it sparked more longing. I wanted his expert thumbs and fingers all over me. He sprang the buttons on my jeans with similar speed and confidence and I willingly slithered out of them. Within seconds he whipped his T-shirt over his head and his jeans were around his ankles.

He pulled me to my feet and hurriedly edged me towards the living-room wall. Passively I allowed him to lead me, enjoying the sensation of someone else taking control for a while. His fingers edged my tarty knickers to one side and slipped inside my body. His cool fingers chilled my hot flesh and for one crazy moment he seemed to be part of me. A missing part that my body had secretly craved forever. The pleasure was astounding. I came almost instantly.

I grabbed, kissed and licked wherever I could reach. His lips, his hair, his shoulders. My fingers shot towards his dick which was now standing proud and magnificent. I slipped out of my knickers as he slipped into a condom, and then I guided him into me. I stared into his eyes and he stared back, never losing me. Not for a moment. It felt incredible. It felt imperative. It felt perfect.

We did it again, after food, this time in the comfort of my bed. A bed that I'd once slept in with Oscar but I've buried his ghost as it's taken me twenty-four hours to stumble upon this realization. We had fierce and fast sex. We had ambling and lingering sex. I came again and then again. He seemed to adore me. His kisses felt like worship on my sexy bits and he kissed my untoned bits and my saggy bits with the same enthusiasm. He also delighted in the squeaky sounds that escaped my mouth when I was overcome with pleasure. He laughed at the squelchy sounds our bodies made as they bashed up against one another in sticky wantonness.

When we were both completely wasted, spent and sore, we nuzzled into one another allowing our bodies to mesh and melt. Despite the heat we did not want to be apart.

Stevie grinned and gazed at me. His eyes were unfocused, a consequence of passion and tiredness.

'Laura, I am so lucky I found you. So, so, so lucky,' he laughed in a whisper. They were the last words I heard before I fell asleep.

That was yesterday.

This is today. Today, the best I can hope for is keeping my desperation at bay. I want to retain my independence and allure. The cab pulls up outside my flat. I gather up my bag and take an extraordinarily long time zipping up my hoody. Stevie doesn't look as though he's going to budge.

'Want to pop up for a coffee?' I grin. I wanted to come across as seductive or at least wry, I think I came across as the dreaded needy and helpless.

'It's late. I need to get to bed.'

'I've got a bed.' The chord I struck was fraught.

'I need to sleep.'

'You can sleep at my place.' Quite definitely without allure, simply desperate.

I sigh and am about to give up when Stevie mutters, 'OK then,' and he leans forward to pay the cabby.

I see the babysitter to her car and then I make coffee. I'm not thirsty but it's something to do. Stevie paces the flat like a caged lion. It's not a great thought.

'Have a seat,' I urge.

He chooses a kitchen chair, a chair that does not facilitate cuddling, canoodling or caressing. I hear his message.

A vile thought grips me. Could Stevie be one of those

178

blokes who's nice until you sleep with him, then turns into a complete shit? It's possible. Past experiences, everything I read in the monthly magazines and pretty much all anecdotal evidence suggests the vast percentage of men are this type. It is possible that I've completely miscalculated him. The way he looked at me as he sank deep inside me was, I thought, communicating sincerity and amazement. What if the only thing he was amazed by was my gullibility and my slightly stretched cervix? I am crippled with shame. Only minutes ago I practically begged him to come up to my flat. Clearly, I wasn't even impressive enough for him to want to bother with a repeat performance. The ignominy of the situation is boundless. I feel like a slug that has just been showered in salt.

I muster the tiny crumbs of dignity that are lurking somewhere very deep inside me and mutter, 'You can go if you want to.'

Stevie looks surprised. Which is natural, considering I practically put him under citizen's arrest to get him upstairs in the first place.

'I don't want to go,' he states. 'Do you want me to go?'

'No, no,' I splutter. 'It's just, you didn't enjoy yourself very much tonight, did you?'

'No, not really.'

At least he's honest. I steel myself. I've always been the sort of person that hoes in, faces things full on. 'Are you the sort of man who treats a girl crash hot until you sleep with her, then you turn into a complete shit? Because if you are, I'm cool with that.'

This is a lie, of course, but at least I sound a bit more

sophisticated and twenty-first century. Depending on his answer I might throw him out or clobber him with my brand new, very heavy Tefal frying pan.

'No, I'm not.' Stevie grins. 'You call a spade a shovel, don't you?'

'I just want to know where I stand.' I fold my arms. I hope I look defiant and even a little intimidating. The stance also hides my shaking hands.

'I'm the sort of man who knows when he's on to a good thing and feels very deeply for the woman he's just started sleeping with. OK?'

Stevie has turned a very deep purple and even if I were to doubt his words I could not have a heart and misinterpret his demeanour. I grin, relieved. Delighted, actually.

He scrapes back his chair and pats his knee, indicating that I should hop on board. I do so and then balance precariously and uncomfortably. I've never liked sitting on a guy's knees. Not even when I was fourteen, which is surely the latest age it is acceptable behaviour. Stevie kisses my neck, which just about makes the whole ordeal bearable.

'I don't like oysters or Roquefort cheese,' he mutters.

'Or my friends,' I add.

'I wouldn't say that, exactly.'

'I know it wasn't a comfortable evening. Bella was being OTT, but honestly she is so lovely when you get to know her. A beaut.'

'Lovely? You say.'

'Yes. And Amelie was being a bit difficult with Bella, they must have had a disagreement.'

'About the temperature of the bread rolls perhaps?' says Stevie with a grin.

'Don't be mean,' I say, hitting him playfully. We kiss. It's a long, slow, lingering kiss.

'Let's go to bed,' he suggests.

'OK.'

I agree without worrying about whether I'm communicating alluring, nonchalant or composed. I suspect I'm communicating gagging for it. I switch out the kitchen light and follow Stevie into the bedroom. He has his back to me and he pulls his T-shirt up over his head. He's beautiful. I want this to work.

'Stevie, don't spit the dummy.'

'What?'

'I mean, don't lose patience. If you could give Bella another chance I know you'd find she's worth it,' I urge.

'You think so.'

'She's my mate.' I don't want to make too big a deal but I do want them to be friends. So it is with quite some relief I hear him say:

'OK, Laura, I'll give her another chance. For you, I'll do that.'

23. How the Web was Woven

Monday 7th June 2004

Bella

'Can I buy you a drink? I think we both need one.'

'It's the least you can do.'

Stevie is right, it is the least I can do but even so I'm not comfortable with him pointing it out. I'm not sure I've handled this correctly, but what's the etiquette for meeting your husband at a dinner party you are hosting with your other husband? I'm not sure if I want to charm him, threaten him or befriend him.

All day I've considered sending someone instead of me to this meeting. But who? Amelie has made it clear that she has no intention of involving herself because I won't take her, frankly, naive advice and 'fess up to Philip. A solicitor is out of the question, since I've broken the law. I don't like handcuffs in the bedroom, not even fur-trimmed ones; the idea of real ones sends me into apoplectic panic. I thought about hiring a private detective but I had visions of a man with a shiny suit, worn through at the knees and elbows, a small, fat man who smokes roll-ups and sprays spittle when he laughs. The vision was so grubby it almost turned my stomach and while this is dirty work to do, Stevie wasn't always a grimy secret. I once loved him very much. The least I can do is turn up in person to offer an explanation.

'I wondered if Laura had spoken about me,' I begin tentatively.

'No. She mentioned her friend Bella Edwards. I know, or knew, a Belinda McDonnel.' He sounds accusing.

'I prefer Bella to Belinda. Bella is just more . . . appropriate.'

'What was wrong with Belinda? Not posh enough for your new London life?'

I glare at Stevie but I can't think of a quick comeback because he's dead right. In truth, even if I'd been christened Flavia, Camilla or Jemima, I would probably have wanted to change my name when I left Edinburgh. Didn't he get it? I wanted to leave it all behind.

'Nice pub you've chosen,' comments Stevie. 'At least I can see a bit of the old you in here.'

I look around and try to decide if Stevie is being deliberately antagonistic. Surely he's trying to insult me. Yes, this pub is a bit like the one in Kirkspey and it has some resemblance to the ones we frequented in our student days, but surely Stevie can't think this is a desirable place to be.

The pub is filthy. Totally depressing and grimy. I can smell stale alcohol and cigarettes in the air, in the carpets, on the seats. I went to the loo a few minutes ago, to splash water on my face, and the stench of vomit, presumably from last night's excesses, wasn't even masked by cheap disinfectant.

Although it is only half past four in the afternoon the pub has a community. A scattering of old ladies, too fat to be comfortable, sit with their legs akimbo, exposing stockings and veined, plump thighs. Their companions are silent old men who look as though they've never eaten a decent meal in their lives; internalizing a vitamin or mineral would probably send them into medical shock. A couple of blokes in their forties are playing dominoes. They are wearing plaster- and paint-splattered jeans and, clearly, have come straight from the building site. Everybody (except me) is drinking pints of beer or dark, rich Guinness. I stick with a Diet Coke. Under normal circumstances I wouldn't be seen dead in here. I chose it because we won't be spotted.

'You could have written,' he says. It appears the small talk has dried up. I don't know how to start to explain myself but I don't insult him by pretending to misunderstand.

'I should have,' I admit.

'Why didn't you?'

'I don't know.'

'Over the years I've sometimes looked back at all that went on and thought it must have been a bad dream.'

'Thanks,' I say, wondering why I sound so huffy. Haven't I had that exact thought?

'I don't mean the marriage, Belinda. I mean the secrecy, then the split – not knowing where you'd gone or what had become of you.'

I shift uncomfortably on my chair. 'It wasn't working.'

'No,' says Stevie. 'It wasn't.'

He doesn't offer any insight into why not. He doesn't utter any regret but then, what was I expecting? It was all a million years ago. I don't want a trip down memory lane. I want a divorce. We have to act as quickly and dispassionately as possible. We have to sever our past and get on with our future.

'It's a long time ago. We've both moved on,' I say.

'*You* certainly have.' Stevie takes a gulp of his pint.

He was always painfully honest, verging on tactless. He didn't give a bugger what anyone thought of him or his opinions, which, oddly, meant everyone thought well of him. I always found his honesty a turn-on, now I fear it might be a nuisance.

I consider how honest *I* ought to be. It's not that I'm an evil cesspit of deceit. In an ideal world I'd rather tell the truth than not, it's just that I don't live in an ideal world and so honesty is often a luxury I can't afford.

I have no idea if Stevie hates me or if he'll be prepared to help me. He might turn nasty – even try to blackmail me or refuse to give me a quick divorce just to pay me back for leaving him. And who would blame him? God, if he'd left me so unceremoniously I'd be looking to hurt, even eight years on. I have to be careful. Philip is a rich man, which leaves me open to exploitation from all sorts of bounders or cads, villains or Elvis impersonators. I don't know Stevie, he might be a nasty piece of work now.

He doesn't look it, I admit. He looks just as sweet and kind and gentle as he always looked. The old Stevie would not turn nasty or awkward. Neither blackmail nor revenge would cross his mind. The Stevie I'm looking at looks just like the old Stevie, except he's a tiny bit broader, not fatter, just more of a man. In a breath I make the decision to play it straight; at the very least it will be a novel approach for me.

'I need a divorce, Stevie. Philip doesn't know about you.'

'Ha.' Beer sprays from Stevie's mouth and falls on to the ugly wooden table between us. He narrowly misses the sleeve of my jacket. I'm not sure if the spraying was accidental, although missing almost certainly was. 'I gathered that much last night. What the hell were you thinking of, marrying someone when you're already married? Is it a scam? Are you planning on ripping him off? For all you've done, I never had you down as an out-and-out criminal.'

'I'm not,' I shout, outraged.

Half a dozen eyes slowly turn in our direction. The oldies aren't particularly curious; they assume they've seen everything before (although I bet they haven't seen this). They are staring at us because we are interrupting their quiet afternoon.

I lean closer to Stevie and mutter, 'Well, yes, technically I am a criminal but my marriage to Philip isn't a scam. It's the real thing. It's love.'

'So, why didn't you divorce me?'

'I . . . I don't know. I didn't know where to find you.' I know it's feeble.

'Did you try looking where you'd left me?'

I won't meet his eyes but I can feel his stare boring into my mind. He's trying to decide if he can trust me and if he wants to help me. Or maybe he'll let me hang.

I wonder how long it took him to get over me. Did he pine for months, or did he go to the pub the very next night and sleep with a random stranger? How long did it take him to fall in love again? Years? Or did he fall for the random stranger? I'm curious; no I am desperate to know. I call upon my honed self-discipline. In this case, there's no such thing as an acceptable amount of delving. If I go down that conversational route I might never be able to clamber back.

Instead I say, 'Laura really likes you.'

As I utter this sentence a slither of shame runs up my spine. It's disloyal to tell a bloke your mate is keen, unless she's expressly asked you to do so, and besides, I know I'm doing it to remind Stevie of what he has to lose. This whole business taints me.

'Is that right?' Stevie feels into his jacket pocket and pulls out a packet of Marlboro Lights. I'm surprised. I know he smoked when we were together, which I hated, but I'd assumed he'd have kicked the habit by now, as everyone with an ounce of common sense has. As he inhales I pointedly waft the smoke away as it is drifting in my direction.

'It's tricky, isn't it? You dating my best friend,' I add.

'I'm not going to stop seeing Laura.'

'I wouldn't ask you to,' I rush to reassure him. 'Are you serious about her?'

'I think so.' Then more definitively he adds, 'Yes.'

Even among this chaos I'm happy about that. It's messy but it is good news. I wish I could tell her. My reaction shows that I'm still a decent person, I was beginning to doubt it.

'We've agreed that we are going to date exclusively and I don't do much exclusive dating. You put me off.'

Suddenly, the ice cube melting in my drink is fascinating. I stare at it. I want to say so much. Too much. 'Laura can't know about us,' I state.

'That puts me in a difficult position.'

'I'm sorry.'

'So you keep saying.' Stevie sighs wearily. 'Do you want another drink?'

I nod. I watch him at the bar. He shares a few words with the barman and they laugh. For a moment I see a glimpse of the animated, happy Stevie I once knew. What have I done? What terrible thing have I done? There's such hurt there. Serious damage. This isn't a game but I fear there may be losers.

He returns to the table, lights another cigarette and takes a large gulp of his drink.

'Are you happy?' he asks.

'Very,' I reply without skipping a beat. Or at least, I was until Stevie came back into my world. 'You?'

'Yes.'

'So it hasn't turned out too badly, has it?' I say stupidly.

Stevie shakes his head – in disgust, I think.

'How old is Philip?'

'Thirty-nine.'

Stevie splutters into his drink.

'Don't be so infantile,' I groan. 'When we were sixteen, thirty-nine might have seemed old, but—'

'When we were sixteen, twenty-three seemed old.'

'Exactly,' I say, thinking he had proven my point for me. But he's grinning as though he's proven his own.

'He's clearly wealthy.'

'We're comfortable, thank you.' Not that it's any of his business.

'You're not working?'

'Not at the moment, but I didn't marry him for his money if that's what you are thinking.'

'No, no, of course not,' Stevie is smirking. I can't be bothered to explain. I owe Stevie a number of explanations but not that one.

'Do you think we can have our marriage annulled?' I ask, trying to get back on track.

'On what grounds? We'd hardly be able to claim non-consummation, would we?'

We fall silent. I wonder if startlingly vivid images of my naked flesh are accosting his mind, the way images of him are demanding my immediate attention.

Oh God, he'd been lovely. Toned and tanned. Fit and lean. Fun and loving. He hasn't changed much.

I lost my virginity to Stevie. Not that it was a loss of any sort, that's a terrible expression. Rather, I chucked my virginity and caution to the wind and I was happy to do so. The funny thing about sex for the first time is that it's such an enormous deal. Stevie, being male, pretty much pushed for sex from the moment he dropped his yellow checker into the blue Connect 4 frame. The onus to resist, to be cautious and careful, fell entirely on to my shoulders because I was the girl. *But* I wanted him just as much as he wanted me. I wanted him so much it hurt. Still, the initial opportunity took some negotiating.

Armed with a three-pack of condoms (purchased from the male loos at the local pub) we set about finding somewhere suitable for the big event. We didn't have a car so we couldn't join most of our classmates who stumbled through their first time parked up at the beach. I didn't want my first time to be up against the bike sheds or in the woods lying on his parka (although subsequently I found these to be more than adequate as venues for love). Stevie's mother never went out so we couldn't do it at his place and while all my brothers and my father went out loads, they didn't coordinate their movements so – rather frustratingly – someone was always at home. Besides, I didn't really fancy shagging in my room. I hadn't changed a thing in there since my mum had died. It was (and as far as I know still is) a tatty and trippy mess of clashing flowery prints. There were flowers on the bedspread, different flowers on the wallpaper and another set on the carpet. There were posters of boy bands on the walls declaring that I was a teenager and dolls on the shelves arguing that I was still a wee girl. I simply would not have been able to concentrate on Stevie with Tiny Tears and Take That smiling down at me.

In the end we caught a train to neighbouring town Newburgh and booked into a bed and breakfast. It was a dingy place with the type of landlady who didn't ask questions providing you paid cash up front. Perfect. Stevie finally relieved me of my virginity on a narrow single bed. The mattress squeaked and the nylon bedspread scratched. Yet, I thought I was in heaven.

Stevie had an enormous penis. Of course, back then I had nothing to compare it with except a picture of Michelangelo's David, so I guess an average-size penis would have seemed gigantic. But I've since done more groundwork and I can confirm I was not wrong. The first time was actually quite uncomfortable and all over in seconds. His size, my nerves and our combined inexperience united to make the entire exercise daunting. So why is it one of my sweetest memories? I still clearly remember the look in his eyes as he rolled off me. Despite the brevity of the act we were both so proud and happy. Stevie almost shouted with excitement that we were lovers. We were grown-up. We were no longer kids whose only entertainment was hanging around the corner shop and the grey granite memorial for the drowned, swigging cider and kicking cans – we were lovers. Stevie promised me that the sex would get better with practice, so we made love twice more that night. Not only did we get our money's worth out of the B&B but he also proved his point; the sex did get better and better with practice.

The issue of where we had sex never appeared again. After the first time we seemed to reach a silent and mutual agreement to make love wherever and whenever we could. I didn't care a jot about sand in my knickers or mud on his parka. Urgently we'd bang out our youthful desire, only pausing momentarily, to wedge a washbasket or other piece of furniture in front of the door. University halls of residence brought a certain level of comfort. At least in those narrow beds we did not have to keep one eye on the door handle. Our lovemaking was passionate, exciting, charged, novel and tender. It was rarely comfortable.

Maybe I should have known that there was bound to come a point when I didn't want carpet burns from thin nylon carpets which smelt of cat pee and had never seen underlay. Every girl dreams that one day she'll slide out of silk underwear and then make love on goose-down duvets, surrounded by satin cushions – just the way I do with Philip.

'Have you ever told anyone about us?' I ask, forcing myself back to the issue I have to deal with.

'No.' Relief squelches through my body. He tilts back his head, blowing out smoke, 'Er, thinking about it, yes, one person.'

I'm immediately erect with tension. 'Who, for God's sake who?'

'I can't remember her name now. Helen or Ellen or Ella. Something like that.' He shrugs, casually dismissing the woman who holds my most important secret. 'We met in Thailand, on a beach. We'd smoked some weed. She asked me to marry her, as a laugh, cos she was mellow and I said no. She took it badly.'

'Of course she did, after such a meaningful relationship,' I snap. Bugger me, I'm jealous that he smoked weed with an anonymous girl on a beach.

'I didn't want to hurt her feelings so I told her that I was already married.'

'You told some bimbo on a beach that we were married! What if I ever meet her? What if Philip does?' I yell angrily.

'She had braids and wore tie-dye. I can't see her turning up at one of your dinner parties.'

'How could you be so—' I am about to call Stevie stupid. I can see from his face that he already expects this, so I resist.

'Don't get arsy with me, Belinda. I'm not the one who

remarried.' He has a point so I have no alternative but to breathe deeply. 'Chill. She didn't believe me anyway. Not even when I showed her your picture.'

'You carry a picture of me?'

'Always.' Stevie coughs and turns away so I can't see his eyes. 'It's just habit,' he assures me.

I don't believe him and, worse, I don't want to believe him.

'It came in useful when I was looking for you.'

I put my head in my hands and allow the full implication of the situation to engulf me. Over the last few weeks I've been so absorbed in my mess and how I can get out of it without affecting my relationship with Philip, only now am I beginning to understand the further consequences of what I did to this man whom I loved and who had loved me. Whose only mistake had been to marry me when we were too young.

'Tell me about loving Philip,' says Stevie, looking into his beer glass.

'You don't want to hear that.'

'I do. I want to understand it. I want to understand you.'

Stevie and I were once so close that we thought our souls had been cut from the same part of the sky. I remember him saying that to me. Now I can't think we have anything in common. I expect he feels the same and wants to reacquaint himself. I'm uneasy but don't see that I am in a position to negotiate.

'We've been married for—'

'You're not married,' says Stevie grimly.

'Well, for the sake of argument.' Stevie shrugs and lets me go ahead. 'We've been married six months.'

'That's no time at all.'

I can hear the jeer in his voice. Stevie doesn't see my marriage to Philip as a real marriage. But he's wrong. My marriage to him was the farce.

'I want to get to our ruby wedding anniversary,' I hiss. I'm irritated. I know I'm on thin ice. Six months *is* no time at all. It's short enough for Philip to write it off as a ghastly mistake, which I'm sure he would, if he found out about my bigamy.

'We'd dated for nearly two years before we got married. All our friends think we're perfect for each other. When we announced our engagement, they asked what had taken us so long.'

'You could have explained, Belinda. You could have said you weren't in a position to commit,' says Stevie sarcastically.

I shift uncomfortably on my chair. 'It was generally expected that when confronted with Philip-the-obvious-catch, I would snap him up after the first post-coital snooze. I live in London, where suitable bachelors are thin on the ground. At twenty-eight, I felt like a baby but was already being referred to as "Madame" by strangers. Philip was heading for *The Times* rich list *and* he's kind.'

'So you didn't fancy him?'

'I did. I do,' I stumble. 'Very much. I'm not blind. I could see that Phil was eminently eligible. He has sense, looks and money enough but I really wasn't planning on marrying. I was trying *not* to fall in love with him.'

I look at Stevie, hoping for a reaction. He sneers, which is not the reaction I was looking for. Fuck me, what did I expect? He can't possibly be understanding.

I hadn't been waiting for a proposal. I was very aware that I was in no position to accept one. And I was planning to tell Philip about Stevie. Or, at the very least, to track down Stevie and sort out a divorce before I moved things on with Philip. I once went as far as to visit Friends Reunited but Stevie wasn't registered. I wouldn't have accepted Phil's proposal if he hadn't asked the night Ben was killed. I'm not saying that I didn't want to marry Phil. I did want to marry Phil. One day.

I can't articulate any of this accurately so I mutter, 'There's no crime in marrying someone who worships you.'

'There is, if you're already married,' points out Stevie.

'Well, yes,' I admit with a reluctant grin. I'm surprised that I feel like grinning at all. 'But if I hadn't been married then it would have been OK.' I touch my temples, I'm exhausted. 'Look, I bath in a loved-up glow and I won't apologize for that. I didn't marry Philip for his money, you know, Stevie. I married his gravitas,' I confess.

I wonder if Stevie will understand this. I wanted to feel safe. Stevie must realize this as he knows me better than anyone else, or at least, used to. He knows where I come from but sadly did not know where I wanted to go.

'Philip is big and strong and—'

'Grey?' says Stevie, rupturing the romantic bubble where he still understands me. I dream of being known and understood, something I've made impossible. Is he jealous of Philip?

'Yes, he is greying but I like that.'

'Older men tend to be richer.'

'Maybe, and they tend to be more mature,' I snap.

Stevie looks offended and I'm glad. 'I don't need to explain my love for Philip. I don't need to explain why I married him. He's a good husband. An excellent one.' I catch sight of Stevie's face. He looks hurt again. I reach out and squeeze his arm, 'I know you loved me too, but we were—' I want to say we were too young but Stevie interrupts.

'We were a mistake. I know, you told me.'

We stay silent for some time as anything I say seems to make matters worse. We drain our drinks and Stevie stubs out his fag. Only as we walk to the pub door dare I ask.

'Will you help me, Stevie?' I put my hand on his arm. His skin feels soft, warm, and pleasant. Stevie pauses and then after the longest time he nods.

'Yes, I will help you, Belinda, because some things never change.'

The relief is enormous, it washes over me although I know I can never be clean again.

'Stevie, one more thing.'

'What?'

'My picture, in your wallet. You have to dump it.'

Stevie nods. 'It's lousy anyway. You're wearing electric-blue mascara.'

24. That's All Right, Mama

Laura

There's a loud knock at our door.

'Stevie, Stevie, Stevie, Stevie,' says Eddie, jumping up from in front of the TV, hopeful and delighted.

I open the door and grin, 'Hi, we weren't expecting to see you tonight.'

'I can leave if you want,' he says, turning away.

'No way, babe – you're here now.' I pull him into the flat and pretend not to have noticed his tetchiness.

'Have you brought your guitar? Are you going to sing?' demands Eddie.

Stevie drops to his knees so that he is at eye level with him, 'Sorry, mate. I did promise to bring it next time I came round, didn't I? I wasn't planning on coming by. It slipped my mind.' Stevie looks gutted at having let Eddie down. Eddie, on the other hand, isn't bothered in the slightest and has already moved on to the next thing.

'Do you like Lego?'

Stevie and Eddie settle down to making Thunderbirds out of Lego and I go back to the ironing. We'd agreed not to meet tonight because following three sleep-deprived nights on the trot, I decided my house needed attention and I needed rest. This was a rational decision made over the phone at lunchtime. However, Stevie's irrational appearance is welcome, despite the fact that he's found me in all my barefaced glory. Then again, he's seen me in all my bare-arsed glory. It isn't logical to worry about lack of make-up.

'Everything OK?' I ask. Clearly it's not. This isn't one of those visits where your new boyfriend tears round to your flat because he can't wait to rip off your clothes and give you a damn good ravishing. He looks tired and stressed. He's come to my flat as a sanctuary. I'm stoked. I mean, obviously, I'm sorry that he's tired and stressed but I can't help being chuffed that he's come to me for a bit of TLC.

'Have those kids been picking on you again?' I ask, with a smile.

Stevie gets up from the floor where he's been playing with Eddie, and throws himself on to the settee. It shakes ever so slightly under his weight. Oscar was much shorter and Stevie looks as though he's going to burst through the ceiling at any moment. All my furniture seems girly and effeminate when he lounges.

He pats the settee. 'Come and give me a hug, Laura.'

I willingly leave my ironing and oblige. 'Tough day?'

'Yes.'

'Kids? Parents? Paperwork? That old guy who eats all the chocolate biscuits in the staff room?'

'Nothing like that,' says Stevie. He's quiet for a long time and just when I'm giving up hope that he's going to tell me what's bugging him, he mutters, 'Neither John nor Dave can make it to Las Vegas.'

'You're kidding?'

'Nope. John can't get time off and Dave has a family party or something that weekend.'

'Can't he get out of it?'

'Sister's wedding, so no, not easily.'

'Oh, babe, that's a shame, I know you wanted them to be there.'

'Yes, it's a shame.'

'Who are you going to ask instead?'

'No idea.'

'You must have other friends. People at school.'

'They're not the type you'd invite to support you as you conquer the world at an Elvis Presley tribute competition. It's such a bloody waste of two tickets and a hotel room,' says Stevie.

I sympathize with his predicament. If I had won a prize to take three friends on an all-expenses-paid trip to Las Vegas I'd ask Bella and Amelie. If they couldn't make it, I'd be struggling. I'm not close enough to Sally or any of the doctors at the surgery to want to dress up in a spangly outfit and sing my guts out in front of them, even if I was talented that way.

I blame TV. We live in a hyperreality. TV has become more real than reality. We all feel we should be living a life like Monica, Rachel or Ross. A life where having cool friends who hang out in coffee bars is the norm. My friends don't have time to live in coffee bars – well, Bella has, recently, but she didn't always live her life that way. If we believed TV (which we do) it would appear that friends who would give their kidneys, as though they were offering a toffee, are queuing at the door. It's not like that in the real world. True friends are harder to come by. I want to assure Stevie that we'll have a wonderful time in Las Vegas alone, but I'm nervous that I'll sound either insensitive or full of bull.

The truth is, I'm not absolutely sure we *will* have a cheer'n time alone. I hope we will but it's all so intense, all very fast forward. Something scary is happening here. And I can't decide if it's the best thing ever or the worst.

I'm falling in love with Stevie.

I know, I know, it's stupidly early to say such a big, out-there thing but how else do I explain the fact that today I caught myself singing, *out loud*, on the tube. I'm almost unhappy with the situation. *Almost*. Part of me wants to kick, scramble, bollocks out of here. I want to sit Stevie down and explain, in words of one syllable, I've closed off that side of me. I no longer trust. I think men are bastards. The odd individual might be able to hide it for a while – give you the impression that they're different from other testosterone-driven fuckwits – but, in the end, they are all the same and they *are* all bastards. I believe this with every rational bone in my body because the evidence is there, isn't it?

But, the thing is, I'm the last of the great romantics.

The irrational bits, my heart and my soul, keep nagging at me. The squishy bits seem to be insisting that *not* all men are bastards. My dad's a nice bloke. Eddie's still cute. And Stevie . . . Stevie seems fine.

I believe in love. The forever kind. It's an enormous inconvenience and you'd think I'd have wised up after the Oscar debacle but I haven't. Stevie is easy and fun. The things that should bother us, don't. Tonight, for instance, he's caught me waist-high in washing, no make-up, hair pulled into an untidy ponytail and he should be put off, but I know he's not. The intimacy is disarmingly easy.

I'd be happier if John and Dave could have made it.

'Eddie's nearly asleep,' says Stevie. 'Why don't you pop him into bed while I scrounge around in your fridge and see if I can rustle up anything that will pass as supper?'

'Deal,' I smile.

After we've had scrambled eggs on toast and a bottle of wine, Stevie and I return to the settee, with a can of beer apiece.

'I like your flat, Laura. I feel happy here.'

'Do you?' I'm particularly open to this line of compliment because Henryk's oft-shared opinion that my entire flat could do with a major overhaul has started to grind me down. I've stopped noticing that my flat is actually kind of cool.

'I like the colours.'

It is colourful. Pretty much every wall is painted differently. This is partly a creative statement and partly the result of watching the pennies. I often buy pots of emulsion that are on the sale rack in B&Q. The paints that people have had mixed up and then backed out of buying because they're too bright, garish or vulgar.

'It's very vibrant,' adds Stevie tactfully.

'I'm lucky that I was able to use up the half or quarter tins that Bella discarded when she decorated her home. Having the odd wall painted in a muted blue or a taupe has helped the overall effect. Calmed it down a bit.'

'I like the bright colours best,' said Stevie. 'I also like your pictures and fairy lights.'

I have pictures all over my home. Posters, bought from markets or galleries, and postcards tucked behind every ornament, book or mug as I keep every single postcard that is sent to me. There are photographs too, mostly of Eddie but quite a few of my family, Bella and other friends. I read in a feng shui book that it's good chi to have pictures of loved ones all around you. Hey, why not? There are times when we need every bit of help that we can get.

I've hung strings of fairy lights everywhere – they're too pretty to keep in a box until Christmas – round doorways and window sills, they decorate vases, frames and shelves. I hang on to things. I find throwing things away, even useless or ugly things, a very difficult exercise (think Oscar). I'm aware that this attitude isn't particularly good for chi. According to Eastern philosophy you are not meant to keep anything in your house that isn't either useful or beautiful, unless it's a ceramic frog.

I've come to regard the overall effect as chaotic – certainly that was Oscar's view. I don't think Henryk approves of my aesthetic choices either, although, to be fair, he limits his criticism to badly hung doors and smelly damp patches. Undeniably, my place is not as cosy and comfy as Amelie's home nor as chic and classy as Bella's. But the effect might be regarded as bohemian. Following Stevie's approving comments I'm more inclined to see that it has a certain lived-in quality.

'When Oscar left, I was determined to hold on to the apartment, mostly because the thought of moving terrified me,' I blurt. I haven't said much about Oscar to Stevie. It's too easy for me to be angry and people like their lemons bitter, not their ladies.

'Why was that?'

'I don't like legal documents, not to mention the scary language exclusive to surveyors and I couldn't face trotting around other people's homes trying to find somewhere suitable for Eddie and me.' Stevie stays silent, which is all the encouragement I need. 'I've house-hunted in the past and the vendors always make an unnatural effort to present their homes and families as perfect.'

'What do you mean?'

'They brew Brazilian coffee, bake bread and give an extra squirt of the potpourri-scented air-freshener. They have vases of freshly cut flowers on every surface. The wives try to be smiley and accommodating, the husbands strive to be at their most witty and affable. I couldn't face it.'

I draw up short of blurting that Eddie and I didn't seem to add up to much of a family without Oscar. Obliterated, we couldn't take on the smell of baked bread and the show of family perfection.

'How did you manage?'

'I bought Oscar out of his share of the apartment by begging the bank to give me a bigger mortgage. We halved our savings, which turned out to be embarrassingly modest, and called it a day.'

'Did you have a good solicitor?'

'I didn't use one. I wanted to make as swift and dignified an exit as possible.'

At the time I'd said there was no point in going to a

solicitor because I didn't care about money. Six months later, I realized that it's only people with loads of money who can say that they don't care about it. Anyway, even if I don't care about money, the gas, water and electricity boards do, the council tax collector does and Visa card do, to name but a few. While it is possible that money doesn't buy happiness, it definitely pays for decent substitutes. I don't say any of this to Stevie, all I mutter is, 'Thank God for Bella.'

'Why do you say that?'

'She helped me out so much.'

She made me get a haircut and buy new clothes; again I keep this information sacrosanct. I don't want to leave Stevie with the impression that I was a smelly, self-neglecting trollop, however accurate. Bella listened to me churn, over and over again, the details of my split from Oscar. She allowed me to rant, weep and despair. Then she encouraged, cajoled and reasoned with me for endless hours. I was a stranger to her and definitely not at my best but she didn't seem to care or even notice. Her heart had room for me. She helped me to find some sort of a sense of humour and sense of self. I limit my explanation to, 'She helped me get my finances in order. She worked out how much I owed and how much money I had coming in, then helped me find a job that covered the shortfall but worked around childcare. Most of which she did anyway.'

'She looked after Eddie?'

'Yes. You sound surprised.'

'She just didn't come across as the kid-loving type.'

'Oh, she is. She's great with kids. Eddie adores her.'

I want to explain that I adore her too. Everyone does. Stevie would, if only he knew her. 'You definitely didn't see her at her best on Saturday night. I can't tell you how fabulous she is. I really want you to get to know her better.'

Stevie looks away. Despite agreeing to give Bella a chance, I don't get the impression he's totally convinced. Suddenly, I have the most amazing idea.

'Let's ask Bella and Phil to come to Las Vegas with us.'

'*What?*'

'You said yourself that the tickets and the hotel room would just go to waste and I can't tell you how much it would mean to me to do something nice for Bella. She's always buying such extravagant gifts for Eddie and my drinks and paying restaurant bills.'

'She can afford to, by the looks of it.'

'But even before she married Philip she was incredibly generous. Not just with cash but with her time. I never have the means or opportunity to pay her back and this would be perfect.'

I'm so excited by the perfectness of the plan that I barely consider how forward I'm being in asking Stevie to give his prize to my friends. In a split second I reason that they will soon be his friends; all the sooner, if we go away together and have a gas. It's my hospitable Aussie spirit taking control; it's ebullient and extends to being hospitable with other people's treats.

'Besides, most importantly you'd have a chance to get to know them better,' I plead.

'I don't know,' says Stevie slowly.

'Can you think of one good reason why not?'

Stevie looks blank, almost scared. For goodness' sake, my friends aren't scary. But he doesn't answer me. I take his silence to mean that he's agreed to my plan and then I pull him towards me and kiss his lips.

Enough talking for one night.

25. Trouble

Bella

'Going away with him is a ridiculous idea,' says Amelie. We are in my local Costa Coffee. I've called an emergency meeting. I gaze out of the window: rain is lashing down and assaulting pedestrians as they scuttle to find shelter. A depressing state of affairs in January, let alone June. Last week I was wearing a T-shirt and contemplating shorts, albeit long ones, and this week I can't leave the house without an umbrella and a raincoat. This tedious situation is only somewhat relieved by the fact that my raincoat is a Burberry raincoat. Christmas 2003's 'must-have' fashion item. I might be cold and wet but I look chic.

Amelie is right, of course, going away with Stevie is a ludicrous idea.

'I know, but I wasn't given any choice in the matter. Laura called and spoke to Philip who, naturally, thought it was a brilliant idea that we join them on an all-expenses-paid trip to Las Vegas. He accepted before I was even consulted.'

'Didn't you try to get out of it?'

'Of course, but he said I've been tetchy for the last three or four weeks and a break would do me good.'

'He knows you well,' observes Amelie.

I scowl. I have been tetchy and both Philip and Amelie have repeatedly commented on it, which naturally has done nothing to alleviate the feelings of irritability. Of *course* I'm prickly. Who wouldn't be when they are married to two men who are mixing in the same social circles and a disastrous exposure seems at every moment probable? No doubt Laura has noticed that I'm being grumpy too, but she has tactfully opted not to discuss the matter with me. I know she's reached her own conclusion i.e. that I don't like Stevie and therefore I am being difficult. She is one hundred per cent correct and one hundred per cent wrong at the same time.

'If you have any suggestions as to how I get out of the trip I'd love to hear them,' I mumble.

'Tell the truth.'

'Any realistic, likely or at least non-suicidal suggestions,' I clarify.

'No.'

'Well, maybe you should keep out of this, Amelie. This isn't a game. This is serious.'

'You've noticed.' Amelie holds my glare longer than I'm comfortable with; I break first and look away.

I wouldn't normally dream of speaking to Amelie so rudely but I'm at snapping point. It's over a week since I met Stevie. Since then, with his agreement, I have made an appointment with a solicitor, which is a step forwards, *and* I have been roped into spending four days away in Las Vegas with my best friend and both my husbands, which is a step backwards. A whole quantum leap backwards, actually. I'm terrified by the prospect.

'I wonder what on earth made Stevie agree to you and Philip joining the Vegas trip,' muses Amelie.

'He was probably railroaded by Laura.'

'That, or he wants to make you sweat,' points out Amelie.

'No, he wouldn't do that. Why would he do that?' I ask.

'Because you've treated him terribly. You secretly married him, you deserted him and now you want to divorce him. Besides this, you are insisting that he lies to his girlfriend and becomes embroiled in all sorts of potentially explosive skulduggery,' states Amelie.

I'm really beginning to dislike her. I realize that this dislike is fuelled entirely by my own inadequacies, which simply makes it more intense. Her goodness makes me feel like the devil has bought my soul. The thing about goodness is that it is only nice to be around if you are good. If you are not good, and right now I'm not, then it's just bloody infuriating.

'I'll ask him what the hell he's playing at when I see him tomorrow,' I say.

'Tomorrow?'

'Yes, we're meeting up again.'

'Why?'

'So I can give him a progress report.'

'I thought you said there hasn't been any progress.'

'Well, there will have been by tomorrow. I'm seeing the solicitor in the morning.'

'Couldn't you send him an e-mail with an update?'

'Too risky.'

'Why? Don't you trust him?'

'No, it's not that. He said he'd help me, so he will. Stevie's a man of his word. But e-mails can be seen by the wrong people.'

'You might be seen meeting him, surely that's more risky,' argues Amelie.

'No, we've picked a venue off the beaten track. Neither of us is in any danger of being spotted.'

'How very clandestine,' she mutters, raising an eyebrow to effectively communicate her distrust and displeasure.

'I'm not enjoying this, Amelie.'

'Make sure you don't. Another coffee?'

I agree, mostly because I want Amelie to leave me alone for a while – even if it's only for the few minutes it takes her to order and collect two lattes. I'm beginning to regret confessing my awful predicament to her. She's behaving like my own personal Jiminy Cricket.

I glance around the coffee house. Normally I love it here. Often, I wander down the high street at about noon and find myself ambling into Costa. Their sandwiches are yummy and I prefer to buy one here than eat alone at home. Usually, I stretch out on one of the big brown leather sofas and sip my coffee while reading a novel. Having been a waitress for more years than I care to add up, there is no other single pleasure quite so great as putting your feet up and taking your time over a cup of coffee. I like to dip amaretti biscuits into my latte. They are expensive and some would argue that they taste like cardboard but I still consider them to be symbolic of urban living and that alone has an overwhelming pull for me.

Only a month ago I remember popping in here for a

spot of lunch following a fairly rigorous exercise class and thinking to myself that my life was damn perfect, utterly, totally enviable. My body felt nicely stretched from my visit to the gym. My stomach felt a little stretched too (skinny café latte and a mozzarella, sun-dried tomatoes and pesto sandwich, tasted all right, a wee bit too salty). I had nowhere I needed to be. No one I owed money, apologies or a time sheet to. I remember thinking that life could not get more ideal. Now, I think my lot is on a par with Job's and Amelie is macabrely expert as Job's comforter. As if to underline my point Amelie returns to the table with three lattes and a smiling Laura.

'Guess who I persuaded to join us?' she beams.

I jump to my feet and hug Laura with mixed emotions. Her beam and cheerful demeanour are, and probably always will be, a pleasure. The guilt that grabs and tugs at my innards, like a bad case of food poisoning, is less welcome.

'What are you doing here?' I hope I sound delighted and curious rather than wary and anxious.

'Amelie texted me this morning that you were getting together and I ought to join you. You don't mind, do you?'

Laura looks momentarily apprehensive. It's a look she used to constantly sport but now is, more or less, banished. It's distressing to see it flash across her face again. She looks uncertain of her welcome and her worth. I'm utterly sorry, particularly because as far as I'm concerned, she *is* unwelcome: through no fault of her own.

'It's fantastic to see you,' I hug her and try to believe what I've said. 'Where's Eddie?'

'At his dad's.'

I wait for a tirade about Oscar. Usually she can't resist recounting the latest insensitivity. There's always something. Besides leaving Laura and Eddie, Oscar's crimes against humanity include repeatedly failing to buy the correct flavour yogurt for Eddie, allowing him to fall off a climbing frame (while everyone knows that Eddie might have fallen no matter who was looking after him, the point is, it happened while he was in Oscar's care), failing to be responsible about bedtime curfews, feeding Eddie goodies packed with salt and additives (which Laura is also guilty of, but . . .), being away for Eddie's birthday, buying Eddie extravagant pressies to try to compensate for the absences . . . I fear and imagine the list is endless. But, today, Laura appears not to have anything to say on the matter of Oscar.

'I can't think of anything except Vegas. To think, in three weeks and a day we'll be on the plane.' She giggles.

'It's always on my mind too,' I admit.

Laura beams and breaks into song. She does a pretty good rendition because she has the singing voice the angels were supposed to give to me.

Laura is glowing and grinning; she has no idea she is grinding me down. I know I should be delighted that she's finally found someone she cares about, someone who cares about her. But all I can see are the problems it will cause. This is never going to go away. Even if Stevie and I manage to secure a secret divorce, and by some amazing stretch of good luck Philip believes my story about sketchy paperwork and we remarry, my life will still be spoilt because Laura is in love with Stevie. And – deep breath – what if Stevie is in love with her too?

It dawns on me that there is a possibility that one day they might want to get married. If they do there will be more paperwork, more questions. Stevie will have to declare that he's been married and that will lead to difficult questions. Even if we negotiate that thorny issue, there will be others. I won't be able to attend their wedding because Stevie's mum will recognize me. How do I explain that to Laura? By the same token Laura and Stevie will never be able to attend any family event I host in case my father or brothers bother to turn up and recognize him. I wonder what scale of miracle I'll need to manage to tiptoe my way through the next forty years to avoid a catastrophic revelation. I don't tell Laura this, instead I say, 'I wondered if you wanted to come over and pick out some clothes for the trip.'

'That's lovely of you, Bella,' grins Laura, 'but you know what? I splashed out.'

'You did?' I'm amazed.

'Yep. I hit Mango and Top Shop. You don't have to spend a fortune. A few T-shirts, a bikini, a little skirt. It's all in the accessorizing.' Then, suddenly, her expression changes to one of concern. 'Isn't it terrible about poor Freya?'

'What about her?' I ask, concerned.

'I haven't had chance to tell Bella,' says Amelie.

'Tell me what?'

'Freya is being bullied at school.'

'She is? By whom? Have you been in to see her teachers? Why didn't you tell me?' I'm outraged on Freya's behalf.

'You've got other things to worry about. Besides, I don't think it's a big deal. She's a strong girl, physically and mentally. I'll keep an eye on it.'

'Amelie!' I'm outraged. Isn't a mother's job to fight their child's battles? How can she be so calm? 'Tell me the details,' I demand.

'One little girl pulls her ponytail and says it looks silly. She's snapped her pencils, that sort of thing. She's bitten her too, which is unacceptable at their age. But the teacher is aware of it. Luckily, Freya has no issues about being a grass. Freya was upset but after a day or two, she decided it was best to wear plaits.'

'Kids can be so cruel, can't they?' I mutter. 'School playgrounds are jungles. I mean, how many adults have bitten you in the last week?' Laura blushes. 'I don't mean in a sexual context,' I snap. 'I mean when they bite and tell you that you smell or ask if your clothes were bought from a jumble sale.'

'Freya has the sense to know this is only about jealousy,' says Amelie. 'It's a storm in a teacup.'

I feel anger sizzling and spitting inside me. Clearly Amelie has never been bullied because if she had she'd want to rip off the head of the ponytail puller.

'Has this bullying started since Ben died?' I ask.

'Why do you think it's related to losing Ben?' asks Amelie.

'Just a guess.'

'Did things get bad for you after your mother died?'

asks Amelie, who is perceptive to the point of being smug.

'We're not talking about me,' I reply, and we're not, but it surprises me to note that tears are welling in my eyes.

'I think we are,' states Amelie, calmly.

'I was a popular kid.' This isn't strictly true. I wasn't *always* popular.

'So you did the bullying?' asks Amelie. She's pretending to be nonchalant by stirring sugar into her coffee but I know she doesn't take sugar.

'No. Definitely not.'

'Well then, you must have been bullied. That's the jungle law, you just about said as much yourself.'

'I don't want to talk about my past.' I glare at Amelie, silently begging her to drop the subject. Why is she pushing this?

'Did you feel abandoned when your mum died?'

I don't move. If I so much as nod the tears will overflow. I'm not going to cry about bullying and neglect that happened over twenty years ago. That would be stupid. The pressures in my life, right now, must be making me feel vulnerable.

'I'm sure your dad and brothers did their best but it must have been difficult growing up in a house full of men.'

Their best was piss-poor actually but I'm not going to say this. The kids used to say I looked like a boy. And I probably did as I wore lots of my brothers' cast-offs. Money was so tight because Dad couldn't work after Mum died – not because he was looking after us kids or because he was grief-stricken – he couldn't work because he was always drunk. The kids said I smelt of dirty boys and beer. They were probably right about that too.

'Who saved you, Bella?' asks Amelie.

'I don't want to talk about this.' I force myself to look at Amelie. She does, at least, have the decency to blanch when she meets my gaze but she's a very determined woman.

'Why not? In all our conversations about my losing Ben, never once have you said, "I relate to that," but you must, mustn't you? On some level? When you lost your mum you must have felt as fucking miserable, angry, and scared as I did when I lost Ben.'

'I was just a kid.'

'You must have felt worse because you were just a kid.'

I slowly draw a deep breath. I need to calm down. I need to remain cool. This isn't the moment to share. I know what Amelie is trying to do and all credit to her for her amateur psychoanalysis. From the things I've told her in the past and, more potently, the things I haven't told her she's worked out that I had a bloody miserable time as a kid from the day Mum's cancer was diagnosed. Until then, my childhood was fantastic, because it was average. I had my fair share of triumphs and disappointments, jelly and ice cream, homework and chickenpox. I was the first kid in my village to have a Raleigh bike. And when I was eight I owned a Cabbage Patch Kid doll, with adoption certificate and everything. It's astounding that you often don't know how wonderful something is until you lose it.

Then Mum got ill. And then she died. I will not talk about it. I will not dwell. It is enough to say the following seven years were filthily sad. I existed in a state of perpetual misery and I would probably still be drowning in that isolated hell if Stevie had not moved to our village. Stevie reintroduced me to kindness and happiness. Stevie.

Clearly Amelie has pieced this much together. She's giving me an opportunity to explain to Laura what I did and why but I wish she'd just back off. Get the hell out of my mess. I don't want to tell Laura any of it. Or Philip. I've been very careful to make light of my father's drinking habit, never labelling it alcoholism. I've kept Philip away from my hometown where all he'd see is poverty, grime and, worst of all, my family's indifference towards me. I don't want it revealed, shared or explained. I simply never want to feel scared again.

'We were talking about Freya.' I try to sound unruffled.

'But that's my point, Bella. We never talk about you. *You* never talk about you. Did you ever come to terms with losing your mum?'

I see Laura squeeze Amelie's arm. She's trying to discreetly communicate that it's best to drop this line of conversation. 'I think you ought to respect Bella's right to privacy,' says Laura.

But Amelie won't be deflected. 'Why don't you ever talk about losing your mum? You never talk about your past at all. It's as though your life didn't start until you arrived in London.'

'Maybe it didn't, Amelie. Not really.' I use the voice I normally reserve for bank managers or traffic wardens. Impervious, distant, polite but entirely 'fuck you'.

'Er, the kids back home called me Jaws because of my brace.' Laura throws in this contribution in an attempt to help me. Ironically, Amelie also thinks she's helping me, she wants to help both of us. We all mean well but are we close to destroying one another?

'You went to a local school, didn't you, Bella? Remind me, what was the name of your village?'

I glare at Amelie, pure toxic. 'Kirkspey,' I say eventually. I know if I don't name it, Amelie will.

'Really?' Laura cries, delighted to have chanced upon what she thinks is a digression. 'That's where Stevie lived as a teenager.'

'Is it really? What a small world,' says Amelie.

'You must be mistaken,' I insist. 'It's a very small village. How old did you say Stevie is?'

'Thirty-one.'

'A year older than me. We'd have known each other. And we don't, so you must be mistaken.'

'I'm sure it was Kirkspey.'

'You should check with Stevie,' says Amelie.

I wish she'd swallow her tongue. 'Kirk means church so there are lots of towns with similar names in Scotland,' I state, coolly. I know Amelie is not going to let this drop so I do the only thing I can. The thing I have always done. I gather up my raincoat and throw a few pounds on to the table and I head for the door. Case closed.

26. I Forgot to Remember to Forget

Wednesday 16th June 2004

Stevie

Bella is wearing a beige halter-neck dress and chunky boots. I'm no fashion guru but I can make a wild stab in the dark and guess that her outfit cost the equivalent of what I'd spend on a second-hand Fiat. The worst thing is my first thought: it was worth every penny. She looks sensational. I have a terrible fleeting thought.

I am proud of my wife.

I pull myself up short and remind myself that (a) she didn't pay for the sexy get-up, her *other* husband did and if anyone should be swelling with pride it's him and (b) Laura. I have Laura. We are an item and therefore I shouldn't be noticing the sexiness or otherwise of other women, especially one I am married to.

'Hi,' I greet her, with studied nonchalance.

It's a terrible thing that I have feelings for her, even jumbled ones, but it would be much, much worse if she knew.

I've always found it one of life's huge bonuses that I've never fancied nasty women. I'm not one of those men who like high-maintenance bitches who bleed you dry and treat you badly. I simply do not have a masochistic streak; life's too bloody short for that sort of effort. Besides, the world is full of decent women who look cute and that is where I like to spend my time. It's odd then that I should think that Belinda, having been transformed into posh totty Bella, is almost irresistible while she is clearly cruel. I don't understand myself.

I force myself to remember the moment I agreed to help her, a euphemism for agreeing to divorce her quietly – to shuffle away like a good little man, denied a scene or any fuss. I saw her slump with relief; clearly, she'd been rigid with tension throughout our meeting. How bloody insulting. Not only did she want rid of me but most embarrassingly of all, she wasn't sure I'd want the same thing. Ha, bloody arrogant bint. Did she think she was such a great catch that I'd break down into an inconsolable heap, that I'd beg her not to divorce me? Did she think that for the last decade I'd been harbouring fantasies about us visiting Ikea together?

I take a macabre pleasure in reminding myself that it is a good thing she has lost her grasp on reality and that she wastes her money on designer clobber and her time at the beauty parlour. It's a good thing she's not a worthwhile person, with ambition or even a job, that she treats her friends in underhand ways, and that she can't offer me anything like a reasonable explanation for her appalling behaviour towards me. This is all to the good because, as Bella Edwards is such a monster, I won't fall for her. I won't become sentimental about her not even if she looks delicious.

I'm thinking all these vicious, stay-at-a-distance thoughts, when she disarms me. She leans in to kiss my cheek. Not two air kisses but a genuine one and all I can see is Belinda McDonnel. Her lips are squashy and smooth. Her cheek soft.

'Can I get you a drink?' I offer and rise out of my chair but she puts a gently restraining hand on my shoulder.

'My shout. What do you want?'

I glance at my bottle. It must have a leak as it is empty, she grins at my evident surprise. 'Another Beck's.'

Bella returns to the table with fresh drinks. Other men in the bar are watching her. They are curious but don't believe they have any real chance of talking to, let alone dating, a woman like Bella Edwards. She's composed, elegant, refined and aloof. I agree, looking at her now she would appear out of their stratosphere, let alone league, and appearances are all in situations such as these. But the men in this pub are like her father, grandfather, uncles and brothers. The men in this pub are like the sort of man her father expected her to marry. They think they exercise because they play darts and therefore aren't worried about the pies and pints they consume. They play dominoes and think that will keep them mentally agile – that and reading the *Sun*.

Belinda hates pubs, always did. I bet Bella likes wine bars. As a child she often sat in her dad's wreck of a car, waiting outside the local, while he had a 'swift one' that always turned into a slow several. If she was lucky, and he remembered that she was there, he'd bring out a bottle of Coke and a bag of crisps. If he forgot about her she might have to sit waiting for him until the early hours. Licensing laws were lax; his ability to drink for his country was notorious. He'd find her curled up in the back of the car, asleep, wrapped in the picnic rug. He'd wake her up and tell her they had to walk the three-and-a-half-mile journey home, he was too drunk to drive. He saw this as responsible parenting. Lots of the other dads tried to negotiate the winding roads despite consuming a skinful. I didn't know Belinda when she was a kid but she told me these stories.

Looking at Bella Edwards it is hard to imagine the woman has ever felt cold, bored, scared or hungry.

Bella tells me she's met with a solicitor today and that getting a divorce will be 'very straightforward'. She's clearly relieved and not a smidgen of uncertainty or regret darts across her face. She wants to discard me as quickly and effortlessly as she can. I can hardly concentrate on her debrief and instructions, as I keep being distracted by visions of her sorting out her wardrobe and throwing last season's clothes into large black sacks, marked 'Charity Shop'. I am last year's 'fab handbag'.

'The courts will recognize an eight-year separation as "irretrievable breakdown",' Bella goes on with a bright smile.

'Who said the law was an ass?' I ask sarcastically.

'We have a choice. We could go for mutual consent after a separation of two years.'

I stare at her in disbelief. She sounds as though she's relaying the agenda for the local residents' association meeting. Her efficiency and enthusiasm are nauseating.

'Or you can divorce me and cite desertion. We only needed to be apart for two years for the courts to be convinced that I . . .' She trails off.

'Definitely wanted to desert me and hadn't just

popped out for a pint of milk and forgotten where we lived.'

'Yes,' she says, flushing to crimson. 'We just have to prove that I haven't been in touch.'

'Not tricky.'

'There's a bit of paperwork. We need to apply for a decree nisi and then —'

'What about adultery?' I ask.

'Adultery?' The crimson blush runs from Bella's face. I look to the floor and expect to see that she is standing in a scarlet pool. Her face is suddenly green.

'Couldn't I cite adultery or unreasonable behaviour? I mean, marrying another man seems pretty unreasonable to me.'

'I thought we wanted a quick no-mess divorce.'

'Well that's definitely what you want.' I don't know why I am saying this. Of course I want a quick no-mess divorce, if I have to be divorced. There's no point in losing my dignity on top of everything else. But I feel sore.

Bella seems to be concentrating on breathing slowly and deeply. Eventually I relent.

'Let's do the mutual consent thing.'

She grabs the ball and runs with it.

'The procedure is the same for all types of divorce. From issuing petition to decree absolute is fourteen weeks. It can all be done through the post. There's no need for any court appearances.'

I sign the paper that will lead to our divorce.

Bella flashes a broad smile and I know I should be sharing her enthusiasm. After all, the divorce will simplify my life too. 'It's a good thing that neither of us owns anything because if we did it gets more complicated.'

'I own my flat and a car,' I tell her.

'Do you really?' She's astonished. 'I was always worried that all you'd ever own was your guitar.'

'I know.'

'Still, it doesn't matter. Both those assets are in your name presumably, and obviously I don't want to make any claim on them.' She blushes again, because we both know she's just said whatever I own Philip can buy and sell ten times over.

'I have a pension too,' I tell her. 'I started it when I was twenty-four. I'm not sure what it will be worth when I retire.' Why am I telling her this? Do I want to impress her with my stab at respectability? Jesus help me, I want to impress her.

'Well, maybe we'll need to draw up a document to say we have no claim on each other's assets. Just to be on the safe side,' says Bella. 'We want to do everything properly.'

I resist adding, 'This time.' I know Bella would never claim any money from me and I don't need a legal document to guarantee that.

'What will you do when we're divorced?' I ask.

'I'll remarry Philip,' she says calmly and then she swallows back her G&T.

'Will you tell him, about . . . me?'

'Good God, no,' she says emphatically. 'I'm planning on telling him there was some hiccup in our paperwork.'

More lies. 'Do you think he'll believe you?'

'I can be very convincing. Another drink?'

I accept. Bella owes me so much that the least she can do is buy me a few lousy drinks.

When she comes back to the table she is carrying the drinks and three large bags of crisps.

'Tomato flavour,' she says with obvious glee. 'I haven't seen tomato flavour crisps since we were about seventeen, so I bought loads. They used to be your favourite.'

'They were your favourite,' I correct her.

She shrugs and smiles, 'Well, we both liked them. Tuck in.'

It amazes me how many truly appalling social situations can be eased by the introduction of food and drink. The annual school production used to be shamefully painful until one of the staff alighted on the idea of selling wine and boxes of Maltesers in the interval. Suddenly, the kids' terrible stutters and two-left-feet syndrome became less insufferable. Would anyone ever manage to get through a funeral without the promise of egg sandwiches and alcohol at the end? Similarly, Bella and I seem to find each other's company more palatable after a few units and a bag of crisps.

'Thanks for asking us to go to Vegas,' says Bella. She's half grimacing and half grinning.

'Laura thinks we need an opportunity to bond,' I explain. 'I was depending on you turning it down.' I'd been furious that Bella hadn't put her famed skill of bullshitting into play and had failed to pull out of the hat an effective excuse for not coming. Things are complicated enough without a cosy holiday for four.

'Sorry. Are you dreading it?'

I was until about three minutes ago when Bella became

Belinda again and bought me three packets of tomato flavour crisps. Crisps which she's munching, and have stuck between her teeth. She puts her finger in her mouth and digs around, presumably for the soft stuff that's stuck at the back. I watch her until she becomes self-conscious. 'Sorry, not very polite of me.'

We both know we've shared intimacies that blow away public tooth-picking. Recently, I've spent a fair amount of time thinking about those intimacies. I've dwelt, with Gollum-like obsession, on our first time and our last time. I've calculated that over the years we must have had sex approximately a thousand times. I'm working on an average of four times a week for the first year, then three times a week for the following five. We cut a lot of classes.

We had sex in every way imaginable, or at least in every way we could have imagined back then. Shy sex, saucy sex, sweet loving, dirty loving, marathon loving, inside, outside, stood up, on chairs, on couches, in cars, on beds, lots of different beds – single beds and friends' parents' beds featured quite heavily in the early years. It all seemed like bloody brilliant sex.

Until Edinburgh. Then we had more and more quick sex, tired sex and angry sex. It is odd, isn't it, that the last time you have sex with anyone you rarely know it's that. We did it the day she left – a duty-fuelled quickie that we pretended was about wishing me luck before the competition. We'd got into the habit of my taking her from behind. She knew that I couldn't last as long in that position, it got it over quicker for her and she didn't have to look at me. Even remembering her firm arse bobbing up and down doesn't make that flashback palatable.

'Do you go home much?' I ask, pushing all carnal thoughts away. Far away.

'No. You?'

'My mum moved back to Blackpool to be near my nan. I visit her every month or so.'

Bella stutters, 'Bloody hell, I do my best to avoid my family for at least a couple of years at a time.'

'You must visit at Christmas?'

'No, actually, the snow always puts me off.'

'What do you do instead?'

'I go skiing.'

'That doesn't make sense.' She shrugs. 'How are your brothers? Are they still fishing?'

'Martin and Iain are. Not on our own boat any more. They work in town for a bigger one. Rob packed it in. He hurt his back somehow. I can't remember the details.'

'What does he do now?'

'Watches TV.'

'And Don?'

'Don's otherwise engaged.'

'They're all well, though, on the whole?'

'I suppose so,' she mutters grumpily. 'To be honest I got fed up of looking after them when I lived with them so I'm quite keen to leave them to their own devices now.'

I ignore her pique. 'Is your dad well?'

'I expect so. I haven't seen him since the wedding.'

'He did come then.' I'm relieved to hear that the re-invention of Belinda found a way to accommodate her father, at least.

'I wasn't keen to break my own precedent,' admits

Bella, alluding, I presume, to our wedding. 'If I could have got away with not inviting my father and my brothers I would have, but Phil insisted. At least Dad managed to appear sober until the reception. Quite an achievement since he'd been drinking since ten in the morning.'

'Did your brothers come?'

'Martin and Iain did. Rob couldn't be bothered and Don, well, as I said he's —'

'Inside?' I guess.

'Yes.' Bella sighs.

'Did they cause any trouble?' We both know that Bella's brothers are awkward when sober, aggressive when drunk.

'No. In all fairness all they wanted was to merge into the wallpaper. Like that was going to happen, with their cheap shirts and dirty hair. They didn't even wear jackets. I'd offered to buy them all suits but they wouldn't let me. It was so obvious that they were fish out of water. But at least that meant they were unsure enough not to kick anything off.'

She's still angry and ashamed of them. I'd hoped she'd grow out of that.

'What do you want from them, Bella?'

'I want them to be altogether different.'

This is possibly the most honest thing Belinda has said to me since we met up again. I pity her for chasing an impossible dream.

'I want them to be charming, involved and fascinating relatives. At my wedding, I wanted Dad to bore the guests with stories about what a darling little girl I was and I wanted my brothers to flirt with my single friends.' She tries to smile but I know her well enough to know that she wants this so much it hurts. Smiling is next to impossible.

'You know that's never going to happen. You'll never change them, however much you change yourself.'

'You're right,' admits Bella, with a sigh. 'My brothers' idea of a charm offensive is to ask a girl if she wants a bag of chips before or after sex. At least my father's indifference towards me came in useful when I told him that a father-of-the-bride speech wasn't required. I didn't want him to walk me down the aisle either, but Philip said it was traditional and respectful. I wanted to say, "Sod respectful. Had my father and brothers ever been respectful towards me when I lived with them? No."'

'Why didn't you say that?'

'I don't talk about my family much to Philip,' she says with a shrug. 'My family are light years away from his; he wouldn't be able to relate to my experiences.'

'You should be more open.'

'Don't you start. Why does everyone always want to rake over the past? The past is just that, *past*. It's where it is for a reason.' Bella looks at her watch. 'Look, I think we've said all we have to say tonight. Thanks for signing the papers. I guess I'll see you at the airport.'

And with that she stood up and took flight.

27. Viva Las Vegas

Wednesday 7th July 2004

Bella

'Oh my God, *first class*. I have never flown first class in my life.'

Laura's grin is so wide I think her face might split and, while I have been imagining all manner of disasters to prevent my having to attend this trip, my best friend's face ripping in two because of the force of her ecstasy, is one I'd not considered.

She's been behaving like an excitable child since the limo picked her up this morning – and who can blame her? Besides the limo, there's free champagne flowing liberally, this is her first holiday abroad in four years, she is travelling with her best friend *and* the man of her dreams.

The only fly in the ointment is that he's the love of my life too.

Oh God, do I mean that?

I am trying to avoid Stevie. I really am but it's not easy. When all the others were enjoying free alcohol in the airport lounge I wandered around the shops. But I panicked when I couldn't get excited about the rows of lotions and perfumes, the discounted leather bags and clothes – this is not just out of character, it must be a seriously worrying clinical condition. I didn't feel the slightest spark of excitement at spending my cash (well, Phil's cash). All I wanted was to be near Stevie. Stevie with his neat, toned body, his broad, full-on grin, his laugh, his wit, his guitar – for God's sake. That shows how desperate things are.

The past six weeks have been the worst of my life.

I've tried not to think about him. I've tried not to want him. But it's like going on a diet; the moment you decide to cut down on fat is the moment you start to fantasize about cream cakes, fish and chips and Mars bars. I'm ashamed to admit that we've met up a few times since we agreed to divorce. One of the meetings was a necessity, the others were luxuries.

At the first meeting we signed the relevant papers within about three minutes. Then I offered him a drink and he agreed, instantly. I should have kept it all business-like and impersonal. But I was enjoying myself. At least, I was until he started going on and on about the past. The worst of it was that I was answering him fully and honestly, just slipping back into the old ways of frank conversations. It is not healthy. It's pretty dangerous, so I buggered off as quickly as possible.

As I left the pub I swore I wouldn't give him another thought and we certainly wouldn't meet up again. We met up again by the end of the same week.

I told him I needed to check a detail with the paper-work. The strange thing was, once we were ensconced in a pub in Covent Garden – a less covert, more comfortable rendezvous than our initial meeting – he didn't refer to the outstanding detail, he knew it was a pretence but he'd come anyway.

During the evening we caught up, like old friends do, with genuine affection. We laughed, chatted and confessed our dreams, achievements and compromises. Stevie talked about his career, his mates and the girls he's dated. He did not talk about Laura. I talked about all my careers, my mates including Laura (I was unilaterally nice, it's easy), and men as a homogeneous group. I didn't mention Philip. We decided we were hungry and chose to eat spaghetti together rather than go home to the people we weren't mentioning.

Then we agreed to meet at All Bar One on Cambridge Circus. An extremely busy venue. I told myself that this underlined that our meeting was innocent and we had nothing to hide. I dismissed as lunacy Amelie's suggestion that I wanted to be caught with Stevie.

The atmosphere was thick with cigarette smoke and curiosity. This time we didn't bother with polite small talk or general enquiries. We sank into a comforting intimacy and picked up where we'd left off years ago. I carefully recounted elusive, long-forgotten memories and he told me his latest theories, ideas and plans. He fidgeted on his chair, but with excitement I think, not nerves or embarrassment. He found it unproblematic to tell me the most tremendous and melancholic thoughts he'd harboured in the last eight years. He was delighted that I was equally interested in both and (at least temporarily) he didn't seem to resent that I wasn't around when he formed his theory on what makes someone happy. Stevie has grown up. This thrilled and saddened me in more or less equal and confusing proportions.

'In the end everyone wants the same thing,' he'd said.

'What's that?' I'd asked.

'Happiness.'

'Well, obviously. But you can't leave it at that. That's too broad.' And while Stevie has great pecs and the T-shirt he was wearing showed them off to perfection, I was mildly impatient that he had failed to develop a more honed argument. Philip would not have tolerated such sloppiness.

'Happiness to some people is scaling mountains. To others it's having mountains of cash. To still others it's having a big family or independence. It's not enough to say everyone wants the same thing.' It terrified me to realize that I wasn't really interested in what Stevie believed made everyone happy, just what made him happy.

'Contentment,' he told me, although I hadn't asked the question. 'I'm happy when I am content with what I have and not longing for something I don't have or I've lost or never had.'

He had lifted his beer bottle to his mouth but he didn't drink, he paused and stared at me. The look sliced me to my core. I felt as if he'd undressed me in that busy pub and exposed me for what I was, someone cruel, someone destructive but someone powerful.

'I don't know if I've ever felt content.'

'I know that, Belinda,' said Stevie, before he coughed, turned away and broke the torturous tension.

Stevie talked about music, novels and poetry. We quoted old poems to one another, poems that we'd memorized at school. I told him I still found T. S. Eliot too much like hard work but I'd since given some more modern poets a chance; Liz Lochhead and Douglas Dunn were my favourites. He told me he still hated Jane Austen and thought she was twee. I told him I still loved her and always would.

'Do you remember hiding in the library? Hiding from the rain? Hiding from your dad and brothers?'

'Bloody hell, yes. I haven't been to a library for years.'

'The one at my school is just like the one back in Kirkspey. The same smell of sticky back plastic and dusty carpets. That smell never leaves you, though, does it?'

Suddenly I was transported back to our school library. It had ugly, serviceable shelving and lighting, damp patches on the ceilings and watermarks in the carpet and yet it was so grand and marvellous. It held such knowledge, entertainment, so many travels and dreams. I have always been happy in libraries.

'It's funny how smells are so evocative,' I comment. 'Your house always used to smell of Pledge.' I laughed.

'And yours always smelt of—'

'Stale fags and dogs,' I interrupted hurriedly.

'I was going to say oil. Do you remember Martin used to keep his motorbike in the sitting room?'

I shifted uncomfortably. Why couldn't we have had a coffee table, like anyone else?

Stevie saw that I was uncomfortable. He leaned forward and tucked a stray strand of hair behind my ear.

The gesture was corny and obvious. But try telling my nipples that. They'd gone hard with desire.

'It wasn't all bad, Belinda,' he said.

'Bella.'

'Bella, whatever. Christ, it doesn't matter what I call you or what you call yourself. I know you. Your childhood wasn't all bad. There must be something you remember fondly about it.'

I thought about this. 'I do miss some things.'

'Such as?' Stevie was grinning like a madman, thrilled that I was prepared to engage.

'Do you remember the old cinema?'

'Yes.'

'Well, I miss the women who sold ice cream in the aisle.'

'Usherettes?'

'Yes. They were charming in an antiquated sort of way. Buying a tub of Häagen-Dazs in the foyer by no way compares,' I pointed out.

'And?'

'Big Wagon Wheels. They used to be massive and they're diddy now. It's impossible to buy them without feeling cheated.'

'And?'

'I miss fighting with my brothers over the Christmas edition of the *Radio Times*. We only got it once a year and it was a big treat. We used to love marking what we wanted to watch over the holidays.'

'And?'

'Getting the bus into Newburgh and buying a new outfit every Saturday from the market, to wear at the local disco.'

'You bought some lovely outfits.'

'Oh, yeah? Short skirts, skimpy tops. I was a class act.'

'You were young. That's how young girls dress. It's called fun.'

I stopped there and offered to buy another drink. I dared not say any more because I knew the next sentence would be the one where I admitted that I miss feeling OK. I want a clean palate. I want not to have made this terrible mistake. Which mistake am I referring to? Marrying Stevie? Leaving Stevie? Marrying Philip?

I became frightened as unformed thoughts drifted into my mind; thoughts about destiny, suggestions of 'the one', hints about the sanctity of marriage. I tried to cast aside the shadowy feelings and refused to examine them thoroughly. Do I even believe in destiny? I decided I don't disbelieve. It's spiky on the fence.

I'm not in the habit of going out in the evening and getting lashed: those days are long gone. Philip and I enjoy the odd glass of wine through the week and get gently sloshed together most Saturday evenings; still I have to lie to my doctor to come in under fifteen units a week. But when I'm with Stevie, it seems the most natural thing in the world to get right royally pissed. Together we feel childishly irresponsible. We always did. It's easy to slip back into old habits, to imagine that we're sparky students full of ill-defined arguments and glorious intentions. We ramble through a vast array of topics – the filthiness of religious wars, the frustration of driving in London, the unflattering nature of boob tubes. Throughout these evenings I reminded myself that the feelings of youth, buoyancy, sparkiness are probably alcohol-induced and that the next day I'd probably feel wretched with a stinking hangover. The day after our meetings I did feel miserable – totally, sickeningly miserable – except when I felt glorious.

I feel miserable when I'm not with him and I feel miserable admitting that. I feel glorious when I am with him or thinking about him. And I feel miserable about that too. My feelings for Stevie are perilous. Illegal. To all intents and purposes, I'm having an affair, but without sex and with my husband. It's off-the-scale confusing. The problem is that besides missing usherettes, Wagon Wheels and giddy shopping trips, I miss Stevie. I miss Stevie so much.

On the flight Philip and I sit behind Stevie and Laura. Stevie is following my instructions to the letter. He's being distant and seems like a different person from the one I have secretly met up with on a number of occasions in the recent past. And while I appreciate that he is following the plan we agreed, I find myself irrationally offended by his coolness towards me and genuinely hurt by his warmth towards Laura. Which makes me a wretched bitch. I watch as they clink glasses, feed one another cashew nuts and watch the same movie as one another – even though they have individual screens and headsets. They choose a romantic comedy, bile rises in my throat. When Philip asks which film I want to watch I tell him I'm going to sleep. He asks if I want a glass of champagne first and, although I never, ever turn down champagne I snap that I'm tired and I can't sleep after alcohol. He's decent enough not to point out the countless occasions I've done exactly that.

Philip is a clever man. He chooses his battles and therefore always lives to fight another day. Recently, he's adopted the strategy of ignoring me. Not ignoring me per se but ignoring the argumentative, stroppy and sullen version of me. He doesn't comment when he finds me staring out the window, when I fail to cook dinner or even order a takeaway. He doesn't yell back when I yell at him for leaving a door open or scattering newspapers around the house. His endless patience shames me and paradoxically goads me on to more and more selfish behaviour. Sometimes, I want him to stand up to me, tell me that my tantrums are insufferable, demand that they stop and demand to know the cause. I want him to force a confession out of me.

At other times this thought terrifies me so I behave like an angel.

So far, Philip hasn't challenged me. But he watches me, all the time: closely, carefully and with eyes that brim concern. He did ask me how I managed at reading group when I'd left my copy of *Captain Corelli's Mandolin* on the table in the dining room.

Fortunately, I find it almost impossible to stay awake when travelling so I sleep for most of the flight to Vegas – welcome rest after weeks staring at my bedroom ceiling. I only wake up when a flight attendant shakes me and asks me to put my chair back into the upright position.

As we taxi towards the gate the passengers, who have been penned into the cabin for several hours, start to move. Slowly I stretch my legs in front of me and circle my feet, clockwise and anticlockwise, just as the in-flight magazine suggests, in an attempt to reduce the risk of a blood clot. I turn my head right and left and catch a glimpse of the economy passengers already standing, ready to disembark. Before I met Philip I rarely travelled and if I did, I travelled economy class with a cheap, inflexible ticket and often on airlines that think loo roll is an unnecessary luxury. I jostled for my place in the queue; I might have inadvertently banged the legs of fellow passengers when I lugged my suitcase (old-fashioned, no wheels) across the conveyor belt and out of the baggage hall. I thought there was a race to the bus stop (not the taxi rank in those days). I believed that the bus might leave without me because that was what life was like. A whole series of buses leaving without me.

Getting a job seemed like a major challenge, as was renting a half-decent apartment. I felt that I was on a treadmill, endlessly running and running but never getting ahead, never winning the big prize. My jobs never fed my soul — they hardly allowed me to feed my body. My apartments usually had dry rot and lecherous landlords. When I arrived at the sales, inevitably, the only thing left was the spangled, lurid orange leg warmers. I was never content.

Philip was the only first prize I've ever won. Calm, strong, understanding Phil was a gold medal.

The aeroplane doors swing open and sunshine floods the cabin. Suddenly things look cleaner and brighter. The passengers in upper class are led politely towards the exit. I stop and turn to Philip.

'I love you, Philip.'

He smiles. He's pleased to hear me say it. I certainly haven't been showing it recently. 'I know you do, darling.'

He kisses me on the lips, a quick but warm kiss. 'Now get a move on, you're holding everyone up. Let's just have a bloody good holiday, shall we?'

As the sunshine and the smell of aviation fuel greet me at the door, I make a decision: after I have divorced Stevie I won't see him *ever* again. If that means I can't see Laura too, then so be it, but I must crush this childish infatuation before it gets out of hand. Again. I can't indulge these trips down memory lane. Why would I even want to? I hate what I came from, that's why I left. I have to avoid any potentially explosive situations. For a start I won't drink – much safer to be abstemious. Many a true word is said in a state of intoxication. Philip is the best thing that ever happened to me and I want to be the best thing that ever happened to him. I want to be a good wife.

28. Can't Help Falling in Love

Laura

Las Vegas is just as exciting, vibrant, glitzy, crazy and wonderful as I'd hoped and imagined it would be.

When we pass through the gates into the terminal we spot a guy holding a sign with Stevie's name on it. The guy is dressed in an old-fashioned chauffeur's suit, but his flat cap — a symbol of the deferential manners of times gone by — looks at odds with his trendy sunglasses and hip, long ponytail.

'Hello, sir,' he greets Stevie. 'I am Adrian and I am delighted to be your chauffeur today. Sir, it is an honour to have such a talented man ride in my limousine. A real honour.' He shakes Stevie's hand vigorously. I am worried that it is his strumming hand and Adrian might inflict serious damage. 'I love a winner, sir. I love that,' Adrian assures Stevie in his lazy drawl.

'I haven't won yet, mate,' says Stevie, who is clearly a bit embarrassed by the fuss his finalist status for the King of Kings competition is bringing him.

'Sir, you're a winner, I can feel it in my blood. Vegas is a city of winners,' insists Adrian.

I feel it would be rude to point out the obvious — that Vegas has far more losers than winners numbering among its visitors and inhabitants and, as there are fifteen

'Elvises' competing, for fourteen of them, Vegas will be a city synonymous with losing after Saturday night. Still, I like the chauffeur's confidence in Stevie and want to believe he really can spot a winner.

We sit in the back of the limo and drink fizzy wine that is not quite champagne; the not-quite status doesn't bother anyone except Bella, who says she can't drink so early in the day anyway, and couldn't even if it had been Cristal. I know this is a lie but haven't the heart to point as much out to her. Besides, I have no idea what time of day it is. Here in Las Vegas it may be two thirty in the afternoon, but back in London it's about ten thirty at night. Surely, that means this is an acceptable time to have a drink.

As we drive I split my time between reading out bits from my guidebook and staring wide-eyed at the scenery. Not that I'm thinking about the arid landscape, spasmodically punctuated with billboards advertising the biggest, best or cheapest of something or other. Instead, I am falling into delicious daydreams about just how brill it is to be me.

The last six weeks have been a total shindig, completely golden. I'm so chuffed by the ease with which Stevie has glided into my life. When he and I are alone, or with Eddie, I find myself thinking lame-brained things like I've found my soulmate. I mean, that's just plain dorkish, isn't it? Soulmates. 'The one.' All that stuff. At my age I should know better. But that's just it, I've never known better! He makes me feel as though I have infinite choices, unlimited possibilities. His smile is a door opening. I am confident about myself, him, our relationship, everything really. It's all effortlessly slipping into place.

I force myself to stop grinning like some sort of imbo and try to concentrate on the guidebook.

'We could catch a show,' I suggest, feeling only the tiniest bit self-conscious about using the expression 'catch' in this context. My philosophy has always been when in Rome, do as the Romans do. I hadn't realized how much I missed travelling until I was on the plane, but I love it. I love everything from the funny smell that lingers on your clothes after you've been in a plane, to the strange coins and notes, the different languages and accents, the wonderful sense of possibility. I love the thrill of arriving in a new country, grabbing a map and starting an adventure. And while first-class travel is new to me, something I only dreamt of in my backpacking days, the excitement at new smells, faces and climates, is just the same.

'We could do, we're free tonight and tomorrow,' says Stevie. 'I have a dress rehearsal on Friday evening and, of course, the main event on Saturday, but there's nothing to stop us seeing a show if that's what you want to do. What were you thinking of?'

'I don't know – there's everything. Music, magic, comedy. Hey, this place offers dirty girls and cold beers.' I point to an advert in the book and giggle at the audacity of such a straightforward appeal.

'There's no Shakespeare or even Noel Coward, though, is there?' Bella cuts through my giggling. 'So there isn't quite everything.'

Bella once saw a production of *The Doll's House* and has an English Lit degree so she's a bit painful when it comes to theatre visits.

'Ah, but did you know that Noel Coward once performed here?' asks Philip.

'No, I didn't,' admits Bella. I see her struggle to adjust
her predetermined view of Vegas as sleezy and cheesy
and reconcile it with this new information. I decide to
help her out by changing the subject.

'Or, we could go to a nightclub. The choice is huge.
Anyone fancy BiKiNiS Beach and Dance Club, a
fourteen-thousand-square-foot indoor beach party? The
mind boggles. Cleopatra's Barge, with a floating lounge,
would you believe?'

'I'm too old for togas,' says Philip with a grin.

'Me too,' I agree.

'You're a baby,' he counters, with his usual charm and
sincere wish to be kind.

'Sadly, it's universal law that women should stop showing spare flesh far earlier than men.'

'I disagree,' chorus Stevie and Philip. We all laugh.

'There's Club Armadillo, a Texas Station gambling
Hall, Club Madrid, Club Rio, Coyote Ugly bar and dance
saloon, somewhere called Curve, where fashionable attire
is required, apparently.' Although I am only up to D in
the alphabetical listing of the clubs available for us to visit,
it's clear that Las Vegas is a playground for grown-ups.
It is a city full of fun and temptations. 'Dragon, that's
in our hotel. Another one called Drais. The guidebook
promises lots of beautiful people at that one.'

'How shallow,' mutters Bella, and then she grins. 'We
should go.'

We drive to our hotel, which is simply called THE
Hotel. I love the arrogance. THE Hotel is a hotel built

within another hotel, the Mandalay Bay – crazy, huh?

The foyer is a mass of stunning slabs of dark marble, we walk for a hundred miles through it to reach the desk. I'm quite surprised at how tasteful it is. The hotels pictured in the guidebook are chintzy and tacky, although sumptuous. This hotel is much more stylish, yet everything is still vast and opulent. The colours are muted and the materials are leather and walnut rather than Dralon and gold-embossed. The plant pots are about a metre wide and two high. The leather armchairs could comfortably seat entire families. I feel like a shrunken Alice in Wonderland.

Two beautiful female receptionists greet us with the kind of cool professionalism I would associate with New York, if TV programmes are anything to go by. They direct us to our suites and tell us our luggage will already be there, which I doubt but turns out to be true. The USA certainly is the country where service is taken seriously. The beautiful receptionists wish us a nice day. We return the pleasantry and they chorus, 'Uh huh.'

The suite is breathtaking, far more palatial than I could have dreamt of. The main bathroom is bigger than my sitting room. I run around opening cupboards and wardrobes. I gasp at the size of the TV and bath. I marvel at the variety of beers in the fridge. I bounce on the bed, climb into the bath (fully clothed) and generally run around behaving like a child on Christmas Eve. I only stop now and again to snog the lips off Stevie.

'I know it sounds naff but I want you to know, Stevie, that you're already the King of Kings in my eyes and you will be no matter what happens on Saturday night,' I say, as I pull away from a clinch.

'Really?' he asks, with great seriousness.

'Really,' I assure him, with a great grin.

I start to rummage through my case, searching for my cozzie. I want to get to the pool as quickly as possible. I have an appointment with the afternoon sun.

'Give me five minutes and then I'll be ready for a dip. I told Bella and Philip we'd meet them by the pool.'

Stevie looks disappointed: clearly after the long lingering kisses, he was imagining we'd christen the suite first. 'Can't we just spend some time alone together?' he asks, as he puts his arms round me and backs me towards the bed.

'No, you randy bugger, we can't. I want a suntan. And despite it being July, because I live in London I haven't changed from my pale blue shade yet and I'm striving for a golden bronze colour.' I gently but firmly push his hands away from my boobs and continue the hunt for my cozzie.

'OK, OK, I know a determined woman when I see one. But I'm too fidgety and excited to sit by the pool. Let's go sightseeing instead. Alone. Alone is the important bit. Selfishly, I want to keep you to myself.'

'Oh, I don't know.' I do, really. I want to be alone with him too, but it seems a bit rude.

'Come on, Laura, we've brought them here, they can look after themselves for a bit. Besides, I bet they fancy a bit of quality couple time too.'

I allow myself to be persuaded, mostly because what Stevie wants is what I want too.

*

Vegas is hysterical.

It's bloody hot without the luxury of air con, even so we reject the monorail and decide to walk along the Strip. We start, as is tradition, at the famous neon sign that states 'Welcome to Fabulous Las Vegas, Nevada' – risking life and limb running in front of cars to secure our photo opportunity – then we cross back to the west side of the street and start to walk north. Instantly we are thrust into one of Vegas's busiest junctions, where Tropicana Avenue crosses the Strip and connects casino hotels on all four corners. Thousands of pedestrians ride up and down elevators and escalators or rush and stride across the elevated walkways. Stevie and I stare at one another slightly fazed and momentarily purposeless.

'Look at that, we're in New York.' I point to a hotel fashioned as the New York skyline.

'That's so Vegas, baby,' laughs Stevie. 'You can see the Statue of Liberty, Brooklyn Bridge, even the Empire State Building and you don't have to leave Nevada. You've always wanted to see the Empire State Building, haven't you?'

'I still do. I'm not going to be fobbed off,' I joke even though I'm secretly pleased that Stevie has remembered my ambition. We spend a few moments admiring the Chrysler Building, Times Square and the Manhattan Express and then wander on. It quickly becomes apparent that Vegas is a city that's all about more. That which could be said is shouted, that which could be sung is belted out. Las Vegas, even on a hot afternoon, is a twinkling, flashing and glittering extravaganza. The city soars and scrambles, up, out and across, while neon signs of every shape and size imaginable jostle for attention.

The fantastical playground is a source of constant surprise. Stevie and I are amused by just about everything we see; it would in fact be impossible to take any of it seriously and still be certifiably sane. Only in Vegas can you see the Arc de Triomphe, Montgolfier's balloon, the Eiffel Tower, the Colosseum and an Egyptian pyramid without having to walk further than twenty metres. Only in Vegas can you watch a perfect dawn and splendid sunset, every hour, indoors, while doing your shopping, or stand by the kerb as a volcano erupts every fifteen minutes, or watch a sea battle between scantily clad sirens and nasty-looking pirates.

During this show a super-fit guy starts chatting to me about the weather (a bit of a non-starter, I thought, as we are in the desert and the weather is basically hot, day in, day out). I hold tightly to my bag, wondering if he's going to grab it and dash off. It's not until Stevie stares him down, and the guy merges back into the throng, that I understand. 'Was he coming on to me?' I ask. Stevie nods and grins. I blush, embarrassed. 'Did I lead him on?' I had chatted in an animated way, it's natural, I'm excited. 'Did I come across as flirty?'

Stevie laughs. 'It's not your fault! The man has eyes, and you're gorgeous. He was bound to try his luck.'

I'm gorgeous. The thought makes me giddy but, even so, I spend the rest of the day avoiding eye-contact with tasty men and worrying about VPL. I have not thought about Visible Panty Line for years. But, if I'm the sort of woman men chat up in the street, I might be the sort whose arse they look at too. No one wants to be objectified but I find it difficult to be indignant. Stevie's attention and affection are creating a halo of attractiveness around me and I like it. I like being desired.

We continue on our sight-seeing tour, stopping to feel (fake) rain fall in The Palms Casino Hotel and to watch the fountains of Bellagio, where a thousand gallons of water spray from thousands of spouts, all of which are choreographed as part of a music and illumination show. We see a double-sized statue of David – like Michelangelo's wasn't impressive enough? We walk by shop after shop after shop. We stop in many of them but even I, with my skill in browsing, feel satiated by about seven thirty, when we find ourselves, hot and sticky, in 'Paris' and desperate for a rest.

'Do you fancy a coffee?' asks Stevie.

'No, something stronger. Let me buy you some champagne. We should celebrate. I'm so thrilled to be here, Stevie.'

We enter Paris, Las Vegas, a hotel casino distinguished by one of the city's more prominent landmarks, a fifty-storey replica of the Eiffel Tower, which thrusts through the roof of the casino and rises 540 ft into the air. We buy a ticket to the eleventh floor where there is a piano bar and a restaurant.

Stevie and I are shown to a window table. It's dark now and we both gaze in amazement at the city below us. The neon city of sin looms below like a large set on a sci-fi movie. It defies belief, an orgy of fantasies made flesh, a place where money is no object but at the same time money is the only object.

'I'm shattered,' I say.

'Still smiling, though?'

'Who wouldn't be? I'm having a blast. I'll work through my tiredness by drinking champagne.'

'I like that sort of stamina,' says Stevie with a grin. I blush as I recall the night before when he and I showcased our stamina in quite a different way. The blush is one of pleasure at the memory, not shyness.

'Do you think we should go back to the hotel and see if we can track down Bella and Philip?' I ask.

'No need to. Let's just enjoy the champers. Do you know what Dom Perignon, the blind, French monk who invented champagne, said on his first tasting?'

'No, I don't.'

'"Brothers, come quick! I am tasting stars!"'

'How did you know that?' I ask, impressed.

'I read it on this matchbox,' Stevie confesses. He shrugs and flicks it towards me. I pick it up and sneakily slip it into my pocket. I already know tonight is the sort of night I want to keep souvenirs from.

I take a sip of the chilled champagne and think how wonderfully accurate the quote is. Life feels so fine. I look at the enormous bags of shopping around us. We've mostly limited ourselves to silly, cheap and cheerful purchases – pressies for Eddie, and for Amelie's kids – but Stevie did insist on buying me a dress in Armani Exchange. I demurred, insisting that the trip was treat enough and that he didn't need to go buying me designer clothes.

'Hardly designer, it's a diffusion brand, darling,' said Stevie with a grin. He was gently mocking Bella, who had explained what a diffusion brand was only earlier that day.

We, the uninitiated into designer wear, were unaware that diffusion brands are the 'more accessible' i.e. cheaper labels within a design house.

'Even so, you can't afford it on your wages,' I insisted.

'The treat will be mine when I see you in it,' insisted Stevie. The dress in question is a backless denim sundress. I couldn't pretend I didn't love it.

The piano tinkles moody lounge music, the neon lights flash below us and Vegas looks like an enormous Santa's grotto. The champagne is cold and Stevie's hot, things could not be more perfect and romantic. Tonight is the type of night when lovers speak of love. I take a deep breath.

'Stevie, I just wanted to say—'

'Hi, guys, how's it going? Of all the bars in all the towns, you had to be in this one.' Philip does a poor Humphrey Bogart but we all understand what he's trying to achieve.

I try to look pleased at the interruption, after all, it was my idea to invite Phil and Bella along on the trip and my main motivation was so that they could bond with Stevie. It would be unfair of me to want to monopolize him now. It's just that we were having such a perfect time. I smile brightly and tell myself we can *all* have a perfect time now. Philip is grinning too. Bella and Stevie are not.

'Can we join you?' asks Philip. He's already pulling up chairs to our table.

Bella sits next to Stevie. She looks fantastic in another designer dress, there's definitely nothing diffusion about it. She looks like she's spent the day in the spa and hairdresser's. I look like I've spent it trawling around a boiling and clammy city. I lament my lack of lipstick.

'So, what have you guys been up to?' asks Phil brightly.

I briefly fill him in on our day's adventures. 'And you two?' I ask politely.

'Well, I've spent it with my nose in a book by the pool and Bella has spent the day at the spa and the hairdresser's, haven't you, darling?'

Figures.

'I'm so nervous of the sun nowadays. I rarely sit out in it. I'd rather go to a spray booth,' says Bella. I think she knows she sounds lame because she looks nervously at Stevie. 'Besides, I wanted to take it easy. I've had a headache ever since we arrived at the airport. It's the Las Vegas theme tune that is doing it.'

'What are you talking about?' asks Stevie.

'The constant, tuneless chords of money dropping into slot machines. It's everywhere and it's horrid.'

I swig back my champagne and cross my fingers that the conversation is going to improve.

29. The Wonder of You

Stevie

I believe there is a God. But he's not a benevolent old chap, a cross between your favourite uncle and Santa Claus. Of course he isn't. If he was, there wouldn't be war, or famine, or Celine Dion's music, would there? The God I believe in is more witty than Oscar Wilde and more implacable and unrelenting than Simon Cowell. Philip was right, 'Of all the bars . . .'

I watch my wife with undeniable fascination. She is a chameleon. One minute she's drinking with me in pubs, treating me to her wit and honesty, trailing me through memories that I'd long ago shut away, allowing me to be delighted by those said memories. The next, she is cold and dull. Or am I being too kind? Calling her a chameleon is too poetic. Is she just a whore?

Obviously, it's unlikely to be a comfortable situation for either of us. But I would understand her better if she stuttered and stammered throughout our meetings. She doesn't. She appears calm, cool and aloof. I'm angry at, and jealous of, her ability to disengage. Am I so disposable? Bella is the ultimate iceberg. When you meet her, you get to see about five per cent of what's available. The rest is submerged in dark, murky waters. I am a fated *Titanic*.

On the other hand, Laura is an open book. She oozes

integrity and sincerity from every pore. She's fun, good in the sack, interesting and no pushover. So why do I find myself continually looking at Belinda's boobs throughout dinner (currently strapped up, high and inviting)?

We eat a bit and drink an enormous amount. Or, at least, everyone except Belinda drinks an enormous amount. Laura and Philip are knocking them back because they are on holiday and are carefree. I drink a lot because I'm in the middle of some sort of ghoulish nightmare and haven't the moral fibre or immoral impudence to manage the situation without the aid of alcohol. I imagine Bella – because, hell, there's no sign of Belinda tonight – isn't drinking to demonstrate how much more self-control she has than me.

I'm insulted and furious that she treats me with such contempt in front of her 'husband'. She practically ignores me. She hasn't congratulated me on winning the King of Kings heats, even though she's here as my guest. She doesn't manage so much as a polite good-mannered chuckle when I make a joke. She can't even be bothered to chat. I can see she might not feel comfortable enquiring about my most wild and romantic moments, my marital status or even which woman first broke my heart. Accepted. But she could chat about some of the non-consequential things that mates chat about – the weather, football results, how to make a decent whisky sour.

Whisky sour. Good idea. I'll have a double as a chaser to this second bottle of champagne.

What power does Belinda McDonnel wield over me? It was the same way back when . . . She was playing out some childish romantic notion of eloping and I was just the sap prepared to go the distance. Why did I instantly agree to tell grade A lies to my new girlfriend to help her out? How did I let her trick me into believing that we were back on a path that was developing into something like a genuine friendship? Because here's the thing, this will make you laugh – I thought I *meant* something to her. The other night, when we were sat in All Bar One, the alcoholic equivalent to Starbucks, cookie-cut but reliable, I believed that there was a connection between us. I thought we'd started to weave gossamer-thin threads of deliberation, laughter and trust that amounted to the beginnings of an authentic relationship. But it was nothing. It meant nothing. I was deluded. Bella Edwards is a hard, manipulative, controlling bitch. And I am a weak, feckless and gullible idiot.

She's got great legs.

Really fantastic for her age. Like, they've got better. I've always found the back of the knee particularly erotic and Bella's is toned and strong-looking.

The whisky sour has been and gone. I've drunk too much.

'How much have you had to drink?' whispers Bella, as if she's read my mind. I didn't think we could still do that. She's taken the opportunity of Philip chatting to the pianist and Laura visiting the loos, to interrogate me.

'Not enough,' I reply sullenly.

'I think you should go easy.'

'I don't give a fuck what you think.'

Bella looks astonished, and that's satisfying. Who is she to tell me how much I should drink? I order a beer just to annoy her.

Laura comes back to the table. 'Stevie, baby, you'd better not drink much more. You have the photo shoot tomorrow. You don't want to feel too rough,' she says, with a smile.

'You might be right, gorgeous,' I lean across the table to kiss her. I kiss her in a way that yells randy. I gently bite her lower lip and push my tongue into her mouth. I let the bottom of my beer glass nudge up against her nipple. I'm not sure who I'm trying to get a reaction from, Laura or Bella. I'm too drunk to care.

Philip rejoins the table. 'Ah, young love.'

'Exactly that,' I agree with a grin.

I still haven't actually told Laura that I love her, not in so many words. I'm not trying to play games. The opposite. I don't want to say anything too definite, with this mess hanging over my head. Laura doesn't play games, she doesn't even want to. It's one of the many great things about her. She's refreshingly uncomplicated.

Women are so unnecessarily complex. I mean besides Belinda – who is off the scale when it comes to creating needless difficulties in her life and the lives of those unfortunate enough to come into contact with her – other birds are not much better. They lie about their age, the number of men they've slept with and their weight, as a matter of course. They lie about fancying married men, their mates' boyfriends and men with money, without batting an eyelid. They lie about the colour of their hair, their ability to eat chocolate and stay thin and how much exercise they do each week. It's so pointless. We know you lie! Men know women lie!

But Laura is different. She thinks like a guy. That first

evening out together, she commented that getting to know someone is complicated enough without pretending to be something you're not. I choked on my beer. She is *so* right. It's so simple. So obvious. Her doctrine is the polar opposite to the doctrine Bella lives by.

And the one I'm living by. Holy fuck. Hardly a comforting thought.

'Hey, buddy, I told them who you are,' says Philip and he points towards the pianist.

'Who I am?' I ask. Who the hell *am* I? Laura's boyfriend or Belinda's husband? My head is spinning.

'An Elvis King of Kings finalist. The pianist was really impressed.' I shrug modestly. 'He wants you to get up and sing something.'

'Go on, baby. Go for it,' Laura screeches excitedly.

'No, I'm too pissed,' I object.

'I've never heard you perform,' says Philip, 'I'd really like to.'

'Please, please, please,' says Laura, giggling.

Other diners tune into the commotion and start to encourage me. They call out tracks they would like me to sing, and it's a buzz, there's no denying it. I've been in similar situations in the UK, at wedding parties if the guests are drunk enough, which they usually are. At the competition heats the crowds get fervent but there's nothing like the enthusiasm of the Yanks. They have no embarrassment about encouraging or complimenting. It's charmingly refreshing. Notably, Bella is not cajoling me on to the stage – she never has. It's her reticence as much as everyone else's encouragement that does it for me.

I walk towards the stage, wobbling slightly, it's alcohol,

not nerves. I'd only noticed a pianist before I stood up, but in true Vegas style, a small band has materialized where it was needed. Beside the pianist, there is now a drummer and some guys on strings. They all flash me hundred-watt grins and ask what's it to be.

Good question.

Drunk, there's a serious chance that I'll become pathetically slushy, indiscreet or angry. It seems impossible to choose a song without it appearing loaded and especially significant. Outright, I reject 'Love Me Tender', 'Don't Be Cruel' and 'Hard Headed Woman' although just thinking about the last option makes me snigger to myself. *And* there's the question who am I singing for? Laura or Belinda? Both will assume I'm singing for them. Whether I belt out a showpiece or croon a ballad, they will layer on tricky significance. As women, they won't be able to help themselves, they will find a deeper meaning where none is intended. So, what I choose matters. I wish I knew the words to 'Old Shep'. That alone would be safe.

I look back at the table. Laura is standing, looking shiny and Amazonian. She grins, waves and then puts her fingers in her mouth to wolf whistle. She looks thrilled for me and thrilled to be with me. I see nothing in her but uncomplicated pleasure. I smile back at her. I turn to Belinda. Bella is looking grave and nervous. She seems to be shrinking before my eyes. She's struggling to meet my stare. I see nothing but regret and mess.

Both women fascinate me.

I start to sing 'The Wonder of You'. I have no idea which one I'm singing to.

30. Good Rocking Tonight

Philip

'Wow, can that man hold a tune!'

'He's not bad,' says Bella.

'Frankly, I'm in awe.'

I unbutton my shirt and fold it carefully before placing it into the laundry bag at the bottom of the wardrobe. Our suite is so stunning that I don't want to mess it up. Bella doesn't have the same scruples; I wander into the bathroom where I'm assaulted by countless lotions and potions that appear to be positively scrambling to make an escape bid from their jars and packaging. It would never cross Bella's mind to put a lid back on a bottle. I reunite various tubes and tubs with their tops, I then wipe away the messy gunk smeared around the jars and start humming 'The Wonder of You' that Stevie sang in the bar. I can't get the tune out of my head. I can't remember the words exactly, something about her love being everything to him, making him feel like a king. Good words. Simple, straightforward, effective.

Stevie is talented, far better than I had anticipated. Not that I'm in any way a connoisseur of Elvis tribute acts but I have seen two or three in my time: one at university, another at a corporate do, and most memorably a cluster of Chinese Elvises – guys who double as waiters at a very trendy (in a kitsch sort of way) restaurant in Clapham. But Stevie is something else, far better than anything I've ever seen, even on TV.

The funny thing is Stevie doesn't even look much like Elvis but when he got hold of the mic tonight, there were moments when I really thought I was in the presence of the King. How crazy is that? He captured the exact melodious tone that Elvis was famous for. A tone that conveyed a blend of sweet, deferential pleading and soulful sincerity. I don't think it was just champers, I felt a huge lump in my throat and for a short time I found that I couldn't swallow, not even alcohol.

'La, la. Laah. La,' I hum.

'Give it a rest, Phil,' says Bella, joining me in the bathroom. It's clear she means the humming rather than my cleaning-up efforts so I stop, except in my head. It's an enormous bathroom with two basins and two mirrors. We stand side by side, her cleaning her teeth, me clearing up her mess. I love the way Bella cleans her teeth. It's so precise, so deliberate and thorough. She always brushes for three whole minutes and she flosses twice a day, unbelievable. I like her purposeful, painstaking approach to cleaning her teeth because it shows she has the ability to be dedicated to something. She may not be dedicated to a career or even to keeping her wardrobe and make-up tidy but she has a high level of personal hygiene and would never go out without lipstick. She's conscientious that way.

'I'm going to have a quick shower,' she says. 'I'm surprised that there's so much smoking allowed. I thought it was outlawed in the US.'

Bella can't stand the smell of smoke and won't be able to sleep unless she's washed the stale lingering smell off her body and hair. I wait for her in bed.

Fifteen minutes later she joins me. She's wearing a matching vest and pants set in a lilac colour. It's cute rather than sexy. She rarely comes to bed naked nowadays. I tell myself that it would be unreasonable to expect it here as the air con is ferocious: she wouldn't want to catch a chill. I put down the guide to Las Vegas and ask, 'Did you have a nice night?'

'Good, thanks. Yes.' She's rubbing cream into her hands.

'Even though you missed out on the champagne?'

'Yes.'

'Why didn't you have a glass?'

'Didn't feel like it.'

'Still got a headache?'

'Something like that.'

I consider leaving my line of questioning. It's possible, likely even, that Bella does have a headache. She's complained about the constant jangle of slot machines and the tinny music from the casinos. But why do I get the feeling that something more than a headache is bothering her?

Of late she's veered – almost hysterically – from shrill and nagging, to silent and uncooperative, from delightful to tearful, then back again. Bella is normally so level, so together, but at the moment I feel I'm married to two women: reliable, kind, calm, even-tempered Bella and the hysterical, cutting, complaining banshee, who jumps when the phone rings and sometimes refuses to answer the door. She's not sleeping well and has got into the habit of skipping meals – and sex too, sadly. Giving up alcohol follows a number of evenings on which she has staggered home seriously drunk.

I've given the matter a great deal of thought and the only possible explanation is that she does not like being idle. Bella may not have ever enjoyed career progression as such, but she has a strong work ethic and had never had a day of unemployment in her life, until we married. I persuaded her to take some time to consider what it is that she wants to do with her life. I'm beginning to think that was a mistake. It pains and worries me to say it, but recently Bella has been showing some of the classic signs of depression, sometimes manic, sometimes lethargic, sometimes ecstatic and other times tearful.

A friend of mine, Bob, is one of those life coach gurus. He worked with me in the City and then when he became a father, he did the standard reevaluation of his life thingy. He came to the conclusion that his life was lacking in some of the essentials; time with family, a sense of pride or fulfilment in his career and a day-to-day sense of meaning. Serious stuff. So he chucked it all in and retrained as a life coach in the hope that he could help other people reach similar conclusions about their lives. I wasn't particularly supportive of his career choice and commented that I hoped everyone he advised had already paid off their mortgage on the six-bedroom pile in Notting Hill before throwing in their lucrative professions, just as he had. Frankly, I've always thought that life coaching was a bit of nonsense. For God's sake, what's the world come to if you need a life coach to help you make every decision – from whom to marry to how you take your tea?

I think it's obvious: this sense of displacement and uselessness that people claim to feel is symptomatic of our hurried and disposable lifestyle *and* the fact that we don't live near our families any more. The art of good old-fashioned chatting is dying out. You don't need an expert to tell you that much. Or maybe you do, as no one talks any more. Anyway, we're blokes so Bob didn't take offence when I said as much.

Frustratingly, it turns out that I was right about one thing, the art of good old-fashioned chatting *is* dying out – at least, it is between me and my wife. Despite repeated enquiries as to what's bothering her, I keep banging up against a fat wall of silence. But it turns out I was wrong about the other thing – a life coach does have his uses.

I found it was helpful to call Bob and tell him about Bella's mood swings. He suggested she might be depressed. I'd never have contemplated depression; she doesn't seem the type. But Bob told me there isn't a type. It's bollocks thinking you have to behave like an extra from *One Flew Over the Cuckoo's Nest* if you suffer from depression. He said her symptoms were typical of someone anxious about their identity. Apparently, newly-weds are vulnerable to this: they struggle to hold on to their identity as they become half of a couple. The other group who are vulnerable to identity issues are the unemployed. My persuading Bella to pack in her waitressing work, just after we married, might have exacerbated the situation. I only wanted to help. Bob said there wasn't much I could do except encourage Bella to draw her own conclusions, and support her all the way. He started talking about love and stuff, the kind of topic blokes normally avoid while enjoying a pint. I appreciated his sacrifice.

I search for ways to support her. 'What's wrong, Bella?'

'Wrong? Nothing.' She smiles at me. 'Why should anything be wrong?'

'I don't know, but I get the feeling something's worrying you? Whatever it is, I'll help. You know that, don't you? Just tell me and I'll help.'

'You're very sweet.' She kisses me on the cheek.

I feel like a Chelsea Pensioner who has just offered to escort her across the road. I sigh and change the subject. 'Laura seems very happy.'

'Yes.'

'She's clearly besotted with Stevie.'

'Yes.'

'And while, as a rule, I don't go in for monitoring the love lives of my friends – woman's work – I'm pleased to note that it's obvious Stevie feels the same about her too. Wouldn't you say so?'

'Do you know, Phil, I'm really sleepy. I'd like to turn the lights out now. A good night's sleep will be the best thing for my headache, don't you think?'

It clearly doesn't matter what I think because Bella gives me another peck on the cheek and flicks out the lights. I'm left staring into the dark.

Ho hum. While it is obvious that Laura is besotted with Stevie, it is just as clear that Bella can't stand the man. She has managed to hide as much from most people, but to me, it's patent. The only thing that is unclear is *why*. Bella vetoed my suggestion of playing a round of golf with him; I only suggested the game to allow her and Laura some girly time. I thought it would cheer her up but she was totally against it. She didn't really want to come on this holiday either. She came up with a number of weak and implausible excuses to get out of it but I'd already accepted Laura's kind invitation. It's obvious to me she needed a break. She's stuck in a rut and doesn't know which way to turn. Bob agreed that a new environment might help her make a decision about her career or, at the very least, stop her being so bloody moody.

Bella's ferocious dislike of Stevie is a mystery to me. He seems like a decent enough bloke to me, even if he has a penchant for wearing silver and white Lycra costumes that are so tight you can see his goosebumps. Gyrating in front of a live audience dressed this way does at least go to prove he has a sense of humour.

'Do you know what I found out tonight?' I ask the hump under the duvet that is Bella feigning sleep.

'What?' she mumbles.

'Stevie went to Aberdeen University too. He *is* one of your fellow alumni.' Bella doesn't comment. 'How old is he, do you know?'

'I'm not sure,' she mumbles.

'About your age, I'd have said.'

'I think he might be younger than me. He certainly acts it,' she snaps.

'I wonder what he studied. Do you think your paths might have crossed? You must at least know people in common.' I'm trying to find mutual ground between Stevie and Bella; it's in short supply.

Bella is reticent about her past, if you judge her against

other women who seem to like nothing better than to talk about themselves – except perhaps to talk about their exes. Bella has the good sense to know that I could not be less interested in her previous sexual encounters; I am distinctly incurious. On the other hand, I would like to meet more of her old friends. They'd interest me.

'I imagine he studied music. That lot kept themselves to themselves. I'm sure I'd have remembered if our paths had crossed.'

'Especially if he was wearing sideburns and gold glasses,' I joke.

'Especially then,' agrees Bella.

And then she surprises me. I suddenly feel her warmth next to my lips. The breath that is escaping from her body is mingling with the breath escaping from mine. She starts to kiss me. Slow, long, probing kisses. In one deft move she wriggles on top of me. Bella is so slight I sometimes barely register her weight but tonight she is pushing down on me, pushing her whole self into me. I can feel her nipples harden under her top, I'm sure she can feel my cock harden and press against her. I wrap my arms around her and squeeze her closer to me. Her fingers are running through my hair and mine are searching for her flesh. She starts to trail kisses down from my lips, past my ear, my neck, my chest, and then her fingers race ahead. She guides my cock into her target and we don't chatter any more. Even if I had the will, her mouth is full.

31. My Happiness

Thursday 8th July 2004

Bella

Stevie has won a seriously amazing prize. Never in a million years would I have imagined that being an Elvis tribute act could be so profitable. I have to admit the hotel is scrumptious; I admit this to no one other than myself, as I stare with amazement around the luxurious, tropically themed out-of-this-world resort.

The Mandalay Bay Hotel has been built around a 'lagoon', it has its own rum distillery (go figure), a couple of pools plus a sandy beach. The beach is swept by waves from a machine that can generate breakers big enough for people to surf. It's all very convincing. I find myself a sunbed, apply sun factor a squillion and settle down to enjoy the rays. I listen to children, screaming and laughing while they play in the pool, and overhear the occasional conversation between dudes who have been catching some waves, and I make-believe that I'm on a real beach.

I concentrate on relaxing, a contradiction I suppose. I will not think about the following: my marital status and the conversation I had the night before with Phil – frankly terrifying. He wanted to know what was wrong with me. I thought I was doing quite well in giving the impression that nothing is wrong with me. Clearly not. He asked if anything was worrying me and said whatever it was, he'd help. Nice sentiment but not one I'm prepared to put to the test. I wish he *could* help. There is nothing I want more than to curl up in his strong arms, and lay my head on his broad chest, and sob. If only he could sort everything out. But he can't. It's not like writing a cheque for a parking fine or telling me that my thighs look positively svelte in the ridiculously expensive pair of leather trousers I impulse-purchased from Joseph and regret doing so. The only person Philip can't save me from is myself.

Oh God. It would be so terrible if he ever got the slightest hint of what's worrying me. How could he begin to understand, forgive or help? The conversation, already difficult, plunged into something far more appalling, when I found myself telling outright lies. So far, I'd been careful to avoid the truth, omit certain details – big details, like marriage ceremonies admittedly – but, until yesterday, I'd never told downright lies. Yesterday I categorically denied that I'd ever known Stevie. Then I initiated sex. Guilty sex, silencing sex. And while Phil was aware only that it was good sex (scared, desperate sex does have a certain edge) he'd hate me if he knew why I was keen to distract him last night. He'd hate me even more if he knew who I was thinking of when I climaxed.

What am I doing thinking about this? I will not think about this.

Other things I will not think about include the fact that Laura and Stevie are clearly getting along like a house on fire. What was it that Philip said? That they were besotted with one another. They must be if Phil has noticed. And that's a good thing. Isn't it?

Finally, I will not think about Stevie.

'Hi.'

I recognize his voice instantly, even though my eyes are closed against the sun. 'Hi,' I mutter. I sit up and pop on my sunglasses. I can't risk my eyes being the window to my soul. Even through rose-tinted glasses Stevie looks a bit pale, but that would be my only criticism. Other than that, he is lean and fit. Gorgeous, frankly. He stands over me holding a towel and suncream. I glance around the poolside and am panicked to observe that the only free sunbed appears to be the one next to mine.

'I didn't realize you were out here,' he mutters, grumpily.

I didn't realize that I had to give him a schedule of my movements. 'Well, yes I am.'

'I can see that.' We both pause. We're unable to grab to mind even the most miniature version of small talk.

'Would you prefer it if I went and sunbathed elsewhere?' I ask eventually.

'Well, you would prefer that, wouldn't you?' His tone is a combination of sharp and sulky.

'We can't sunbathe together,' I point out.

'No, I suppose not.' Stevie looks around and discerns what I already know about the scarcity of sunbeds. 'But then again, what harm will it do?' He shrugs.

It smarts that he is totally apathetic towards my presence. I get the distinct impression that it makes no difference to him whether I sunbathe next to him or on the other side of the globe. What can I say? 'Sorry, babe, you can't lie down next to me as you are almost naked and I'm already entertaining inappropriate thoughts about you, I'm not sure I'll be able to control myself.' No. Of course not. The only dignified thing to do is give the impression that I'm as unaffected by him as he is by me.

'No harm at all. We only have to avoid each other in front of Laura and Philip. Anything that goes on between the two of us is our little secret, hey?'

How did such an unfortunate sentence form in my brain, never mind struggle into existence? That sounded one hundred per cent come-on. I'm wrestling with playing by the rules I set, within the game I created. I know that I ought to just pick up my towel and go and track down Phil in the gambling hall, but something glues me to the sunbed. I blush furiously. Stevie looks momentarily bemused, then dismisses me. He places his towel on the bed next to mine and sits down. I pick up my novel. He picks up his suncream. Out of the corner of my eye I watch as he rubs lotion on his thighs, arms, face and stomach. It's quite a show.

'God, I could never imagine you using suncream,' I blurt.

Wrong, wrong, wrong! That sentence was, once again, totally unsuitable. For a start, it implied criticism – the Stevie Jones I knew and loved was too ridiculously macho for anything as sensible as sun protection. For a second, it alluded to the fact there once was a Stevie Jones that I knew. And *loved*.

'What do you mean? That I'm too thick to take on board government warnings about global warming and skin cancer?' asks Stevie snidely.

'No, not that. It just . . . Well . . . It just wasn't something we ever thought about when we were kids, was it?' I'm beginning to wonder if there are any 'safe' topics of conversation for us or if we are wading through the verbal equivalent of a crocodile-infested swamp. 'I mean too much sun wasn't something that kept anyone awake at night in Kirkspey, was it?' I grin, hoping that Stevie realizes I'm not sarcastic or critical. I'm nothing other than nervous.

He looks at me for a long time, about two hours or maybe thirty seconds. 'Suppose not. Will you do my back?' He offers me the sun lotion as though his request is a reasonable one.

I take the lotion as I can't see an alternative. What can I plead? Cramp in my arm? Allergy towards sun lotion? Inability to touch my husband's back without remembering just how physically attractive I always found him? None of these excuses seem quite right, especially not the truth.

Stevie flips on to his stomach. I hover above him. What to do? What I want to do is straddle him. Gently lower my crotch on to his bum, one leg dangling on either side of him so that he sees my neatly manicured, scarlet toenails and my smooth, bronzed legs. I want to rub lotion up and down his taut, muscled back – gratuitously massaging the cream until he's fighting an erection. Ideally, I'd like to take off my bikini top and lean into him allowing my breasts to push against his back and shoulders, I'd like us to be upstairs in the privacy of a suite.

Obviously I've had too much sun.

I shake my head and try to dislodge the disgusting fantasy. Then I slap a bit of lotion on his back and shoulders. I hope he doesn't get burnt because I hardly did what you'd call a thorough job and even then I had to force myself to think of cleaning underneath the fridge and behind the loo. Ugly thoughts to neutralize the fabulousness of touching him.

I sit back on my sunbed and grab my novel. Stevie flips on to his back, which is a good thing because he's less likely to burn that way, and yet not such a good thing because he notices, 'Your book is upside down.'

'Oh,' I say, turning it quickly. 'It's not very good anyway.'

'What is it?'

'Oh, something light.' I try to hide the cover from him.

'Tolstoy's *Anna Karenina*,' he observes.

'Yes,' I admit.

'A great work.'

'Yes,' I admit.

'Not light, really.'

'No,' I admit.

Stevie pauses, then smiles. 'This is really awkward, isn't it?'

'Yes.' I grin widely, relieved I'm not the only one to find this whole situation impossible.

'Do you want a drink?' he offers.

'I'm trying not to.'

'Why? You're on holiday.'

'Because I don't want to do anything I'd regret,' I answer. That's the thing with Stevie – it's easy to be honest around him.

'What could you possibly do that you'd regret?' asks Stevie.

He smiles at me, a slow sexy smile. If anyone else had treated me to that same smile I'd be sure there was a tiny bit of flirtation going on. But there can't be. There mustn't be.

'What's left for you to do? It's not as though you could get drunk and marry impulsively just because you're in Vegas. You're already married to both your travel companions. Unless, of course, you go for the hat-trick and do the lesbian marriage thing with Laura.'

I stare at Stevie weighing up whether he is being cruel or spiteful. But his eyes are sparkling with mischief. He's trying to laugh at our situation because what else can we do? If we didn't laugh then we'd most definitely cry. I choose to burst into slightly hysterical peals. It is some sort of a relief.

'I'm not sure that lesbian marriages are legal, even here, in the state of Nevada,' I say with a giggle.

'Oh, legality has never held you back,' says Stevie and laughs uproariously. He waves at a passing waiter and orders a bottle of white wine and two glasses. I don't object as the resolve I had, in shovel-loads on the plane, has melted away.

Stevie and I spend two glorious hours together. We hire a huge tyre-shaped float. It's big enough to allow us both to bob inside and we drift around the loop-shaped pool, screaming every time we coast under the 'waterfall'. We paddle in the 'sea', we drink wine and eat enormous club sandwiches because it transpires that neither of us had breakfast. It's very hot, so we also become more confident at rubbing on sun lotion for one another. The conversation flows as rapidly as the surrounding fountains. We chat about nothing much: places we've visited, hotels we've stayed in, bars we've drunk in. I haven't backpacked or stayed in a youth hostel, Stevie hasn't drunk in the Sanderson or the Ice Hotel in Sweden, so we both have a lot to say.

We joke and occasionally we disagree, but only gently. For example, I believe that there comes a certain age when women ought not to wear bikinis and ought gracefully to adopt the single-piece suit and a sarong. Stevie laughed at this and said fat, ugly and old people were just as entitled to feel warm sun on their skin as lithe, young beauties.

We hold stupid competitions to see who can float on their backs for the longest time (boredom breaks me and Stevie is the acknowledged champion). Stevie shows off doing underwater handstands and swimming between my legs. To the casual onlookers we probably seem to be the epitome of a deliriously happy couple. I bet people think we are honeymooners. Yet, even as I enjoy the morning, I mourn because I know it does not belong to me: I've stolen it. The thought sobers me so I swim to the edge of the pool.

'I fancy drying off,' I say, as I haul myself out of the pool. Stevie does the same and I become momentarily mesmerized as I watch the sparkly water that clings to his shoulders and legs. I'd sparkle too, if I clung to him like a second skin. He has a broad chest, much more man and less boy than I remembered, probably because the hair there has thickened but, thank God, it's not a rug. His shoulders are square and strong-looking.

'Do you work out?' I ask, not considering the implied compliment.

'What do you think?' asks Stevie as he flashes me a cocky grin and winks. I pull my eyes away.

I am aware that I am practising the same trick I tried to employ at my wedding to Phil. Everyone warned me (correctly) that the big day would speed by in a flurry of smiles and excitement and before I knew it the whole thing would be over. Amelie advised me not to drink too much and concentrate on preserving two or three unforgettable things that can't be captured on film – a particularly provocative smell, touch or taste. She said I was to make them my own and keep them as treasure to unearth whenever I needed them later. Right now, I am breathing in the smell of sunshine and sun lotion on warm flesh, and drinking in the image of flickering sunlight on the pool surface and I'm trying to hold on to it. I'd like to capture *every* sound, glance, smell, sensation and store them up because I'm on borrowed time. I'm having fun with a borrowed man. The thought hits me, with a sledgehammer whack. I force myself to address the issues we've been avoiding.

'Where's Laura this morning?'

Stevie's posture becomes rigid. We both know that the mention of her name is a rebuke. 'I left her on the phone to Eddie and I booked her into the spa. By now she'll be having a facial or a massage.'

'That's very thoughtful.' I force a smile.

Stevie shrugs. 'It's not easy being a single mum.'

'I guess not.'

'Where's Phil?' he asks to chide me.

'Playing the slots.'

'No, actually I think that's him over there, with Laura,' says Stevie.

I look towards the direction he's pointing in and sure enough, Phil and Laura are threading their way through the sunbeds, towards us. It's as though we summoned them up through a voodoo spell. They are both grinning and waving happily. Laura looks relaxed after her spa treatments and Phil is shouting something about winning $380. I only wish I felt happier to see them.

32. Treat Me Nice

Laura

I can't remember when I last had such a riotous time. I spent the morning in a spa, a treat paid for by my truly legend boyfriend, and the afternoon by the pool with said truly legend boyfriend and Phil. Bella went shopping and only came back to the pool late afternoon. Then she slept in the shade insisting that the sun was her worst enemy. An eminently sensible attitude, no doubt, but not one I'm prepared to adopt, considering the dearth of sunshine in my life. Phil, Stevie and I had a hoot. We played cards – practising for tonight when we plan to hit the casinos big-style. We splashed around in the pool and enjoyed vibrant-coloured cocktails. At about four Stevie dragged himself away for the PR photo shoot. A bit of a bore but we can hardly complain – a few duty calls while we enjoy all this seems fair enough.

'I'm going to go shopping. Do you want to come?' I ask Bella.

She squints at me, then feels around for her book, which is lying beside her sunbed.

'I'd love to, but I'm dying to know what happens in my novel and can't leave it alone.'

I don't comment on the fact that she wasn't reading it

when I approached her but instead I ask, 'What are you reading?'

'*Anna Karenina.*'

'Come shopping, Bella. You've read it before – you know how it ends. She shags the cute guy, can't live with the guilt of being an adulteress and tops herself.'

'It's not as straightforward as that. She was a martyr to her passionate nature. She tried and tragically failed to live outside the customs of her time,' says Bella, with more commitment than I was expecting.

'No doubt, I must have missed something when I read it. The thing is, adulterers always dress up their sleaze, but in the end it's the same thing – horrible,' I say. 'Anyway, on to brighter things, why don't we hit the shops? I want to surprise Stevie and buy something really glamorous to wear tonight. I want to look fabulous for him.'

Bella stares at me for the longest time, then asks, 'Can you afford it?'

I fight a blush. 'Well, no, not really. Not in the sense that the money is in my bank account but there's still space on my plastic and I *so* want to look sensational.'

'Come with me.' Bella takes my hand and leads me back to the hotel.

'It's stunning,' I gasp.

We are in Bella's suite and the item I am referring to is a fuchsia-pink dress laid out on her bed. It's Matthew Williamson's peony dress that, to my certain knowledge, both Kate Beckinsale and Laura Bailey have been spotted in this spring. It's flirty and fun, and without doubt the most sexy number I have ever had pleasure to set eyes on.

While I am thrilled for Bella, it must be a joy to own such a fabulous item, inwardly my heart sinks. Obviously, if she's wearing this tonight my need to shop is not only dire, it is life and death. I have nothing that can complement, let alone compete with, this dress. I surreptitiously check my watch. It's ten to five and we're meeting Stevie in the bar at nine. Do I even have time to find something so wonderful? Is there anything else quite so lovely on the planet or, more practically, in the Vegas shopping malls? I am not normally this giddy over clothes and I'm not especially competitive – over the last few years I've got used to Bella looking a million dollars and me looking . . . well, considerably less. But tonight I want to shine. Tonight, I want to stand out. Because, tonight, I'm planning to tell Stevie *exactly* how I feel about him.

I know, I know, a girl is supposed to wait until the guy's made a declaration. It's more elegant, it's more refined and it's probably a damn sight more sensible – no one likes a knock-back. But I *can't* wait. I nearly blurted it out last night – I would have, too, if Bella and Phil hadn't interrupted us. But maybe it's better that I've had to wait till tonight when I look groomed and cool. Last night I was shiny and glowing – in the wrong sort of way.

I'm actually looking forward to telling him that since he came into my life everything has gone topsy-turvy. Everything that was dull and grim, has vanished. Everything that was fun and good, is better. I love the way he listens with seriousness to anything I have to say – even crap, like my ideas on where the storyline in *Corrie* is going. I love the way *he* has an opinion on where the storyline on *Corrie* is going. It's a genuine skill to be able to chatter nonsense and yet ask questions which show perception and intelligence. He thinks I have that skill. I think he has. He is funny, very, very funny. In a belly laugh type of way, not in the nasty too-clever-for-your-own-good type of way, which is so popular in London. He is razor-sharp, totally on the ball about all sorts of stuff. Music, the national curriculum and what's on at the movies are topics that are bound to be discussed in the staff room, but Stevie also knows about the latest white paper the government is trying to push through, literature, motorbikes, hunting rituals of ancient, nomadic African tribes. It might just be that the Scottish education system is broad, but it impresses me.

Then there's the other stuff. He looks at me and his eyes scorch my soul. Tattooing my heart and mind with a message of hope and promise. Plus, he is so crash hot in the sack it would be impossible not to love him. Vegas is the place where people come to gamble and to take risks. I'm placing my bet on the King of Hearts. The fact is, I will burst if I don't tell him.

'Are you wearing that dress tonight?' I ask, as I sit down on the bed. I'm still sticky with sun oil and sweat so I'm careful not to touch it. Typically Bella has laid the dress alongside beautifully coordinated accessories: a pair of killer heels, a sparkly bag and earrings. It looks like a fashion shoot. 'You could be a stylist, you know,' I tell her. I often suggest careers to Bella. It is a mystery to me how a woman so brimming with talent and intelligence has avoided making anything of herself.

'I don't think fuchsia pink is my colour,' says Bella.

I look at her quizzically. 'You *have* to wear it. This dress deserves an outing. It's an insult to the designer to leave it at home.'

'And it's a tiny bit long for me. Pink's your favourite colour, though, isn't it?' Bella delivers these lines with a broad grin.

'You're kidding!' The penny drops. She's offering it to me.

'No, I'm not kidding. I bought it for you – or at least, Phil did. His cash, my choice. We wanted to thank you for bringing us on this fantastic break. That's what I've been doing all afternoon, shopping for you. Look, it's your size, the shoes too.'

I pick up the dainty, strappy shoes and carefully inspect them. They are beautiful, a spangled mix of diamanté and satin, and entirely to my taste. Not quite as high as Bella would wear. She's put a great deal of thought into this gift. 'Oh my God,' I squeal. 'I'm going to look stunning.'

Bella starts to laugh. 'I like the modest you, it's refreshing,' she teases.

And then we hug each other. We often hug each other – hello and goodbye, when Eddie says something super-sweet, or when either of us just needs a hug. But there hasn't been much hugging between us recently and I only realize as much when Bella grasps me. The hug started with me grabbing her but now she won't let me go. Slowly, carefully, I break away from her. I look down at the girl in front of me. It must be the height thing because she looks as vulnerable as a brittle stick. One blow and she'd snap.

'Hey, Bella, are you OK?' She looks close to tears.

'I'm glad you like it. I didn't want you to think I was being flash.'

'Be as flash as you like, babe, especially since you have such great taste,' I joke. I sit on the bed and start mooning over the dress. I can't believe it's mine, I can't wait to try it on but I need a shower first.

'I do remember, you know,' says Bella. 'I remember wanting to buy expensive things and not being able to afford them.'

'Hey, babe, I know. We've spent many a happy hour playing imaginary purchasing,' I grin.

Bella and I used to play a game where we'd sit and flick through a magazine, *Vogue* or even the Argos catalogue, it didn't matter. The idea was we'd choose one item from each page as our imaginary purchase. The rules were, only one item – however many you coveted on a particular page – and you *had* to have something, even if it was a page selling the latest range of commodes.

'No, I mean before that. You and I were always broke but we weren't *poor*. We could pay our rent and buy food. I'm talking about being poor. As a kid, after my mum died and my dad stopped going out on the boat. Without him fishing, we had no money. I mean no money, Laura.' Bella turns to me and looks me straight in the eye. 'We couldn't afford any new clothes, not even pants and socks.'

'How did you manage?'

'We had good neighbours. They gave us stuff to tide us over until the boys were old enough to work. I just—' She can't finish the sentence. 'It was pretty miserable.

Things aren't always what they seem. Not everything is straightforward. That's all I'm trying to say.'

I have no idea why Bella chooses to confide this in me now, especially after years of being very closed about her childhood but I know it's important. I also know she's not prepared to share any more when she says, 'Anyway, go and get your gladrags on. I need a bath.'

33. Hard Headed Woman

Bella

'Hi, Amelie, it's me.'

'Ermph?' Amelie makes a sound that isn't a recognizable word. I check my watch.

'Oh, shit, sorry. I forgot all about the time difference. It must be . . . what?'

'One in the morning,' she mumbles.

'Sorry, I'll go.'

'Don't you dare! I want the latest instalment. Wait till I get a glass of water.' After a minute, she returns to the phone somewhat refreshed. 'So what's up? Has it all gone bang yet?'

'No.' I can barely disguise my irritation. I wish Amelie wasn't quite so certain that this situation is going to explode. Why won't she humour me and let me believe there might be a pain-free exit?

'So, what have you been doing?'

'I spent the morning by the pool.'

'Alone?' she asks suspiciously. How does she know?

'With Stevie.'

'Nice,' she mutters, with heavy sarcasm.

'And this afternoon I went shopping for Laura.'

'A guilt purchase?'

'No. A thank-you present,' I insist, huffily.

'Having a good time then?'

'Sort of.' I pause.

Where do I begin? I am so confused. I cannot find any clarity no matter how much I search my head or even my heart. I need to talk to someone about this but my usual options of Phil or Laura are non-starters. I don't get the feeling that Amelie is going to be especially sympathetic either but I'm so desperate I blurt out what's in my mind.

'What if I've married the wrong one?'

'Which one are you talking about? You're married to both of them,' replies Amelie flatly.

'I have feelings for Stevie,' I confess.

'What sort of feelings?'

I can't tell Amelie that I keep stealing glances at Stevie's muscled arms, chest and shoulders or admit that I find his lean stomach fascinating and the thin line of hair that leads to the contents of his swimwear is as enticing as the Yellow Brick Road. The problem is he's sexy. Not in an obvious way – well, actually yes, he's sexy in an obvious way – but he's also sexy in a funny, quirky way. He's what he always was. I squirm on my seat and concentrate on the feelings I *can* tell Amelie.

'He's easy to talk to. After all, I've known him forever.'

'You haven't spoken to the man for eight years. You don't know him. It's a common desire – endless intimacy. But you haven't known anyone forever and nor has anyone known you that long.'

'I think about him all the time,' I whisper.

'In what way?' she asks, seriously.

'In *that* way. The way women think about men.' I'm hedging. 'Being with him feels special. Do you think that's telling?'

'What do you want to be told?' asks Amelie. 'I can't answer the question, Bella. I'm as new to this situation as you are. I don't know how you're supposed to feel.'

I'm probably not supposed to feel lust, or longing or loyalty, I'm almost certain of that. 'I don't want to think about Stevie. I'm trying not to.'

'But you have to try?'

'Yes, and even then I fail. I'm really trying to be sensible. I'm not drinking.'

'Good idea.'

'Well, at least, not when I'm with Phil.'

'Wouldn't it be more sensible not to drink around Stevie?'

'Maybe.' I own up. 'I'm so confused. I've changed my mind about five times since I arrived here.'

'Where does that leave you? Back where you started?'

'I don't know. Dizzy. Today, when we were alone together in the pool I found myself employing that trick you taught me for my wedding day.'

'What?'

'Preserving two or three unforgettable details that can't be captured on film.'

'And what did you capture?'

'The smell of sunshine and sun lotion on warm flesh and the sunlight on the pool surface.'

'I meant on your wedding day to Phil,' clarifies Amelie, starkly.

'Oh.' I'm startled. 'Erm, lilies, I think, and the feel of

Phil's jacket when he put it round my shoulders in the car as we left the reception.'

'That's what you need to be concentrating on,' advises Amelie sternly.

I rush at the only question I really want an answer to, 'Do you think it's possible to be in love with two men at the same time?'

'No,' she replies flatly.

'But people are!' I insist. 'That's why there's that song, "Torn Between Two Lovers".' I start to hum the lines about not knowing who to choose and breaking rules.

Amelie impatiently interrupts me, 'You asked if *I* believe it's possible to love two people and I don't. True love is all-absorbing. It's possible to be curious, infatuated, wistful maybe . . .'

I get the point she's making but I don't like it much. I try to ignite her sympathies. 'It must be a truly pitiful position to be in, though, don't you think? If, say, inadvertently you found yourself in love with two men at the same time. I mean, especially if you were married to both of them as well.'

'Bella! All I can see here is how awful it is to be Laura or Philip. You're not in love with Stevie. I don't even believe you're particularly well suited. It's easy to be sentimental when you're striving for closure.'

'But he's really hot!' I blurt.

'Closure is always more tricky to attain with sex-god types but don't get it mixed up, Bella. Don't risk everything you have with Phil, just for sex.'

'If it's only sexual attraction then maybe I should just shag him and be done with it. That would help me put

287

an end to it, hey?' I've expressed my most secret fantasy in the guise of a jest.

Amelie isn't fooled. 'Don't joke about affairs, Bella.'

'It wouldn't be an affair. I'm married to them both.'

'Think about what you've just said, Bella. For God's sake, *think*.'

'Yes, yes,' I mumble. I don't convince myself so I'm certain I haven't persuaded her. 'Got to go.'

I hang up as Phil walks into the room.

34. Shake, Rattle and Roll

Laura

When I enter the hotel bar at precisely 8.45 p.m. Bella and Phil are already waiting for me. Phil gives a low wolf whistle and Bella claps.

'You look wonderful,' says Phil.

'Perfect fit. Aren't I clever?' says Bella, smiling. 'You look stunning.'

And they're right. The dress is a winner. It swishes, whooshes and swirls in all the right places. I feel very sexy and very feminine. It's backless and my back is one of my strong points (many a joke has been made about that over the years – glad to see the back of you etc etc, ho ho ho). Bella is wearing a black cocktail dress, classical and understated. I get the feeling she's being deliberately discreet so that I can shine. I'm touched by the completeness of her generosity.

Stevie returns from his photo shoot at exactly nine o'clock, as promised. It's immediately clear that the dress has the desired effect.

'Wow! You are beautiful.'

'Thank you, sir.' I play with an earring and try to act cool, calm and collected.

Stevie swoops in to kiss me on the cheek and whispers, 'One hundred per cent knockout.'

I grin. 'You're looking quite gorgeous yourself.'

Stevie is still wearing his Elvis costume. For the purpose of the PR shoot the contestants were all provided with identical outfits, although I understand that in the actual competition they can rediscover a little individuality. No doubt to amuse us, Stevie has met us in the bar wearing his costume.

'Pretty fly for a white guy,' I laugh. And I can't resist flinging my arms around him. Sod cool, calm and collected.

'Are you going to get changed?' asks Bella.

'Don't. We'll get free drinks all night if you wear that get-up,' says Phil, laughing.

'I imagine I'll have to sing for my supper if I do,' says Stevie. 'It might get a bit tedious when we arrive at the third bar of the evening and another bouncer insists I do "Jailhouse Rock" and the guy behind the bar wants "Hound Dog".'

And as if to prove his point we are immediately interrupted.

'Oh. My. God. You are *so* the real thing!'

While not strictly accurate, obviously, Stevie is not the real thing – Elvis is dead and even if you buy into the conspiracy theories and believe that he's not dead, just living as an obese geriatric on some island somewhere – it's patent that Stevie is not your man. Stevie weighs only about a hundred and seventy pounds and there isn't a single indication of rigor mortis.

'Can we have our picture with you?'

The gaggle of tiny, skinny, blonde women hand Bella the camera and barge past me as though I am invisible, despite the designer dress. For all their size, smiles and giggles it's clear that these women are tough. They have hard bodies that have trod mills and participated in endless aerobic classes; their cumulative total of time spent in gyms must be decades. I am somewhat comforted to see that they are not as young as I thought on first impression. The expertly applied make-up, long manicured nails and bleached hair are smoke and mirrors, which means they pass for late twenties at a distance but up close they have at least ten years on that.

They pout and preen and pose. They kiss Stevie's cheek, take photos and liberties – one of them pinches his butt, another pinches his crotch. I'd say he enjoyed it up until the crotch pinching then he hurriedly shooed them on their way.

I breezily laugh at the incident, hoping to disguise the fact that I want to drill my stiletto heels into their faces.

Stevie decides to have a drink in his suit but it soon becomes apparent that we aren't going to get much peace. Everyone behaves as though he is godfather to their child. Some buy drinks and beg him to sing a verse. Others push past us, his *girlfriend* and friends, and demand photos. One couple has heard about the King of Kings final.

'Really?' says Stevie, clearly awash with pride but trying to look nonchalant. 'So, erm, did you see an advert or a press article? I understand that they are really pushing the event in local papers and radio. I'm not blowing my own trumpet but I do think that the organizers have done a good job with bringing a certain amount of gravitas to the whole event.'

'Actually, we are here with the Italian King,' says the guy.

'He's my brother,' says the girl, smiling. 'We will be supporting him.'

'Oh. Of course,' says Stevie, nodding his head with understanding. Stevie looks around, 'Is he here now? I think I know the guy you mean. I met an Italian at the photo shoot.'

'No, he is not here now. He is resting. Tomorrow is the dress rehearsal show. He does not want a hangover.'

I wonder if Stevie feels chided. 'Erm, tell him good luck.'

'He doesn't need luck. He is very good,' smiles the loyal sister.

I resist challenging her to a duel at dawn as I'm pretty sure that Stevie will hold his own when it comes to the competition. Instead I say we have to go: we're keen to get to the casino.

We can't decide which one to visit, we're spoilt for choice. In the end, we opt for Bally's: it isn't a million miles away and Phil wants to see the showgirls. Stevie doesn't seem as interested, but then he's swilling in the attention from the groupies. We decide to walk there rather than take a cab as it's a lovely, mild evening and we all agree a walk would be pleasant. To tell all, I'm enjoying turning heads and I know we are a mesmerizing spectacle. Stevie is Elvis, I am the lady in red (or at least fuchsia pink) and Bella and Phil are just their usual gorgeous selves.

The approach to Bally's is dramatic. We travel up a very long escalator flanked by cascading water, lighted pylons and giant palm trees. It almost bothers me that I am becoming acclimatized to such ostentatious nonsense.

As we approach the entrance, a sound and water show – involving a wave machine and fountains – erupts. No doubt a wonderful spectacle although I imagine it becomes a tiny bit repetitive and annoying if you are staying here.

'Water is very much the flavour here,' comments Bella. 'Apparently, in the multi-million-dollar show *Jubilee*, the "Titanic" sinks every night on stage.' She is reading this from a poster that depicts scantily clad ladies – unsuitable dress for the Titanic, I would have thought.

'What a giggle. We'll have to go,' I say.

'Yes, let's do that later, but where to now?' asks Stevie.

We are faced with the most enormous mash of lights, signs, slot machines, craps tables, roulette wheels and poker games. Everything is reddish-pink: the people playing, the drinks, the walls, the dealers and the machines. I'm not sure if the ruddy complexions are the result of the hue cast by the lights or the possibility of winning cold, hard cash. It's a noisy, rowdy, exciting spectacle.

'Well, not to the baccarat room,' says Phil. 'I've been reading about it and apparently that's where players go if they are willing to wager hundreds of thousands of dollars on a single hand. These guys are called "whales" in gaming parlance.'

We all agree that such high rolling is astounding. Bella looks white with shock: she isn't keen on gambling – she won't even buy a lottery ticket.

'That's madness,' she cries. 'No one wins but the house. Gambling is for losers, in the harshest sense of the word.'

'Not the most helpful attitude, darling,' Phil points out. 'Not here, in Las Vegas – in the middle of a casino.'

'I can't help myself, I hate these places,' she mutters.

It's clear that Bella is not going to feel comfortable on the green baize map but after some time we collectively persuade her that a hand of blackjack, or twenty-one as it's known to some, is worth a shot. The odds are better. Bella's competitive spirit kicks in and she starts to enjoy playing against the dealer, particularly when she can set her bet as low as five dollars. I want to try poker but Stevie teases me and says it won't be my game.

'Why not?'

'Well, most people make unconscious revelations through body language – tics, twitches, nervous laughs or something that gives them away – your face is an open book.'

'I can be deceptive when I want to be,' I argue.

'No, you can't,' smiles Stevie, as he leans in to kiss me. 'Every one of your expressions is there for the world to read.'

I stare up at him and wonder if he is reading my face now. Does he know that I think I'm holding a great hand. A straight flush. Can he read my face and know that it's saying, I love you?

Probably not, because he turns to Bella and says, 'I think you'd be good at poker.' She doesn't appear to hear him.

We each allot ourselves a modest sum of money and then embark on losing it. Stevie sensibly points out that the money we lose is just the fee for this particular form of entertainment and we should view it as we would the entry fee to a theme park. It makes me feel better as I slip my last allotted dollar into the slot machine. At one point I had been seventeen dollars up, but now I'm wiped out. Still, I enjoyed the ride.

Elvis imitators pop up everywhere in Vegas. Just yesterday I spotted an Elvis accompanying two showgirls, another stood outside a chapel (it was unclear whether he was the groom or vicar) and a third was washing cars in the parking lots near the helicopter base. So, I am surprised by how much attention Stevie grabs tonight. We get free throws on the craps – although they are not lucky throws – plenty of free drinks, and the stream of well-wishers is almost constant. Largely, the interest is great fun. With the exception of the blondes that swamp him. They flirt, flatter, fawn and they fuck me off.

They are so focused on Stevie that I don't even register on their radar. As they crowd around him I am edged out. Bella scowls; obviously she feels sorry for me and she's noticed that I've all but disappeared. She suggests we retire from the casino and find a bar. She, Phil and I march ahead, Stevie follows, trying to shake off his groupies.

'It must be ace being a man,' I mutter to Phil, as he passes me a large martini.

'Why do you say that?' he asks.

'Well, there are so many more attractive women than there are men,' I grumble.

'Do you think you have lesbian tendencies?' Phil asks jokingly, he's looking hopeful and I just know he will offer the use of his videocam.

'I wish I did.' I wonder if it's apparent that I am

insecure. How terrible that I'm insecure when I'm wearing this gorgeous dress. I wish Bella would say something reassuring; instead she is watching Stevie being photographed with his arms around another two blondes. She looks worried. Phil follows her gaze.

'Ah, I see. Don't worry, Laura. The women surrounding Stevie are professional blondes, not a threat at all.'

'Professional blondes?' I ask. 'You mean hookers?' I'm horrified and a little curious.

'No,' he grins. 'Not as such. You don't recognize that sort of woman because she's almost extinct in the UK. Or at least in Shepherd's Bush, the surgery and Eddie's nursery where you spend most of your time. Those women devote their entire lives to pleasing men. Or at least, rich or famous men.'

'That's meant to cheer me up?' I ask, glugging back my martini and ordering another. 'Won't Stevie like that? I mean from a guy's point of view, women that devote their entire lives to pleasing men, that sounds like a good thing.'

'In truth, there isn't a man out there who doesn't miss that breed of woman. He might not admit as much, too PC, too afraid of his wife . . .' He winks at Bella, who is listening intently. 'I should add that professional blondes don't have to be blonde. Brunettes and redheads can apply, but chances are they'll end up blonde, no matter what colour hair they were born with.'

'You're on about dumb blondes then; these girls don't look dumb to me,' I point out.

'The PB isn't stupid. The opposite. She has enough guile and confidence to hide her brains, so as not to appear threatening to any of the rich men she knows or hopes to get to know better. The professional blonde knows that, secretly, we guys are an insecure bunch.'

I wait for Bella to punch Phil playfully and tell him to get off his soapbox but she doesn't. She is more patient than she usually is when he's waxing lyrical with one of his pop-culture-psychoanalytical theories. Could be she's genuinely interested. I hope to God that she doesn't think there's something in it, as I really respect Bella's opinion when it comes to eternal negotiations of the peace treaty between the sexes. The war isn't quite over.

'This woman doesn't work – her profession is to look good for her man. PBs are fit, with lean hard bodies and boobs bought in Harley Street. They are devoted to their personal trainers, their hairstylist and colourist, their pilates and yoga instructors, their platinum Visa card, their personal shopper and their self-image. But even if a guy is bright enough to work this out, the sad truth is he doesn't much care because his girl looks good. It could be viewed as a fair financial arrangement.'

'Phil, do you think I'm a professional blonde?' asks Bella, unable to conceal her horror.

Phil kisses his wife's lips. 'No, my love. Of course not.'

'But I don't work and I have a trainer and yoga classes and all that stuff. I'm not like that, Phil.'

I am so glad that Bella hasn't had anything to drink. If she had, she would not be behaving quite so reasonably by now, she might have flung a glass of wine or at least a tantrum.

'My love, the reason Laura didn't recognize this type of woman is because they are very different from you two. You are the new breed of pleasers. You please yourselves, and in doing so, please your men. The new breed is a sassier, more hip type of girl who still visits the hairdresser with indecent frequency but carries slightly more body fat and is likely to have floppier boobs. She likes to look adorable for herself and her mates; what her guy thinks is a lower priority. On the whole I prefer this type of woman, she's more fun in a heated debate and less likely to cry if you don't buy her the latest six-grand handbag, as seen in *Vogue*.'

Phil leans forward on his barstool and kisses Bella again. This time it's a long, intimate kiss and I feel distinctly uncomfortable and closed out.

'I know you better than you think, Bella,' I hear him mutter. 'Better than you know yourself sometimes.' Then he turns to me and says, 'I don't think PBs are Stevie's cup of tea either, Laura. You are. Now, shall we go and rescue him and find somewhere to eat?'

35. Always On My Mind

Bella

Suddenly, it is two in the morning. Time has sped away. Most of the evening has been spent on an exhausting quest for food. Phil and Stevie concocted a bizarre plan to eat at three different venues. It was partially inspired by Phil's obsession with recommended eateries and partially an attempt to shake Stevie's groupies. Phil's guidebook recommends where to eat by course, so he thought it would be a good idea if we managed to sample three of the recommended specialities in one night, therefore three restaurants. He argued that as we are not staying here very long we should try to pack as much in as possible. It seemed something like sense. I agreed because this plan means there's little chance of conversation running dry or deep, both terrifying prospects. Instead, most of the evening was passed making comments about the decor of a venue, the distance to the next venue or asking for directions. All of which was innocuous enough.

We had our appetizers at Delmonico Steakhouse, apparently famous for rock shrimp salad dusted with Parmesan cheese and served with truffle potato chips. It looked delicious; I managed a couple of mouthfuls. Then we moved to Nobu, in the Hard Rock Hotel, for sushi. They had my favourite black cod marinated in white miso but I didn't have a hunger. The sushi actually was a poor call all round. It turns out Stevie's dislike of oysters stretches to a dislike of all fish other than battered cod. It's funny that his tastes haven't particularly developed in over eight years; I love sushi. Plus Laura commented that it was impossible to feel satiated after a sushi meal. Her mentioning appetites that are in need of meeting was no doubt an innocent comment but I couldn't take it as such. I kept imagining the cravings Stevie is gratifying for her and felt sick, with jealousy and pain.

We finished our gourmet tour at the MGM Grand, with satiny bread and butter pudding; even that didn't tempt me. Phil and Laura who had been drinking steadily all night devoured my portion between them. The MGM Grand Hotel offers a wide range of entertainment – anything from live lions in the reception to showgirls on the stage (who look more ferocious than the lions in many cases) but at 1 a.m. we agreed that it's time to turn in and head back to the hotel. Our motivations for this decision are diverse.

Stevie has the dress rehearsal gig tomorrow night and had started to obsess that he hadn't been conscientious like the Italian contestant. Phil wanted to go back to our room because he was drunk and woozy and hoping to get lucky again tonight. He has no idea what made me jump him last night. The unexpected nature of the encounter, which defied probability or recent patterns, has encouraged him to hope that he might get a chance to do it again. He's definitely a glass-half-full sort of guy.

Laura was clearly thinking along the same lines. I constantly caught her staring adoringly at Stevie. I don't know which bothers me most: the idea of making love with Phil or the idea of Stevie making love with Laura. Both acts ought to be part of the proper order of things. Neither ought to bother me at all. But they do. Filthy as it is to admit to myself, Stevie having groupies is annoying, Stevie having Laura is devastating.

Sex is becoming an increasingly sticky area for me, no pun intended – not at all. I'm barely having any with Phil, as I keep finding myself thinking about Stevie, and I feel like a miserable, treacherous cow for doing so. Feeling like a miserable, treacherous cow tends to ruin the mood. Obviously I'm not having any with Stevie because, what can I say? Because he's with Laura, because I'm with Phil, because the opportunity hasn't arisen? I'm beginning to hate myself as it dawns on me that the real reason is the latter.

For me, sex has always been hand in glove with love. Of course, I've had two or three loveless fucks in my time but that can be attributed to my eternal optimism overriding the blatant evidence. It's my rule, I don't go to bed with men I'm not in love with, or on the way to being in love with, or at least *expect* to be in love with by the time we share breakfast. It was important to have criteria while I was working in bars and dives otherwise there was the temptation to take home a different cute smile every time I felt lonely. I've never had sex just because I feel like sex. It's not like hunger, thirst or tiredness, it's not an appetite that demands instant gratification; not in my book.

So, I *must* be falling back in love with Stevie, mustn't I? Because all I think about is sex and him. Having sex with him. How it was and how it could be. Last night I had this amazing, pretty filthy dream about us doing it up against a wall. Predictably, when the dream started out it was the wall in the gymnasium at school. The sex was frantic, hurried and amazing. His kisses were strong and dark. Engulfing. His lips meshed into mine and we were kissing with such power and conviction I felt bruised. He scrabbled with his flies and then he sank into me. He was staring into my eyes, never losing me. Not for a second. It felt incredible, essential and right. By then the wall had changed to one here, in the hotel reception, and somewhere in my consciousness I realized that my erotic dream wasn't just a trip down memory dirty back alley, I was dreaming about doing it with him *now*. I woke myself up and Phil too as he was concerned that I was sweating and panting and looking so scared.

I've always had quite a respect for the subconscious.

I spent most of this evening trying not to think about sex with Stevie. God, you'd think it would be easy, with him dressed as Elvis.

When we got back to the hotel I told Phil I wasn't tired and I wanted to stretch my legs before going up. He looked disappointed but agreed.

After an evening spent in noisy, garish, blaring casinos, restaurants and the Strip, the sanctuary of the hotel's gardens is a relief. I amble around the modern sculptured bushes for a while, vaguely admiring the black bamboo and the slate pathways, but it only takes a couple of minutes before I stumble across an outside bar. In Las Vegas there isn't an opportunity missed to make money, to intoxicate, to entertain, entice and excite. I'd wanted to clear my head and get away from all the garish and ghastly glitter, so it doesn't make sense that I flop on to a barstool as soon as I see one.

I am all out of willpower and ask the barman for a brandy. I never drink brandy but it seems like the sort of drink you order while wandering around a Vegas hotel garden in the small hours of the morning. The bartender pours me a generous measure; generous measures are a Vegas trademark.

'Had a busy night?' I ask him. I know that right now what I need, more than anything, is to spend some time alone, with nothing other than my thoughts for company. The idea appals me, so instead I choose to trill pointlessly to a complete stranger. Hardly improving, and that's probably the attraction.

It goes two ways when talking to bar and waiting staff in the USA and part of the fun is you never know which one it will be. They will either act as though you are their long-lost sibling, who has been tragically separated at birth, and they then warmly rush to fill you in on their life story. Or, they will treat you like something smelly that they've stepped in by accident. I'm gratified that this bartender is the first type. I don't think I could have coped with someone confirming what I suspect about myself.

'Not so busy, just three wedding parties in here tonight.'

'Three?' I ask, surprised. 'Seems a lot to me.'

'At weekends we sometimes have five or six. Midweek, things are quieter. It was pleasant this evening. One of them was very touching – the bride and groom actually knew each other quite well.' The bartender gives a sort of smile that turns into a shrug.

'Right,' I reply, although clearly things are not particularly right, if the only qualifier for a 'touching' wedding is that the bride and groom know each other 'quite well'. But then, who am I to talk? I'm hardly the gold standard.

'It's not always the case, believe me,' says the bartender in a conspiratorial tone. 'Vegas has about fifty chapels, most of which are open daily from eight in the morning to midnight and twenty-four hours on legal holidays,' he tuts. 'The invitation to impulsiveness is too much for so many weak or thoughtless people. Do you know that on average three hundred and seventy-seven couples marry in Vegas every day? On Valentine's Day you can't move for white frocks. I wonder how many of them last.'

'Impossible to say or judge,' I comment.

'With respect, ma'am, that's bull.'

I don't see anything respectful about a bartender who says bull, but the guy is probably tired after a long shift.

'It's easy to judge. The majority of couples who want a quickie wedding aren't serious about each other or the commitment of holy matrimony. There's one chapel that offers rooms themed with headstone headboards and coffin bathtubs. Now what does that tell you about the sort of people who marry in Vegas?'

'Great if you're a Goth,' I point out, suddenly feeling defensive for all the Goths on earth who love each other dearly but don't want to marry in a church. An odd response because, up until this moment, I'd always thought Goths were slightly mad and a bit unhygienic.

'In the same chapel there is an Al Capone room,

with an image of a bound and gagged bellboy inside a closet. Who is that appropriate for? America's would-be murderers and masters of organized crime?'

I find the Al Capone room harder to defend so I silently sip my brandy.

'I bet a classy broad like you did it properly, surrounded by friends and family, flowers and confetti. I bet you married in a church and had a sit-down meal in a marquee. Right?'

The bartender is describing my wedding to Phil, to the letter. I could add that I glided down the aisle to Wagner's Bridal Chorus and back up it to Mendelssohn's Wedding March, with church bells pealing in the background. I had confetti and champagne, a sit-down five-course dinner, a band, a string quartet and a guy singing Sinatra tunes. At midnight we had fireworks and bacon butties. It was, in every way, a perfect wedding, a huge celebration and spectacle.

Normally, when talking to strangers – and, indeed, some of my nearest and dearest – I find the best road to follow is the one that causes the least sensation. When the old dear in the dry-cleaner's assumed that I was 'one of those high-flying exec career girls' I didn't contradict her. There are cab drivers driving around London who think I agree that every kid needs a 'thick ear now and again'. I don't, I am a fully signed-up member to the NSPCC Full Stop campaign, but I didn't have the courage to say so. I've met people at parties who think I'm interested in where to source the most divine piqué waffle bedlinen, that artichoke is an effective natural remedy for bad indigestion, or that vine weevils are a great menace for container gardens, as there are no chemical controls. It's disgusting. I'm not interested in any of these things. Phil thinks that I agree a minimum of four children would be desirable; in fact I think two would be the ideal number. I wonder how many I'll end up with?

I have never examined why I am reticent to share my beliefs and true feelings beyond telling myself that at best I am being polite and at worst I can't be bothered to explain myself to these people who have, frankly, ludicrous views and interests.

But I wonder.

I slip off my shoes and rub the aching arches of my feet. Why do women still wear stilettos? Can't someone invent something sexy and comfortable?

The truth is, my opinions are in a constant state of flux – I don't know what I believe, what I stand for or even who I am – because I am two people.

I am Belinda McDonnel, a skinny kid from Kirkspey. I wear ugly hand-me-downs or at best cheap slutty fashion clothes bought on market stalls. I live in a two-bedroom house so tiny that the front room, as my mum called it, has been converted into a bedroom for me. It's our family's grasp at respectability; the alternative would be sharing a bedroom with my brothers. The TV and the knackered dining table are crammed into the living room with my brother's bike and a settee – it's certainly a lived-in room. We don't have so much as a washing machine, the lino is sticky on the kitchen floor, the carpets threadbare and there is still a working toilet in the yard. Would anyone believe they still exist?

And I am Bella Edwards, a sophisticated woman dripping in designer labels with a wardrobe just to house my handbags and shoes. I live in an enormous fourteen-room house. The kitchen and utility rooms are fitted out with all the latest state-of-the-art mod cons – waste disposal units, under-floor heating and a fridge that dispenses ice. There are four toilets in my home. All of them are inside. They even have heated seats. Frankly, I've always thought heated seats were a step too far when it comes to luxury. It suggests to me that someone has been there just before me and stayed long enough to warm the seat. A truly unpleasant thought. One that puts me in mind of Kirkspey. I didn't tell Phil that I hated heated loo seats when he was having them installed at great expense. I wish I had.

How is it possible that I am still Belinda McDonnel? Why can't the designer labels protect me like a suit of armour, as I had hoped?

I am not prepared to answer these questions now or maybe ever. But nor am I prepared to let this smug barman make judgements and pronouncements, assumptions and assassinations, without treating him to a real account of my *legal* marriage.

I launch into my reply. 'Actually, this "classy broad" married in a registry office in Aberdeen. That's Scotland,' I tell him helpfully. 'I was wearing second-hand Levi's. They were turn-ups, very fashionable at the time, and I had Doc Marten boots with tartan laces. I did nod towards tradition in so much as I was wearing a blue blouse. It was sheer and pretty and it had belonged to my mother.' One of the few pretty things she'd ever owned. 'I carried a bunch of carnations. Bought, at considerable expense, in relative terms, from a high-street florist – not a garage – but still they were not what you'd describe as a bouquet, definitely more of a bunch. We pulled witnesses off the street. One was on the way to the dentist but said she didn't mind being late to her appointment. She was in her forties and commented that she'd never liked the dentist and rarely got invited to weddings these days. The other witness was a guy in his thirties. He was unemployed and had nothing better to do. The whole process took about ten minutes. Then we swapped addresses with the witnesses and for a couple of years afterwards we sent them Christmas cards. Our wedding breakfast was in Pizza Hut. Even back then they had an all-you-can-eat salad bar. We were students and such touches were important. We also had sticky toffee pudding. I was nineteen and very much in love.'

Despite the length of my diatribe, the bartender is rapt. He beams at me, pours two more large glasses of brandy and pushes them towards me.

'Wow, great story, lady. You've restored my faith in young and impetuous love. It's great you guys are together after all these years. Have these drinks on me.' He wanders away to polish glasses.

I'm totally bemused until I notice that an arm is round my waist. I turn, and am face to face with a grinning Stevie.

'Oh, thank God it's you,' I say. The relief is violent, I think I might faint. 'Imagine if Phil had sneaked up on me and heard all that.'

'I didn't sneak. I couldn't sleep so I wandered down here. I wasn't looking for you.' He says this with too much conviction and so I doubt him. 'Good story.'

I blush. 'I got a bit carried away.' I rerun in my head all that I've just said to the barman. It's slightly mortifying that Stevie heard me reminisce with such attention to detail. I've tried to give him the impression that I hardly remember the day. *And* if that wasn't disconcerting enough, his arm is still round my waist.

It excites me.

His touch blisters through my dress. I actually flinch. Shaking, I sip my brandy.

'The guy was having a go about people who marry impetuously. It didn't seem right to let him assume that all these marriages are a complete joke and that they'll all end in disaster.'

'Oh, but you do think ours *was* a complete joke and it *has* ended in disaster.'

'I've never said that, exactly.'

Stevie isn't going to let me off the hook, 'So, it's OK to let him assume we're still happily married over a decade later.'

I shrug, realizing that once again I have failed to be totally honest and committed to the reality of a situation. A particularly bitter pill considering I was briefly experimenting with truthful self-expression.

'I only got so far with the story. Every happy ending is dependent on where you close the book,' I comment breezily. Then I deftly turn the subject, 'You've changed out of your Elvis costume.'

'Yeah, the competition organizers borrowed it from some sponsoring supplier and it had to be returned in pristine condition. I shouldn't have risked wearing it tonight. It would have been a disaster if I'd spilt anything down it.'

'So why did you wear it?'

'I think Laura liked the buzz it caused.'

I tut. 'I think Laura found the constant presence of your groupies a real pain.' I certainly had. 'It was you who liked being the centre of attention.'

'No, really. Unlike you, Laura really digs my Elvis thing. She really gets it. Laura likes me for what I am. She doesn't care if I'm an Elvis impersonator, a teacher, a tinker, tailor, soldier, sailor. It's all the same to her.'

I hear the criticism loud and clear and choose not to say anything else on the subject – it would only come out sounding undignified. We pick up the glasses of brandy and wander towards a metal table with two chairs. Without saying anything we've tactically agreed on the table furthest away from the few remaining revellers who are noisily gathered around beer bottles and the DJ decks.

We sit under an olive tree. I know olive trees have recently become very fashionable and are found in dozens of trendy bars so it's just coincidence that we've found ourselves sitting under one but I can't help but think of the symbolic nature and I have to suppress a giggle.

'What are you grinning at?' asks Stevie.

'Nothing,' I smile and for no reason at all I playfully stick my tongue out at him.

'You can be so age twelve,' he says, but he's smiling too and I know that we're OK.

'It's lovely out here, isn't it? Such a luxury to sit out in warm air so late at night.'

'Quite good to be away from the air con and the noise too,' adds Stevie.

I totally agree with him and find I don't even have to say so. 'Have you had a fun day?' I ask.

'I liked being with you by the pool this morning,' he says.

How is it that time after time I can still forget how dangerous it is to have a conversation with Stevie? He always insists on being hideously straightforward.

'And I liked being by the pool with Laura this afternoon,' he adds.

As I said, hideously straightforward. I look away so that my eyes don't betray the hurt I feel. I shouldn't be hurt. Stevie is supposed to enjoy the company of his girlfriend. That's a good thing.

For a good thing, it hurts like hell.

'Did you like playing the casinos?' I ask.

'Fantastic laugh,' he confirms. 'You?'

'Hated it,' I reply frankly. 'My problem with casinos is that they remind me of amusement arcades – horrible places. Cheap, tatty prizes, the incessant clatter of the machines, lousy music, glowing coloured lights, and chewing gum stuck to the floor that looks like loose change. I hate it when you see drunken people scrabbling around trying to pick it up, thinking they've got lucky, but they never have – and they never will. It's anything but glamorous,' I mutter.

'You're talking about Blackpool,' says Stevie astutely.

I shuffle uncomfortably. How did he work that out? I don't want to talk about Blackpool. We never have and that's fine by me.

'Vegas is just like Blackpool,' I grumble.

'No, it's not. It's glamorous here and exciting. No one's hometown is ever glamorous.'

'It's the same hopeless hope,' I reply definitively.

Stevie sighs and gives up arguing with me. We sit silently until he quietly adds, 'This evening was difficult, though. The whole situation is killing me.'

Did he feel it too? Was he uncomfortable every time Laura touched or kissed him, the way I was when Phil lavished attention or affection on me? Did he sometimes want to turn to me and share a joke or a thought but knew that he had to gag himself or risk exposure? Did he watch the couples on the dance floor and wonder what it would be like to hold each other? He might have.

'It's a hideous, miserable situation and I wish to hell I wasn't in it. I wish you hadn't put me in it,' he clarifies.

'I'm sorry,' I say for about the millionth time.

'So you've said, about a million times.'

Inappropriately, I start to giggle.

'What are you laughing at now?'

'Just that I was thinking the same thing. I've noticed that we often think the same thing.' I don't mention or acknowledge that sometimes we disagree over fundamental and petty things too. That's not so important right now.

Stevie looks up at the black sky and sighs. 'I'm so confused, Belinda. One moment we're fine. We're friends, right?'

'Right.' I smile.

'But then suddenly, without warning, we're enemies.' He turns to me now, 'Which *are* we? What can we be?'

'I don't know,' I reply. There is another option, of course, but it's X-rated and I can't bring myself to suggest it. I reach out and squeeze Stevie's arm. But then I can't seem to move my hand away. I wait for him to pull away from me. He doesn't.

We fall back into a silence. I hope he believes it's a comfortable silence. For me, it's a silence fraught with sexual tension, which I know is wrong but feels a little like something that's right. I am staring at his mouth and thinking about kissing his lips. I'm not imagining gentle, tender kisses. I want to thrust myself hard against him. I notice that his strong, muscled arms are now tanned from the day in the sun and a bit pink at the crook of the elbow. I want to kiss him there, in the crook, I want to kiss him everywhere.

These brandies have gone to my head; now I remember why I am supposed to be off the booze.

I pull my hand away from his arm, and sit on it. Being here with Stevie is exciting; the warming trickle of brandy in my stomach, which is already melting my brain cells, is delicious and the warm summer night is a delight. It's a moment in time that, taken in isolation, is perfect. Considered on the grand scale, it's disastrous.

Time is running out for Stevie and me. This morning was borrowed time, tonight it's stolen. Somewhere, lodged in a court (whatever that means) back in London, are the papers we signed saying we want to divorce each other. In the same way that, for years, a paper sat in a registry office in Aberdeen saying we once had wanted to be married to each other. Both papers mean nothing and everything, at the same time. In two months' time a decree absolute will declare that our muddled paths are legally dissolved. And that will be that. Suddenly, I see tonight as my last opportunity to ask the questions that used to keep me awake at night, when I first upped sticks, and ran away to London.

'What pulled you to it, Stevie? How come you wanted to be an Elvis tribute act so badly?'

'So badly that I drove you away, you mean?'

He's right. Without Elvis we might have made it work. That's why I need an answer to my question. I start to retrace his history, hoping to jog his mind into offering me long overdue insight.

'You always liked Elvis, even when you were a child. You were a big fan by the time you moved to Kirkspey.'

'Definitely. Do you remember the hours we spent watching his old movies, listening to his tracks?'

'Yes.' Back then Stevie's near obsessive knowledge of and great love for Elvis had been endearing. 'You went to university—'

'Yes, and it was great.'

'But you didn't do gigs then.'

'No. I got to know lots about the Trojan wooden horse and I got to spend lots of time in the Coach and Horses.'

'Exactly my point, Stevie. I thought you were a Renaissance man. You studied music, you read *The Iliad* and *The Odyssey* in your spare time, yet still went to the pub with your mates. You got a really good degree – and then you wanted to be an Elvis impersonator.' I try, but fail, to hide my exasperation.

Stevie smiles thinly, 'Tribute act, if you please. Believe me, Belinda—'

'Bella, if you please,' I say, playing tit for tat.

'Bella, believe me, belting out a couple of verses of "Love Me Tender" is far more relevant than most of the stuff I learnt at university. Even if I'm wearing a wig and flares.'

I'm aware that he's trying to keep things light, but his jokey attitude towards his career only riles me more. 'Why can't you just fulfil your potential, be yourself?'

'That from a girl who changed her name, her haircut, her accent and home but failed to leave a forwarding address for her husband.'

Suddenly, the night air doesn't feel quite so warm. I can see his point but it doesn't stop me staring crossly at him. Indeed, it's probably because I can see his point that I'm so churlish. I notice my brandy glass is empty so I signal to the bartender, who brings us colourful cocktails. I have no idea what I'm drinking; I should probably have eaten the bread and butter pudding to line my stomach. The bartender must think so too because he places a small bowl of nuts on the table. I scoop a handful into my mouth but know they can't help me.

I breathe deeply and try to hide my discomposure.

'Can I ask *you* something, Belinda?'

'Anything,' I agree rashly.

'If I hadn't met Laura and stumbled into your life, when would you have got around to contacting me? Or were you hoping the whole messy business would just disappear?'

'The latter, I suppose.' I sigh. 'Although the situation was coming to a head. Time was ticking on.'

'Biological clock?' he asks.

I seethe. I hate it when men talk about biological clocks, or hormones, or the time of the month. They wear that supercilious expression and nod as though they understand everything. When in fact the opposite is true.

'Not mine,' I snap. 'Phil's.'

'No. You were never maternal,' mutters Stevie. He sips his cocktail, clearly oblivious to the threat of my blinding him with a colourful, paper umbrella. Our confidence and cosiness is easily threatened. 'You know nothing about me,' I bite.

'I'm your husband,' he states.

'Technically. Nothing more.' Suddenly, I want to pick up my bag and storm out of the garden back up to my room. I want to run away from this horrible creeping intimacy, this straight talking, this dangerously explorative mood. I want to run fast, my feet pounding on the pavement, over and over again, just to put some distance between us. But I stay put.

'Philip is desperate for children. It was becoming increasingly difficult to explain my reluctance. But how could I have children with him when I'd simply be inviting those new lives to join my old mess. Parents shouldn't do that. A parent's role is to sort out the messes. I knew I couldn't be legally married to you and have a child with Phil. Besides—' Do I want to go on?

'What?'

'Well, even assuming I get this bigamy thing sorted out, I'm still nervous of how adequate I'll be as a parent. I'm a bit short on role models,' I confess.

'You'll be a great mum, Belinda,' Stevie assures, with seriousness.

'Thanks,' I grin. 'You'll be a great dad.' Obviously my brain hadn't been consulted before my tongue threw out this rash statement. Stevie is glowing in the light of my compliment.

I snap my mouth shut at just about the exact moment his lips meet mine.

We kiss – for how long? I don't know – a fraction of a second or several minutes. The kiss is such a delight. It zooms past the last eight years, erasing my history, erasing my responsibilities and, oh God, erasing my morality. He *is* sex. He always was. I craved him when I was young. Ached for him on warm summer nights when I slept alone in my dad's home. The window open, letting in the sounds of the evening and the promise of a future. A breeze, that was all about promise and the question, what if? What if?

I'm not going to. I want to. Oh yes, I want to and that's bad enough, but not as bad as actually doing it. I know how he feels (firm) and how he tastes (salty, sexy). I know every curve, niche and crevice of his lovely, lovely body. And there's something else. I know that the sex we had – as good as it was – would be *even* better now. I've had other men to practise on, not loads but a few. Way back when . . . I probably got marks for energy, rather than expertise. I'm more confident about my body now – mystifying, considering my skin is not as soft and my boobs have . . . what should I say? Relaxed? But at least I now know exactly how to get the right bits to start jumping.

And let's face it; he's probably learnt a trick or two.

Oh God, we could have excellent sex. Intense and passionate sex.

'Phil,' I say, pushing Stevie away at about the exact same moment I hear him mutter, 'Laura.'

We separate and I grab my cocktail – better that than Stevie's body.

'We can't, Stevie.'

'We're married. Legally we wouldn't be doing anything wrong,' he says, articulating the loophole that has occurred to us both.

'Morally we'd stink,' I point out.

Stevie sighs. 'I'm confused about your moral code, Bella. Did you find it easy to stand at an altar and agree to marry Phil? Did you sail through that bit about "if anyone knows of any legal reason why this marriage can't go ahead" etc etc?'

'I know I'm confusing you, Stevie. I'm confused too.'

I push back my chair and unsteadily totter to my feet. I sway slightly, Stevie probably assumes that's the effect of the alcohol which is better than him knowing the truth. His kiss was the most overwhelming of my life and I think it is stamped upon me for ever.

He grabs my hand and our fingers entwine; finding each other swiftly and naturally, as though they had memories of their own.

'Why are you having such an effect on me, after all these years? If I was truly happy with Philip, you wouldn't get near me,' I mutter.

'I agree.'

'Why do I want you?'

'I'm irresistible.' Stevie wants to appear cocky and confident but it's an act. I know him: he's lost and forlorn.

'I have to go to bed.'

'Good idea.'

'*Alone*, Stevie.'

Stevie squeezes my hand, then kisses it, 'I shouldn't be thinking about you either. I should be thinking about Laura – or focusing on the competition – but you plague me. You play me. I wish I hadn't heard you talking to the barman.'

'I didn't know you were listening.'

'True enough. If you had, the last thing you'd have been was honest.' His eyes drill through any semblance of sense I possess. 'Meet me tomorrow, Belinda. We still have so much to deal with. There's so much I don't understand.'

'That's madness,' I insist, pulling my hand away from his. This was just a drunken kiss. We've overstepped the mark, yes. But it's a bungle, not a premeditated cruelty. 'I can't meet you,' I say, shaking my head.

'You owe me, Belinda. This isn't just about you. I'll be in reception at nine. I'll wait for you,' states Stevie firmly.

36. Any Day Now

Friday 9th July 2004

Stevie

Bollocks, bollocks, bollocks.

Could this possibly get any messier? What have I done? What have I said?

'Morning, gorgeous,' Laura mutters, as she opens one eye. She doesn't lift her head – she also drank a shedload last night and she's only human. She does, however, launch the widest beam and set it sailing in my direction.

I am leaning against the dressing table, as this is the point in the room furthest from the bed. I move my fingers in a feeble wave and say nothing. She widens her grin a fraction, closes her eye and drifts back to sleep. She'll assume my reticence is because I'm hungover too, or nervous about today's impending rehearsal, or that I didn't want to wake her from her drowsy slumber. Whatever conclusion she reaches, it will be generous and I don't deserve her benevolence.

Nearly every day, for several weeks now, I have been lucky enough to wake up to Laura's beam. It's a wide, very even grin and while I'm aware that it's fashionable to describe desirable women's smiles as 'cookie' or 'lop-sided', 'slow' or 'reluctant', Laura's is an absolutely straight grin that is fast and ready. She has fleshy pink lips and Hollywood-white, uniform teeth. Her parents must have spent a stack of dollars at the dentist. This morning, like all the other mornings, her smile radiates and fills the entire room. That and the blinding sunshine streaming through the window are clearly signs from God that I am a condemned man. I know that, generally speaking, sunshine and a dazzling smile from your girlfriend are seen as fortuitous but in my case I see them for what they are. Aggravators of the world's most vicious hangover, sent to spitefully suck the last drops of moisture out of my frazzled and parched brain. Timely reminders sent to nip and snarl at my malfunctioning conscience.

I've lain awake for practically the entire night when what I needed most was to sleep. Well, I needed sleep about as much as I needed a lobotomy, a kick up the derrière, to turn back time or a life swap. Sleep has to be deemed the most accessible of the above choices, and yet even that eluded me.

All night I lay awake next to beautiful Laura and thought of beautiful Belinda. Laura's long, lithe limbs were stretched out next to me and I carefully studied the wonder of her – her grace, poise, strength and athleticism. But while I could see her beauty I felt unable to enjoy it. I have betrayed her.

Some would argue that as I've failed to mention my secret marriage to Belinda, for the entire duration of our relationship, that I had already betrayed Laura on a number of occasions. Whenever I surreptitiously sneaked off to meet Belinda in some warm old pub or snug thirty-something bar, I betrayed her. Whenever I was vague about the 'significant others' in my past, I betrayed her. Whenever I fudged the details of where and when I went to university I was less than honourable. However, in my heart I had not betrayed Laura. Until last night. I believed that I was protecting her. I told myself that I was only involved in this messy subterfuge at Belinda's insistence *and* Belinda isn't some malevolent force – she's Laura's best friend. I did a pretty good job of convincing myself that keeping a secret from Laura was for her own good. After all, the secret did not relate to her, directly. And, well, if I was protecting myself a little bit – because once I'd sat through oysters and linguini at Bella's and stayed schtum, I was involved – then no harm done. What else could I do? I honestly believed that my situation was messy but not irretrievable and, significantly, not of my own making.

Until last night.

I kissed Belinda. It is impossible to fudge, to excuse, to defend or vindicate. I betrayed Laura. OK, I'd had lots to drink and I am confused. This whole *thing* is just scrambling my head. And Belinda is my wife. But, oh shit, shit. That sounds like I'm trying to fudge, to excuse, to defend or vindicate and as expected, it doesn't hold up.

I feel dirty so I slip into the bathroom and quietly start to take a shower. Well, as quiet as it is possible to be; the shower is a power shower with jets that almost blow me clean away, right down the plughole. No more than I'd deserve under the circumstances.

Do I or don't I love Belinda? I did once. Do I still?

Do I or don't I love Laura? I thought I did, I was about to tell her I did. But then I kissed Belinda.

How is it possible to think so much of two women at the same time? To want two women so much at the same time? Answer: annoyingly, it's easy. The issue is who do I want to spend my foreseeable future with? Because while having feelings for two women at the same time is feasible, it's certainly not advisable and not the sort of situation that can be allowed to endure. Bigamy is a crime and despite the precedent Belinda has set I cannot see it as anything other than morally reprehensible. Adultery – the same. I don't want to have an affair with Belinda. I don't want to cheat on Laura. But I don't want to be with the wrong woman either.

I stand with my face towards the shower faucet and let the hot jets spray and splash water on to my face. Who *is* the right woman? I had no idea that life could be so difficult. What would my mates, Dave and John, make of this? Well, John would probably take the piss: he'd insist that there is no dilemma when choosing between two hot women, that it's a win/win situation. Dave would see it as the horrible drama it is. I don't know what to think, except that I have to go to Belinda. I need some answers.

I'm not proud of what I decide to do next but I can't find a solution that would earn me a medal. This one might, at least, help me find some peace of mind. I dry and dress as quietly as possible. I write a note telling Laura that I'm going to spend the day at rehearsals. I hate lying to her but I think it's better than leaving her without any explanation and I'm talking from experience. Then I sneak out of the bedroom, gently closing the door behind me.

37. Memories

Bella

'I wasn't sure you'd turn up,' says Stevie.

'Nor was I,' I shrug.

I'm not sure I had any choice in the matter. Last night I lay awake, putting all my energy into not touching Phil. I was terrified that if I touched him, a touch would lead to a hug, a hug to a kiss, and then what? Would he be able to tell I'd kissed another man that night? Of course not. Not possible. Not feasible. But somehow believable. A terrifying thought. I don't want to hurt Phil. I've never wanted to hurt him. I've been trying to avoid that all along. That, and losing him.

Last night I repeatedly told myself I had no choice but to meet Stevie. I reminded myself that he could blow the whole situation sky-high by exposing me as the fake I am, if he so chooses. And, I also argued to myself that he has a point, I *do* owe him some more answers and further explanations; it's a miracle I've avoided giving them out so far. Finally, I want to. I can't think of a better way to spend my day. The entire position is terrifying.

'Have you eaten?' asks Stevie. He takes a sweeping glance around the hotel reception. 'We could have a pastry in the café or go to a diner.'

I shake my head. 'No appetite.' Besides, I have no

intention of hanging around where Laura or Phil might spot us. I don't have a death wish.

'Me neither. What do you want to do?'

'Something fun. Come with me.'

We walk out of the reception and step into a waiting limo. I joke with Stevie that I now believe there is no other way to travel since Adrian picked us up from the airport. Stevie looks thrilled that I'm being kind about the trip which, after all, he did win. I haven't been demonstratively appreciative, I know. I'm not really in a position to be especially gushing in my compliments.

I tell the driver to go west of the Strip, via Desert Inn Road and then out on to Industrial Road.

'Where are we going?' asks Stevie.

'Wait and see. Don't worry, I'm not taking you to one of those pay-by-the-hour hotel rooms or even to a tattoo parlour to have my name emblazoned across your chest.'

'That's a relief.' He smiles and pretends to mop his brow.

I was trying to hit a note of flippancy, in an attempt to keep the mood light, but of course I simply sounded flirty and suggestive. How is it possible to keep the mood light under the circumstances? For a start we both feel extremely uncomfortable that we are lying to our partners in order to be together and I, for one, am fighting lusciously, filthy thoughts. *Again.*

It's got to be illegal, or at least unusual, to think your husband is as sexy as I think Stevie is. He licks his lips and I practically gasp imagining him running his tongue between my legs. He stretches out his legs, casually, in front of him and I catch a glimpse of his ankle. Not an obviously provocative part of the body under normal circumstances but I have to exercise superhuman restraint, in order not to swoop down on my hands and knees and start kissing him there. I don't even like feet; I'm definitely not a toe-sucking type. I'd always thought women who fantasized about giving blow jobs in the back of limos were cheap or weird. I don't want to consciously focus on the fact that I'm currently working out the logistics of doing just that. I wonder if he's having equally erotic thoughts. I steal a sly glance and catch him grinning at me, but it turns out that we're not thinking along the same lines, because when he does interrupt the silence, it transpires he's been thinking about Kirkspey. Kirkspey is always far from my mind.

'If they could see us now.'

'Who?'

'My mum, your dad, your brothers, anyone from Kirkspey.' I shudder at the thought. Stevie is smiling affably. 'What do you think they'd say?' he muses.

'I think they'd be shocked,' I comment pragmatically. 'For a start none of them know that we've had anything to do with each other for eight years. And my family thinks I'm married to Phil. So I guess they'd be a bit surprised to see us riding in the back of a stretch limo, in Las Vegas.'

'Yeah, but besides all that stuff about who knows what and—' he starts to grin '—and who is married to whom.' How can he find that amusing? 'I bet they never thought my Elvis gigs would get us so far.'

'No. I guess not.'

This scenario is so far out of their realm of experience

that they couldn't even begin to imagine the sumptuousness, the glitter and the glitz. They could not visualize the enormous hotel rooms, the marble slabs in the lobby that have no discernible use but are purely decorative. They could not imagine riding in a limousine, dipping in a Jacuzzi or drinking cocktails in a bar. My dad wouldn't believe that Stevie was living a life that only fictional characters like James Bond are entitled to. Even the filthy underbelly, the gore attached to Vegas, the prostitutes, the drugs, the gambling addicts, would be beyond the imagination of most Kirkspey inhabitants.

'Here we are,' I say, with a beam, as we reach our destination. I'm glad to move off the subject of Kirkspey. And I'll be glad to get out of the limo. Although it has a huge interior, we were still too close for comfort in it. I need my self-control to go the distance, I'm only human, there's no sense in putting it through unnecessary stress.

'Where are we?' asks Stevie.

'Elvis-A-Rama,' I say proudly. Stevie must see that my bringing him to the Elvis museum is a treat for him.

'Really? Wow.' He grins and almost jumps out of the limo before it draws to a halt.

We're the first ones into the museum and, somewhat surprisingly, even I find it reasonably interesting. Stevie finds it fascinating. He salivates over the exhibits, working himself up to a frenzy over certain artifacts. There is a boat, an ancient Cadillac and a piano. When the curator is not looking Stevie reverently caresses the steering wheel, door handles and ivory keys. I try not to giggle as he tenderly strokes these cold objects. I also try not to feel jealous, lucky bloody piano keys.

There is a display devoted to Elvis's army career, showcasing his uniform and letters that he wrote to his manager at that time. There's a fetching red-trimmed karate robe; predictably there are a couple of rhinestone-speckled jumpsuits that Elvis wore to perform and there is a pair of blue suede shoes, which are apparently insured for one million dollars. There's a soundtrack playing, so I hum along, as I walk past countless walls plastered with movie posters and record-album covers. After about an hour and a half I'm flagging but Stevie has only just begun to pay homage. I didn't spend this long in the Louvre. I find a seat in front of a video screen and lose myself in a film with shallow plot and questionable dialogue.

I just don't get it. Stevie's enduring passion flies right over my head. Elvis was cute and talented and, from all accounts, a nice enough guy to be around, but why would you want to devote your life to looking like him and singing his songs? Why would Stevie want to do that? Stevie and tens of thousands of other people? I don't understand. I shrug and add this question to my pile of unanswered whys.

I wait as long as I can bear to, then check my watch. It's nearly midday. I congratulate myself because I've sidestepped any big talks with Stevie, I've resisted falling into his arms and avoided discussing last night when I didn't resist falling into his arms. So far so good. Also, Phil thinks I'm shopping and has no idea that I'm a bigamist, which is undoubtedly a result. So why don't I feel better or calmer?

I blame Amelie for lots of my discord. I made the mistake of calling her this morning and even though I didn't wake her this time, she was no more sympathetic or helpful than the last time I called. When I tried to explain that Phil made me feel content and secure and Stevie's kisses had sent fireworks to my heart and other less romantic parts of my body, she had tutted impatiently.

'You seem to think your husbands are there to provide answers or to complete you. It doesn't work like that. You have to be a complete being and soul before you can love properly. Phil wasn't put on this earth to make you feel secure nor was Stevie sent to make you feel wild and limitless. Why don't you work out who you are first? Think about it.'

I'm sick of her sanctimonious attitude. She's self-appointed in the role of my conscience and she's unwelcome.

'Amelie, why are you so cross? You and Ben didn't even bother to marry because you don't believe in the institution,' I'd argued.

'You do, presumably, since you've chosen that route twice. And, for the record, we did believe in integrity, loyalty and commitment.' I think she would have hung up on me at that point but I didn't give her the opportunity: Phil emerged from the bathroom so I had to cut her off.

Amelie isn't helping matters by constantly insisting that I need to think about things. What I really need is for her, or someone, anyone really, to give me some answers. I'm working against the clock here and I need help.

I stand up and go to hunt down Stevie – it's time for lunch.

There's a smart diner next door to the museum. The

menu is the same as in all other diners i.e. extensive as long as you fancy something that comes served with chips or maple syrup. As it happens, that's exactly what I fancy, so Stevie and I settle down to large burgers (his chicken, mine bean) with side orders of fries and huge, creamy strawberry milkshakes.

'Should I put something on the jukebox?' asks Stevie.

'Yes.'

'Any requests?'

'Anything but Elvis,' I say.

He must think I'm joking because he chooses 'Viva Las Vegas'. I bite my tongue. I can deal with it. How long does one track last? Three minutes, tops. We are friendly and relaxed while we talk about music, the museum and the menu. I think we can manage to stay affable – as long as we keep away from the subject of my multiple marriages.

'About last night,' says Stevie, who perhaps has not drawn the same conclusions.

'I'm not sure we have anything to say, do we?' I hope this sounds like a closing statement rather than a question.

Stevie overrules me. 'I think we do.'

'We'd both drunk too much. It's easy to do silly things when there's moonlight and . . . cashew nuts and things.' I'm not making sense.

'I see,' says Stevie. He seems reluctant to let the incident lie, but lie it must. I mean, what's the alternative? My grabbing Stevie now, climbing across the Formica table and snogging his face off? Hitching up my skirt and riding him till I'm raw?

'Have you had fun this morning?' I ask, pushing the porn-style vision from my head.

'Yeah.' I'm grateful that he's allowing me to change the subject. 'But even that's confusing, isn't it? How much fun we have together?'

So we're not changing the subject then. I try again. 'You've won a great prize, Stevie. Did I ever say congratulations?'

'No, you never did,' he says. 'You never thought I'd amount to much,' he adds. His tone is observational rather than offended or bitter.

Inwardly, I smile. 'Amount to much'; a one hundred per cent Kirkspey expression if ever I've heard one. 'I didn't think you'd amount to *enough*,' I clarify.

'Explain,' instructs Stevie.

He is sat with his elbows on the table and stirring his milkshake with a straw. As he issues his one-word instruction he is staring out of the window, seemingly concentrating on a flashing neon sign that reads: 'Life is Fragile, Handle with Care'. Like so many of those trite little sayings that you find on fridge magnets and Hallmark cards, the message suddenly seems scarily pertinent.

To most people Stevie no doubt looks the epitome of relaxed cool. But I spot the muscle at the side of his mouth twitch; what was it that he'd said about poker faces, last night? I know that Stevie is tensely sat on tenterhooks. My answer matters to him. My answer is important. I take a deep breath. He's right. I do owe him and I get the impression that he's telling me that now is the time I have to pay. I plough in.

'You were on about the people in Kirkspey earlier. The

thing is, you were all mixed up with how I feel about them. You still are.'

'Go on.'

'They're not normal and I just wanted to be normal. At one point, you seemed like an escape and I was wild about you. Then you seemed to be part of their clan and I was just . . . wild at you, I guess.'

'You've lost me. Rewind.'

'Do you want more music? I think I've enough quarters.'

Stevie sees this as the diversionary tactic it is and says no. 'Explain what you mean, Belinda, please.'

He's asking Belinda and she could never resist him.

'OK. When I was sixteen and petting heavily with you in the front room of my dad's house, you seemed like an exotic creature. You'd come to Kirkspey from Blackpool, England.'

'Blackpool? Exotic?' asks Stevie, quite reasonably confused.

'I hadn't been there then,' I mutter, more than a bit embarrassed about my appalling lack of knowledge and sophistication at the time. Was there ever such a naive girl?

'Loving you, having sex with you, seemed rebellious, unruly and promising.' I take a sip of my milkshake. 'For the first time since my mum had died I felt excited about my life and, specifically, about my future. I hadn't even thought of university until you assumed that I'd be going.'

'I know, your dad hadn't suggested it,' comments Stevie.

'You know that my dad rarely spoke to me at all.'

'And you know that fishermen are very superstitious about women,' says Stevie. 'It wasn't personal.'

It felt personal. Stevie is trying, as he always did, to defend my father's indifference towards me. I shrug, and don't bother to point out I wasn't some remote unlucky woman, I was his daughter. It's an old wound; I'd rather not pick at the scar tissue.

'You paid me attention when no one else did. You opened my mind. You had all these ideas and plans and hopes. I thought that we'd help each other to scramble out of Kirkspey and that you'd help me shake off the loneliness and sense of otherness that I'd always carried.'

I pause and half-heartedly pick up a chip, dip it into ketchup, but haven't the required keenness to get it to my mouth. We both know that when I say 'always' I mean since my mum died.

'When we were at university together you helped me fit in. I just wanted to be normal, like all the other normal middle-class students. You were much more confident than I was.' I pause and then ask, 'Do you remember we used to sit up all night reading poetry? Do you think my father's ever done that?'

I give Stevie a moment to call up my father's image. Mr McDonnel, a flat-capped, no-nonsense Scotsman known for his gigantic size (six foot four, and eighteen stone, naked, not that anyone ever wanted to even imagine the man naked, he was scary enough in his clothes). He's a hard, dour fisherman. He breaks chickens' necks with his bare hands. He courted my mum by taking pounds of knock-off black pudding to her mother's house on a Saturday teatime; his brother worked in a butcher's.

I remember my mum relaying this fact with such pride to a young me. I thought the pride was misplaced back then and I still think so now. Of course, Stevie would not be able to imagine my dad opening a poetry book as part of his seduction technique. I don't want to imagine my parents' coital act at all, but if I have to I imagine the act was silent, perfunctory, distinctly unflowery.

'But then we married and all you wanted to do was go home and tell everyone.' I sigh because I feel as defeated and exasperated as I did eleven years ago.

'Isn't that the usual thing to do when you get married? Isn't that the *normal* thing, Little Miss I-Aspire-To-Be-Normal?' asks Stevie. And now he does sound a bit peeved. Lost, maybe? Confused?

'Well, we hadn't been normal, had we? We'd eloped. And the "normal" I aspire to is hosting dinner parties in Wimbledon, eating meals that require a cluster of knives and forks and discussing current affairs. Not three nights a week in the pub, big night out on Saturday when you get sausage and chips at the chippie and eat them as you stagger home. I didn't want to spend my life eating fish fingers off a tray on my lap, while watching TV. I didn't want to wear a nylon tracksuit and look forward to Christmas when you'd buy me a piece of jewellery from the Argos catalogue.'

'You're a snob.'

'Maybe. But I'm thirty years old now and I have to accept myself and my faults or just give up the ghost.'

I could let the discussion drop. Stevie would for evermore think of me as a snooty cow who's ashamed of her background. He'd probably hate me a little bit more but I wouldn't have to delve any deeper. Or (the scary alternative) I could push through this awkwardness and try to explain the small print. I could be courageous and tell Stevie that my discontent was not about the lack of money but about something far more obscure and defining.

'Kirkspey makes me feel limited,' I explain. 'Hemmed in. Underused. They don't expect much from me and when I'm with them I'm not much.'

'They?'

'My family, my childhood friends, even the teachers. They didn't expect much from me or anyone else for that matter. No one from Kirkspey believes anyone from Kirkspey can be anything at all. They are dead before they've lived. You didn't see them as I did. It became impossible for me to imagine our life together.'

'You saw me as one of them? A deadbeat?' he asks, with a perception I could have done without.

'Sometimes.' He looks hurt and drains his milkshake. 'Not always. But more and more often towards the end. You ignored my suggestions to move down south.'

'We couldn't afford it.'

'The day you said we could move back to Kirkspey and live with your mum was particularly bleak.'

'My mum's a lovely lady,' said Stevie, understandably defensive.

'She is, but it would have been such a terrible leap backwards for me.'

'But there was work there.'

'In the post office!'

'A steady income. I thought that was what you wanted.'

'I still don't know what I want.'

But even back then I knew what I didn't want. I didn't want my children to grow up in a house where the white paintwork is yellowed with cigarette smoke and people use the loo as an ashtray so there are always stray fags floating in the water. I didn't want a household where no one bothers to say 'excuse me', 'pardon' or 'what?', let alone knows whether it's to negotiate body space, beg forgiveness for an embarrassing bodily function or ask if a question can be repeated in a louder voice. I didn't want my daughters to be considered unlucky. I didn't want my sons to feel the need to mindlessly beat other women's sons, just for something to do on a Friday night. It all seemed pagan. I just wanted things to be different.

'And now?' asks Stevie.

'Now, what?'

'Now do you see me as one of them? Do you see me as someone who would want to hold you back? Limit your potential?'

'For fuck's sake, Stevie, you are an Elvis impersonator. You wear jewellery and flares. What makes you think you could ever show your face in Kirkspey local again? You're not one of them. I was wrong about that.'

Stevie smiles, a broad forgiving grin. He recognizes my backhanded compliment. His pleasure encourages me to be kinder.

'You've done really well, Stevie. I wish I'd had teachers like you when I was at school. And the Elvis thing's turned out OK, hasn't it? Don't get me wrong, I still fundamentally disbelieve in what you are trying to achieve. Why be an imitation when—'

'Stop, stop, quit while you're ahead,' Stevie laughs. 'Please don't pour any cold water on the compliment. Leave me with the warm glow.'

We smile at one another and I feel a great sense of relief. Telling Stevie how I felt, and why I acted as I did, is a stupendous release. I had not realized that I was so burdened by guilt and shame until now. Now I feel a tiny bit calmer. Stevie's relationship to me is a little bit straighter and clearer: he's an ex and I've just articulated all the reasons why he's an ex. I feel such a surge of wellbeing that I stretch out my hand and grab his. I squeeze it tightly, hoping he'll understand how I feel. I hope that somehow he sees that there has been a monumental shift.

'About last night, Belinda.'

'Do we have to talk about it?' I ask. I mean, one step at a time.

'I think we do,' says Stevie who is obviously keen for quantum leaps.

'I'm so sorry, Stevie, but I don't want to.' It terrifies me that last night Stevie kissed me, and not only did I kiss a man other than my husband but I kissed a man who is my other husband.

And I liked it.

Very much.

I don't want to lose Philip but I can't quite let Stevie go. Of course my actions are stupendously flawed. Kissing Stevie is a direct route to losing Phil, and signing decree absolute papers is the sort of thing you do when you are letting go. I can't have both men but will one of them ever be enough?

'*I* need to, Belinda. I'm totally thrown. Here's the thing. Last night Laura looked sensational. She looked more—'

'More beautiful than I did.' I help him out. Of course she did, that had been my plan. I didn't want him to notice me because I knew I was unlikely to resist the onslaught of his attention.

'Different. She always looks lovely but last night she was beautiful. And she's easier going than you. She's not married to someone else. She's not even married to me, for God's sake. And yet in the garden all I wanted was you.' Stevie pulls his hand out of mine and his head sinks into his hands. For one really awful minute I think he might cry. 'I didn't want to fall in love with you again. But it's you. It's always been you. But then . . . it can't be you because although we're married, you're off limits. We're getting divorced.'

The pain and pleasure of hearing Stevie say this explodes inside my head and heart simultaneously. It's a rush of emotions and I'm unable to fathom which is dominant and where the feelings were launched from. Damn, just when I was making some progress. Is it as clear-cut as my head fighting my heart? I don't think so. I think my heart is fighting a savage civil war and my head is a barbarous, invading foreigner. I rush round the table and bend down to wrap his sad bulk in my arms.

Then, when I think things cannot possibly get any more fraught and confused, I hear a familiar voice boom, 'Hello, my loves. Who would have bloody believed it? After all these years, who would have thought it?'

38. Devil in Disguise

Stevie

The situation is out of my control and even out of the seemingly all-governing control of Bella Edwards – because the secret is no longer *our* little secret.

In vivid technicolour he lumbers through the diner towards us. He's beaming at the serendipity of our meeting; Belinda and I only see the face of the Grim Reaper.

'Bloody hell, me loves. Stevie, me lad! Belinda! I wouldn't have known you, lass. You've gone skinny. How bloody brilliant to see you both.'

Neil Curran slaps me on the back, hugs Belinda and then, in a rare moment of northern man showing affection, hugs me too. Belinda and I rise from our compromising position and accept the hugs but our tongues freeze. Neil Curran, never the most observant of men, doesn't notice our silence.

'How many years must it be now?' he asks. 'Six? Seven?'

'Eight,' mutters Belinda. I feel very sorry for her. There's no opportunity to pull on her poker face. The expression she's wearing shows that she's completely distraught and out of options.

'And is that a wedding ring I see?' laughs Neil, grabbing hold of Belinda's left hand. 'Nice.' He lets out a low and long whistle, 'A carat. You must have done well for yourself, Stevie. All of that off an Elvis tribute act's salary? I'm impressed.' Neil's vulgar reference to the cost of Belinda's ring is not meant to be offensive; it's supposed to be the opposite. Of course, under the circumstances it's pretty vile. I thought I'd stopped being bitter a long time ago that Belinda rarely wore my plain gold band.

'Any kiddies?'

'No', Belinda and I chorus quickly. I look at her, waiting for a signal as to what we should do next. She struggles to take control of the situation by turning the conversation away from us and focusing on Neil. I suppose, the less we say about ourselves the fewer lies we'll have to tell.

'So, Neil, Neil Curran,' she repeats his name and – credit where it's due – she does a plausible impression of being pleased to see him and overwhelmed by the coincidence of meeting him. The latter sentiment requires less acting talent, of course. 'After all these years you haven't changed a bit,' she says, turning on the charm. If I remember correctly, she never actually liked the man. She thought he was a slimy tosser. 'What are you up to nowadays?'

'Still the same stuff, Bel-Girl.' Belinda shrivels a fraction on hearing the nickname he'd given her several years back. I've always thought it was rather witty on a number of levels – she always hated it. 'That's right, same stuff. It's in the blood, isn't it? Elvis, showbiz the whole shebang. It's in y' blood. You know that, with your Stevie. Still doing the circuit after a decade. Bet you didn't imagine that way back when?'

'No,' says Belinda, drily. 'So, are you here for the Greatest European Tribute Artist Convention and

Competition?' Somehow she manages to inject enthusiasm into the question.

'Of course. I'm the compère. I saw the list of finalists and your name, Stevie. But I wasn't sure it was you, lad. Common name, Stevie Jones, might have been one of a number,' says Neil. 'You haven't been so big on the UK scene for quite some time now, have you, Stevie? Didn't know what you were up to. Have you been earning your cash abroad? This your comeback gig?'

'Something like that,' I mutter.

'Very appropriate, lad. The King himself did exactly the same thing in Vegas on July the thirty-first, in nineteen sixty-nine. He performed at the Hilton, an off-Strip hotel that depended on the showroom as its major draw. Hundreds were turned away almost every night, even though there were two shows. One at eight in the evening and another at midnight.'

I know everything Neil is telling me about Elvis and he probably knows that but he likes the sound of his own voice far too much to shut up. Besides, he's clearly had a few too many already and makes the mistake most drunks make: he thinks what he has to say is fascinating. I tune out and spend a few moments in unprofitable panic worrying about the things I've just said to Belinda, the fact that last night we kissed and the fact that someone from our past is here, very much in our present. I look at Belinda and I figure that she's doing the same. She's alabaster white.

'Have you had a flutter?' he asks.

'Small one,' I confirm.

'What about you, Bel-Girl? I'd have you down as a bit

341

of a secret gambler. The quiet ones are always the worst.' Neil nudges me in the ribs.

Belinda stares at him, clearly stunned that he has made such an accurate appraisal of her character. She may hate gambling on the tables and slots but he's right, she's the biggest risk-taker I know.

'Have a go on the slots, little lady. That's my tip. The three-coin jackpot often pays a hundred and fifty per cent of a two-coin win. Theoretically costing a quarter of a dollar per play. The trick is, Bel-Girl, to know that they only pay out substantial sums if two or three coins are deposited instead of one. But, and here's the rub, less than a quarter of slot players play with more than one coin at a time. That's knowledge for those in the know, that is.' He winks at her, she doesn't respond and I doubt she appreciates the tip. 'It's grand bumping into you. It will be just like old times tomorrow. Best of luck to you, Stevie. Best of luck, lad,' says Neil, who always had a habit of repeating a sentiment several times.

'Thank you,' I stutter. If ever a man needed luck . . .

'Well, we need to get going,' says Belinda, signalling frantically to the waitress for the bill. She knows Neil Curran well enough to guess that he could keep chatting all afternoon; our participation in the conversation would not be required. 'Stevie needs to try his costume on. We don't want to be late for the dress rehearsal.'

'Oh, yes. We're taking it all very seriously. The rehearsal's an event in itself. Ticketed, you know,' says Neil, proudly.

'I guess that's so the organizers can make twice as much, is it?' asks Belinda.

'Aye.' Neil smiles, 'My idea.' He doesn't seem to hear her dig. She was forever complaining that the organizers of these events were exploitative and the prizes weren't up to much. She could never see the fun in just being part of it.

'I helped find a number of the sponsors too, mind,' adds Neil. A northern man, in his fifties, who isn't shy about his canniness with money. If he'd been born in the south, as likely as not Neil Curran would have been running a cutting-edge advertising agency or made a fortune as a City trader.

'This bash has cost a bob or two with every finalist bringing three friends.' And then he asks the question I didn't want to answer in this lifetime, 'Who did you bring with you, if you haven't bairns?'

I don't think the truth – my girlfriend and Belinda's other husband – would make appropriate small talk so I'm grateful that Belinda takes control.

She kisses Neil's cheek.

'Really fantastic to see you,' she lies. 'We'll leave you to your lunch and er . . .' She glances at the booth that Neil emerged from; it's littered with empty beer bottles but he's eating alone. 'And er . . . your beer,' she adds, as she grabs my hand and starts to lead me away. She appears every inch the devoted Elvis-wife, who sees to it that I leave plenty of time to style my quiff before big gigs, sews sequins on my costume, spends hours on the Internet sourcing the most authentic gold glasses available, that sort of thing. Exactly the type of wife Belinda did not want to be. 'See you at the rehearsals, tonight, I expect,' she calls over her shoulder.

'I'll be there, lass. You can count on me. Goodbye.'

We pay the bill at the counter and then leave the diner. Belinda manages to keep smiling until we are safely in a taxi, then she immediately lets go of my hand as though it is scalding her and rounds on me like Attila the Hun.

'Fuck, Stevie, what have you done now?' she spits, in an angry whisper.

'Me?' I'm more than surprised.

'Didn't you check to see if you knew any of the personnel running the competition?'

I feel stupid. There's an information pack in my room with brief biographies of the competitors, the other entertainment acts and the compère. I hadn't read it.

'This is all your fault,' says Belinda emphatically and somewhat unfairly.

'*My* fault?'

'It was you who brought us here,' she snaps angrily.

'Oh, I'm so sorry,' I mutter sarcastically. 'But you weren't forced to accept the freebie holiday, you could have said you had a previous engagement.'

'I wish I had,' she barks.

Hell, of course this was always going to go tits up. How could I, of all people, have fallen for the pseudo-sophistication of Bella Edwards when I knew it was just Belinda McDonnel in a posh frock. Belinda never had the luck to get away with anything as conniving as this. Belinda was the kid in class who always got caught when she copied her homework, the kid who missed the hockey goal on an important penalty point, the kid whose mum died of lung cancer. How did she manage to get away with bigamy for this long with luck like hers?

Bickering isn't going to help.

'Bloody hell, Belinda, what are we going to do?' I have no idea why I've asked her. She's hardly been a leading beacon when it comes to good ideas and foolproof plans to date, but then I am struggling for alternatives.

'You'll have to pull out of the competition.'

'What?' I'm astounded.

'There's no alternative. He thinks we're married.'

'We are.'

'Be serious, Stevie.'

Belinda has disappeared. The woman who wrapped her arms around me and wanted to comfort me in the diner, just ten minutes ago, recedes in front of my eyes and instead Bella, the I-will-survive queen, comes to the forefront. In my head she is wearing one of those T-shirts that read 'It's All About Me'.

'If you go ahead with the show, Laura, Phil and I will be in the audience. Neil's bound to come over to our table after the show and he'll let the cat out of the bag.'

'Well, you and Phil don't have to come to the competition, we might get away with it.'

'We won't,' says Belinda. 'Things are getting out of hand.' I'm not sure if she's referring to the unfortunate meeting with Neil Curran or our snog last night.

'Promise me you'll pull out,' she says.

'Don't ask me to do that.'

'I *am* asking. I'm pleading.'

'I can't do that, Belinda. This means too much to me.'

'As much as I mean to you?' she demands. I pause for a moment and wonder how I can explain.

Eventually I mutter, 'You're not mine.'

'Just a few minutes ago you said you were in love with me. Was that just something to say at the time, to increase your chances of getting your hand down my knickers, or did you mean it?'

A number of things go through my mind. Whether I've ever had even the slightest chance of getting my hand down her knickers is, I'm ashamed to admit, one of the thoughts. The others are a little more pragmatic as I struggle with the nub of the question. Did I mean it when I said I loved her? And, if I did, how much am I prepared to do in the name of love?

'I think I meant it,' I say weakly.

Not exactly impressive, I know. Not the sort of fighting talk that wins the lady. I watch Belinda struggling with indignation and common sense. I realize she's probably heard more romantic propositions but I don't want to say anything I might regret. Anything *more* that I might regret.

'Sort it out, Stevie,' she says, and then she tells the taxi driver to stop.

'But, lady, you're nowhere near the Mandalay Bay,' says the driver.

'I can walk a few blocks. I need to shop,' she tells him. Then she turns to me, repeats her instruction, 'Sort it out,' and flounces out of the car and in the direction of an enormous shopping mall.

I stay in the taxi and as we edge through traffic on the Strip, I ask myself, can I sort it out?

Neil Curran is a loud, diehard compère who, in another lifetime, had a stand-up act at seaside resorts such as Blackpool and Yarmouth. We got to know him when

I was trying for the Greatest European Tribute Artist Convention and Competition in 1996. Funny that he should be compèring the competition this year as he did on the night that Belinda did her bunk. Of course, Belinda would argue that this isn't so much a coincidence as indicative of the fact that the job of a tribute artist is small-time and the circles I mix in are small too. She won't accept, or even acknowledge, that the Elvis tribute industry is massive. Facts aren't going to get in her way.

The mini-drama that ensued after Belinda walked out was the talk of the town for several days and the talk of the circuit for ... well, longer than I was prepared to keep track of. Belinda doesn't know, she's never asked, but I did not win the King of Kings title that night in Blackpool. I did not even compete.

We weren't having a good night, or a good year, come to that. I'm not a bloody fool, I knew that much. We were forever rowing about our secret marriage, our lack of cash and where and how we should best earn our livings. Even so, nothing could have prepared me for what she did that night.

I will never forget the humiliation as I sat at the table, nursing a warm pint and a glass of crap white wine, waiting for her to return from the loo. After twenty minutes I sent someone to look for her, I was concerned, not worried. I thought she must have an upset stomach or something. I became more than concerned, more than frenzied with anxiety in fact, when she wasn't in the Ladies, or anywhere else in the hotel.

Neil kept insisting that there was nothing to worry about and that the show must go on but I couldn't do it.

It was obviously serious. Your wife doesn't go to the Ladies and then just forget to come back.

How could she have left me on the most important night of my career to date? How could she think that was an acceptable way to end a relationship? A marriage. There wasn't even a note. Nothing. Zero. Zilch. Diddly-squat. Fuck all.

I have never felt lonelier than I felt that night; the night I slept alone in the grotty B&B, on a hard narrow bed. Blackpool is my hometown and while my mum was still living up in Kirkspey at that time, I had other relatives – aunties, uncles, cousins – who I could have called on. Any one of them would have happily loaned me a bed and even made me a fry-up the next day, but I stayed put. I slept in scratchy sheets, in a room with malfunctioning central heating because I thought – I hoped – that she might come back to me. Her clothes were gone but it didn't have to mean she had indisputably, literally quit. I told myself that maybe she'd get as far as the coach station and then she'd find out there wasn't a bus to Edinburgh until the next day so she'd come back to the B&B. We'd talk about what was wrong and we'd put it right. It might be OK. It didn't have to be a big deal.

She didn't come back to the B&B nor was she waiting for me in our flat when I returned to Edinburgh. I will never forget – and God knows I've tried to – the wave of fear, panic and then unadulterated terror that swept over me when I opened the door to our flat and there it was – nothing. Total and complete nothingness. No letter. No missing possessions, no trace, no clues, no reasons, no explanations.

I contacted the police. I told them it was possible my wife had been abducted; neither they nor I believed that to be the case. They added her name to a long list of people who had done a 'Reginald Perrin' as they called it and said they'd check the hospitals. But as she was an adult and there were no signs of foul play there was little they could seriously be expected to do.

No signs of foul play? Even if Belinda had left of her own free will and no crime had been committed, the foul play quota was still off the scale. What she had done to me was so intensely cruel and profoundly wicked that it was categorically unforgivable. That's what I told myself, *unforgivable*. Then I spent weeks, months, and eventually years thinking of ways to forgive her.

Nothing comforted or helped me. Belinda would probably laugh if I ever tried to explain to her that even Elvis Presley's music failed to console me in those bleakest months. I didn't think he'd suffered as much as I had. I didn't think he'd ever been so totally humiliated.

For ages Belinda had been trying to get me to give up Elvis. It was ironic that her departure achieved what she had longed for, and yet she never knew it. My greatest love had stolen the joy I had in my other great love. It appeared that one could not exist without the other. Not for me. For several years I couldn't even listen to an Elvis song. I hated the man, or at least the music. If ever I was in a shop and an Elvis track drifted through the sound system, I would leave the shop. I've walked out of quite a number of karaoke bars and wedding receptions in my time. I thought it was meaningless pap and even 'Heartbreak Hotel' and 'My Baby Left Me' did not scratch the surface of agony at being so unceremoniously binned.

After about four weeks, she sent me a postcard so that I knew she was alive – and that she didn't feel alive near me.

For some time I thought I was rubbish, crap, leftovers. I endlessly mulled over the self-indulgent, self-destructive questions that all dumpees ponder, regardless of gender. I found the answers a year and a half later, after I'd been travelling abroad for some time. What did I do to deserve this? Nothing. What is wrong with me? Nothing. Why would she treat me like this? Madness.

Look, it's all water under the bridge now. But, I'm just saying at the time it was hard. Granite.

When I came back to the UK I decided to study for a PGCE so I could teach music. It took a further two years before I could let Elvis back into my life.

But when he returned, he returned with a vengeance. My music had matured. I thought as much and others confirmed it to be the case. I had more to put into the lyrics because loss has a whimsical way of making some people bigger. Having loved and lost was good for my art – much better than good old-fashioned happiness or contentment. Although, to this day, I'd have preferred to be a 'not bad' tribute act with a wife and kids at home, rather than a 'sensational' one with a different cutie from the crowd in my bed each night. I guess I'm just an old-fashioned guy at heart.

The thing is, I hankered after winning the heats and the trip away to Vegas but I covet and crave winning the final competition, with an undignified longing that borders on an obsessive need.

Of course, I don't believe I can turn the clock back. It will never be January 1996 in Blackpool again. I will never have the opportunity to say to Belinda, 'Don't go to the loo. Talk to me, tell me what's wrong.' I cannot change the sequence of events that followed that fateful trip to the Ladies. Events that cascaded into the casual heap that – for want of a better term – I call my life. However, if I compete and win this time, I might just be able to jump-start my life again and put myself back on track. I might regain some dignity.

I threw the competition for her once. And I threw my life away too. But I won't do it again.

I am going to go to the rehearsal and I am going to be good. Seriously, intensely good. I am going to be the King of Kings European Tribute Artist Act 2004. Belinda McDonnel and Bella Edwards will have to find a way to live with it.

I sneak into my hotel room and pick up my costume and leave again without being spotted by Laura. I leave her tickets for tonight's dress rehearsal show and a note telling her I'm missing her. Which is only part of the story.

I catch the monorail and as I hop on board it crosses my mind, what am I thinking of? Do I really believe that winning the competition would win me back some dignity when I consider that I have wrapped my arms around two women in twenty-four hours? While I am determined to attend the rehearsals and enter the competition I know that to sing or not to sing is not the difficult question. And probably, for that reason alone, it's the question I decide to focus on.

39. Stuck On You

Laura

'Can I get you another drink, Laura?'

'No, I'm all right, ta, Phil. I don't want to start on the turps just yet.'

'So what was that vodka and tomato juice?' He points to the empty glass on the table next to me.

'Hair of the dog.'

'Fair enough.' He lies back on his sun lounger, clearly unprepared to drink alone but I can't keep him company today, even to be polite.

'Just how much did I drink last night?' I ask Philip, as I reach for my sun lotion and slap a dollop of factor fifteen on to my thighs. It's the third time I've reapplied cream in about half an hour. I'm not thinking clearly.

'About as much as me.' He grimaces.

'So, too much is the easy answer then.'

Normally I can hold my own against Phil and I never have to drive the porcelain bus. But Lord knows, I'm thirty-two not twenty-two and I really think I'm getting a tiny bit long in the tooth for experimenting with cocktails that are the same colour as my mouthwash.

Philip and I pass a comfortable couple of hours lolling next to the pool, having a bit of a yarn about various hangover cures. He favours a large breakfast, I prefer popping a couple of painkillers. We give both methods a go as desperate times call for desperate measures. We also try hair of the dog, sleep and lots of good old-fashioned glugging of mineral water. By three o'clock I can give a reasonable impression of a fully functioning human being. I put down my novel and announce as much to Philip.

'I'm feeling better too,' he confirms. 'Which is bad news, really, because by tonight I'll have forgotten how awful I felt this morning and I'll do the whole thing all over again.'

'Not me. I'm taking it easy tonight. I want to feel tip-top tomorrow for Stevie.' I beam at Philip. I love the role of supporting girlfriend; it's a novelty.

'Do you think he has a good chance of winning the title?'

'Of course,' I say instantly and loyally. Then I pause to consider a more reasoned response. 'Well, I haven't seen any of the other competitors perform, but he's brilliant – you've seen him.'

'I was very impressed,' smiles Phil. 'But they all must be good for them to have got this far,' he adds cautiously. I know he's trying to temper my expectations.

'I know the standard of entertainment must be high. They are charging thirty bucks entry just for the dress rehearsal tonight.'

'What's the difference between tonight's show and the final tomorrow?'

'None as far as the contestants are concerned. They have to sing the same two songs at both shows. But tomorrow there will be warm-up acts, showgirls and judges.'

Phil is squinting against the sun. 'Being part of something so big is impressive, isn't it?'

'What is?' asks Bella, interrupting our conversation. She's suddenly hovering in front of our loungers, blocking my sun.

'Hi,' Phil and I chorus. 'We were talking about Stevie and the competition.'

Bella scowls. She is so not impressed with Elvis tribute acts and nothing anyone can say will change her mind.

'Where have you been all day?' I ask, changing the subject. I really haven't the energy to hear her bad-mouth tribute acts, indirectly pouring scorn on Stevie.

'Shopping.'

'Where are your bags?' Phil and I ask in unison again. I'm pretty sure the same reasoning does not motivate our curiosity. I'm keen to see the fabulous stuff she'll have bought. Phil will be worrying about his credit-card bill.

'I didn't find anything I liked,' says Bella.

'Nothing?' I'm stunned.

'You've been shopping all morning and most of the afternoon and you haven't bought a single thing?' asks Phil. He can't believe his ears. Or his luck.

'That's right.' Bella drops into the sun lounger next to him. 'I think I'll go and change into my swimsuit and take a dip,' she says. But she doesn't make a move. Instead she waves to a waiter and orders an orange juice.

'Still not drinking?' I ask.

'No.'

'Detoxing?'

'Hmmm,' she murmurs but she doesn't tell me what programme she's on.

'Very sensible,' I comment. 'I felt as rough as a badger's arse all morning.'

Actually, I find Bella's sudden sober behaviour rather irritating. It's as though she's determined to have as little fun as possible on this holiday. Also, it's embarrassing that she can remember more than me about my singing 'My Way' in the bar at the MGM Grand last night. What possessed me? Daft question, lots of alcohol possessed me. When I'm sober I can hold a tune; I'm not so confident about my abilities when I'm under the influence.

'Are you excited for Stevie, Laura?' asks Phil.

'Yes, very,' I pause. 'Well, mostly. A little bit of me is dreading the shows,' I confess.

'Are you worried he'll be disappointed if he doesn't win?' enquires Phil sympathetically.

'He'll win,' I say with a confident grin. I'm a big one for positive thinking. 'No, it's not that.' I sigh and then admit, 'I'm getting a bit fed up of the groupies. I found their constant presence a little overwhelming last night.' I've been waiting for Bella's return to air my grievances, but I put on my sunglasses because I'm not sure I can cope with even her seeing my eyes as I say what I need to say. 'I can't put my finger on it but last night we had all the ingredients to have a stupendous time and yet the evening was more . . . fair to middling.'

'I thought you were having a brilliant time,' says Phil, clearly hurt.

'Oh, Phil, don't get me wrong. I loved the venues you picked, the food was delicious.' I turn to Bella, 'And please don't think I'm undervaluing your generosity because the dress is stunning. I love it.'

Bella waves my comments away and stares back out to the pool. She's intently watching a group of kids horse about – pushing and splashing one another.

'But that's my point. We're in Vegas, I was with my best mates in all the world, wearing the most gorgeous dress I've ever worn . . .'

'You did look hot,' confirms Philip.

That's the kind of interruption I like. 'Yet at times I felt Stevie gently drift away from me.'

'Rubbish,' says Phil, who knows nothing about these things.

Bella, who knows everything about these things, stays silent. I continue, 'It felt a bit like discovering your new Louis Vuitton handbag is an imitation. One moment you think it's the most fab thing on earth, the next it's slightly shaming. It's the same bag but you can't carry it around with the same swagger when you know it's not the genuine article. Last night Stevie was mostly attentive, kind, funny and considerate but on occasion, without any perceivable provocation, he became distant, distracted, discouraging.'

'Nonsense,' says Philip again. 'If he is at all distracted it's probably because the big competition is coming up tomorrow. He's just nervous, right?'

I want to believe this so much. Too much.

The thing is, and there is no way I can say this in front of Phil, last night Stevie did not want to come to bed with me. Despite my peony dress. Hasn't he read the script? Cinderella gets to go to the ball in a pretty gown, the prince falls in love with her and they live happily ever after. I'd make do with the modern equivalent. Cinderella gets to go to the ball in a pretty gown, the prince falls in lust and can't keep his hands off her. After several months of hot sex they move in together because they can share the washing-up and it cuts down on phone bills. Some would think it's a sad day when even your daydreams take on such a practical skew but I'm more comfortable with realistic aspirations. The days of dizzy dreaming are long gone for me. Either way – Stevie hadn't read the script. Last night he walked me to our room, came in, changed out of his Elvis costume then made up some story about wanting to clear his head.

Was I born yesterday? I've always believed that no man turns down a warm bed unless he has another waiting. Is that very paranoid of me, just a little bit paranoid or sound judgement?

'Last night he sneaked off at some ridiculously late hour. He said he had this pre-gig lucky-habit thingy to do. He had to have a walk late at night and do some voice exercises. He said I couldn't go with him because he'd be self-conscious about doing tongue twisters in front of me. I'm not convinced. Could it be true?'

'Yes!' says Bella, with huge conviction. 'Creative types do have their good-luck routines and funny rituals. I once read that Mariah Carey insists on having Labrador puppies in her dressing room before every performance.'

I instantly feel better. For about a moment.

'Look over there.' I hiss and nod my head sidewards in the direction of a skinny, toned blonde, one of the groupies who had practically sexually assaulted Stevie last night. Right now, she is massaging sun oil into some other guy who just happens to have a quiff and is wearing large gold sunglasses.

'She's one of those hussies from last night. Look at her – she's as good as having sex on a sun lounger.'

'Don't be silly,' says Bella. But she is straining to see over Phil's shoulder.

I turn just in time to see the hussy whip off her bikini top. She is uncomplicated sex on a plate. A fabulous dish, most men would agree.

'That could have been Stevie,' I screech.

'But it's not,' points out Phil, calmly.

'Those women don't even care which Elvis they get to shag!' I yell indignantly.

'You don't have to worry about Stevie.'

'Of course I do, Philip. He's a man. Be honest! If you were single and you were offered no-strings-attached sex, would you turn it down?'

'Stevie is not single,' says Philip. 'He's seeing you. And, for the record, yes, I might turn it down. Men are not all led by their penises, despite what popular culture would have you believe.'

'Under what circumstances would you say no?' I ask, wanting to see a glimmer of hope.

'Well, if the lady in question was nuts or ugly, then I'd pass.' Philip takes a sip of his water, he clearly thinks he's being rather noble. I'm not so sure. But then, I'm not thinking straight about anything much.

Am I being ridiculous? This morning I lay pretending to be asleep as my boyfriend sneaked around the bedroom, getting showered and dressed as quietly as possible. At one point it was obvious he had lost something. I guessed it was his wallet and I knew it was in the top drawer of the dressing table, I'd watched him put it there the night before when he finally returned from his walk and practising his voice projection. I'd pretended to be asleep then too. Stevie searched in his jacket pocket, his jeans pockets and his bedside drawer before he found the wallet. Why didn't I ask what he was looking for and point him in the right direction to save him several minutes of panic? The answer is: I was scared.

I did not want to talk to Stevie this morning because I am scared of what I think he has to say. I don't want to hear it.

'I'm not sure Stevie's good for me,' I say.

I don't mean this. I'm being dramatic. I always feel blue after I have had a skinful. I think Stevie is remarkably good for me. But I care so much that I'm madly jealous.

'I've started to watch other women all the time. I notice how they wear their jeans, if they have jutting-out hip bones, if they have shining hair, clear skin, big tits. I couldn't admit this to anyone other than you two but I'm almost overcome with curiosity and jealousy. A consequence of my relationship with Oscar, no doubt. It seems foolish to trust a second time but then it would be more foolish never to trust again, wouldn't it? I'm losing my mind. The truth is I am so head over heels into him, you know? I don't want to think about ever losing him.'

'Bella, are you OK, darling?' asks Philip.

I follow his gaze. Bella is a putrid shade of green.

'It's sticky out here,' she says. She tries to stand up and stumbles. 'I need shade.' She straightens up. Philip rises to follow her, but she brushes him aside.

'Stay with Laura. I'll be fine, really, it's nothing.'

He drops back into his sun lounger, defeated, and watches Bella as she heads for the hotel.

'Do you think—'

'What?' I ask.

'Oh, nothing.' He waves to a waiter and orders two G&Ts. I don't object, despite my plans to be bright-eyed and bushy-tailed tonight. That conversation has left me in need of a drink. We are lost in our own thoughts and say nothing to one another until the drinks arrive. Philip picks up his drink and swizzles the ice around his glass. I know something is bugging him when he fails to say cheers. Philip is a stickler for form and has impeccable manners.

'Do you think Bella is OK?' he asks.

I glance in the direction she bolted. 'Yeah, she'll be apples. She doesn't like the sun much. She just needs to cool down, like she said.'

'You don't think she's been behaving oddly recently?'

'No.' My answer is automatic and not absolutely honest. She has been behaving like an impossible snob with her loathing of Elvis impersonators and all associated, but that's not something I'd feel comfortable discussing with Philip.

'If there was anything wrong and she'd confided in you, would you tell me?' he asks.

The truthful answer to this question is, 'No.' I'm not sure if keeping my best friend's secrets makes me a terrible person or an excellent one.

'Of course,' I lie because Bella hasn't confided anything in me so this is an academic exercise. It's on a par with your boyfriend flipping his lid because you want a free pass to sleep with Robbie Williams or some other A-lister. It's daft, since there's no real possibility of it happening.

'Can I talk to you about something?' asks Philip.

'Fire away.' He doesn't and I listen to the people around us having a good time, splashing, laughing, chatting. Phil's stillness is heightened by contrast.

Eventually he says, 'Look, I don't want you to think I'm crazy but, well, I wouldn't have said anything except I thought you might understand.'

'What?'

'That thing you said about watching other women all the time . . . well, I do it.'

'Philip!' I'm shocked and don't bother to hide it.

'Not other women,' he adds hastily. 'Other men.'

'Philip!' I'm doubly shocked.

'Not for *me*. I watch and monitor through jealousy.'

'You what?' I start to laugh, which possibly isn't the empathetic and sensitive reaction Philip was hoping for.

'I think Bella is having an affair.'

I stare at him with disbelief. 'You're losing your mind,' I declare flatly.

Philip stares at me, evidently longing for reassurance. He looks like I often did when I asked Oscar to come up with innocent explanations for late nights in the office and lost weekends. I'm overwhelmed with pity and want to assure Phil that he has nothing to fear from Bella on that front. His case is quite unlike mine was with Oscar.

Simultaneously, I'm also pretty miffed with him for being so ludicrous. 'Bella is devoted to you. She would never stray.'

'I always thought so but she's been so edgy and secretive recently. She keeps making calls when I'm in the shower or hanging up when I walk into the room.'

'Who does she say she's calling?'

'Amelie.'

'Well, in that case she'll be calling Amelie, probably about watering the plants or something anal. You know what a perfectionist Bella is.'

'I'd hoped this trip would be an opportunity for Bella and me to talk. I know something is bothering her and has been for a while. I wanted to find out what it is and put it right with her but she won't talk to me. I've tried.'

'Maybe she's considering her next steps. You know, her career and everything. I think she wants to work it all out for herself without anyone's help. She's always been independent. That's her style. She is supposed to be having time off to do some thinking, isn't she?'

Philip shrugs sadly. 'Maybe. I have considered that, but she is so distant and strange. The truth is I miss her. I sense she's keeping a secret from me.'

'It's nearly your fortieth birthday. No doubt she has secrets,' I point out.

'But she's moody, tearful and melancholic. She keeps calling off whenever we four are due to meet up, saying she's tired. Have you ever known Bella to prefer to lounge around in her room rather than go out to play? And last night *she* didn't come to bed either. She sat downstairs and had a drink at the bar in the garden.'

'And that's it? That's your evidence for thinking my best friend is having an affair?' I'm mortally offended for

Bella and pissed off at Philip. When did he turn into such a doubting Thomas?

'It's more evidence than you have to suspect Stevie, yet you're suspicious of him.'

'Yes, and you think I'm being ridiculous,' I argue crossly. I instantly realize that part of me is narky with myself. Having heard Philip's paranoid ramblings I'm embarrassed by my own: lack of trust is horrible to witness in a relationship. I'm also fed up because I know I am a bit circumspect about the longevity of relationships, but I mean *my* relationships, I firmly believe other people might thrive and I'm depressed to be faced with Philip's qualms.

Philip can see my outrage and is hurried into an un-characteristic confession. 'She's gone off sex,' he mumbles into his glass.

I give this piece of information the consideration it deserves. I know it will have cost Philip dearly to confide such a thing. The truth is Bella has been acting weirdly for a number of weeks. She's been snippy with me and Amelie but I'd put it all down to my meeting Stevie. Evidently that's not so. Suddenly it dawns on me.

'Oh my God, Philip!' I yell. I can hardly believe I haven't worked this out before. It's so obvious. All the pieces fall together. 'Don't you see? She's moody, secret-ive, exhausted and a bit lacklustre in the bedroom?' Philip raises his gaze and waits for me to spell it out. 'Phil, you're going to be a daddy.'

40. Suspicious Minds

Philip

Could Laura be right? Well technically, of course she *could*. It's possible . . . Is it probable? Who knows? Maybe. I hum to myself as I shave and shower. Bella lies on the bed flicking through a million satellite TV channels, none of which seem to hold her attention. I watch her from the bathroom, as the door is ajar. There's a large tin of jelly beans on the bedside table – she's eaten two thirds plus she's munched her way through a gigantic packet of crisps and half a Hershey bar. She doesn't even like Hershey bars – could this be the start of eating for two? Shouldn't she be eating fish or broccoli, something with more nutritional value and less gelatin?

As I towel myself dry I reflect on the past couple of months in light of Laura's suggestion. Pregnancy would explain the mood swings and her resistance to settling on a career. She obviously doesn't want to get her teeth into something only to have to start all over again. It would explain why she didn't want to come on this trip – some women are nervous of flying in the early stages – and why she's given up the booze; I did think a holiday was an odd time to ditch the poison. It would also explain why she hasn't bought any clothes this holiday and the dizzy spell by the pool.

But if she's pregnant, why wouldn't she tell me?

She's probably just being considerate to Stevie and Laura. She won't want to steal their thunder, this trip is supposed to be about them, not us. Isn't that just typically sweet of Bella?

The more I think about it, the more I see that it makes absolute sense. I am light-headed with relief and joy. It's now ridiculous to think that last night I lay alone in bed and dwelt on terrible, ugly thoughts. How could I have imagined she was having an affair? Madness. We're in the desert for God's sake; the only people she knows in the state of Nevada are Laura, Stevie and me.

I emerge from the bathroom – a dripping cloud of love – with a towel wrapped around my waist. I've caught a few rays and Bella loves to see me wet and freshly shaved, she's told me so on a number of occasions. I stride to the bed and then carefully lean in to kiss the top of her head. To think this woman is carrying my child! This amazing, beautiful, interesting woman is going to be the mother of my babies. I think I might explode with pride. I hover above her, waiting for her to turn away from the TV, and towards me, so that I can kiss her on the lips.

'You're making the bed wet,' she mumbles, without taking her eyes off the screen. I look up to see what's captivating her. A minute-long advert for kitchen knives? I pick up the remote and press the 'off' button.

'I was watching that,' she grumbles with undisguised irritation. She turns to stare at me crossly, which gives me the opportunity to plant a smacker on her lips. Bella allows the kiss but keeps her mouth firmly closed, which inhibits my seduction plans.

'If you were drinking alcohol, I'd say this was a champagne moment, wouldn't you, gorgeous?' I ask. Then I grin and add, 'But if you were drinking, it probably wouldn't be a champagne moment.'

'What are you talking about?' asks Bella. She squeezes her hand into the tin of jelly beans and scratches around for another large handful. 'I don't know why I keep eating these. They're making me feel sick.'

She feels sick! I could kiss her. I lie down beside her and prop myself up on one elbow, facing her. 'I have something really funny to tell you,' I say.

'I could do with a laugh,' replies Bella. But she doesn't let me tell her the funny thing, instead she says, 'I'm really tired, do you think there's any way we could give tonight a miss?'

She stares at me. Her enormous brown eyes, framed with thick, long lashes, have never looked more beautifully Bambi-like. She's exhausted. Confirmation of everything I've been hoping for. It's as though she's shown me the funny white stick with the blue line. A family is just what I want. What we want. I'm so thrilled, I could burst. Knowing her secret is enough to make me explode.

'We can't miss the show unless we have a really good excuse,' I reply. 'After all, the main reason we're here is to support Stevie. We're his guests. We can't fail to show up at the dress rehearsal. Tonight will be important for his morale and confidence.' I pause dramatically, 'We'd need a really, really excellent reason to miss it.'

Like my wife is feeling nauseous carrying our first baby! I wait for her to confirm my suspicions but she doesn't. Bella sighs and mutters something about the best reason in the world. 'What is it?' I almost yell my question as excitement has made it impossible for me to control my voice. Bella looks startled.

She doesn't answer, she just rolls off the bed and opens her wardrobe door. She pulls out a top – the first one that comes to hand. It's unlike her not to spend hours agonizing over what to wear. Maybe she already knows that some of her clingy numbers won't fit any more. Has she changed shape yet? Not to my eye, but then I'm not really sure when women start to 'show'. Oh hell, this is exciting. My wife is going to bloom. I'm certain that she's going to be one of those beautiful and serene mothers-to-be. I imagine she'll glow rather than puke. But if she does puke I'll be right by her side holding her hair. I want to be with her every step of the way. I want to massage her achy back and I definitely want to be at the birth. But most of all I want her to tell me she's pregnant! I can't wait another second. I want to start our future now.

'Bella.'

She pauses at the bathroom door. 'If we have to go to this thing I need to get ready.'

'Bella, are you pregnant?'

'What?'

I sit up on the bed and grin helplessly, waiting for her to make all my dreams come true.

'I'm right, aren't I? You're pregnant. The tiredness, the dizziness, the moods. Not that I mind you being moody. I mean, I understand. It must be hormones.' I'm gabbling because I'm deliriously excited but I don't want to upset her, she has been *very* irritable recently, so I tread carefully. '*And* it's extremely noble of you to wait until after the competition to make the announcement, rather than stealing Stevie's thunder. But, sweetheart, you can tell me! I'm so thrilled.' I stop gabbling.

Bella is silent. She's frozen, one hand on the bathroom door handle. She's looking at the floor. 'You're mad, Philip. Insane.'

She pops my dreams. Like balloons jabbed with a pin, they bang and disappear.

'You're not then,' I mutter, sadly.

'No, of course I'm not. Whatever gave you that idea?'

I lie on my back and stare at the ceiling. Of course Bella isn't pregnant. She'd have told me if she was. She wouldn't have cared about Stevie's competition. In fact, I don't think there is anything on this earth she cares *less* about than Stevie's competition. How could I have allowed myself to get so carried away? How could I have imagined something so important to be fact, based on nothing other than flimsy hypothesis and conjecture?

Because I wanted to believe it. I want us to be a family so much – more than anything. More than common sense, or caution, can control.

Besides, if Bella isn't pregnant then I am once again face-to-face with a number of very worrying issues. The alternative to pregnancy appals me.

I lie in silence except for the sound of running water as Bella showers. I hear her dry her hair and listen to the familiar sounds of her rattling around in her vanity case. I sit on the edge of the bed waiting for her. The sun is setting so the room is washed in a warm golden glow. The occasional reflection from the neon lights in the street darts crazily around the room, ricocheting off the furniture. The warm glow and the coloured lights suggest we ought to be having a better time than we are.

It takes Bella longer than usual to apply her make-up, more than enough time for me to pull on some chinos and a shirt. When she emerges from the bathroom I see that the extra effort has been worthwhile.

I'm always proud of my wife. She's strong, funny and gorgeous. But tonight she is something more; tonight she is dazzling. She's wearing a casual enough get-up. A red, funky sheer top and a beige skirt. I bought both garments for her from Diesel one Saturday afternoon when we were killing some time in Covent Garden. I've seen her wear the outfit two or three times already and it's 'reluctantly sexy' – it allows a flash of taut stomach rather than anything obvious – plus, she's wearing high strappy shoes, always a winner. Her hair is glossy and straight, like a sheet of ice, and her fingernails are freshly painted a very obvious scarlet that she normally confines to her toes.

I know a lot of 'stuff' about Bella. Our friends often joke that we'd be really great candidates for that old show *Mr and Mrs*. We know all the trivia about each other, trivia that holds lives together and gives them some form.

She takes skimmed milk in her tea, semi on her cereal and the full-fat stuff in coffee. She wears a Jo Malone perfume, except it's very trendy so it's called cologne, not perfume. She uses Jurlique skincare products. Her favourite smell is basil. Her favourite cheese is Gorgonzola. Her favourite dessert is a bowl of strawberries and melted chocolate. Whenever she buys a new outfit she absolutely *has* to wear it that night, even if she is just sat at home, with me, watching a DVD. She likes the feeling of warm sand between her toes when she's walking on a beach but prefers to sunbathe by a pool. She often laughs so hard that she is helpless and feels sick – although not that often, not recently. She loves being met at stations or airports. She gets a kick out of sticking her knife into a new jar of honey and eating from the blade, even though she knows she shouldn't. She prefers instant coffee to filter because she loves to 'pop' the seal on a new jar of coffee. She could recite a similar list of my preferences too. I know she could, because the fridge always boasts my favourite foodstuffs, her arse is often to be found in the lingerie that I find sexiest. She buys me video games I haven't got but do covet, she can choose me a book or a tie and knows all the names, ages and birthdays of my nieces, nephews and godchildren.

But suddenly, I'm paralyzed with fear because I wonder is this all I know? 'Stuff?'

I'm not so sure I know any of the big things about Bella, the things that give a life meaning. We have form but no meaning. How does she vote? Would she even get off her backside to cast a vote? Probably, for general elections but maybe not for local ones. How shocking. Does she want four kids? Does she want one? Why can't she figure out what she wants to do from nine till five? Is it really *that* hard? What's making her sad at the moment? How is it possible to know so much about a person and yet know nothing at all?

She's made an effort with her make-up. I know that because I know she doesn't normally wear eyeshadow, but today she is wearing two colours, carefully blended together and the liner stuff, and mascara. I know that she's wearing Perfect Pout gloss on her lips and Eyeko bronzer on her cheeks. I've been with her when she's scoured shelves for these products. I know so much. I know nothing at all. Because, the question that I cannot answer is whether the make-up is a mask to hide her? Armour to protect her? Camouflage to disguise her? Or is she painted like a flower to attract a passing bee?

I don't know my wife and the pain of admitting such a thing is almost beyond my capacity. I'm struggling to behave with a semblance of rationalism.

'Do we have to go to the show?' she asks again.

'You're all dressed up,' I point out.

'We could go somewhere else.'

I ignore her and pick up the door key and my wallet. 'Bella?'

'What?'

'Are you having an affair?'

'No.' She stares at my left ear, for about a minute, then she looks me straight in the eye and repeats, 'No.'

But I don't believe her.

41. One Night

Bella

We arrive at the hotel hosting the gig at 8.45 p.m. I have done my best to delay the inevitable – I've never taken so long to get ready for something, not even on my wedding days. However, Phil's beautiful manners mean that my death warrant is signed. I swear I can hear the blade of the guillotine being sharpened. I thought that looking sexy might distract him and that he'd pounce on me, putting all thoughts of supporting Stevie out of his mind. But the conversation about my phantom pregnancy well and truly ruined the mood. Where the hell had that ludicrous idea come from?

In the taxi I said I was feeling dizzy again. He grunted that he was sure it was nothing a stiff drink wouldn't cure. It seems he is all out of consideration and thoughtfulness as far as I'm concerned. Understandable, I suppose, but lousy timing. If ever I needed Phil to be dependable, solicitous and kind, it's tonight. Bad luck. Bad timing. Very Vegas.

Neil Curran will expose Stevie and me tonight. Besides the imminent exposure – too terrible and traumatic to contemplate – there'll also be a certain amount of torture beforehand. A little like bad foreplay before miserable sex, only hundreds of times worse. I am going to have to sit through fifteen Elvis tribute acts. I am about to be hauled – lashing and biting – down memory lane. It's almost enough to make me want to confess all to Philip right now. Why put myself through the horror of drawing out the experience?

Survival instinct, I suppose.

Despite the odds, a tiny defiant (deluded?) part of me wonders if it is possible that I'll get away with this. I'm hoping that somehow Neil Curran won't spot me in the crowd, or if he does, he might not want to mention his ancient association with Stevie, in case it's viewed as nepotism. I still hope against hope that I'll leave tonight's gig as Phil's wife.

The hotel is as flashy and gaudy as all the others I've seen on this trip, they're beginning to blur into one homogeneous mass of neon. We flash our VIP tickets to an earnest and efficient member of the waiting staff and we're swiftly ushered through a series of dark corridors and back doors, until double doors are pushed open and we are in a lavish and remarkable concert room.

The carpets are plush. The flowers, lights, candles and glittering backdrop on the stage are impressive. The tables and chairs have been set up, in tight clusters around the stage, and stretching as far back into the hall as possible; I'd guess there is a capacity of six hundred. It's a long way from the King's Arms Hotel in Blackpool. Undeniably, it's striking.

We are late so the venue is already heaving. At first glance I think every chair is full but the usher points towards a table near the stage, where Laura is sitting alone, watching a Mediterranean-looking Elvis singing

'Blue Suede Shoes'. He's thrashing manically about the stage and the kindest thing I can say about him is that his costume is very glittery. Laura turns, spots us and then beams and waves enthusiastically. Phil and I thread our way through the tables and join her. She jumps up and kisses us both, giggling with anticipation.

'Have we missed much?' asks Phil.

'This is the fourth contestant; he's from Greece.'

'Were any of the others any good?' I ask, more out of politeness than genuine curiosity.

'Good enough but no real competition,' says Laura with a grin. '"All Shook Up" has already been done twice. Poor choice because the song has become so recognized that it's difficult to recall or recapture its initial impact. A German contestant did "Wooden Heart", which is a bit predictable, as it was originally a German song for kids. One guy did a neat rendition of "Good Luck Charm" but that's not a crowd-pleaser. It doesn't showcase Elvis's tenderness or the command and control he had over his voice.'

Laura has become quite the expert on Elvis. I never had the same interest.

'When's Stevie appearing?' asks Phil.

'He's tenth.'

I groan inwardly. The row will have erupted way before then. Poor Stevie won't even have the opportunity to perform because it would be very callous to carry on after the revelation that we're married. Looking at it like that it seems all the more stupid that he's insisting on taking part at all.

There are a large number of Elvises in the crowd. Some are supporters and some are performers, who come to the front of house once they have done their spot, to watch the rest of the show and monitor the standard of the competition. They congratulate one another on their performance, which is genuine: they all admire Elvis so much that they like to see his work performed well. They also hate each other. Life is complex.

Phil is following my gaze and muses, 'What's the collective noun for a group of Elvises? A gaggle? A gang? A flock? A group?'

'A travesty,' I say firmly.

Phil ignores my comment and suggests ordering a bottle of champagne; Laura agrees. I decide to have a glass even though I'm not in the mood for celebrating; I hope it will numb the pain. Although the hall is rammed with waiting staff I make a big thing of going to the bar, which is not visible from the stage. I time my exit to coincide with the Greek Elvis finishing 'Blue Suede Shoes', at least this way I can avoid being spotted by Neil Curran for another act. I wonder how many reasons I can make up for leaving the table. I could buy snacks, reorder drinks, I could go to the loo (my old favourite). Could it possibly work?

I manage my mission of ordering drinks from the bar, even though it means that I have to argue with three waiters who all think I am sabotaging any chance they have at making decent money from tips tonight. The last thing these guys need is customers who are keen to serve themselves. My ploy works for now – by the time I return to the table Neil has been and gone, the coast is clear.

I check the commemorative programme (Laura's

bought three) and find out that the guy currently performing is Danish. Fair enough, I'm genuinely impressed by the European nature of the competition. In Blackpool fourteen of the fifteen 'European' finalists were British. Here in Vegas there are only eight British guys.

The guy on the stage is bald and fat. OK, I accept that Elvis became a bit of a lard boy towards the end of his life but he was never bald. I'm unreasonably offended on Elvis's behalf that this, frankly, plain – no, I might as well be honest – this *ugly* guy thinks he's anything like Elvis. Whatever grievances I have against Elvis, everyone knows he was sex on legs.

I close my eyes in frustration – a feeble attempt to blank out my surroundings. Then, a funny thing happens, I start to think, maybe – just maybe – the Danish Elvis is good. His 'Crying in the Chapel' is just like Elvis's. There's something raw and awkward about his performance that has a distinct authenticity. I open my eyes again and this time I don't see a bald, fat guy. I see a talented man who has the audience rapt. He's shaking with nerves, and although I am officially as hard as nails, he affects me by bending down (a struggle, the costume is tight) to shake hands with a wee bairn who is sat by the stage. She can't be more than seven years old and she melts – bloody hell – I do too. Towards the end of his second song I rush off to buy plates of pitta bread and hummus, claiming that I'm starving, and from a distance I listen to the explosive applause his act inspires. I find myself clapping too.

Once again I avoid Neil and return to the table to catch the sixth act singing 'GI Blues'. He's wearing a uniform. Good ploy, I concede. He certainly cuts through the clutter of white suits with diamanté and feathers. Laura loves this act and claps in time to the music. Then she catches herself and stops abruptly.

'Don't think I'm being disloyal,' she says. 'I'm fully behind Stevie, but this guy is pretty good.'

'They're all good,' I grant. 'The quality of the contestants is really impressive. It's a decent show.'

Laura is delighted that I'm showing any sign of enthusiasm for the event. I have to confess I am surprised. In Blackpool the show was depressingly amateur and I loathed it. Microphones fell apart, the techies buggered up the intro of some acts and cut off the final notes of others. Neil Curran drank one too many and pronounced the contestants' names incorrectly, even the judges were more worried about getting their next pint in than they were about the acts.

Here in Vegas there is a large orchestra, not a bashed-up beatbox. The audience contains some friends and family but is mostly made up of card-carrying members of the public, who want to be professionally entertained. They number in the hundreds, not an embarrassing fifty or so. The bar sells Moët not Blue Nun. There is a stage, curtains, theatre make-up and backdrops. The performances are convincing. Things have changed.

'I'd hate to judge anything,' Laura says. 'They are *all* so good and so devoted.'

Whereas I judge all the time.

The GI Elvis must have something special because I forget to dash out of the room as his act closes. I'm left with no alternative but to duck under the table as the compère strides on to the stage.

'What are you doing?' demands Phil.

'I've lost an earring,' I say, swiftly swiping one from my right lobe. Laura and Philip immediately start to hunt for the earring, causing more disruption than I want.

'No, no, you watch the show,' I instruct. But it's too late.

'What's going on over there?' demands the compère. 'Avoiding a debt collector?'

The joke is pretty shoddy and could easily be one of Neil Curran's but the accent's not his. This compère is American. I peep out above the table and almost collapse with relief. He's in his mid-thirties, slim with teeth so white they sparkle. Definitely not Neil Curran.

Where is Neil Curran and his endless pit of dirty jokes? I don't understand. Why the reprieve? I grab the programme and rapidly flick through it until I find the page that lists the personnel involved in the competition. Sure enough, in black and white, Neil Curran is billed as the compère. He's almost unrecognizable, billed as a 'stupendous and special guest, the great and the good, Neil Curran, brought over by popular demand' (his, no doubt) *and* the accompanying photo is at least fifteen years old. Still, despite the generous intro and the old photo, it *is* Neil. So what's going on?

'It says here that a Neil Curran is compèring. Who's the American guy with the smile?' I ask Laura.

'Wow, yes. You missed a full-on drama earlier on. Apparently the billed compère is one hundred per cent mank, pissed as a parrot. He's been drinking all day. The competition organizers have insisted that he goes to bed and sleeps it off. According to Stevie he's practically under armed guard, because they don't want him to fluff up tomorrow's big show.'

'Stevie told you that?'

'Yes. He popped by the table before the show started. He said you'd be interested. Said you'd think it was bewdy.'

Laura smiles and doesn't understand the magnificent significance of the information she has just imparted to me. Bless her, why would she? And bless Stevie. He must have come by to try to put my mind at rest. I am so relieved, my body melts like warm wax. Neil *was* a bit merry at lunchtime – situation normal. Thank God, Americans have principles about such things. I don't deserve to be this lucky but I am so, so grateful that I am. I beam at Laura and she smiles back. I beam at Phil, he's cagier.

Oh shit, yes. Philip is suspicious. The question about whether I'm having a baby (way off mark) and the question about whether I'm having an affair (not so way off mark) demand my attention.

I lean towards him and whisper, 'You OK?' He nods but without much enthusiasm. 'I'm sorry you had your hopes up about me being pregnant,' I whisper.

He shrugs but the hurt is visible. I lean close to him and kiss him – for the first time since I kissed Stevie. I hope the kiss conveys warmth, promise, an apology and love. I hope he doesn't sense any guilt, fear, deceit or pity. I wait nervously for his response. Under the table Phil squeezes my knee and mouths, 'Love you.'

Relieved, I sit back and decide that since I've been touched by this crazy piece of good fortune, then I might as well try to enjoy the show.

The eighth Elvis appears to be quite the professional.

As he walks on to the stage he starts to chat to the audience in role. Something I approve of. I mean, if you are going to do this thing, then you ought to go the whole hog. He swaggers on to the stage in a blur of, 'OK, baby?' and, 'Uh huh.' But, in fact, his performance is not so strong. I can't make out the words he's singing. I think he's saying, 'Mumble, mumble, mumble, murmmmmble.' It is a professional hazard that some Elvises go too far on the low gravelly thing and are barely audible. Still, I find I am tapping my foot and having what must look like a good time, to the outside world.

By the time the ninth Elvis is performing (the Italian who is, as his sister promised, very good) I am genuinely excited about seeing Stevie's act. Laura is giddy with nerves. She wants Stevie's to be the performance of a lifetime. Unsurprisingly, she's not especially bothered about the pinwheel suit (black this year, I'm led to believe) or even the prize money. Nor do I think she's itching for Stevie to become a full-time Elvis tribute act. She just wants him to win because it will make him happy. She wants him to be happy.

And I do too.

Who would have thought it? How can events keep changing, twisting, turning, morphing with such speed, after standing so still for years. Now that I think we have a reasonable chance of remaining undetected this evening, I find myself wanting Stevie to perform brilliantly. Perhaps I can persuade Phil that we don't need to attend tomorrow's show and maybe Stevie will win. Yeah, why not? He wants it enough. He's talented enough. And then after he wins we can all go home to—

To what?

To how it was. I finally did it. I've started to think about who I am and what I want. The last couple of months have been a rollercoaster but there has been one constant, and tonight, while I was applying my make-up, I reminded myself of it: I don't want to lose Phil. I don't.

My thoughts are interrupted as the compère announces Stevie Jones.

He's wearing a sky-blue jumpsuit, the most flamboyant costume I have seen tonight. It has a fur and feather collar, the neckline plunges to meet a wide, diamanté belt at his waist. I think anyone else would struggle to carry it off but Stevie looks wonderfully sexy. He hesitates as he walks on to the stage but I know that the timidity is fake: he's already in role. Elvis was always endearingly shy. Then he switches on the charm, full beam. He grins at the audience, curls his lip and mutters, 'Thank you very much, ladies and gentlemen.'

The room erupts into wild applause.

Stevie is fit, tall, dressed to kill, and he's given the audience what they want: Elvis at his best, Elvis in his heyday and all of this before he even sings a note.

I find I am on my feet cheering and clapping, I only notice when I realize my hands are stinging.

Stevie starts with 'Jailhouse Rock'. It is impossible to resist from the moment the first distinctive lines and chords slam on to the stage. He howls the intricate and complex lyrics with exuberance and sincerity. He is on his toes, moving with confidence and rhythm, flinging his body around the stage in exactly the way Elvis did. When did Stevie become so good? He's far better than

I remembered or imagined. Like the King himself, he gets the crowd hot and bothered and young and old alike swoon. His foray into the audience is the best-received segment of the night so far.

He closes the song to riotous applause pounding up to the chandeliers.

Stevie pauses to wipe his face on the silk scarf he's wearing round his neck and gives it to a middle-aged woman, *à la* the King himself. The old girl looks like she might explode with glee now that she is wrapped in his sweat.

I wonder what he'll perform next. The entire room is waiting with bated breath: it's almost possible to see, taste and smell the anticipation.

Are you lonesome tonight? The question bounces from Stevie's lips and squarely hits his target – the hearts of every single member of the audience. Even the tiny minority of eternally confident, supremely content individuals – who had never missed a soul or regretted drifting apart from any lover – felt they were being directly besieged by his intense tenderness. The song effectively demonstrates his versatility. He isn't an Elvis tribute act that can do either rock 'n' roll, or ballads: he has the talent to tackle both.

Stevie's deep-voiced narration in the middle of the song is a confident move. It's a brave tribute act that relies on nothing but his voice; no fancy moves, no whizzy lyrics, no distractions at all, just a simple riff, delivered with almost painful sincerity and yet Stevie does it. Stevie pulls it off.

Everyone in the room believes that Elvis is singing to

them: I know that Stevie is singing to *me*. It's our song. Well, as good as. All the lyrics are scarily pertinent. Stevie is appealing to me, the woman who strangely changed and left him surrounded by a perpetual emptiness. I hear him. I hear the pain of eight years' confusion, heartache and misery, which I caused. The whole room hears it because when Stevie finishes, the applause and stamping of feet, the standing ovation and the delirious screams for more almost bring the roof down.

'He's excellent! Easily the best!' exclaims Philip, confidently. He's on his feet, beaming and clapping.

'Do you think?' Laura is wiping away tears of joy that are squeezing out of her eyes and running down her face. 'I agree. He's gold,' she laughs in a rare moment of absolute certainty that her opinions stand solid. She's clapping so rapidly her hands are a blur.

'You can tell he was brought up to do this,' I enthuse. 'His mum would be so proud. All those years of practice. When Stevie was as young as eight his mum dressed him up in the suits and stuff and took him to competitions.' I beam and the smile is so wide it hurts my cheek muscles. Laura nods, I'm not telling her anything new.

Phil stares at me, 'How do you know that?'

'He told me,' I answer without skipping a beat. I'm not lying but I was careless. This moment of jubilation and triumph has made me let my guard down. How stupid of me. How careless! I stare at the stage, not daring to turn back to Phil because I know he is watching me, very, very carefully, and I'm terrified of what he might see.

42. I'll Remember You

Stevie

I actually feel quite sorry for the guy who has to go on stage after me. The audience doesn't want to know. They only want me. I have them eating out of my hand. I know that sounds really big-headed – and I try not to look too cocky when I'm backstage – but it must be pretty clear to everyone that there hasn't been a better performance tonight. I have never given a better performance in my life.

Belinda came.

She risked everyone finding out that she is a bigamist to watch me perform tonight. What does that mean? It has to be good, doesn't it? Assuming Belinda wanting me is good. It has to mean *something*. It has to mean *we* mean something. Today she begged me to throw the competition but I could not do that, not even for her; I had to go ahead and it was the right decision. Tomorrow, if I perform as well, the title will be mine. After all these years, some things will be put straight.

I join Laura, Belinda and Philip front of house. It takes ages to walk the fifty or so yards to their table, because everyone wants a piece of me. People ask for autographs, reach out to touch me, women jump around me and plant quick pecks on my face and hands – it's surreal.

When I reach the table, Laura falls on me and hugs me tightly. Bella smiles shyly over her shoulder. Her straight hair and smart clothes don't fool me: I can see Belinda McDonnel's unsophisticated delight shining through. I bask in it. Phil, a true gent, has bought a bottle of champagne and Laura has bought a bottle of water. She smiles and tells me that she doesn't want me hungover tomorrow.

'You were brilliant tonight,' says Belinda, as we all settle into our chairs.

'Thank you.' I meet her eye, glug a large glass of water and then sip some champagne. I'm really only drinking it to be polite. It feels weird drinking the guy's champagne when I'm married to his wife and feeling ambivalent about it. I mean – he's a good bloke – under any other circumstances we might have become mates.

'If you can be half as good tomorrow you'll walk it,' says Belinda. She's actually giggling. She's genuinely enthusiastic. I'd begun to doubt I would ever see the day.

'Well, it's never over until it's over. Nothing in life is a certainty,' I caution. I'm nervous with her assumption that the competition is in the bag, even though I've had the same thought. I have a good chance, I know that, but Belinda of all people must know that you can't predict anything in life.

'You'll win, I know you will,' says Laura leaning in to kiss me. Awkwardly, I shift my face so that her kiss falls on my cheek. It's not that I don't want to kiss Laura. She's gorgeous and any man in his right mind would want to kiss her. It's just that I feel distinctly caddish kissing her in front of Belinda. I feel the full weight of the deceit I'm practising. It's crippling.

I turn to Laura and say, 'Babe, you know what? I need an early night.' She grins assuming – not unreasonably but still inaccurately – that I'm feeling frisky. I mean I need *sleep*.

'Well, if you're sure you don't want to stay and watch the competition.'

'I'm sure.'

'I'll get my wrap.' Laura leaps up and dashes off to the cloakroom. Philip mutters something about needing a pee and exits the table in the same instant, leaving Belinda and me, face-to-face, and alone.

'I've never seen it before, your talent. I think I've refused to see it – but you were right to perform tonight,' she says.

Even after the rapturous and universal applause, her praise is possibly the most flattering thing I've ever heard. It's certainly the most coveted.

'Good choice of tunes. Brave and different.' She takes a deep breath. 'Stevie, I know what you were saying but—'

'What I was saying?' She's lost me.

She takes a quick look over her shoulder, scouring for Laura and Phil, neither of them is in sight. Bella recognizes that we have only snatched moments and decides to be bold.

'I'm very flattered that you sang to me, Stevie. It means a lot, whatever happens.'

'I have no idea what you are talking about,' I state flatly.

'"Are You Lonesome Tonight?" It was for me, wasn't it?'

Awkward pause. I can see why she might think that. The lyrics, I guess, could be interpreted as pertinent to our situation but I chose my songs months ago, way before Belinda re-entered my life. I run through the lyrics in my head. Oh God, I can be stupendously thick sometimes. The song is all about a woman who ups and offs without any reasonable explanation. The singer – this bit is really mortifying – pleads to her through a series of questions clearly articulating his pain and longing. What was I thinking of? Not Belinda – obviously. Which is a bit surprising, actually.

I could let it go. I could let Belinda think that my performance of a lifetime was inspired by her, but it wouldn't be fair. My performance of a lifetime occurred *despite* her. I've never lied to Belinda: it would be lunacy to start now when things are already so murky.

'I didn't choose that song with you in mind. I didn't choose it with anyone in mind,' I blurt.

'Oh.' Belinda physically pulls back from me, she looks startled. Hurt? 'I thought—'

'Years ago, you taught me not to be overly emotional about this business. You berated me for picking my numbers for sentimental reasons. I chose to sing those two particular tracks tonight because I knew they contrasted and complemented each other. They showcased my range. That's all.'

Belinda picks up her champagne glass and takes a sip. She's considering what I've just said. I study her face. It's almost impossible to read. Is that relief I see?

'Stevie, you must perform tomorrow. I meant what I said before, you'll win. I won't be there tomorrow. Somehow, and I'm not sure how yet, I'll persuade Philip that we don't need to attend the competition. It's not going to be easy, he's a big fan of yours.' Belinda flashes me a quick grin as I try to digest what she is saying. 'We are unlikely to get as lucky again. Neil Curran will be sober for sure. His salary depends on it.'

I am stunned and saddened. Belinda thinks I'm great. She thinks I'm the best Elvis tribute act ever but it hasn't changed her mind. She doesn't want me. The disappointment is . . .

. . . not as devastating as it was eight years ago. I wait to feel the onslaught of pain. The bloody agony of being rejected, the relentless misery and confusion brought on by being deserted, but it doesn't happen.

I have to get this clear. 'Why did you come tonight?'

'I couldn't get out of it. Phil insisted,' Belinda shrugs.

'Phil did?'

Yes.' Belinda catches sight of my face. 'Oh, no. You thought I'd chosen you?' she asks carefully. I nod. Belinda looks mortified. 'I'm sorry, Stevie. It's not a choice I can make.'

She's holding the long stem of the champagne glass, I notice that the liquid is moving – she's shaking, ever so slightly. She looks directly into my eyes and I know what's coming. Way back in Blackpool she wasn't able to look me in the face. She could not finish us cleanly, let alone battle for us. I always thought that was the worst thing about our break-up. I respect her for doing it differently this time.

'If I could turn back time, if I'd had more confidence in you, things might have been different,' she says slowly. 'But it's too late now. Too late for us.'

These are the most desolate and cruel words in the English language, naturally, they were always going to end up in our relationship at some point. Too late.

'Oh, this is such a mess and it's all my fault,' she cries, frustrated.

I'm not going to argue with her.

She stutters on with her explanation. 'It's not that I'm choosing Phil over you, Stevie.'

'It seems that way.'

'I've been thinking about this all afternoon. In theory we could just walk away – legally you are my husband – we could just run away and start up again as a married couple. At the very least we'd avoid all this mess, and isn't running away my forte?' I sense a *but* coming. 'But we'd never recover. We'd feel too guilty. The past always catches up. I've learnt that much.' Belinda is still staring directly into my eyes, she isn't ducking this one. When I try to look away she takes my face in her hands and forces me to hold her gaze. 'It's not a level playing field. I can't hurt anyone else. I can't hurt Phil and I can't hurt Laura.'

'But it's OK to hurt me.' I know I sound petulant; a silly, sulky boy, but no one likes being brushed off. 'Don't tell me I'm too good for you.'

'I wasn't going to.' She grins. 'I've hurt you so much already but largely you were over it. This unfortunate shove down memory lane has been disturbing and distressing, but it's not real. It's a flirtation, or a letting-go ritual, or something – but it's not real.'

I consider what she's saying and a tiny part of me, buried about five fathoms deep, reckons that she might just be talking sense. Unprecedented but not impossible.

'What you have with Laura is real. You said yourself she adores you, tinker, tailor, soldier, sailor. She's interested in your music. You both like travelling. The same things make you laugh. I think you have a promising start. And what I have with Phil is —'

'Patchy,' I point out because someone has to.

We were making real progress along the road of 'tell it how it is', up until a moment ago. I feel duty bound to shove her a few more steps along the path. I'm bound through love. I'm not sure I can categorize the love I feel for Belinda, this mixed-up beauty. I'm not sure if love ought ever to be labelled and put in tidy boxes. I might love Belinda because she is an old flame and we have so much shared history. My love might be attributable to friendship. Or she might just appeal to the macho bit in me, the bit that wants to help out a confused but attractive woman. I don't know. Right now, it hardly matters. Belinda, the vulnerable, neglected, grief-stricken girl floats in front of me. Bella the woman, the survivor and product of all that has gone before, is sitting with me too. I like them both. It's a revelation.

It's almost indiscernible – something in the eyes, perhaps, or a shift in the demeanour – but slowly the woman starts to emerge and grow in front of me and the girl is fading away. This is the natural order of things.

'Come on, Belinda, you're kidding yourself. Philip doesn't know anything about you. Your entire relationship is based on a huge lie.'

'And good intention,' she defends.

'It doesn't cut it. You don't cut it as his wife.' I'm being cruel to be kind and she seems to understand this.

'I will, though, Stevie. If I get the chance.'

I look at my wife across the table, nervously sipping champagne to buy time – time that is priceless to her – and I see that she means this with every fibre of her soul. She means it so much that in that instant my wife vanishes and my ex-wife – with all the closeness and distance that that implies – shrugs at me.

'You have to tell him about your past, Bella. About me and about your dad. You have to talk to him about how much you miss your mum and why you're scared of having babies. You have to tell him that as a young kid you were bullied at school. You have to tell him everything and give him the chance and honour of knowing you in your entirety. Because, if you don't, none of this makes any sense at all and the pair of you won't make it.'

43. That's When Your Heartaches Begin

Bella

Stevie's right, of course. Despite the fact that this salient piece of advice is delivered to me by a man wearing a flared, beaded catsuit and stick-on sideburns, I recognize that it's the best advice I've had for a long time. I determine to do exactly as he suggests – and I would have if, at that moment, our table hadn't been invaded by my worst nightmare. In a rush – similar to that of the opening of the doors to Harrods on sale day – we are suddenly deluged with company.

Laura and Phil have come back. Laura is holding her wrap and Phil a glass of whisky, a double by the looks of it. And Neil Curran is holding court.

'Bloody cheek of them! Said I was pissed. Put me under lock and key, they did. That's an infringement of my human rights, that is. I'll bloody sue. Every bugger is suing every other bugger over here, aren't they? Well, I'll bloody sue them.' Neil's indignation dissolves when he lays eyes on Laura. He always was a dirty old flirt with a keen eye for a pretty lady. 'Aren't you going to introduce me to your lovely friend, Bel-Girl?' he asks me.

I struggle to find words because I know that everything is now out of my hands. I sink back into my chair and watch in amazed horror; aware that the situation is past rescue.

Laura beams at Neil and says, 'I'm Laura Ingalls. Hold the name jokes.' She puts up her pretty hands and metaphorically brushes away the expected jokes. She's obviously got Neil's number and knows he'll tease her mercilessly about her name. 'You, on the other hand, don't need any introduction.' She knows instinctively that the compère is someone an Elvis-wife/girlfriend ought to befriend. Funny, as I'd always found it easier to be rude to Neil Curran. 'You are the infamous compère, Neil Curran,' she says with her widest beam.

'Not so infamous, darlin'. Just a bit fond of the bottle. But, bloody hell, lassie, I'm on holiday. Well, as near as damn it.' He plonks himself into a chair next to mine, then asks Laura the question I'm dreading: 'So, how do you know this lovely couple?'

Laura looks a wee bit confused that Neil has referred to Stevie and me as a couple. In the longest moment of my life I see her decide that the drunken compère has jumped to a conclusion, then she strives for what she believes is clarity. 'Bella's my best friend and I'm Stevie's girlfriend.'

'Fucking hell. Pardon my French,' says Neil, spluttering. 'That's all a bit cosy, isn't it?'

'Philip Edwards,' says Phil, holding out his hand for Neil to shake. 'Bella's husband.'

Weakly, Neil shakes it and turns to stare at Stevie and me. 'Who the hell is Bella?'

I think he knows.

'I am,' I mutter. Choiceless.

'But you're married to Stevie,' says Neil, 'not this one.' He points at Phil.

'No, no,' giggles Laura. 'Stevie and Bella have just met through me. Bella is with Phil, I'm with Stevie.'

I can see her trying to be patient – she thinks he's still under the influence. Sadly, I know that Neil Curran has never been more sober. I daren't look at Stevie but I sense movement. I think he is dropping his head into his hands, adopting the pose common to utterly and completely fucked members of mankind.

'Er lass. I don't know what's the do 'ere, but as true as I'm standing in front of you, I can tell you Belinda McDonnel and Stevie Jones are married. They told me so. We're old mates, you see. We go back over a decade.' Maybe Neil thinks Laura is trying to pull his leg and while Neil likes to dish out the gags, he doesn't like to be the butt of others' jokes. He becomes more adamant. 'Couple of lovebirds these two. Even after all these years. I caught them canoodling in the diner next to the Elvis-A-Rama Museum, just today.'

'What's he talking about?' Laura throws the question at Stevie and me. 'Tell me he's wrong. Tell me he's lying. He's drunk, isn't he?'

'I'm sorry, I—' I stop. I can't very well say, 'I'm sorry, I can explain.' My actions are beyond explanation.

'You are married to my boyfriend?' asks Laura, incredulous.

I nod my head, too ashamed to speak.

As it happens, Laura doesn't require me to say anything more, she flings the contents of the nearest glass over me and charges out of the room, sobbing. Stevie follows her.

'There's never a dull moment around you two, I'll say that for you,' says Neil. His eyes are twinkling. 'I best be on my way. Likely as not, you've a bit of explaining to do, Bel-Girl.'

And so he shuffles off, leaving me alone with Philip.

44. Heartbreak Hotel

Philip

I'd guessed. About eighteen minutes before the brassy compère confirmed the status quo, I'd guessed that there was something between Bella and Stevie. I hadn't thought they were married. No. No, that was too much for my imagination to conjure. But as I'd watched Bella watch Stevie sing 'Are You Lonesome Tonight?' I'd reached the conclusion that they were probably going at it like rabbits behind Laura's and my backs.

Sorry to be vulgar. But it throws a man, somewhat, hearing that his wife is a bigamist. Quite an assault on my dignity, I think most would agree. And needless to say there's the little fact that my life has been snatched away. My being crushed.

'Get your wrap, Bella,' I instruct. She does so without argument or attempting an explanation. For this, at least, I'm grateful. I'd rather we played out the rest of our drama in private. I wait for her to return to the table with her wrap. For a fleeting moment I consider there's a real possibility that she won't return. Bella has a history of walking away from problems. An extensive history, from what I can gather. She does, however, reappear at my side. She looks tiny and transparent as she hovers waiting to catch my attention. Which is ironic, no? The one thing she's definitely not, is transparent. I finish my whisky, as I anticipate a need to fortify myself, and then we thread our way through the tables to the exit and catch a cab back to the hotel.

45. My Baby Left Me

Stevie

Laura can really move. She'd slipped through the crowds and outside into a waiting taxi within moments of Neil Curran's horrendous revelation. I try, but miserably fail, to keep up with her. What is it with me and women slipping from my grasp at the final of the annual European King of Kings Tribute Artist Convention and Competition? Except, this time, I know that Laura didn't so much slip from my grasp. The most charitable description is that I carelessly dropped her – some would say I flung her away. I tell myself not to make flip comments about déjà vu, not even to myself, it's mindless and disrespectful. I deserve this lousy predicament but Laura doesn't.

I run back to the hotel – I might move faster on foot than she will in a cab and maybe I can head her off, although I'm not sure what I can say or do to fix this situation. Belinda was right – she's finally started to talk some sense – this whole crazy episode has been a diversion but it's not real. When I said that stuff to Belinda in the diner I was talking idiotic, indulgent crap. It's not as though I thought of her every day for years and years. If we hadn't come on this holiday together I wouldn't have thought of kissing her and I wouldn't have missed kissing her. But I'm missing Laura already.

Laura's taxi beats me back to the hotel and by the time I push open the door to our suite, she's packing.

'Don't go,' I plead.

'Fuck off,' she says. Neat, succinct, to the point. 'You miserable, lying bastard,' she adds, in case there was any need for clarity.

'Laura, please. I am so sorry.' I rush towards her, but she backs away, glaring.

Her patent disgust turns me to stone. I decide against trying to put my arms around her, instead I drop into a chair in the corner of the bedroom. For some minutes I am silent, trying to gather my thoughts. In the meantime she dashes around the room, grabbing knickers off the floor and tiny tops from drawers. She bundles them into her case, not giving a thought to creasing. At this rate she might have moved out before I've built a compelling defence. What am I talking about? She might have married someone she hasn't even met yet before I build a *reasonable* defence. I start blathering, all I have as a vindication might not be too compelling or reasonable, because even the truth exposes me as an arse, but I have to try.

'I am so, so sorry.' I sound like Bella. 'I didn't mean to hurt you.' That old cliché. 'I didn't plan any of this. It just sort of happened.' I sound pathetic to me too.

'*What* sort of happened?' screams Laura. 'You stupid wanker. Are you saying you sort of married my best mate? I'm right, aren't I? You are married to my best friend?'

'Technically,' I admit.

'A bona fide, full on, one hundred bloody per cent commitment.'

'Yes.'

'Fuck! It's one up on an affair. You almost make Oscar look like a good guy.'

'Sorry.'

'But Bella is married to Philip.' The good news is Laura has stopped packing. Her outrage at the complex state of affairs has, at least, distracted her from that.

'Not technically.'

'How long have you been married?'

'Erm, eleven years, I suppose.'

'Holy fuck. An eternity. But it was one of those passport marriages or something, right?'

I can hear the hope in her voice. I wish I could justify it. 'No.'

'You bastard. Are you saying it's a love match?'

'Yes. *Was*. It was.'

'I hate you,' she says. Simple enough.

'Please, please let me explain, Laura.' I jump up from my seat and move towards her. 'This is why you and I had such a slow start. I was trying to find a way to describe my weird marital status. I wanted to tell you on the very first night. I tried to but you didn't let me – you rushed ahead with your own assumptions.'

'Don't you dare try to blame this on me, you twat.'

'No, no, I'm not trying to blame you. Of course I'm not.'

I can't help but notice how determined and confident Laura is. I've seen flashes of this in her before and I've always found it attractive. I know it's an inapt thought but I find I'm turned on by the fact that she's giving me a hard time and fighting her corner with such steely fortitude. I can't help but admire her. Not that it will do me any good. I realize the time for my cashing in on admiration for Laura is long gone. I've blown this. I have no chance of winning her back. I daren't even hope for that. Right now, I just want to apologize.

'And that bogan drongo said you were acting like a couple of lovebirds today. What did he mean?'

'We bumped into him at a diner.'

'You've been rooting us both all along?' Her disgust whips me.

'No! For a time I got muddled and last night I kissed Belinda. We needed to talk about it so we met up today.'

'You've been kissing who?'

'Bella. She was called Belinda when I knew her. She changed her name.'

'That scheming bitch.'

'Please let me explain,' I implore. I don't know how it happened but I'm on my knees, prostrate in front of Laura, literally begging for a chance. This might seem ridiculous considering I'm wearing a skin-tight, sky-blue, catsuit, but I don't have much right to dignity at this precise moment in time.

'Explain,' instructs Laura.

It's the first time, since Neil Curran's revelation, that she's said something to me without feeling the need to cuss or yell. I see this as progress of sorts. Laura flops on the edge of the bed. She looks so miserable, lost and wounded. Again this is something I have caught a glimpse of in the past. Occasionally, when Laura has talked about Oscar and how badly he let her down I've seen the same expression of sorrow flicker across her face. I used to burn with fury against a man I'd never met because he'd hurt Laura. Watching her pain now is about a million times worse because I know I caused this. More than anything I want her pain to stop.

I present the facts of Belinda's and my story as fairly and honestly as I can. I take care not to imply that the entire sorry mess is Bella's fault and take full responsibility for my part in it. I make a big blunder when I point out that I've always been uncomfortable with the situation and only backed Bella's plan because Laura had begged me to give her friend a chance.

'You lousy sod! I said that without any knowledge of the actual situation. You're a pathetic bastard, trying to offload this crap on me.' Spot on.

This is a difficult conversation and it becomes almost impossible when I get to the bit where I snogged Bella. Laura's intelligent, she wouldn't believe me if I said it had been solely the result of too much alcohol and, besides, that isn't true. On the other hand, I don't want to give the impression that I am still infatuated with Bella.

'Who did you bring here? Me or her?' Laura asks suddenly.

'You. I brought you. I didn't want to bring Belinda, Bella. That was your idea.'

'More fool me.'

'You're no fool.'

'I am. I bloody am.' Laura looks away and I catch the grief and regret in her face, just punishment for what I've done.

'When I first came to Vegas I didn't want to start anything up.' My voice cracks and squeaks reflecting how important the clarity of this explanation is to me. 'The opposite. I wanted to draw a firm line under everything between me and Bella. I wanted to end it.' My breath stumbles in my chest, making it difficult for me to breathe, I so want Laura to believe me. I so want my explanation to add up.

'I was having such a marvellous time. I thought we were falling in love but all along you were hankering after an old flame. How is that possible?' asks Laura, miserable and confused. 'You've ruined everything. Pissed on everything. This hasn't been our story. It hasn't been about our beginning. Even if I believe you, this is Bella's and your end.'

'It can be both things.'

'No, it can't.'

Laura stood up, zipped her suitcase and walked towards the door. 'I've booked my own room for tonight. I imagine it goes without saying but I won't be staying for the final. I'm going to try to change my ticket so that I can fly back tomorrow.' She glances around the room. 'If I've forgotten anything post it to me. I don't want to see you ever again, Stevie. Do you understand? I *never* want to see you again.'

The door bangs behind her. A dull, definitive bang.

46. I'm Leavin'

Saturday 10th July, 2004

Laura

I spent the night crying. Not only is it traditional but it's also my due. I cannot believe the scale of the deceit that has been played out in front of me. I called the travel agent and the airport and got my ticket transferred so that I could fly home today. After sobbing and pleading and 'holding the line' for over an hour, it was confirmed that I can fly home today as long as I'm prepared to transfer in Amsterdam. I'd transfer in Timbuktu if it was a speedy way to exit this hellhole. I call Amelie to tell her my change of plan.

'Why are you coming home early? Have you had a row with Stevie? Is everything OK?' she asks. I almost melt at hearing her concern ooze down the telephone line. I am so glad that I have sensible Amelie to comfort and help me. I can't wait to curl up on her comfy, squashy settee and spill out my news. I can already imagine her outrage on my behalf.

'You wouldn't believe me if I told you,' I reply.

'I think I might,' she sighs.

There's something in her tone, sad acceptance perhaps, that makes me ask, 'You know?'

'Yes.'

'How do you know?'

'I've known all along.'

I hang up. Amelie knows, she knew *all along*. Amelie, who is decent and honourable and I thought was my friend, was part of this foul sham and she didn't think to tell me, to warn me. She is not decent, or honourable, or a friend. I am so alone. Once again, I have no one to turn to and I am so sick of having to stand on my own two feet.

I don't call Oscar to tell him that I'm coming home early. I still have a smidgen of pride and I can't bring myself to admit to him that the man I've been dating, who I thought was the man of my dreams, was actually my best friend's husband. I'll leave Eddie with him until Monday as planned, even though I ache to wrap my arms round my little boy. I know that I'll be comforted by the smell of his hair and skin and the warmth of his clumsy, casual hugs.

The thought of my journey home is depressing. I had imagined that by the time Stevie and I flew back to England we would be sweet as. We would sit back in our comfy, up-front seats, sipping free champagne, confident in the knowledge that we had exchanged promises of love. Do I ever learn? I know it's dangerous to project. So what was I thinking of when I allowed myself to indulge in fantasies where Stevie and I would drive to Oscar's to pick up Eddie? I'd taken great pleasure in imagining Oscar's face as I introduced him to Stevie. I confess I got a certain amount of satisfaction envisaging my average ex, shaking hands with my gorgeous present.

That'll learn me! I'd been especially excited anticipating the pleasure on Eddie's face as he unwrapped the mountain of pressies that Stevie and I have chosen for him. Now, I'm not even certain where those pressies are, I left Stevie's room in such a hurry.

Stevie's room.

Because it doesn't feel like mine any more. In fact, the truth of the matter is, nothing is mine. Nothing ever was. Bella wasn't my friend and Stevie wasn't my boyfriend – he's Bella's husband, so even the memories aren't mine.

My head aches with lack of sleep and excessive bawling. My eyes sting and my throat is raw. I am famished, yet I feel sick when I try to eat. I can't think how to fill my day. Stevie and I had talked about sightseeing. We were going to do either the Hoover Dam or the Grand Canyon. I guess I could go on my own but I can't rally. I have a lifetime of doing things on my own ahead of me. I don't see the rush.

I don't want to sunbathe, or drink, or gamble. Vegas truly is a desert.

I sit in the lobby café and sip coffee. I buy myself an enormous slice of carrot cake but don't touch it. Yesterday, I walked past the café several times and coveted the delicious cakes stashed behind the glass counter. Stevie and I had promised to indulge ourselves on the way home from last night's gig. We'd thought that the cream icing and the light sponge would be perfect for soaking up the champagne that we would have drunk. How can things change so dramatically in such a short space of time? One minute, so close it's almost impossible to know where one person's dreams, thoughts and laughter start and the other's end, then the next – total strangers.

'Hi, Laura, I've been looking for you.'

'Oh God, that's all I need. Bella Edwards, or should I call you Belinda McDonnel?' I say without turning to face her. She slips on to the stool in front of me.

I'm surprised she's hunted me down. Clearly, she's underestimated my murderous feelings towards her. I kind of admire her audacity for meeting me face-to-face; on the other hand after hearing of her antics over the last eight years, and in particular the last few months, her audacity can't be hyped.

'I wanted to talk to you.'

'Bit late.' I force myself to look at her. She's blushing, furiously. Good. Hope she spontaneously combusts.

After about two billion years of silence Bella drags her gaze to meet mine. Bugger me, she looks awful. Good. I wasn't the only one who didn't get a decent night's kip. I've never, ever seen her look so dog rough. My first instinct is to feel sorry for her and then I remember how much I hate her. I wonder what Phil has made of her frolics? Poor man, he's in a worse position than I am. Maybe I should call him. We could appear on one of those awful daytime TV programmes together.

'Shouldn't you be talking to Phil?' I ask.

'Yes.' Her hands are shaking. I watch as she tips three sugars into her coffee. Normally she doesn't take sugar. 'I really wanted to talk to him last night but he couldn't face it.'

'Well, you're no longer the one calling the shots are you?'

'No, I'm not,' she admits. 'We've an appointment, at noon, to talk.'

'How very civilized,' I mutter.

I think back to the night before. I thought *I'd* reached new levels of maturity when I'd only flung insults and expletives at Stevie. If I'd been in my own apartment, or his, I would have flung an entire dinner service, lamps, books, you name it. As it was, nearly everything in THE Hotel is pinned down or prohibitively expensive to replace. How can Phil and Bella be so grown-up that they pre-book their rows? Doesn't Phil want to wring her scrawny neck?

'I'm sorry I've ruined everything for you and Stevie,' says Bella. 'I never wanted to.'

'How do you know you have?' I demand. 'Maybe we're going to muddle through.' I don't think this for a nanosecond but I don't want to give her the satisfaction of knowing she's ruined my life.

'I saw Stevie this morning. He seems to think things between you are pretty bleak.' I glare daggers. How dare she sit there and add insult to injury? Where does she get off on telling me she's still having cosy little one-to-ones with Stevie? Hasn't she done enough damage?

'Stevie is truly sorry,' says Bella. 'None of this is his fault.'

'Don't sweat it, forget it,' I mutter, with more bravado than I feel. 'He's a bloke, invariably they lob-in to a girl's life bringing with them a shitload of trouble, it's almost to be expected.'

'He didn't mean to let you down.'

'Let's put Stevie to one side, shall we, Bella? I want to

talk about you and about how *you* let me down.' Bella looks like an accident victim, traumatized and stressed.

Bewdy. It's undoubtedly really ignoble that I want her to suffer – so hang me. 'How could you have done this to me? Why didn't you tell me who he was when you first saw him at The Bell and Long Wheat?'

'I thought I'd get away with it.'

'I admire your honesty,' I comment sarcastically. Then a thought strikes and saddens me. I drop the sarcastic tone. 'Oh, shit, Bella, I've always admired your honesty and now it turns out that you haven't any. I based our friendship on the knowledge you gave me of yourself, which, I think you will agree, was at best sketchy.'

'I'm sorry,' she repeats.

I swear if she says she's sorry one more time I'll ram the ashtray down her throat. Neither of us smokes anyway – she can have it as a souvenir. I take a deep breath and make a mental note to buy some Bach Flower Remedies. I understand they're good for nervous tension.

'You were insulted that it took me five days to tell you I'd had a brief encounter on the Piccadilly line but it's taken you *three years* to mention that you're married!'

'Look, Laura, I didn't plan any of this and I am as sorry as I can be that you got hurt. I know things are tough for you, what with you bringing up Eddie on your own and everything. I never wanted to make it harder.'

'Don't you dare feel sorry for me,' I hiss. 'I'm so sick of your obsession with my single-mum status. I'm exhausted by being defined that way. You'd think in the twenty-first century everyone would have got over it a bit. So my marriage didn't work. So what? My kid is fantastic. I've moved on and for that matter, I've moved up too. I wish everyone else could move on. If I was a nubile twenty-year-old supermodel with three trust funds, your betrayal would be just as bad. Why can't you see this is about your actions, not my circumstances?'

'I don't know what to say,' admits Bella. 'I never wanted to come to Vegas,' she stutters.

'I'm surprised. I'd have thought Vegas would be the perfect place for you. A place where it's legal to plight your troth on a bungee jump, in a drive-thru chapel or in a hot tub. You could have got married a couple more times.' It's a cheap shot, therefore irresistible. No one has yet mentioned the fact that her situation is not only immoral, it's illegal.

'I wish you hadn't invited me,' she groans.

I wish I hadn't invited her too, so at least we agree on that.

'It wouldn't have mattered,' I say. 'You'd still have been married to my boyfriend. I just wouldn't have known it. Have you any idea what you've done to Phil and me?' She doesn't get it, does she? She still thinks the issue here is that she was caught out, not that she has done a terrible thing. She is eternally elusive. 'Oh my God, the peony dress. It was a guilt purchase,' I cry.

'No. I wanted you to have something nice.'

'I had Stevie!'

'I tried to explain,' she stumbles.

'You sound like him. You're well suited.'

Bella takes a deep breath and then says, 'No, we're not. Listen to me, Laura, we don't match any more. We disagree about everything: Elvis, Vegas, travel, sushi, ambitions, money, people. We don't want to live our lives in the same way. He's gorgeous, and once upon a time I loved him very much. A little bit of me will always love him.'

I mash my carrot cake with the back of my fork. I long to be doing something more menacing, mashing her face perhaps. I have no sympathy for her even though it's clear she's fighting tears.

'But we're not right for each other *now* and he knows it.'

I look around for something to throw or somewhere to run. I don't want to hear this.

'He suits you, Laura, and I suit Phil. You're Stevie's. He's not mine and, believe me, I so wanted him to be mine. I wanted something from Kirkspey to be mine. But he's not.'

'What is it with you and your hometown? Don't you know that everyone has a love/hate relationship with their hometown? It's part of growing up.'

'Mine's just hate/hate.'

'You have serious issues. You have no idea when to let things go, yet you're incapable of tackling anything head-on. Instead, you duck, dive or dodge.'

I expect Bella to wave away my observation, to duck, dive or dodge it but she surprises me by asking, 'What do you mean?'

'Well, besides the entire Stevie episode and your prolonged loathing of your hometown, there's the issue of how you constantly focus on everyone else's problems rather than deal with your own.'

'I don't.'

'You do. You're always asking Amelie how she is.'

'That's because I care,' says Bella, with indignation.

'I know you do, but what can she say to you? She'll tell you she's fine and clearly she's not. If she ever wants to talk she calls you. I just think that sometimes she'd like to talk about something other than losing her partner. Sometimes she doesn't want to feel like a victim. Ditto me with the single-mum thing. *And* why the hell can't you just decide which office you want to go to during the week and just go there like everyone else?'

I'm not sure where all this resentment has come from. I thought I was angry with Bella for being married to my boyfriend but it appears my irritation and frustration are much more far-reaching. I'm angry with her because she refuses to grow up.

'What do you want, Bella? I just want a healthy child, to travel a bit, to fall in love. You know, the usual stuff. Not to have an absolutely boring time at work. But you! You want all sorts of ill-defined illusions. Fame, glamour, guarantees, stupendous wealth. I'm not sure they'll ever add up to happiness. I think that's why you can't stick a job for more than five minutes. You want to be running the company before you've discovered how to work the photocopier. You want to control everyone and every-thing but you abdicate all responsibility in your own world.'

It's a strange beast, female friendship. We are so embroiled in one another we can psychoanalyse with ease but we struggle to be straight with one another. Why, in all our years of friendship, hadn't I said any of this to Bella before? Had I pussyfooted around her because I was eternally grateful for her friendship and didn't want to upset the apple cart? Was I scared of hurting her? Or just scared of her? Did I love her too much? Or not enough?

'What do you want?' I yell.

Bella looks wounded and startled but remains silent. For a moment I assume she's not going to answer. But then she does, and her answer knocks me for six. 'I just want to feel safe.'

I don't yell at her any more because fat tears are rolling down her cheeks. I get up and walk away. I'd prefer to spend my last few hours in Vegas at the airport than drown in Bella's self-pity.

47. Stranger in My Hometown

Bella

I splash cold water on my face and stare at myself. Not a pretty sight. My skin is grey and drawn. My eyes are wee, nasty, red slits. My lips are white. I consider hunting for a lipstick in my handbag. I know Phil always likes the fact that I make an effort but I can't muster the necessary boldness. I'd rather tackle this one barefaced, naked, stripped. It seems more appropriate.

Oh my God, what is Phil going to say to me? Laura has already put me through the emotional mill, justifiably throwing acute observation and brazen home truths. I'm not sure I can take much more.

But wasn't that her point – I don't deal with things. Could she be right that I only involve myself with other people's lives as a sophisticated avoidance technique?

I straighten my shoulders, puff out my chest and exit the cloakroom. I have an appointment to meet Phil in the hotel restaurant at noon. The chosen time puts me in mind of shoot-outs at the High Chaparral. Despite this, I know that I have to keep to the arrangement. I can't run away this time. Indeed, it is possible that Phil is testing me. I expect he knows it's fifty-fifty whether I'll turn up at all, but he's always been a bit of a gambler. He took me on, didn't he?

Will Phil press charges? It's possible; he's so upstanding and correct about everything. Ironically it's one of the many things I love about him. I have broken the law, he might feel obliged to turn me in. Oh fuck it. I might as well be in prison if I haven't got Phil or Laura or Stevie or Amelie.

I tell the maître d' that I have a reservation under the name of Edwards and that I'm meeting my . . . who? I think I'm meeting my husband. But he's not that any more. Strictly speaking he never was. I say I'm meeting a friend. I'm told that I'm the first to arrive and I'm shown to my seat.

The restaurant is already busy as Americans tend to eat lunch earlier than Europeans. I'm grateful for the crowds. I know that Phil won't want a scene so our discussion will be just that and not a bunfight. I *think* it's unlikely that Phil will arrive with a gang of police officers because he doesn't like drama.

I'm grateful he decided that it wasn't sensible to talk last night. Anything said in haste would, likely as not, be damning. I admired his dignified silence and respect the fact that he needs time to think about our situation. We both needed some thinking time. I used every moment of mine. Last night I wanted to roll into a ball of self-pity, turn out the lights and simply wait until the morning when the maid would knock on my door and announce that the longest night of my life had been endured, but I realized I didn't have a moment to waste. I had to try to order my thoughts and to understand my actions.

When Phil is fifteen minutes late for our appointment, I start to panic. He prides himself on his punctuality. Does he want to make me sweat? It would be understandable. I wait another ten minutes. Maybe *he's* not going to show. He might want to give me a taste of my own medicine. Would he do that? No, it's not his style, he isn't vindictive. I pull apart a bread roll and drink two large glasses of iced water but there's still no sign of him. If we don't talk soon I'll implode. Another five minutes later he finally joins me at the table.

'Oh, thank God. I was imagining something terrible had happened to you,' I gush.

'More terrible than my wife being a bigamist?' asks Phil.

I blush. 'I was about to start calling hospitals.'

'I'm not the type to self-harm,' he observes.

'No, I didn't mean that. I thought you might have been run over or something.'

'Life isn't that convenient, Bella,' states Phil. He sits down and carefully lays his napkin on his knee.

This conversation definitely hasn't got off to the start I was hoping for.

The waiter appears, he gives us our menus and runs through the specials. I have no idea what is on offer, although Phil asks what the vegetables of the day are. I marvel at his presence of mind. He says no to the wine menu, and when I order a gin and tonic he asks for lemonade. I change my order to a tomato juice.

'Drink what you like, Bella,' he says. 'It's all the same to me.'

Is it? How depressing. 'I owe you a clear head,' I mutter.

Phil orders two courses, for which I'm grateful. It

appears that he intends to hear me out. Of course he does. Phil is a gentleman. I tell the waiter to bring me whatever Phil's ordered, until Phil points out that I don't like bean sprouts. Embarrassed, I scan the menu and select something else, I have no idea what.

'Do you want to lay out the facts for me, Bella?' asks Phil.

I do exactly that. I resist justifications, excuses, defences, apologies or pleas. I stick to dates, times and geography. I tell him when and where I got married and how far along I am in the process of getting divorced. I tell him about all the meetings I had with Stevie and, although it is an uncomfortable confession, I tell him that I let Stevie kiss me once.

When Phil is in possession of the facts, he asks, 'And why do you think you got yourself into this mess?'

I'm taken aback. I hadn't ever considered that I'd actively got myself into this mess. 'I didn't choose it. It happened to me,' I say.

'That's not true, is it?' He forks a pile of bean sprouts into his mouth and chews.

'I'm not great at dealing with trials and tribulations, I see that now. Laura said I dodge them and Stevie . . .' I steal a glance at Phil. He doesn't falter but continues chewing. I can't decide if his cool, calm and collected response is good news or dire. Is he jealous, or angry, or just curious about my muddled life? I plough on. 'Stevie thinks I have a lot of unresolved issues with regard to my mum's death and my home life.' I choose formal distancing words but Phil sees through my ploy.

'What do *you* think?' he asks.

'It's possible.' I pick up my tomato juice and sip.

'Has it ever crossed your mind that the thing that attracts you to Stevie is that he is a little piece of your home?'

'Way off mark,' I say dismissively. 'There's not a single thing I like about my home and—'

'And you like Stevie?'

'Yes.' It's difficult to admit but impossible to deny.

'How much do you like him, Bella?' Phil has asked this question without skipping a beat but there's something about the area below his eye that gives him away. It contracts a fraction, betraying that my answer is important to him.

'I know that I felt comfortable exploring my past with someone who knew who I'd been before. You don't know me, Phil. I didn't even want you to know me.' This confession costs.

'Are you so terrible?' Phil tries to grin but since he thinks I am pretty terrible, his grin is weak.

So I tell him. I tell him everything. I tell him that my dad thinks I'm unlucky to the point of doomed. I tell him that as a child I thought he was perhaps right – maybe my misdemeanour of combing my hair when the boat was at sea did have something to do with my mother's death.

'You don't believe that now, do you?' he asks.

'No. I'd have to be certifiable. But I felt sad and guilty for the longest time.'

I tell him about the outside khazi and my brother's criminal record. I tell him that I resent everyone in Kirkspey for their lack of ambition and I hate myself for being no different – I'm just as unfocused, only I wear designer clothes. I tell him that I have no sense of self. I'm not even sure if I have opinions because that would mean I had beliefs and, most importantly, that I had self-belief.

'I disagree, Bella. You are extremely opinionated about a number of subjects.'

'Name one.'

'You think smoking should be banned in public areas.'

I do. But would I tell a cab driver this if he asked me? Not if I thought he was a smoker. I wouldn't want to offend him.

I notice that Philip has stopped eating. He lays his knife and fork neatly across his plate and gives me his undivided attention. It takes hours to recount the lost memories, the buried embarrassments and my countless failures and disappointments. I describe jobs I walked away from, was sent away from and the interviews I forgot to turn up for.

'I'm not very good with numbers or deadlines, people management, customer complaints or schedules,' I admit, with a sigh.

Phil waves his hand with a dismissive air. 'Schedules are for those who can't handle spontaneity. You might appear to be a flake, but really, you're multitasking at levels that most people don't notice,' he says kindly. How is it possible he thinks that there's anything good about me under the circumstances?

I keep talking but pause, several times, to check if he's bored. He always shakes his head and urges me to carry on. At first, the recounting is awkward and self-conscious. I struggle with chronology and self-pity but, in a peculiar way, talking is a relief. I'm exhausted with pretending to be something and someone I'm not. The waiter clears away our plates and we order coffees, but I don't stop talking. He wanders by with a heavily stacked dessert trolley, we wave it away and I'm still talking. The truth of me, unabridged and with gory detail, spills out on to the table between us.

Eventually, I run out of relevant anecdotes, I take a deep breath and ask, 'I bet you're glad you're not married to me, now you know I'm not what you thought I was.'

'You're exactly what I thought you were, Bella, except that there's more of you,' replies Phil. 'I can't see what has made you so sad and ashamed. So your family was strapped. So what? Lots of people are poor, Bella. It's not a crime. It's just a shame. You've got to roll with the punches and accept that some hands that are dealt are pretty miserable. You know, all low numbers from different sets.'

'Which only works if you are playing Twenty-one,' I say, picking up on his gambling analogy.

'See, that's a good attitude,' he smiles. He seems pleased with me, which is of course impossible. 'That hand wouldn't win if you were playing poker but it would if you were playing Twenty-one. It depends on your game.'

'It wasn't just that they were poor. My father and brothers loathed me. I was just a scruffy nuisance, who was forever in the way. My father's greatest filial ambition for me was that I'd get out the road or disappear altogether.'

'Which you did, when you married Stevie.'

'The funny thing is my father liked Stevie. He'd have approved of the marriage, if he'd known.'

'Did you keep the wedding quiet to punish him?'

'Maybe. I don't know.' I sigh. This is hard, sorry work. Yet I know that I can't quit, not this time. I take a deep breath and then galvanize. 'I think it's more complicated than that. My father's approval of Stevie might have been a tiny part of why I married him in the first place. Maybe there was a time when I still wanted my father's approval, I really don't know. All I know is that I soon knew it was a mistake. I didn't want my father's approval and I didn't want to be part of their world, which Stevie certainly was. And I'm sorry if that makes me a terrible person but that's the truth of it.'

'That doesn't make you a terrible person, not in my book,' says Phil. I beam at him until he adds, 'Failing to divorce Stevie is what makes you a terrible person. Marrying me in front of all our friends and family while you were married to someone else makes you a horrendous person.'

It's true, then, what I've long suspected: I am worthless. Kind, generous, intelligent, thoughtful Phil thinks I'm horrendous.

'Why didn't you divorce?' he asks. His voice is a pitiful groan and I long to put my arms around him and comfort him. More, I long to turn back the hands of time and divorce Stevie before I marry Phil. Both wishes are impossible.

There are a myriad of answers to that question. Are any of them good enough?

'I didn't know how to do it. I was scared of the cost

of a lawyer. I had no one to advise me. It was easier not to,' I reply simply. They are all true and were all factors, to a greater or lesser extent.

Phil looks bitterly disappointed. Had he been expecting something that would absolve me, paint me in a fairer light?

There's nothing more that Phil wants to hear. He signals to the waiter for the bill. I'm pretty sure he's not going to report me to the police. But, I'm equally sure, he never wants to see me again and that's penalty enough. I've had two great chances in my life, with two great men, more than most women get and I've fucked them both up. Circumstances have not conspired against me. I've been responsible for my own downfall.

Phil puts his platinum Amex on top of the bill and pushes it towards the waiter. 'I think we're all done here,' he comments.

Almost. But there is one last thing I need to say. I know it can't make any material difference but it has to be said.

'Phil, do you remember on our wedding day that my father thanked you for taking me off his hands? As though I'd been some sort of financial drain or sad old spinster?'

'When really you were a frisky old bigamist.'

I stare at him and try to weigh up the comment. He smiles, helping me decide that he is trying to be kind or at least funny, his smile gives me the courage to plough on.

'Marrying you has helped. My father is intimidated by your wealth and lifestyle. He thinks I must have some talent – well hidden, admittedly – to land such an eligible man, and I live more comfortably now than I ever imagined possible. But you need to know, Phil, that neither my father nor my background had any influence on why I married you. I did not marry you to impress or suppress my father. I did not marry you to avoid waiting tables for the rest of my life. I married you because I love you. I've always loved you. It's not even difficult. I was so happy on our wedding day. I am so, so sorry that I've caused this terrible mess and that my secret has seeped, leaking insidiously into everyone's lives, infecting everyone.' I daren't pause. If I do I risk him walking away. 'If there was anything I could do to change things, I'd do it but I don't think there is so I just need you to know that I love you. I was not planning on hurting you. I might often be confused, lacking in conviction and chaotic but that's one thing I'm certain of.'

I am sobbing so I hope he understood my enunciation. I hope he understood the sentiment. Despite my resolve to avoid a scene, I think I've made one. From out of nowhere, a waiter passes me a clean napkin, presumably so I can blow my nose, and the guy pushing the heaving dessert trolley hands me an enormous slice of chocolate cake. He mouths, 'On the house,' and scowls at Phil.

Phil nods curtly, excuses himself from the table and leaves me to cry into my mountain of sticky gateau.

48. It Hurts Me

Friday 13th August 2004

Laura

It's a traditional British August, so today it drizzled from sunup to sundown and yesterday rain poured so heavily there were government warnings about flash floods – again. Unlike everyone else, I like the miserable weather. It's appropriate. For me, summer was well and truly over by the time my plane from Vegas touched down and there is nothing worse than feeling depressed when you are surrounded by Londoners wearing bikinis in public parks.

How could I have been so stupid? So gormlessly trusting? *Again*. Again is the worst bit. When I split up from Oscar I thought I'd never be fool enough to trust another man. I swore I'd never allow myself to be exposed to such heartache. But Stevie wormed his way into my trust, my consciousness and my heart. Then he unexpectedly blew up; smattering my self-esteem, self-knowledge and my ability to love, across all of America.

After Oscar left I often said I'd never fall in love again. I repeatedly told anyone who would listen (limited audience, Eddie and Bella) that I would *never* love again, that I didn't even want to.

But I was lying.

I only repeated the mantra to double bluff Fate. I vacillate and can't decide if fate is a misogynistic bastard or a spiteful cow. Fate is probably female because sometimes the jokes she plays are surprisingly witty, and women, on the whole, have a more creative bent when it comes to revenge.

Anyway, I thought if I said I didn't believe love was possible, then sly Old Maid Fate might forget about me and somehow then her nemesis, Lady Luck, would sneak into my life again or, better yet, Cupid would get a straight shot and I would find someone new. And it worked, didn't it? Or at least, for a time I thought it had.

I thought I was the luckiest woman in the world to meet a man like Stevie. But that man never existed. The sexy soulmate with a fondness for my kid was a figment of my imagination. Stevie was as deceitful as Oscar. His infidelity may have varied in the details but was essentially the same. There are a million ways to leave someone but in the end they are all cruel.

This time, when I say enough is enough, I mean it because what *is* the point? If Stevie and Oscar are the same (as different as they appeared to be) then the obvious conclusion to draw is that *all* men are the same. Oh God help me. God help us all. Womankind has nothing to look forward to. The awfulness of this logic sits, like a stone, in my gut. As much as I believe it, I still don't want to. It's such a bleak, wretched, dismal, desolate, cheerless, mean thought. It's up there with four-leaf clovers being nothing but weeds and Santa Claus being nothing other than the fat pervert hired by the local department store. There is no magic.

For a month now, I've thought about this all day, every day, which makes me poor company and a lousy receptionist. Incessantly, I mull over, and over, and over Stevie's betrayal. He is a married man. A *married* man. And if that wasn't bad enough he is married to my *best friend*. Make that ex-best friend. I could have forgiven the married thing, if he'd told me right at the beginning. He was, after all, separated – that is, if his and Bella's story can be believed. A big *if*: they're hardly what you'd call reliable witnesses. I might even have been able to reconcile myself to the fact that he was once married to *Bella*. Maybe, given time and if they had been honest in the first place.

But they weren't, were they? They both lied to me and made a fool of me. And that leads to the question, why weren't they honest? And it's obvious, isn't it? Because he still loves her. He must, he *must*. There is no other explanation for his loyalty to her. He was shagging me either to annoy her, to stay close to her or as a cover for their affair. I'm not sure which of these dreadful possibilities is correct, but one of them has to be.

If only I was dealing with just *his* betrayal. Then I would, at least, have a survival plan and a way to build up my trampled self-esteem. I'd call Bella and she'd invite me over to her house or she'd rush over to my flat. We'd drink a week's worth of units in one night, eat pizza and chocolate, call him a faithless, cheating bastard and then I'd break down in tears and sob that I still love him. She'd pop me into bed, smooth my hair and mutter, 'Of course you do,' (without sounding patronizing or despairing) because that's what she did last time. But, now I've got no one to turn to and I'm missing Bella just as much as I'm missing Stevie.

Today, leaving work on the dot doesn't make me feel guilty, even though I have failed to complete the filing. Sally can do it on Monday. I'm always carrying her and it's time this job-share was just that. I traipse to the station and follow the hordes underground. We stomp after one another into the greyness, avoiding eye-contact by staring at one another's shoes. I'm so numb I can't even feel enthusiastic when I spot a Japanese girl sporting a pair of Jimmy Choos. She's wearing them with ankle socks, which is a fashion statement that leaves me flabbergasted. Normally, I'd make a mental note to tell Bella about this sighting. It's the kind of nonsensical chatter we always enjoyed. It's a bleak day when there's no one to talk Jimmy Choo to.

I've eaten next to nothing all day. Or at least, nothing in the least bit nutritional. I wonder when I had my last packet of wine gums (lunchtime) and I wonder when I can have my next (does four packets of wine gums in one day indicate an addiction, or simply culinary laziness?). I worry over whether you really can get BSE from the gelatin in wine gums. It was a bad day for me when whoever it is that makes these decisions, decided that the vending machines on the London Underground platforms ought to dispense wine gums. Until then I'd resisted chocolate bars (too messy) but I can't get a fellow commuter gunky with a packet of wine gums and therefore they are irresistible to me.

I put a pound in the vending machine. Only after the coin slips from my grasp do I see the tiny sign advising that no change is available. A pound is a lot to pay for a tube of sweets. The electronic letters line up to read 'Sold out, make another selection'. I don't have the will. How come the little irritations that are part and parcel of life seem insurmountable nowadays?

I get on the train and find standing space at the end of the carriage. Hundreds more passengers follow me. The doors try to close twice. I watch as a busy commuter pushes unreasonably, to squeeze on to the packed carriage. As he jostles he knocks into a middle-aged woman with lots of shopping bags. In turn, she jolts the arm of a girl in a beige raincoat who spills her Diet Coke. While on the one hand I am sympathetic (if ever I do have a light coat I always spill things on it), on the other hand I have a malevolent sense of satisfaction when I consider that someone else is having a difficult day too. Suffering is not making me a nicer person.

I pick Eddie up from kindie and, only just, manage to fake an interest in his latest artistic offering. Today Eddie has spent his time gluing dried pasta to a sheet of paper, his sweatshirt and his hair. My faked enthusiasm (at best lukewarm) is dampened further by Eddie's opening question.

'Where's Stevie?'

He's asked the same question every time I've picked him up since I came back from Vegas: four weeks, six days and about ten hours ago. A lifetime in the world of a four-year-old. I give him the usual answer.

'We're back to normal now. Stevie doesn't pick you up any more. I'll be picking you up from now on. *Every day*,' I say firmly.

Before Vegas we had fallen into the habit of Stevie

collecting Eddie whenever he could. It made sense with Stevie's working hours, it made us seem like a normal family. But we weren't any kind of a family and I should have remembered that we weren't, rather than becoming lulled into a false sense of security. Ironic that Bella warned me not to let Stevie get too close to Eddie. Well, clearly she had her reasons.

'I miss him,' says Eddie. 'I don't like normal.'

I should probably think of something wise and consoling to say to my son right now. Instead I squeak, 'I miss him too.' And I don't risk another word all the way home: it would be unhelpful to sob.

I open the door to my flat and am surprised to see Henryk waiting for me in the kitchen. Surprised and a little bit irritated, I thought he'd cleared out. To his credit, over the last six months he and his team have fixed the proverbial House-That-Jack-Built and transformed it into, if not a sumptuous apartment, then at least a safe, functional, pleasant environment. I may be alone in thinking luxury is level shelves, flushing toilets and windows that open and close.

Henryk's presence here can only mean one thing – he's hoping to be paid. Inwardly I cringe. While I have always been aware that Henryk wasn't renovating my entire flat for the sake of Anglo–Polish relations or indeed as a charitable enterprise, I haven't quite thought through exactly how I am going to pay him for all he has done. The nearest I've ever got to forward financial planning is buying two lottery tickets rather than one.

'Hiya, Henryk. Do you want a cup of tea?' I ask, without any real sense of hospitality.

'No, thank you. I have just come to drop off your key. I don't want to take up too much of your time.'

'I'm putting the kettle on.' It's all he needs, by way of persuasion.

'OK, I take it very—'

'Sweet. I know.' I smile and accept that maybe it isn't such a terrible thing to find Henryk in my kitchen. An empty kitchen would mock me more.

Today I haven't received any personal calls or e-mails. All that was in this morning's post was a circular addressed to Oscar. Of course, I was hoping for long, heartfelt letters, offering apologies and solutions, from both Stevie and Bella and I was hoping for a string of pleading phone calls. I wasn't *expecting* either, which was just as well. Today would have been a good day to receive an airmail letter from my folks, or one of those girl-power e-mails that are sometimes forwarded to my mailbox. Nothing. Fate was reminding me how lonely my life was before Stevie and Bella. See, fate's a bitch.

I spend a few moments settling Eddie in front of the TV, then I throw a couple of fat sausages under the grill. I know that if I don't eat with Eddie I'll be eating alone tonight but I can't bring myself to betray as much to Henryk and so I only cook enough sausages for my son.

'Did you enjoy your holiday?' Henryk asks.

'Not really.' I don't see the point in lying.

'You fall out with your boyfriend?'

'How did you know that?'

'You hesitated when cooking sausages, which tells me cosy dinner for two is not on your cards tonight. Besides, recently you have been listening to lots of slow, sad records by way of making point that you are broken-hearted. I turn on your radio. It is Heart FM. The CDs piled by the side of the stereo: Dido, Ella Fitzgerald and Celine Dion.'

'Quite the detective, aren't you?' I'm not sure whether to feel annoyed by the invasion of privacy, impressed by his perceptiveness or flattered that someone is taking an interest in me.

'Do you want to talk about it?'

It turns out that I do. We share two pots of tea and four beers as I tell Henryk all the gruesome details. In the main he stays quiet, only interrupting to say 'Jesus H. Christ' when absolutely necessary. When I reveal my boyfriend's married status and the fact that my best friend is a bigamist, for example.

'So why did she marry the old guy when she was married to your guy?' asks Big H. Despite the serious nature of this question, it makes me smile. The old guy, Philip, is at least ten years younger than Henryk.

'I don't know. I don't think she does. Philip proposed, who'd have thought she'd accept it? What with her talent for evasion. She says she loves him.'

'Maybe she does.'

'I think she loves Stevie.'

'I am confused. She left Stevie.'

'*Then* she did. Because things were a bit tough. They were very young and poor.'

'Lots of people are very young and poor and they make it. Maybe there is an attraction but that doesn't mean they are in love.'

I really hope Henryk isn't going to talk about sex. I've had a difficult enough day as it is.

'A shared history is valuable but maybe those two weren't right for each other and they know it,' he adds.

'It is true that when things aren't right for her she moves on. Jobs, homes, friends. I just never expected her nomadic ways to stretch as far as husbands.'

'You disapprove of her?'

'Yes, I do.'

'Are you jealous?' asks Big H as he sips his beer.

'Most definitely.' I smile, 'I don't have the ability to move on, call it a day and learn from experience. Bella is the opposite. She can't stick with anything for more than five minutes.'

'You make her sound unpleasant.'

'Do I? Well, she isn't. I wish she was. She's decent opposition in the struggle for Stevie's affections.'

'Is that what you are doing? Fighting for his affections?'

I decide not to answer this one. It's a little too foreign and direct. Instead, I stick to describing Bella. 'She's fun, clever and beautiful. When she talks to you, you feel flattered, singled out, appreciated.'

'And this Stevie, how did he make you feel?'

I consider this for a moment. Is it worth explaining to Henryk that Stevie made me feel alive, vibrant, understood and valuable? Or should I tell him that the biggest thrill was that Stevie made me feel normal and confident, both in myself and in my future.

In the end I say, 'Happy. He made me feel so happy.'

'Is it so impossible to imagine this thing fixed?' asks Big H.

I glare at him. Emotions are tender, sacrosanct and ephemeral. A situation as messy and complex as this can't be fixed like a damp patch or a broken lock. Some cracks are just too huge to paper over. Henryk pushes on: 'Has either Bella or the boyfriend been in touch?'

'Bella called me a lot in the beginning. Whenever I saw her ID on the phone I let the machine pick up. I didn't listen to her messages, just erased them. She has nothing to say that I want to hear. And Stevie only tried once. He sent a letter.'

'What did it say?'

'I don't know. I put it in the bin, unopened. I was tempted to write "Return to sender" on it and post it back to him but I decided against it. I didn't want to seem playful.'

'Why didn't you read it?'

'I don't need to read his bloody letter. He's told me everything I need to know by the fact that he only tried to get in touch once! He doesn't care.'

Besides, if I'd read the letter I might have weakened. If it was full of entreaties and pleas, who's to know that I'd have the strength to resist? And resist I must.

'You are a tough woman,' says Henryk.

Am I? I'm amazed. I've been worrying that I'm a bit of a pushover. Stevie and Bella certainly saw me as a sap.

'You need to talk to him.'

'I'm never going to talk to him again,' I say categorically.

'Not the boyfriend. The old one. You have to speak to Philip.'

'Oh, Henryk, you haven't got some half-arsed plan that

433

Phil and I will get it together. Life doesn't work out like that. He's a nice guy but I don't even fancy him. Besides, I'm in—'

'In love with Stevie,' says Henryk. 'I know.' He holds my gaze with his old soul eyes. The guy smells of cement and is wearing a lumberjack shirt yet he has more depth and sensitivity than a nineteenth-century romantic poet. It is a bit of a shame that there aren't more men like Henryk around. Like him, but in their thirties and without the moustache.

'Jesus H. Christ, of course I don't think you get romantic with the other husband. This situation is big mess enough. But maybe you help each other.' Henryk looks at his watch and seems startled. 'I must get home. It is good to speak with you, Laura, but my wife doesn't like me late and in truth, I don't like being late to her. I must go and you must get your son to bed.'

Henryk leaves my key, tells me he'll be in touch regarding the invoice but he has a good enough heart not to mention a figure now. I see him to the door and thank him for taking the time to talk to me.

'It is a pleasure. You are good woman and you'll make good man happy, I know it.'

Then he rushes away, taking the stairs two at a time, to hurry home to his wife. As his green and purple checked shirt fades into the distance, I decide what I want. I want what Henryk and his wife have. I don't want to just get old in someone's company, I want to grow old being adored. I want my husband to rush home to me, long after he's in his fifties, two stairs at a time.

Does that mean I still believe it might happen? Damn

me, for being an eternal optimist. I *have* to learn. I must not have these thoughts.

I drag Eddie out from the makeshift cubby he's built under the dining table with a picnic rug and an assortment of cushions. I force him to brush his teeth but let him forgo his bath as it is already a quarter to eight. He lugs his little body into his favourite Spider-man jim-jams and unusually, falls into a heavy sleep the moment I ease him into his bed.

I sit by his side, stroking his dark curls, which defiantly refuse to be tamed, and listen to the sounds that are drifting through the open window. I can hear a neighbour's TV blaring; someone else is considering lighting a barbie. I've got to hand it to the Brits, there's no holding them back when it comes to making use of every second of summer. It only stopped raining about an hour ago – how can a barbie seem like a reasonable idea? A couple pass by and I listen to them bickering about what to watch on TV tonight. Just as they are moving out of earshot I hear the bloke yell, 'OK, OK, we'll watch your crap.' His words are stroppy but his tone of voice is affectionate.

And I wonder.

Is this it for me?

Am I destined to sit forever on the sidelines, watching my son grow up and listening to my neighbours' squabbles? Will I get the chance to grow old disgracefully in the arms of someone who adores me? Or is it really two strikes and you're out?

Bleak, bleak thought.

I wander into the kitchen, stick my head in the fridge

and consider what I should eat for supper. Nothing looks especially inviting as my appetite is subdued, but my belly is rumbling and thinks my throat has been cut, I need fuel. I settle on a tin of beans. I pop a couple of slices of bread into the toaster and the beans into a saucepan.

I scrabble around the kitchen drawer for a box of matches to light the gas ring. Sod's law springs into action. Of course, I couldn't stumble across a box of Swan: I had to find the ones from the champagne bar at Paris, Las Vegas.

I read the quote on the box: 'Brothers, come quick! I am tasting stars!' I bitterly regret sneaking these into my pocket. I do not need to be reminded of that wonderful night. I need to forget it. I, too, thought I was tasting stars. I believed that Stevie was a miracle. A stupendous, delicious, bubbly miracle, all mine to enjoy.

And I thought he felt the same about me.

But he didn't.

So I need to stamp out any latent affection that might be smugly hanging around, waiting to develop into something even more dangerous – longing, for example. Because if Stevie doesn't adore me and doesn't want to grow old being adored by me, then bugger him. It would be such a mistake to flog a dead horse. I am not some imbo who is prepared to hang around wanting and waiting for Stevie, since he's clearly a bastard. Besides, who am I kidding? He's probably rooting Bella right this moment. They are probably enjoying some amazing date in a fabulous restaurant, bar or club, while I'm here, alone in my kitchen with my tin of beans and box of matches. It's worth remembering that I couldn't hang around him, even if I wanted to, as he wants nothing to do with me. Which is a good thing because he's the lame-brained one. He's unworthy.

It would be a big, big mistake to want to be with him. Huge. Catastrophic.

The only mistake I could think of making that would be quite as catastrophic would be *not* hanging around Stevie if he did want something to do with me.

Bugger it, why is it so easy to imagine being adored by him? Growing old with him? That mental picture should have been well and truly shunted from my mind now. It's over four weeks since we broke up. I sigh.

Still, since the picture of domestic harmony and ancient dotage is still lodged firmly in my mind, what harm can it do ringing Phil?

49. Reconsider Baby

Saturday 14th August 2004

Philip

I wasn't surprised to receive Laura's call, but then again, little surprises me nowadays. I was pleased she rang. I've missed her. She's a great girl, a decent laugh; you know, fun. Of course, I'm not expecting her to be much fun today. Not under the circumstances.

She didn't bother with excuses or a preamble. She barely paused to politely ask after me. She went directly for the jugular and said that she needed to talk to me. I suggested dinner or lunch, she reminded me that she struggles to get childcare cover at the weekend, so I suggested we meet in Kew Gardens, that way she can bring Eddie with her. He can terrorize geese while we talk about life.

She's late – situation normal – and I feel strangely comforted by this constant in a world that is in such disarray. Finally, she strides through the gates, a striking silhouette against the rare sunshine this summer. She looks lovely. She's wearing a dress, a floating, girly thing that is an effective complement to her strong, defined, almost masculine limbs. Eddie is trailing behind her. He looks hot and bothered; stubborn and fed up. I kiss her hello, on the cheek, and offer to buy him an ice cream.

It's like flicking a switch: suddenly, he is wearing the widest, most angelic beam. If only it was so easy to make his mum smile.

We find a cafeteria, choose an ice each and, thus fortified, Eddie gamely charges in front of us, happy to amuse himself.

'How have you been?' I ask.

'Miserable,' replies Laura. She grins, there's not a jot of self-pity about her, she's simply stating a fact. 'How about you?'

'Up and down.'

'I bet,' she says licking her chocolate ice cream (two scoops and a Flake).

I take the bull by the horns. We might as well get on with it. 'I understand you won't speak to Bella or Stevie.' I bite into my more modest choice, a fruit-flavoured ice lolly.

'Do you bloody blame me?' she asks, outraged. 'You of all people can't think I owe them a hearing or anything else for that matter.'

'No, but you might owe it to yourself.'

'Fuck 'em, I say. They deserve each other. I don't want to have to listen to either of them bleating on about how they couldn't resist each other, or that they were destined for one another, or that they tried to stop themselves but couldn't, or some other predictable pig's arse.'

Laura says this at reasonably high volume. Even though I've sat through, and actively contributed to, some fairly loud debates in the past month, I still shy away from publicity. I take a glance around us and then start to lead her along a less populated walkway.

'Neither of them wants to say any of those things to you, Laura.'

'Yeah. I bet they don't think they even have to justify it to me,' she says bitterly. 'Too busy rooting.'

'They haven't shagged for many years.'

'Who told you that?'

'They did.'

'And you believe them?'

'I do, as it happens.' Laura flashes me a strange look. It's hard to decipher. It's somewhere between incredulous and pitying. 'I've talked to them both at some length over the last month and I think I have a clearer picture of what went on than you have.'

'I suppose Bella managed to convince you that she wasn't about to run off with Stevie. That she'd made a choice to be with you even before Neil Curran spilt the beans.'

'Just so.'

'Ha.' Pure contempt spurts out of Laura's mouth.

'Do you want me to tell you what I found out?'

'No,' she says firmly.

'Then why did you call me?'

Laura plonks herself on the nearest bench. Eddie runs to us and insists his mum holds his ice cream. She takes it from him and continues to lick her own as she watches him attempt forward rolls, cartwheels and handstands just in front of us. He's only four, so not in the slightest bit accomplished.

'It's great being a kid, isn't it?' she muses. 'Look at him, not a thought for injury, mud or goose shit. He's just having a laugh. I'd give anything to be that carefree.'

Eddie waves and instructs us to watch him do a forward roll. Which we do; he performs it badly then stands up and beams, 'I'm brilliant at those, aren't I?'

His mother and I laugh and assure him he's the world champion.

'You're giving him a lovely childhood, Laura,' I say.

'Thanks.' She pauses, then adds, 'He's missing Stevie. He was really shattered for days. Even though Stevie was only around for a couple of months, they really liked each other. Did I ever cock that up. I should never have let Stevie get his feet so far under our table. Especially since he was getting other bits of his anatomy up your wife.'

I swallow. This isn't an easy conversation to have.

Laura sees my discomfort. 'Sorry, mate. This is obviously lousy for you too. You know I'm not delicate.'

'They didn't have sex,' I repeat.

'What makes you so sure?' asks Laura. She still sounds doubtful but something in her voice suggests she wants to be convinced.

'I trust Bella on this.'

'Right!' The word explodes in a derisive and indignant snort.

'I do. I talked and talked to her. She went into detail about their encounters, so much detail that what she said had to be true.'

Laura seems to consider this. Eddie retrieves his ice cream from her and I think she's admiring the flower beds but it appears she's watching the visitors. 'What a drama. I didn't want my life to be so full of drama and disappointment. I just want the chance to be normal, like that family over there. Is that so much to ask?' She points, apparently randomly, to a couple sat on a picnic rug under a large birch tree. They look as though they've set up camp for a week. Besides the enormous double buggy and picnic basket, they are weighed down with umbrellas, parasols, suncream, raincoats, spare clothes, three children and a baby.

The mother opens an endless stream of Tupperware boxes, and dishes out food to her family while breastfeeding. She looks frazzled. The father appears to be equally irritated. He keeps insisting that the children ought to sit down and shut up but he's ignored. His broadsheet is flapping in the wind and several pages escape. He chases them, muttering obscenities. The family is boisterous and fraught. But I still know why Laura envies them.

'They weren't having an affair, Laura. They had a flirtation with their past. Not even with their present. I don't believe either of them is attracted to what and who they are now. They fell, briefly, for the sixteen-year-old versions of each other.'

'Nice theory,' says Laura, sarcastically. 'Very convenient.'

'It's what I believe,' I reply.

'So, they're not together now?'

'No.'

'I take it you've forgiven her then?' asks Laura. I can almost smell her disapproval, it's so raw and unmanageable.

'The thing is, Laura, not many people have me down as a romantic. It's one of the drawbacks of being practical when it comes to DIY,' I say, trying to make light of seriously heavy subject matter. 'But I am a romantic. I loved Bella from first sight and I still love her.'

'Well then, I'm sorry for you.'

'Don't be.'

I wonder how far I want to involve myself in this. Should I just leave Laura to her own savage pit of despair or should I try to get her out of there? Over the last month I've got pretty good at these big emotional talks, but hell, they are draining and not what you'd call second nature to me. I decide I'm prepared to give it one more push.

'I know you're hurt because you feel betrayed by Stevie.'

'And Bella.'

Women!

'And Bella,' I add carefully, in an effort to placate. 'And I know you're scared. Damn, Laura, believe me, there's nothing you can tell me about fear. When I remember Bella and I are not husband and wife, I think I might stop breathing. Understanding that fact might make my lungs collapse. I don't want to lose her. I understand scared.'

Laura shakes her head in disbelief. 'Lucky, bloody Bella. She always falls on her feet. Before she met you she stumbled into opportunity after opportunity, even though she always blew it. Then she met you and you adore her. But does she appreciate you? No, she pisses you about to the extent of marrying you while she's married to *my* boyfriend and you still don't think that's a sacking offence. Astounding. Just thinking about it makes me want to spit chips.'

'Stop ranting, Laura.' I've had my fill of hysterical

443

women for the moment. 'Love is more important than anything, more important than a marriage certificate for a dead marriage or an absent decree absolute. Love is the only thing that counts and I love Bella.'

How embarrassing is this? What happened in my life that it seems to be a sensible thing that I am sat on a park bench in a botanical garden and instead of discussing the seasonal blooms and asking for advice on invaluable gap fillers for my borders, I am talking about love. The answer is patent: Bella happened.

Since Bella opened up that lunchtime in THE Hotel in Las Vegas we have had countless 'long chats'. I have spent an inordinate amount of the past month talking about feelings, thoughts, beliefs and, well, love, essentially. It's not too awful, I suppose. But I hope to draw a line under the entire exercise as soon as possible. It's women's work. The thing I need to say to Laura is very straightforward.

'Being with Bella makes me happy. She wants to be with me, I want to be with her. I'm going to find a way to make that happen.'

'Are you going to get married again?' asks Laura. From her tone, I'm pretty sure she doesn't want to be bridesmaid.

'When the decree absolute comes through, I'll ask her to marry me again.'

Laura glares at me. 'Sucker,' she snarls.

'Laura, happiness or unhappiness is a choice and I'm far too sensible to choose unhappiness.'

Laura looks as though I have slapped her face. 'You think this is my fault.'

'Not at all.'

'You do. You think I'm sulking, unnecessarily.'

'No, Laura, I think you're scared senseless.'

'You're on her side.'

'There are no sides. I'm Switzerland, totally neutral about everything and quite keen on peace and trade treaties.' Laura looks infuriated. I'm sorry I always resort to joking when I'm agitated, especially as they are never remarkably spectacular jokes. 'I can love Bella and like you too, you know.'

'I do know. Stevie set the precedent for that.'

'Laura, you're not thinking clearly. You're angry with Bella for not sorting out her past and getting everything muddled, but you're guilty of the same thing. You were hurt so badly by Oscar that now you're pulling out of anything you and Stevie might have going because you're scared of being hurt again.'

'Stevie pulled out of that by lying to me. By kissing my best friend and—' Laura stumbles to a halt.

If she accepts that Stevie and Bella weren't having an affair, which I think she might now, Stevie's misdemeanours are significantly less appalling.

'What are you saying?' she asks.

'It might not be a bad idea to have a think about whether Stevie made you happy.'

'You know he did.'

'And ask yourself whether you really have to throw that away.'

After a few moments Laura says, 'OK, I'll think about what you've said. I'm not promising anything.'

'It would make me very happy if you did think it over.'

I push my luck and add, 'It would make Bella happy too. She's worried about you. That thing you accused her of, the displacement compassion – when you said she was only bothered about people as a way to avoid sorting out her own mess – it can't be true. She's sorting out her problems but still worries about you.'

There are tears in Laura's eyes. Anger? Frustration? Indignation? Sadness? I'm clueless. 'I was a bit harsh,' she acknowledges. 'I was so angry.'

'With good reason. And shocked,' I add.

'Yes.'

'But?'

'But, I know she's not as horrible as I want her to be. I almost wish she was. I know she was very good to me, when it mattered. A total beaut. I wish I could see it all just the way you do. So simply.'

'Everyone deserves a second chance, Laura. Bella, me, Stevie and you – most of all you.'

'I'm not even sure Stevie wants a second chance,' says Laura.

A comment on this is beyond my remit, so instead I suggest we go to the Orangerie café and buy cake. Laura agrees, and Eddie takes no persuading either.

50. You Don't Have to Say
You Love Me

Friday 22nd October 2004

Stevie

I am a single man. I am a free man. I am an uncomplicated soul. I know what to write in the box when marital status is requested on some or other red-tape form. I am no longer lying to my employers, my friends, my family or myself. And it feels good. I am in possession of one bona fide decree absolute.

If only I'd thought to get it a year ago.

Or even five months and two days ago, which was the day before I met Laura. Not that I've had that calculation readily to hand, I hasten to add. I'm not turning into a girl or a lunatic, I've just sat and calculated the exact date on a calendar. Just over a month and a half of which was spent with Laura. Three and a half without. That last bit is quite girly. I'll have to watch that tendency.

Bella and Philip seem to be doing OK now. They've managed to put the whole rotten mess behind them, which is admirable. I'm chuffed for Bella. There's no denying that she means a lot to me, and always will, so I'm glad she's happy. But equally, in the cold light of day, away from all the energy and razzmatazz and emotions of Las Vegas, I'm sure she's not the girl for me. I could sit here and list the reasons we're incompatible but it's all old news, not interesting to me or anyone else. Except Laura perhaps. Maybe, if I'm truly, thoroughly, especially lucky, she'll give me the chance to tell her why Bella and I are incompatible.

Or, more importantly, a chance to tell her why she and I *are* compatible.

Or, more potently, why we ought never to be apart again. Well, except for work, meeting our mates, going to the loo and things like that. But in a more general sense, we should never be apart again. I'm sure of it.

Way back in 1996, when Bella split, I did all the despairing stuff that the unceremoniously dumped tend to indulge in. I endlessly recounted every moment spent together. I reran every row, obsessing about how they could have been played out in a way that would have altered the outcome. When Bella left I was heartbroken, sick to the pit of my existence. It was a big deal and I'm not going to pretend otherwise now, even after so much water has passed under the bridge. *Especially* after so much water has passed under the bridge.

In some ways, it has been just the same since Laura binned me, but in other ways it's completely different. I have recounted every moment, time and time again. But this time the memories don't slash me to the core, they don't make me recoil and cringe. I actually take pleasure in them. I haven't been replaying every row, because there was only ever one row. The final, unyielding, definitive row. Admittedly, I have been doing a fair bit of obsessing about how that could have been played out differently but, it pains me to admit, I haven't the imagination to conjure up a scenario with a happy ending.

Whenever I think of my time with Laura, or Laura and Eddie, I feel fantastic. I feel one hundred per cent hero – totally happy in my own life and skin. I'm proud, buoyant and jaunty. And then reality crashes in blasting apart soothing memories, forcing me to confront the fact that I have only *memories* – and not enough of those: memories that will undoubtedly fade and ultimately disappear altogether. I haven't got the girl. The misery gets pretty vivid at that point.

The circumstances of the two monumental dumpings are totally dissimilar. Laura dumping me was not only justifiable, but understandable. I'd almost go as far as to say she was without choice in the matter. I know what I did was twatish. What would Laura call it? Bogan. That's it, I was totally bogan. I should never have agreed to keep Bella's secret. I should have blurted out our history all over her and Phil's pure wool rug, the moment I was invited into their sitting room way back in June. I should not have been intimidated by a plate of oysters.

Should have, what ifs, could have, would do if I had my time over . . . all the old excuses. But I didn't, did I? And that is the salient fact as far as Laura's concerned.

I wrote to her and laid my cards on the table. I told her I loved her. Big news. I should have told her a long time ago (should have, what ifs, could have, blah, blah). By the time I told her I had nothing to lose, now I'd lost everything. Hardly romantic or positive, I know. Why didn't I tell her one night when we lay in a post-coital glow, or when we were flying to Vegas, or even that final night as she was packing? Would it have made any difference?

In the letter I told her exactly how I feel about her, why I thought we were so good together and why I thought we deserved another chance etc etc. I threw away all semblance of pride and just begged. Sod it, pride doesn't keep you warm at night.

I tried hard to see it from her point of view and to do what was best for her. I realized that I'd put her through a shocking time and so in the letter I made it clear that I'd leave her alone until the divorce was complete. Then, and only then, I would present myself to her as a single man, a free agent, so to speak. I told her I knew she needed time to consider everything, that she wouldn't want me to bombard her with loads of irritating texts, calls, letters, visits and stuff. I promised her that I wouldn't do any of that. I did weaken, just a smidgen. At the bottom of the letter, by way of a P.S. I wrote that if she *ever* wanted to contact me, day or night, I'd be at her side faster than she could say 'All Shook Up'.

It appears she never felt the urge.

It took me over twelve attempts to get that letter into a fit state to post.

I stood by the bit about giving her space. It wasn't easy. Daily, I've had to fight the impulse to haul my arse round to her flat, kick the door down and demand she take me back. But, I decided that macho crap is the last thing a woman wants in a situation like this. It's imperative that I show her I can be considerate, careful and sympathetic because there hasn't been much evidence of that of late. So, with amazing acts of restraint (Dave and John have to confiscate my phone every time we go out on the lash, to avoid my making drunken, heartfelt but annoying calls) I have managed to stick by my promise and I have not pestered her.

But today's the day.

I get a bus to Shepherd's Bush. I'm going to the surgery to see her. At least there she can't ignore me. If I went to her home she might just refuse to answer the door. I'm timing my visit so that I arrive just before her lunch-break. She won't want to discuss her private life in public so maybe she'll agree to have a sandwich with me.

I just need fifteen minutes. I just need a lifetime.

I hate visiting doctors. I'm always certain I'm going to leave with a more dreadful disease than the one I arrived with. Sure enough, the moment I step inside the tiny reception, someone coughs. It's a nasty, wracking, rattling cough and I feel their germs winging their way towards me, rushing up my nostrils and down my throat. It's disgusting. I don't know how Laura does the job she does. Still, faint heart never won fair maid. I galvanize.

Laura is on the phone, booking an appointment. I'd like to say she looks wonderful but she doesn't. She looks tired and drawn. I'm not sure if she's suffering from a late summer cold or an early winter one (hazard of the job) but I am sure that she could do with some chicken soup. I'd like to be the one to bring it to her, on a tray, up to her bedroom. Her nose is red and her skin is sallow. She's wearing a nice top, though. I haven't seen it before. I feel mildly alarmed by this. New clothes are insurmount-able proof that her life has gone on without me. Of course I knew this but I'm terrified. I wanted her to be frozen in time until I'd sorted out my messy life. What if she's not only got a new top but a new bloke as well? It's possible. It's horrible. Bugger, did I ever balls this up.

The surgery is fairly quiet, which is a relief. If I am about to endure the humiliation of a lifetime, it's a comfort to know that there will be only three independent witnesses, one of whom has a hearing aid.

I walk to the reception desk and wait until Laura finishes her call. She does so, writes something in a diary. Without looking up she asks, 'Do you have an appointment?'

'No, but I think you were expecting me,' I reply.

Her head jerks up. I smile. She scowls. I hold out the flowers I've brought. An enormous bunch of sunflowers, with lots of green foliage. They are wrapped in cellophane and tied with string of gigantic, almost rope-like, proportions. They look expensive because they were.

'I'm not expecting you. If I had been expecting you, and your predictable peace offering, it would have been over three months ago,' she snaps. She yanks the sunflowers out of my hands and tosses them into the bin under her desk. They don't fit, so she struggles and violently shoves them for a few moments, some petals fall off. Having dealt with the flowers she turns back to me, 'Now sling your hook.'

'But I wrote to you!' I have so much to explain and seemingly little time to do it. 'You did get my letter?'

'I got it. Never read it. Now go.'

'You never read it?' I ask in disbelief. Hours of work? Months of hope?

'No.' She's staring at something just past my ear lobe,

I turn round to see what's holding her attention. I can't see anything obvious. Then I realize, she's just avoiding my gaze.

'Why didn't you read my letter?' I hope I sound as hurt as I feel.

'I figured if you had anything you really wanted to say to me you'd say it more than once.'

What sort of woman logic is that? I decide not to spill that exact sentiment. I confine myself to commenting, 'That doesn't make sense.'

'If you'd wanted me, Stevie, you would have bombarded me with texts, calls, letters and visits.' Laura is no longer pale and drawn, she is flushed and furious. 'You are such an arrogant bloody drongo. A lazy, arrogant, bloody drongo.'

I'm not one hundred per cent sure of the exact nature of the insult, but I get the gist.

'You sent me one lousy letter and then gave up. Now you have the audacity to swing by three and a half months later with a crappy bunch of flowers, and what? What am I supposed to do? Swoon? Run to you?'

Well, yes.

I need to get a few things straight. First, the flowers are not crappy. I put a lot of thought into those. I avoided anything obvious, like roses, or cheap, like carnations. And I thought I was acting decently by giving her some space.

'I told you in the letter I wouldn't pester you.' I take a quick glance over my shoulder at the waiting patients. I hope Laura sees this as a hint to calm down a bit, or at least wait until we are alone and then she can unleash the full fury. She thinks I'm reminding her that she's neglecting her duties.

'Mrs Williams, you can go and see the nurse now,' she says.

'No hurry, love,' says Mrs Williams, who clearly finds the floor show Laura and I are providing is a far better tonic than anything the nurse could provide.

'Will you come for lunch with me?' I ask.

'No,' says Laura.

I shift from foot to foot. That was not the response I was hoping for but it was not totally unexpected. Well, this may not be the most romantic or appropriate place for big declarations, but I'm left with little choice. Laura starts to play with the paperclips and the staple gun on her desk. She's a little menacing, but even so I lean close to her and whisper, 'If you'd read the letter you wouldn't have expected any more correspondence from me. I said I wouldn't be in touch again until I was a free man.'

I can sense the waiting patients strain to hear my whispers.

'By a free man, you mean after you'd divorced my best friend?' asks Laura loudly.

There is an audible intake of breath from our audience.

I nod, slowly, somewhat defeated.

'Big of you,' mutters Laura. She's being sarcastic but I pretend to interpret her comment at face value, at least that gives me the opportunity to be self-effacing.

'No, Laura. Nothing I've done throughout our relationship has been particularly big or grown-up. Except messing up, that was big time. But I'm sorry.'

'What for?' asks Laura, cannily.

'Everything.'

Laura sighs. After some moments of silence she asks, 'Did you win?'

For a moment I have no idea what she is referring to and then I work it out. 'No.'

She looks up at me now. There's real shock in her face, and maybe disappointment too. 'You didn't?'

'No.'

'Why not?' She sounds stunned.

'I only sang one song, which is against competition rules. I sang "Love Me Tender" instead of "Jailhouse Rock" or "Are You Lonesome Tonight?", my declared, and therefore billed pieces, so I was disqualified.'

'That's terrible.'

'Not really.' When I lost the competition in 1996 I blamed Bella. This time I don't blame Laura. I don't even waste time blaming myself. There are more important losses. 'Anyway, even if I hadn't been disqualified I wouldn't have won. "Love Me Tender" on its own doesn't do enough to showcase a range and, besides, I was under-rehearsed.' The competition seems light years ago. I've barely given it a thought since I left Vegas. My head has been too full of Laura.

'Why the hell didn't you sing your rehearsed songs?' she asks. 'You were brilliant at performing those. You'd definitely have won.'

'Thanks.' The warm glow stretches right through my body and settles in my boxers. It feels good to know Laura admires something, *anything* about me.

I cough. '"Love Me Tender" was for you. I thought there was an outside chance that you might just have been in the audience. And if you were, you might have . . . I don't know . . . been moved or something. Maybe even have forgiven me. It was an appeal.' I shrug.

It sounds weak and hopeless thousands of miles away from Vegas, months after Neil Curran's revelation, but at the time I'd been compelled to sing that song and just that song.

'You prat, Stevie. You threw away the prize.' She's shaking her head in amazement.

'Yes, I did,' I agree. 'Because you are the prize, Laura. And I threw you away. After that, losing the competition hardly mattered.'

'Me and a sixteen-hundred-dollar catsuit. Tough night,' mumbles Laura but she isn't quite as biting as before. Always one for surprises, she suddenly demands, 'Sing it to me now.'

'What?'

'Sing it to me now.'

I'd heard correctly the first time, I just hoped I hadn't. I don't have any music. Or inclination. For God's sake, I'm in the reception of a GP surgery. Three old dears and my angry ex are hardly what you'd call an encouraging audience. I haven't got my guitar or even a background CD. I'm not sure I have the required confidence.

Laura has folded her arms across her chest. Good tits. Inappropriate thought, but honest. I've missed them and the heart behind them. Sod it, singing in a doctor's reception isn't such a weird request. If singing is what the lady wants.

I clear my throat.

'Is he going to sing?' asks a woman with swollen ankles.

456

'I think he is,' says the woman with the hacking cough.

The woman with the hearing aid starts to play with the dial.

I launch into 'Love Me Tender'.

What choice do I have? Flowers failed, chocolates would be an insult. I owe her this much. There are three simple, four-line verses with a chorus in between each. The ballad is deep, rich and emotional, if you get it right. Or, deconstructed ruthlessly, the lyrics can appear naff. I ask her to love me true. I beg her to love me long. I plead for her to love me dear. On top of that I promise to love her too. I swear I always will.

The song lasts a couple of minutes in real time. In Stevie-time it seems like weeks. This is it. *This* is the performance of my life. It's imperative that I seduce my audience. Obviously, I'm not focusing on the coffin dodgers, they melt away, they disappear. There is only Laura and me. It's Laura I have to convince, sway, satisfy and assure. This is all about Laura.

When I finish Laura says, 'Not as good as "Are You Lonesome Tonight?"'

'No. Evidently not.' After all she has not fallen into my arms and she is not applauding riotously the way she did when I performed in Vegas. In fact, to all outward appearances, she is unmoved.

'What are you doing here, Stevie? What do you want?' she asks.

I could buy time. I could ask how Eddie is doing because I really miss him and would like to know. I could take a chance and lean across the desk and kiss her, crush her body tightly against mine, remind myself how wonderful it is to feel her against my chest. Or I could tell her I want to be happy again and I need her for that. I don't do any of this.

Something tells me that the next sentence out of my mouth is the most important I'll ever utter. The pressure is almost unsustainable. My fear is reaching new levels. I give it my best shot. Because after all, that's all we can ever do.

'When you are young, falling in love is more or less random. Who you end up marrying is random. The act means little, the staying is the important thing and Bella and I didn't stay together. Any history we have is ancient and irrelevant.'

'But documented,' she points out, quite correctly.

'That's all it is. A couple of pieces of paper.'

'What changes as you get older?' she asks.

'I'm choosing you. I've had a look around, a fairly extensive look, actually, and I'm choosing you above all others and I'm asking you to choose me,' I say.

'What do you mean?'

Deep breath. 'I want you to marry me, Laura.'

'For fuck's sake, what is it with you two? Why do you have to keep getting married? Why can't you be like a normal person and just say you want to be with me?' she demands crossly. Her outrage at my suggestion has at least and at last drawn her from her desk seat. She marches around to my side of the reception desk. She's within grabbing distance.

'Do I take that as a no?' I ask. I hope she can't hear any self-pity in my voice.

She pauses. 'No, don't take that as a no. It's definitely

not a yes, though. It's not even a maybe. It's a . . .' She looks around her, perhaps searching for inspiration or clarity. 'I'll think about it. Because while part of me hates you and is furious with you, another bit still thinks you're the best thing ever.'

I'm not sure who's clapping. It might be any one of the three old dears. It might even be the nurse or the doctor, both of whom have ventured out of their office to discover why their patients have dried up. It might even be me. I pull Laura towards me and kiss her. It's a good kiss. Strong, certain, passionate. It goes on and on and on. It's the sort of kiss I want never to end.

Eventually, Laura breaks away and says, 'I'll want a copy of the letter, though. And some assurances. A little more detail about the last few months. But yes, OK, you can buy me lunch.'

And I grin at her, helplessly, because I am one hunk of love.

Epilogue

Tuesday 7th December 2004

Bella

I married Phil yesterday. We carried through my initial plan, in so much as we haven't told anyone that our first marriage wasn't legal. We're going to let the vast majority carry on in blissful ignorance. So, it was unlike our first wedding. We did not have two hundred guests; we had two witnesses. Amelie and a guy called Freddie, who is Phil's solicitor. For the last few months Freddie and Phil have been working on the legalities of my situation. Understandably, Phil was keen to ensure that our marriage was legal this time. Me too. My crime had to be reported but, luckily, neither Phil nor the police wanted to press charges so I don't have a record.

We married in a registry office, not a church. I wore a red trouser suit. There were no large hats, no morning suits, no confetti, no bridesmaids or pageboys in cute kilts. I did not throw a bouquet. It was a perfunctory affair. It did not have the illicit excitement of my marriage to Stevie, or the splendour and romance of my first ceremony with Phil, yet it felt more serious and important than either of those occasions.

We had a sensational celebratory lunch in Claridges,

just the two of us. Amelie couldn't join us because she had to collect the kids from school and Freddie had to get back to the office. We drank plenty of champagne and there were big, white lilies on the table. We married for the second time exactly a year after the first. So we'll have the same anniversary, just a different year, which will hardly matter by the time we reach our ruby wedding anniversary. And we will make our ruby anniversary, I'm sure of it. Because, while all the details are different when comparing our first wedding ceremony to our second, one fundamental thing has not changed. I love Phil. I want to be his wife, more than anything I want that. I love him more than I did before. I value, trust and appreciate him. Also, we both know a lot more about me so our love is deeper and more complete.

Since meeting Phil I've suspected that I'm the luckiest woman on the planet and yesterday proved that to be the case.

Laura and Stevie are an item again. I understand from Amelie and Phil that Laura made him sweat for a month but in the end her optimism at life in general and her love for him, specifically, won the day. She lost interest in being peeved; she just wanted to spend some time being happy. In the New Year they are going to Australia together, to live. Oscar got a job in Singapore so Laura is no longer tied to London. She admitted to Stevie that her wanderlust was exhausted and that she was ready for a bit of homespun support and affection from her family. I guess the events of the last few months had taken their toll. According to Amelie, a reliable source, Stevie begged to join her. Laura nearly burst with joy. Apparently, she'd been thinking about moving back to Oz since July but couldn't bring herself to go without having sorted things out with Stevie.

It looks like Laura's got her happy ending, which is good news. And Stevie too, he's found someone who appreciates him and wants him just the way he is. That person was never going to be me. I'm not the type of girl to share my man's love with a dead rock 'n' roller, even the King of rock 'n' roll.

So the tangled mess I caused is being resolved. The bewilderment is fading, the hurt receding. It hasn't been easy. But then nothing of any true value is ever easily attained.

When Phil left me to my gooey gateau in the restaurant in THE Hotel, in Vegas, I was hardly able to breathe for shame, sorrow, grief and regret. I thought my world had ground to a halt. I could not imagine a time when the pain would stop, my pain and everyone else's. Unsurprisingly, I did not eat the cake. I left the dining room and I wandered around the hotel garden. When I'd passed every tree and bush about fifty times, I walked along the Strip. I'm not sure how far I walked or for how long. I had nowhere to go and no one to go to. I'd never felt so alone. The loneliness chilled me to my core.

I had very little money on me and after I'd bought a bottle of water I was flat broke. It struck me how easy it would be to just drop out, to become nothing, to disappear altogether. I had run away and reinvented myself once before, but this time I did not have the buoyancy to run towards a new life or even the grim determination, born from dissatisfaction, to run away from an old life.

Without Phil I had nothing. I had no career, no sense of purpose, direction or self. I had no friends, no family, no money, and no home. Worse, I realized that even if I had a career, money and home, without Phil I still had nothing.

I stood on the walkway surrounded by neon lights flashing, promising wealth, sex and helicopter rides and I almost laughed at the weirdness of a life where everything can be bought, except for peace of mind. I had learnt to live with a certain amount of confusion, I'd almost become anaesthetized to it, but suddenly the enormous mess I'd made of my life hit me and threatened to knock me out cold.

My eyes fell on a tramp shuffling along searching trash cans, presumably for food and bottles that he could collect a dime on. I'd seen a number of people in similarly desperate circumstances in Edinburgh, London and every other city I'd ever visited. I'd *seen* them but I'd never really *noticed* them before. He was wearing plastic bags on his feet and, even though Vegas is hot all year round, he was dressed in layer after layer of filthy, tatty clothes. Wherever he walked people made space for him as they moved away from his smell and poverty. I wondered how *he'd* fallen so low? It was easy for me to imagine a million ways to mess up. He sensed me staring at him, turned, glared and then erupted into furious yelling. He didn't want my pity.

In that moment I saw what I wanted from my life and found the energy to fight for it. I turned and started to dash back to the hotel. I rushed through the hordes, refusing to be distracted or delayed by ambling tourists or pushy touts, I ran back to my love.

When I opened the door of our room Philip had his back to me. He was looking out on to the dazzling lights below, watching hundreds of cars moving up and down the Strip. He was watching people shouting, laughing, crying, drunken people, sober people, the happy ones and the heartbroken. He didn't turn to face me, although he must have heard the key in the lock.

'Give me one more chance, Phil. I know I don't deserve it but I'll make sure you never regret it. Please, Phil,' I blurted.

I was prepared to humiliate myself, over and over if necessary. I'd plead, petition, reason, explain and even fight tooth and nail if I had to. I was determined I would not lose Phil. I refused to be that unlucky. You have to make your own luck in this world.

When he turned to me I saw he'd been crying.

He gave me the chance I didn't deserve, because love allows that to happen.

When we got back to England, Phil suggested I see a counsellor. Bloody hell, as if I hadn't been through enough shocks! Philip Edwards suggested a counsellor, like he was a woman or one of my gay friends. I said no and insisted we'd sort it out between us. He argued that we might be able to sort ourselves out but then he asked, 'What about all the other issues, Bella?'

'What issues?' I replied, disingenuously. After all, I'd been burying my head in the sand for years; I was the reigning champion of avoidance.

Phil pointed out that as we'd got a second chance perhaps everyone deserved the same, even my father. He was getting carried away. I really can't envisage a big

Surprise, Surprise type of family reunion, even after intensive therapy, but I saw that a counsellor might help me find a way to reconcile myself with my past. That would be enough. That would be a lot, because maybe then I would be able to move on into my future. A future with a career, and babies, and opinions that I express honestly and openly. Even to taxi drivers.

Phil looked a bit nervous when I told him that was one of my aims but I think he'll be supportive, even in the mini cabs.

I'm retraining. Again. I'm doing a degree in child psychology. No one believes I'll finish the course, except Phil, and I'll prove him right. I'm determined to.

It turns out that I was wrong about what makes you a grown-up. It's not keeping spare loo rolls in the bathroom cupboard and light bulbs in a box in the garage. It's about being comfortable with yourself. I've finally realized that being grown up involves having the guts to make a difference and the humility to accept that it will mean making mistakes. Growing up means living a full life; having the courage to own up, stand up, shout up, calm down and go down on bended knee if necessary. Yesterday at our simple marriage ceremony I felt entirely grown-up.

There's only one more thing I need to do. I pick up the phone, speed-dial number 1.

'Hello, Laura, it's me, Bella.'

Great. Even my opener sounds dubious. Will she be kind and understand that I'm telling her it's Bella because we haven't spoken for so many months and I'm neurotic that she'll have forgotten my voice, or will she be harsh and assume I'm distinguishing between Bella and Belinda?

For several moments she says nothing at all.

And then, at last, 'Hi.'

'How are you?' I ask lamely.

'Great, thanks.' She's not cutting me any slack.

'Me too.' Not that she asked.

'And the reason for your call is . . . ?'

I like the fact that's she's so gutsy and tough. It shows she's recovered from her three-year confidence crisis. It's ironic though, isn't it, that I did everything to bring her out of that pit when we were friends and it turns out all I had to do was be married to the love of her life. Just kidding.

'I wanted to tell you that Phil and I remarried.'

'I heard you were going to.'

'Right.' I pause again.

'You want me to say congratulations?' she asks.

It is traditional. 'I don't mind. I just wanted you to hear it from me.'

'Everything has turned out OK for you, hasn't it, Bella?' She doesn't sound thrilled about this.

'I understand things are good for you and Stevie too,' I point out.

'Oh, they are,' she says, with a gush of genuine enthusiasm, then she checks herself and adds, 'no thanks to you.'

'I suppose not.'

This conversation is agony. No matter how many times I'd prepared for it with my counsellor or practised it in my head I could not have anticipated how bad Laura is making me feel. In the past, we only ever made each other happy.

A fat tear falls on to the magazine that is propped, unopened, on my knee. Oh God, I am so weepy at the moment. I really don't want to cry in front of her. That would be so mortifying, so indulgent.

'Are you crying?' she demands.

'Yes,' I mutter, reluctantly.

'Are you pregnant?' she asks, with the intuition of a best friend.

'Maybe,' I admit. I snuffle and laugh down the phone. 'You're the first person I've told, I haven't even done a test yet and I haven't mentioned it to Phil. I didn't want to get his hopes up but—'

'Oh my God, that's amazing!' Laura laughs. 'Isn't it?' she adds, a little more cautiously, but reasonably, considering the views I've articulated to her on motherhood in the past. The conversation is a rollercoaster. Neither of us is sure of the other, but we are heading in the right direction. I'm not certain how long I need to apologize for; Laura is not firm about how long she needs to stay angry with me.

'Yes, it is amazing. I really want to be pregnant,' I assure her and I'm blubbering again. It might be at the idea of a baby and all that means – or because I can hear genuine warmth in Laura's voice.

'But what about your course as a child psychologist?'

'Have you been keeping tabs on me?'

'Well, obviously,' she giggles.

'I'll still do the course even if I am pregnant. Part time, if necessary. It will take longer but people manage these things. You do your course, with Eddie and a job. I'll be fine. How is Eddie?'

'Really great.'

Dare I tell her that I miss him loads? Or did I relinquish that right?

Suddenly, we have run out of things to say. I could ask what her plans are for Christmas or how things are at the surgery, but in this case I think small talk would do more harm than good. We both know what I need to say.

'I'm sorry.'

'Yes, I imagine you are.'

We hesitate, allowing those two sentences to settle into our history.

'So, you're off to Australia.' I try to inject as much eagerness as I can into my comment. The thought of her leaving makes me feel incredibly sad but I can see why it's the right thing for her to do.

'Yes.'

'Do you think we might e-mail?'

I don't want to lose contact with her. Bella Edwards has spent a lifetime losing people and leaving people behind but I suddenly want to hold on to Laura, very tightly. 'We've got so much history,' I mutter.

'In this case I think there might be too much history,' says Laura. 'I still can't quite believe that you were once married to my Stevie.'

'It was a long time ago. Everything changes. We've moved on,' I remind her.

'I'm beginning to get that,' she admits. 'I'll say one thing. It's been one hell of a ride knowing you, Bella.'

I don't know what to say. Am I consigned to the past tense for her? 'We'll send each other Christmas cards, though? Hey? And photos of Eddie and Baby Edwards, as and when?' I ask desperately.

'That would be OK,' concedes Laura. She adds, 'I think you'll have a girl.'

'Or a boy,' I suggest.

'Yes.' Laura giggles again. We've both always thought old wives' tales for predicting a baby's sex were ridiculous. I mean, it's going to be one or the other, isn't it?

'I know it can never be the same,' I state. 'I've made that impossible.'

'It would be difficult. I can't imagine inviting you and Phil over to visit me and Stevie.'

'No. But, wherever you are, Laura, I hope you're happy.'

'Yes, you too.' And now Laura sounds as though she's choked up as well. 'Before you ask, I'm not pregnant,' she sniffles down the line, 'just moved.'

We talk for a few minutes more. We chat about Eddie, my counsellor, whether she is going to sell or lease her flat, about our plans for Christmas. I ask her what haulage company she's using because I know someone who is in the business who can probably do her a deal. We amble in and out of the conversation the way we have, almost daily, for the last three years.

And finally we say goodbye. And I don't know if that's the end, or just the beginning of another chapter.

Glossary of Australian terms

Australian	English
Australian	**English**
Beaut	Marvellous
Beauty	Marvellous person
Bewdy	Wonderful
Bezzie	Best
Big bikkies	Worth a lot of money
Bit of a yarn	Chat
Bogan	Stupid or uncouth
Brekkie/brekky	Breakfast
Bull	Not true
Bushed	Tired
Champion	Nice person
Cheer'n	Happy
Chockers	Full
Cozzie	Swimming costume
Crash hot	Very good or well
Cubby	Child's playhouse
Daks	Trousers
Dig	Like
Dork	Idiot
Drive the porcelain bus	Vomit in the loo (after too much to drink)
Drongo	Idiot
Dunny	Loo
Fair dinkum	Cannot be faulted

Flips his lid	Loses his temper
Friggn' A	Excellent
G'day	Hello
Give it a bash	Have a go
Good as gold	It's very good
Hoe into	To tackle or attack energetically
Humdinger	Big row
Imbo	Imbecile
It's gold	It's very good
Jim-jams	Pyjamas
Kick on	Stay and party
Kindie	Nursery
King hit	To hit or punch someone forcefully, usually from behind
Lame-brained	Stupid
Larrikin	Wild, unruly
Legend	Nice person
Let me have a squiz	Let me have a look
Lob-in	To arrive unexpectedly
Mank	Drunk
Mind your own bizzo	Mind your own business
Narky	Angry
Nong	Stupid
Not the full quid	Bit daft
Off her lolly	She's very angry
On the turps	Drinking alcohol
On ya or Good on you	Encouragement
Pig's arse	Rubbish
Pissed	Angry

Pissed as a parrot	Drunk
Pull your head in	Mind your own business
Rat shit	Awful
Rooting	Shagging
Scrungy	Messy
Shattered	Upset
She'll be apples	She'll be fine
Shindig	Party
Shit-faced	Drunk
Smashed	Drunk
Snitchy	Narky
Spit the dummy	Lose patience
Spitting chips	Very angry
Square shooter	Honest person
Squiz	Look at
Stoked	Happy
Sweet as	Lovely
Tanked	Drunk
What a legend	What a nice person
What a purler	What a great thing or person
Wing-ding	Argument
Yak	Talk

Acknowledgements

Thank you to Aly Barr for helping me check facts about fishing communities, weather and dialogues in Scotland and to Kerry Barr for explaining the Scottish exam system. Thank you to Nicole Byford for doing the same with regard to Australia.

Thank you to all my readers, each and every one of you.

Thanks to my family for constant encouragement and support, childcare, anecdotes and love.

The biggest thank-you has to go to Jim. Thank you for your love, patience and assistance: particularly for coming up with fantastic marketing ideas, designing my website, searching out Elvis tribute banks, driving to Blackpool, reading my scripts over and over again, propping me up, picking me up, slaying dragons and generally ensuring that my life is so crammed full of purpose and unadulterated bliss that I'm in serious danger of exploding.

HUSBANDS

Bonus material

Reading Group Questions

- Bella is sometimes difficult to like. Do you think that she is a sympathetic character?

- Laura and Philip both feel, at points in the novel, that they have been betrayed by Bella and Stevie. How did you think the subject of betrayal was portrayed?

- Amelie is the only major character whose narrative voice we do not hear. What do you think of the characterisation of Amelie? Is she right to be so critical of Bella?

- How is female friendship portrayed in the novel?

- What kind of insight do you think the novel offers into the psychology of a bigamist?

- The novel is told through the eyes of the four main characters. What effect do you think this split perspective has?

- Do you think that Bella's difficult childhood in Kirkspey excuses her later actions?

- Philip is able to forgive Bella at the end of the novel. What to you think of his decision to remarry her?

- The novel revolves around two major coincidences. What role do fate and coincidence play throughout?

Have you read all of Adele's fabulously addictive novels?

ABOUT LAST NIGHT

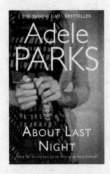

There is nothing best friends Steph and Pip wouldn't do for one another. That is, until Steph begs Pip to lie to the police as she's desperately trying to conceal not one but two scandalous secrets to protect her family. Her perfect life will be torn apart unless Pip agrees to this lie. But lying will jeopardise everything Pip's recently achieved after years of struggle. It's a big ask. How far would you go to save your best friend?

MEN I'VE LOVED BEFORE

Nat doesn't want babies; she accepts this is unusual but not unnatural. She has her reasons; deeply private and personal which she doesn't feel able to share. Luckily her husband Neil has always been in complete agreement, but when he begins to show signs of changing his mind, Nat is faced with a terrible dilemma. She begins to question if the man she has married is really the man she's meant to be with . . .

LOVE LIES

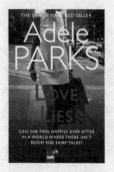

It's a girl's ultimate fantasy – being swept away by Prince Charming and living a life of luxury, wealth and celebrity. But after a whirlwind romance with pop star Scottie Taylor, modern-day Cinderella Fern must ask herself if love is telling the truth. Can she find her Happily Ever After in a world where there isn't much room for fairy tales?

YOUNG WIVES' TALES

Lucy stole her friend Rose's 'happily ever after' because she wanted Rose's husband – and Lucy always gets what she wants. Big mistake. Rose was the ideal wife and is the ideal mother; Lucy was the perfect mistress. Now neither can find domestic bliss playing each other's roles. They need more than blind belief to negotiate their way through modern life. And there are more twists in the tale to come . . .

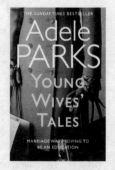

STILL THINKING OF YOU

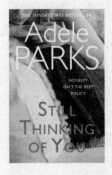

Tash and Rich are wild about each other; their relationship is honest, fresh and magical, so they dash towards a romantic elopement in the French Alps. However, five of Rich's old university friends crash the wedding holiday and they bring with them a whole load of ancient baggage. Can Tash hold on to Rich when she's challenged by years of complicated yet binding history and a dense web of dark secrets and intrigues? Does she even want to?

THE OTHER WOMAN'S SHOES

The Evergreen sisters have always been opposites with little in common. Until one day, Eliza walks out on her boyfriend the very same day Martha's husband leaves her. Now the Evergreen sisters are united by separation, suddenly free to pursue the lifestyles they think they always wanted. So, when both find exactly what they're looking for, everybody's happy . . . aren't they? Or does chasing love only get more complicated when you're wearing another woman's shoes?

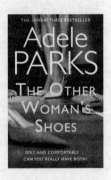

LARGER THAN LIFE

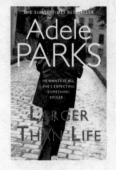

Georgina fell in love with Hugh the moment she first saw him and she's never loved another man. Unfortunately, for all that time he's been someone else's husband and father. After years of waiting on the sidelines, Georgina finally gets him when his marriage breaks down. But her dream come true turns into a nightmare when she falls pregnant and Hugh makes it clear he's been there, done that and doesn't want to do it all again. Georgina has to ask herself, is this baby bigger than the biggest love of her life?

GAME OVER

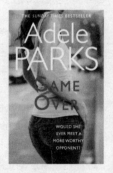

Cas Perry doesn't want a relationship. When her father walked out on her and her mother she decided love and marriage simply weren't worth the heartache. Cas, immoral most of the time and amoral when it comes to business, ruthlessly manipulates everyone she comes into contact with. Until she meets Darren. He believes in love, marriage, fidelity and constancy, so can he believe in Cas? Is it possible the world is a better place than she imagined? And if it is, after a lifetime of playing games, is this discovery too late?

Playing Away

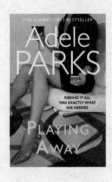

Connie has been happily married for a year. But she's just met John Harding. Imagine the sexiest man you can think of. He's a walking stag weekend. He's a funny, disrespectful, fast, confident, irreverent pub crawl. He is also completely unscrupulous. He is about to destroy Connie's peace of mind and her grand plan for living happily ever after with her loving husband Luke. Written through the eyes of the adulteress, *Playing Away* is the closest thing you'll get to an affair without actually having one.

One word was all that mattered . . .

Read on for a preview of
Adele Parks' novel
TELL ME SOMETHING

I

I fell in love with Roberto twice.

The first time was twelve years before I met him.

I was on holiday with my parents in Padova, north Italy. I was fourteen, sulky, brooding and romantic. The second time was twelve years later, in a pub, in south-west London. He was watching a football match on the large screen. I was pulling pints. By then I was more gregarious and thoughtless but still astonishingly romantic.

Before Padova, holidays with my parents (and there was no other kind) had been limited to the British Isles. I grew up accepting that foreign holidays were something that everyone else did but, for me, they were out of the question.

My parents were a traditional pair and they were careful with their money. Both facts can be quickly explained and possibly excused if I tell you that my mother and father were forty-four and forty-nine respectively when the stork dropped me on their doorstep. Today they would not be considered horribly geriatric parents but back then they were regarded as such. Some of my mum's friends were grandmothers. Besides, they'd previously had two stork visits, nineteen and seventeen years earlier. My father always joked that the bird assigned to our family had no sense of direction or urgency and it had been late by about fifteen years. He maintained that he and my mother had always wanted three children and a little girl was especially welcome; which was very kind of him although unlikely to be strictly accurate.

No one in my family can have been particularly over-joyed by my tardy arrival. My brothers, Max and Thomas, must have felt vaguely uncomfortable with this obvious proof that their parents still indulged in sex. No doubt both of them were happy to rush off to university as soon as feasibly possible in order to put distance between themselves and the whole messy business. It would have been quite reasonable for my parents to have assumed that the broken nights' sleep and soiled nappies part of their lives was well and truly behind them, at least until grandchildren arrived. My father had just made partner at his accountancy firm and he was the captain of the golf club that year; both time-consuming, demanding roles. My mother had her bridge and now she had me.

Still, they made the best of it. I was healthy and my mother found pleasure in dressing me up in party frocks, something that had not been available to her while parenting Max and Thomas, obviously.

But family legend suggests I was not so much a bundle of joy, rather a bundle of trouble; a poor sleeper, picky eater and angry while teething. It wasn't a picnic. I grew up believing resentment silently slept with us all. I believed that their ideas were out-dated and overly fussy in comparison to other parents. My father played the oboe and called boys chaps. He often corrected my friends' use of the auxiliary verbs 'can' and 'may'. My mother was more embarrassing still, just because her exposure to my classmates was more regular.

She was not as pretty as all the other mothers who

clustered at the school gate. Her clothes, shoes and complete ignorance about who Paul Young was set her a generation apart. Looking back I can see that she was a careful and concerned mother but at the time I gave her no credit for this, only grief. She regularly invited my friends around for tea but refused to serve fish fingers or Angel Delight, as the other mums would. Instead she made huge stews and persisted in serving sprouts or cabbage. She had no idea. She also insisted on collecting me from the school gate even when I was at senior school. Sometimes, if I thought I could get away with it, I pretended she was my batty grandmother (a batty grandmother being infinitely more acceptable than an interfering mother) and I would join the other children in laughing at her sensible shoes and practical mackintosh before I was in her hearing range.

I was always vaguely embarrassed by my parents and I was ashamed of myself for being so, which in turn made me even angrier at them for being the source of my ugly emotion in the first place. They weren't draconian; they were just wrong. While the pocket money they gave me was slightly below class average, they (theoretically at least) allowed me to spend it on whatever I chose. But their obvious disappointment if I chose a *Jackie* comic and a stack of sweets rather than an edifying classic novel always diminished the pleasure of those treats. Clothes were an issue. I was twelve before I was allowed to own a pair of jeans, fifteen before I was allowed mascara (although I secretly applied it at school long before that), seventeen before I was allowed to have my ears pierced. OK, I'm looking back at these grievances from a wiser age (just thirty-two) and I admit that my parents didn't exactly commit war crimes but, at the time, in my view, they might as well have done.

The main focus of contention was holidays. Other parents took their kids to Costa del somewhere or other or even (the pinnacle of cool) Disney in America. My classmates tried sticky liqueurs on holiday and spent their money on stuffed toy donkeys and jars full of coloured sand. Their sunbathing was injudicious and they often returned home with sore sunburnt limbs but exciting stories about flirtations with foreign boys to make up for the pain.

My parents were more interested in National Trust buildings than busy beaches. Their idea of a superb holiday was to hitch up the caravan to a site along the southern coast (preferably near a castle and a decent tea shop that sold a light sponge cake). I endured countless wet weeks watching my parents struggle with an Ordnance Survey map in an attempt to find the footpath that took us to yet another dull relic.

When I was fourteen it was my parents' thirty-fifth wedding anniversary, and Max and Thomas (who were already enjoying successful careers as a journalist and a doctor, respectively) thought that the anniversary was excuse enough to treat our parents to their first holiday abroad. My father had been to Germany to complete his National Service but my mother had only ever crossed the Channel to go to the Isle of Wight (terrific bird-watching, apparently).

My parents' reaction was guarded. Max spent hours drawing attention to the numerous places of historical and archaeological interest and Thomas calmed their fears about drinking tap water or attacks from mosquitoes, and slowly my parents started to accept – and then finally enjoy – the idea. I was to be included in my parents' anniversary trip, as they would never have allowed me to stay at home under the supervision of my big brothers, let alone by myself. My reaction was one of unequivocal joy.

I got a paper round and began regularly babysitting for neighbours' kids, as I longed for a wardrobe boasting bikinis and shorts. I was thrilled at the idea of owning a passport. I pored over maps and guidebooks. I became silly with excitement when my father and I finally visited the bank to exchange our currency. I marvelled at the strange money and couldn't resist sniffing it. It felt warm and peppery; somehow promising and mysterious. Obviously, I had less interest in churches or art galleries than my parents and I was more focused on getting a tan, eating ice-cream and making eye contact with Italian boys. My targets were modest – I wasn't even expecting to speak to anyone other than the hotel receptionist – and still I was fizzing with the excitement of the adventure.

By some miracle our holiday managed to surpass even my lofty expectations. I delighted in everything strange, new and foreign. The duty-free shops at the airport seemed glamorous beyond compare and I coveted the enormous Toblerone bars that were not so freely available in UK supermarkets in those days. I was disproportionately pleased with the wet paper towels that the friendly air hostess doled out with free (*free!*) drinks of cola on the flight. From the moment the aeroplane doors swung open when we touched down and the sun slammed into the plane and cocooned me, I was in love.

2

I wasn't in love with the guy ushering us down the plane steps and towards the airport bus, or anything prosaic like that (although he was cute). I was in love with *Italy*. A wall of thick heat slapped on to my pale, gangly limbs and I wanted to sing because suddenly I felt at home.

I lived in a clean, functional house which groaned with healthy food, music practice and educational games. We were comfortably off. We had everything we could ever have needed but nothing that I wanted. We had fitted carpets, a microwave, hot water bottles, silver cutlery (that had been handed down to my parents from my mother's grandmother), but we did not have a TV in the sitting room (just a very tiny one tucked away in the spare bedroom, pulled out on special occasions); we had a piano, we had net curtains, for goodness sake; the very epitome of a middle-class British existence in all its insipid glory.

Suddenly I felt warm, colourful and impassioned. I'd never got excited about anything in my life until that point. Without a TV I had no idea who Duran Duran really were, and had faked a crush on 'the drummer' to blend in at school, but I couldn't have picked him out in a line-up of Thai lady boys. I did not excel at a particular sport or a subject. I was not the type of child to have found solace in books. My few friends were equally dull and ill-defined. We didn't even choose to be one another's friends – we were sort of the left-over kids that no one really wanted to be pals with. I'd never had a boyfriend or even been kissed.

And suddenly there was Italy.

A country of warmth. A country that smelt of sweet, strong coffee. A country full of noise, chaos, chat and energetic and constant hand gestures. I was heartened by the abundance of flowers, festivals and flowing ribbons pinned to doors to announce the birth of a baby. It seemed to me that the Italians knew how to squeeze every ounce of juice out of life. And best yet – even better than the squeals of delight expelled from the kids chasing pigeons in the piazza – it seemed that every boy and man looked at me in a way that suggested I was interesting, appreciated and alive. In England my curly hair, fair skin and splattering of freckles were tragically unfashionable. But Italian men didn't seem to mind that I didn't sport a sleek, dark bob; quite the opposite.

My infatuation grew deeper and more serious with every espresso I gulped. For ten days as I wandered around the narrow medieval streets of Padova I did not feel the ghosts of Giotto, Dante or Petrarch, as my parents did; I felt the weight of appreciative glances from the city's Giovannis, Davidos and Paulos. While my parents discussed the beatific smiles great artists had given the Virgin and Jesus, I wallowed in the much more salacious smiles secretly bestowed on me by waiters and boys lounging outside souvenir shops. I was too shy to actually talk to anyone else, tourist or local, so for hours I licked ice-creams or drank coke and stared.

I watched the girls who giggled in gaggles yet managed to attain a level of sophistication that even the sixth-formers I knew could only long for. Was it their high heels? Or the tight belts? Their thin wrists or mascara? I did not know. All I knew was that I wanted to be one of them. I wanted to join an enormous, noisy family for the *passeggiata* parade at five o'clock; it was marvellous that even something as simple as an evening stroll seemed to be a celebration. I wanted to buy cakes as a Sunday morning gift for my friends; cakes that were presented in a cardboard box, wrapped with cheerful ribbons. I wanted to live among ancient history and serious style. I wanted their sociability to be mine. I wanted to eat their food and to bask in their civic pride and cultural interests. I wanted to live in Italy. I wanted to be Italian. It was obvious what I needed to do. I would marry an Italian.

I came back to England with bagfuls of *Oggi*, the Italian equivalent of *Hello!* magazine. I vowed to teach myself Italian from those glossy pages; it would do – at least until I could find a formal tutor. But, as my tan wore off, so did my keenness to self-teach. While I continued to nurture my passion for all things Italian in terms of food, style and coffee, I'm afraid I did nothing about actually learning to speak the language. I pushed the *Oggi* under my bed and they stayed there gathering dust for several years.

I did intend to study Italian at university, but my grade C at French GCSE didn't convince the necessary academic authorities that I had a talent for languages. The university admissions tutors were not in the least impressed when I tried to explain my motivation; apparently 'desire to marry an Italian' is not a compelling enough reason to be accepted on to a degree course. I considered moving to Italy to teach English. I'd heard about a course where the teacher doesn't even have to know the native tongue but instead can teach students through full immersion; but then I discovered that getting this TEFL qualification would cost thousands, so I decided that my best bet was to work for a year or so and save up. Mum and Dad were devastated when I told them I planned to move to London. My father said he feared I'd drift. He repeatedly pointed out that my brothers had always been terrifically motivated and decisive and had never presented him or Mum with a moment's worry. I was also motivated and decisive, but it was impossible to explain as much to my father. I was certain that he, like the university admissions tutors, would not accept my ambition to marry an Italian as a legitimate career plan. Luckily, that year Max's wife, Sophie, presented Mum and Dad with another grandchild and Thomas got married to a scary paediatrician, Eileen MacKinnan, who impressed and bossed my parents in equal measures. They had plenty to keep them occupied.

When I got off the National Express coach I immediately headed to Covent Garden, where I knew there were enough authentic Italian bars and restaurants to allow me to pretend I was in the country that flew the tricolour. I told myself that it would do until I'd saved up enough money to actually go there. I quickly found work waiting tables and pulling pints, yet somehow I never managed to gather together the money necessary for the teaching course. One year drifted into the next and then merged into another, almost without my noticing. My father got to say 'I told you so' on an indecent amount of occasions. If I ever gave any thought to my just-out-of-grasp TEFL qualification I reasoned that there was no particular hurry; there would always be Italians needing to learn English. I was happy as long as I earned enough money to buy fashionable shoes and handbags and pay the rent on a scruffy bed-sit in Earls Court which I shared with my friend Alison, a girl I met through one of the waitressing jobs.

Despite the ordinary jobs and the tiny, scruffy flat I remember my early twenties as marvellous years; it's criminal to do anything other. I may not have been committed to earning a TEFL qualification but I was still resolute in my vow to marry an Italian, and I soon discovered that there were plenty of Italian guys to date here in the UK; I didn't really have to have the upheaval and inconvenience of going abroad alone. I dated a series of Giancarlos, Massimos and Angelos. They did not disappoint. They flattered and were attentive; they fed me pasta and enormous compliments and I had a ball. Admittedly, sooner or later, they inevitably returned to Italy or the intensity burned out after only a few short weeks. This wasn't much of a problem; while I had a tendency to instantly fall in love with every one of these guys, I fell out of love relatively quickly too. I never allowed myself to be heartbroken for anything longer than a week. Alison called me shallow but I liked to think of myself as adjusted. I was aware that my youth was to be enjoyed and I saw so many girls wasting night after night crying into their pillows because of some guy or other. Ridiculous! There were always plenty more *pesce* in the *mare*.

Alison suggested that I try to date men who were more likely to stay in the country but she was missing the point. I was spoilt for life and found it disappointing to date anyone other than Italians. I didn't even want to. I did try, once or twice, but what came after was always *after*. English men simply didn't know about intense stares. They became tongue-tied when issuing compliments. By comparison, their dress sense was poor. Tailored shirts versus saggy football tops, reciting poetry or the words of some dated *Monty Python* sketch, drinking champagne out of my shoe or necking lager out of pint glasses; there was no competition.

So eight years passed, filled, but not punctuated, by a blur of intense but short-lived love affairs. Maybe I *was* shallow, or maybe I was perfectly average. I don't know. I just had a type.

Then Roberto walked into my bar and my life.

I watched him watching the football match on the TV screen. Even before he said a word it was instantly clear to me that he was Italian (his shoes shone and he was wearing a pink shirt with a confidence that eludes English blokes); besides, he had a unique energy and appetite that seemed to ricochet through the bar and then ping right into my being. I watched as he cheered his team when they made a decent pass, as he pulled at his hair when they let a goal slip through, as he hugged his friend with delightful, firm enthusiasm when his team equalized – and I was mesmerized.

The excitable and exciting stranger seemed to sense I was watching him. He turned and caught me undressing him with my eyes. I wondered whether he knew I was projecting way past the first carnal encounter, down the aisle and straight into the maternity hospital. I was defenceless; his deep, dark eyes stripped me of any ability I had to feign indifference. I fought my instinct to reach out and stroke his glorious bronzed skin. I wanted to run my hands over his well-defined and athletic body. While not especially tall, everything about his presence seemed purposeful and powerful. His being in the bar made me feel strangely safe and excited all at once.

He pulled himself away from watching the football and came over to where I was standing behind the bar. Alison would probably have described him as swaggering, I saw a saunter. He leaned close enough for his citrus cologne to drift into my consciousness.

'I take a beer and, you too, if you are available,' he said. He held my eye, and despite my best intention of dragging my gaze away from his, I found I could not. Did he mean he wanted to buy me a beer? Did he mean he wanted to take me somewhere? Could he mean he wanted to take me sexually? Could he possibly be being so brazen? I hoped so.

'Where would you take me?' I asked, choosing to understand his comment to mean more than an offer of a beer.

'Wherever you want. To a restaurant. To a movie. To a new sort of ecstasy.'

He dropped the last suggestion with indecent aplomb and waited for my response with a cool confidence. I should have been offended or outraged. At the very least I should have *pretended* to be one of those things; instead I offered my phone number.

'No. I won't take your number,' he said firmly.

'You won't?' Suddenly I was embarrassed. Had I got it completely wrong? Had I misheard him? Had I imagined the chemistry which was zinging between the two of us? Had the lethal dart of attraction just struck me?

'I wait here with you until your shift is finished.'

'But that's five more hours,' I objected gently, grinning, not trying to hide my amusement.

'I have forever. I know you are worth the wait. If you give me a number, I call, you might have met another man by that time. I can't risk it. Rather I wait for you. I must not let this go. I sense it is important.'

I had heard similar before. Italians are prone to this sort of impassioned announcement – it's one of the things I like about them. But I had never felt such chemistry before. Roberto's presence made my throat dry. He'd detonated a bomb of unprecedented excitement. I felt sparkling shafts of exhilaration shoot and spread through my body. Lust lodged in my skull. Desire drenched my innards. Longing shuddered down every nerve in every limb.

The bar rapidly receded. I didn't care if there were customers to serve or crisps to fetch from the storeroom. Suddenly there was only me and this Italian man; everything other was a dull, sludgy irrelevance.

We cleaved to one another for the following five hours. By turn we chatted, laughed and silently stared at one another. He told me of his love of fast cars and football. He introduced two or three of his pals but I could barely harness their names to my memory, as he was all-consuming and everything other was less. He told me that he'd only been living in England a week but already had an interview for a job in an advertising agency in Soho.

'And your family?' I probed.

'My family have a business in the wine trade,' he said simply; then he sipped his beer in a manner which suggested he found the turn in the conversation difficult.

'A vineyard, how amazing.' I imagined rows of green vine things, like soldiers in the sunshine.

He shrugged. 'Not really. Quite normal.'

I could not comprehend how he could describe running a vineyard as normal. It must be the most romantic thing in the world. I assumed he was attempting to be modest. I wondered if they still crushed grapes by stamping in them. Probably not, some European regulation doubtless prevents it, but maybe they still celebrated festivals by producing wine through the traditional methods. The Italians are big on festivals. Not that I was sure that I'd actually want to feel grapes oozing through my toes. I'm not really that earthy. Worse yet, someone else's toes. Yuk. It's enough to send you teetotal.

He sighed. 'Actually, I have come to England after terrible argues with my family. I need to prove myself. Make career here.' I admired his independent spirit and didn't need to ask for any detail on the nature of the arguments as he added, 'Sometimes families are stifling. I need to be away from my family for a time. You understand?' I nodded enthusiastically. Yes, yes, I understood. I understood everything about this man. 'I think you really do,' he said with a gravelly voice that shook with sincerity.

A sincerity that transcended all that had gone before.